# Shatter the Night

Also by Emily Littlejohn

*Inherit the Bones*

*A Season to Lie*

*Lost Lake*

# Shatter the Night

## Emily Littlejohn

MINOTAUR BOOKS

NEW YORK

First published in the United States by Minotaur Books,
an imprint of St. Martin's Publishing Group

SHATTER THE NIGHT. Copyright © 2019 by Emily
Littlejohn. All rights reserved. Printed in the United States of
America. For information, address St. Martin's Publishing
Group, 120 Broadway, New York, NY 10271.

www.minotaurbooks.com

Library of Congress Cataloging-in-Publication Data:

Names: Littlejohn, Emily, author.
Title: Shatter the night : a Detective Gemma Monroe mystery / Emily Littlejohn.
Description: First Edition. | New York : Minotaur Books, [2019]
Identifiers: LCCN 2019019599| ISBN 9781250178329 (hardcover) | ISBN
    9781250178336 (ebook)
Subjects: LCSH: Women detectives—Colorado—Fiction. | Murder—
    Investigation—Fiction. | GSAFD: Mystery fiction.
Classification: LCC PS3612.I8823 S53 2019 | DDC 813/.6—dc23
LC record available at https://lccn.loc.gov/2019019599

Our books may be purchased in bulk for promotional,
educational, or business use. Please contact your local
bookseller or the Macmillan Corporate and Premium Sales
Department at 1-800-221-7945, extension 5442, or by email
at MacmillanSpecialMarkets@macmillan.com.

First Edition: December 2019

10  9  8  7  6  5  4  3  2  1

This book is dedicated to my father

and my grandfather, both veterans.

We miss you terribly.

# Acknowledgments

If writing is a solitary activity, publishing a book is truly a team effort. Chris, you've stayed grounded so that I can chase my dreams. Thank you for loving me while my head is in the clouds. Pam Ahearn, my friend and agent, I wouldn't want to be on this journey without you. Catherine Richards, Nettie Finn, Linda Sawicki, and the rest of the team at Minotaur, thank you for continuing to trust me to tell Gemma's story the best way I know how. Claire and the Peanut, you are my life's greatest joy.

# Shatter the Night

# Prologue

**The night was full of terrible things,** shrouded creatures with dagger-sharp teeth and ghostly beings that seemed to float on air, their sneaker-clad feet hidden under long white sheets pilfered from linen closets all over town.

The creatures moved quickly, freely; the night belonged to them.

It was Halloween, and the quaint mountain town of Cedar Valley, Colorado, held more than tricks and treats. There was a dark energy, a dark spirit, summoned from the past that moved through the roaming packs of shrieking children.

No one saw it, of course, or likely even felt it. We lead self-absorbed lives, after all; we rarely notice when forces of darkness crouch in our shadows.

It was only later that I would be able to name the energy; name it, know it for what it was, and direct my rage and grief at it in equal parts.

It was evil, and it had crept into our town unannounced and unwelcome, though not unexpected. Towns, villages . . . they're living things, and like attracts like.

We had summoned the evil to our town just as surely as if we'd mailed an invitation. We just didn't know it yet, and by the time we did know it, the damage would already be done.

People would be killed.

Lives would be changed.

And Cedar Valley would never be the same again.

# Chapter One

**Halloween.**

Since becoming a cop six years prior, I'd grown to dread the thirty-first day of October. I could no longer believe the holiday was simply a night of innocent fun. I'd been witness to desecrated graves and smashed pumpkins; violent bar brawls and deadly DUIs. The night gave liberty to all sorts of spooks and ghouls, not only encouraging them to come out and play but practically daring them not to.

I was also a parent, though, and slowly learning that Halloween was a night I needed to tolerate, if not someday even embrace. My daughter, Grace, was nearly a year old and already she was captivated by the glowing pumpkins and toddler-size spider webs that adorned front porches and yards all over town.

Luckily, because Grace was so young, my fiancé, Brody Sutherland, and I still had full control over what she wore. He wanted to dress her as a witch, while I was leaning toward a cute bunny. After a heated discussion in the back aisle of a costume shop on Colfax in Denver, where the three of us had gone for a quick weekend getaway in late September, we split the difference and paid forty bucks for a zombie llama costume.

It was as ridiculous as it sounded. By the time we got her ears on, Grace looked like a rabid camel. But I'm nothing if not stubborn and by God, we were going to get our money's worth. Brody threw on an old monkey suit and I slipped a pair of cat ears over my dark hair and called it good.

We'd been out an hour; it was well past dusk and we were nearly done trick-or-treating. The sky had turned a violent deep purple, a shade of eggplant that seemed both ominous and watchful. The full moon was still low, gradually beginning its climb up past the clouds. We were lucky; though the forecast had predicted an early-morning snowfall, none had come and the night was merely cold instead of both cold and snowy.

Cedar Valley, like most mountain towns in Colorado, was both blessed and cursed with a population that was widely spread out; even our own nearest neighbors in the canyon were a good quarter mile away. And so, every Halloween, the town's city council sponsored a Spooks' Night Out. Up and down Main Street, merchants and shop clerks decorated their storefronts and competed to see who could give out the most coveted treats. This year, word on the street was that Old Man Brewer at the bookshop had a seemingly endless supply of full-size candy bars.

We reached the end of Main Street, where the businesses faded into stately residential homes and low-slung bungalows. Grace was sleepy, her eyes nearly shut.

It was quieter here, with the bulk of the trick-or-treaters still to the north.

Brody adjusted his monkey suit and moved Grace higher on his shoulder. "What do you say? It's been a long evening."

It had, but we had one more stop to make. "I promised Caleb we would come by. He's dying to see Grace in costume. Anyway, it's just up here."

The small, tidy, single-story redbrick bungalow was set back from the street on a quarter-acre lot. A gleaming white Mercedes sedan, parked along the sidewalk, got an appreciative whistle from Brody. Together, we read the placard mounted on the black wrought-iron fence: *Montgomery and Sons, Estate Planning and Legal Services*, though I, and everyone in town, knew there were no sons to be found inside. There was only retired Judge Caleb Montgomery and a part-time paralegal who favored heavy gray cardigans, even in the heat of summer, and smelled, incongruously, of coconuts and tropical sunscreen.

We pushed open the gate, wincing as the rusty bolts screeched, and stepped onto a narrow path that led from the gate to the front door. Caleb, or most likely his wife, Edith, had lined the path with carved pumpkins. They glowed, lit from within by tea lights.

The door opened slowly as we reached the front porch. Caleb Montgomery greeted us with a smile and a bowl of hard butterscotch candies.

"Come in, come in!" he called softly, noting the nearly-sleeping Grace in Brody's arms. "A rabid camel! How original! Wherever did you find a costume like that?"

I shrugged. "Colfax, of course."

"Beautiful car, Caleb," Brody said and shook the older man's hand. "Early Christmas present?"

Caleb grinned. "You could call it that. A man's got to live a little, right?"

"Absolutely."

The house was small; the front living area had been converted into a reception area, and the two bedrooms turned into Caleb's office and an office for his paralegal. In the rear of the house, closed French doors likely led to a kitchen, bathroom, and perhaps a closet or two.

A small white dog dressed in a bee costume darted toward us. The dog's bark was all Grace needed to perk up; she squealed with delight and then fussed in Brody's arms until he relented and set her down. The dog fell over with happiness, squashed its tiny wings, and offered up its pale speckled belly for rubs.

"When did you get a dog?" I asked.

"I didn't. It's the neighbor's, but Cricket—the dog—prefers to hang out with me. He's highly intelligent that way. I'll take him home before I leave for the night."

We watched dog and baby play for a few moments, then Caleb cleared his throat. "May I speak to you a moment, Gemma? In private?"

He gestured to his office. I followed him, smiling at the white lab coat he wore. The retired judge had always reminded me of Albert Einstein, with his shock of white hair and matching mustache. The costume he wore now only served to reinforce the image. Once we were inside his office, Caleb gently closed the door and slipped into the enormous chair behind his desk. A slight man, he was nearly swallowed by the leather and brass-studded throne.

He rubbed at his face. "This life. It's exhausting, isn't it? When I was a kid, I was terrified of dying. Now, the thought of living forever is enough to make me want to scream. Mankind was created with an expiration date, and for good reason. Our hearts are too soft, our emotions too brittle to go on forever."

I took a seat across from him in one of the two guest chairs. A single nine-by-twelve manila envelope lay on the mahogany desk and Caleb stared at it, falling silent. For the first time, I felt a sense of trepidation at what he might wish to discuss. It was unlike him to be especially morose or sentimental; seeing him this way was unsettling.

It was almost as though he were afraid.

I'd known Caleb most of my life, after all; he and my grandfather Buford "Bull" Weston had been colleagues and friends for decades. Both men had started their careers as attorneys and then moved into judgeships in Cedar Valley. Caleb was armed with an analytical mind and a sharp wit. Years in the courtroom had left him all too aware of the darkness that lies in the hearts of every one of us, but he was more likely to seek scientific explanations (nature versus nurture, that sort of thing) than find refuge in melancholy musings.

I realized suddenly that it had in fact been months since I'd seen Caleb or his wife. Perhaps there was something going on in their family, an illness or a financial worry.

I tried to lighten the mood. "You're not getting soft on me, are you?"

Caleb smiled grimly. With the tip of his finger, he pushed the manila envelope across the desk to me. I picked it up, noting a tiny spot of blood at the edge of the flap.

"Paper cut?"

"Nosebleed." Caleb grew impatient. "I didn't call you in to discuss my health, dear. There are letters in there, letters you should read. Though they might give you nightmares." I didn't bother telling him that come dark, nightmares were my most constant companion. I'd been living with them for years. Part of it stemmed from my work as a detective in Cedar Valley, work that had led me down bleak, hopeless roads. In my dreams I often found myself stuck on those same roads, traveling them over and over again, walking alongside the dead, the victimized. Never far behind us were the murderers, the rapists, the men and women who had black clouds in their heads and hearts.

And some of the nightmares had planted their seeds the terrible night my parents were killed in a car accident. Just a child, I was in the station wagon with them, and I knew the images and sounds from that night would stay with me forever, even as the days and years took me farther and farther from that time.

I glanced at the large manila envelope again. "I take it they're not love notes?"

Caleb sighed. He slumped down even farther into the chair. "They're threats. Death threats. It's ridiculous—it's been six months since I left the bench. I'm out of the game, I have no influence. My clients now are widows who want to amend their wills and bored divorcées looking to squeeze a few more pennies out of their ex-husbands. You make a threat if you want something done, an opinion swayed, a conviction overturned. Me? I'm powerless."

"Did the threats start arriving before or after you left the bench?"

"Just after." Caleb leaned forward and rested his hands on the desk. They were pale, like his hair, and as I saw now, like his face. He was a washed-out version of himself, a faded man.

It was a strange thought to have; Caleb was, to my knowledge, healthy. He wasn't quite seventy, and while he carried an extra ten or fifteen pounds on his belly, he was an avid hiker and fly fisherman. The man before me looked as though he hadn't seen the sun in weeks.

Caleb continued speaking. "The first letter showed up four, maybe five months ago, at the house. Since then, I've gotten one every couple of weeks."

"Do you have gloves?" Not expecting to be involved in official business that night, I'd left my small evidence kit in the trunk of my car.

Caleb retrieved an old pair of leather driving gloves from a drawer in a file cabinet behind him. He handed them to me and as I slipped them on, I asked the obvious question.

"Why haven't you turned these over the police?"

"This will sound crazy, but . . . well, they're like a puzzle. There's something so familiar about the words, the language, and yet it's just out of my grasp. I guess I've been reluctant because I have to know who's sending them. I have to know, Gemma. And I thought I could figure it out myself."

I upturned the manila envelope on the desk, wondering just how ugly of a business I was about to step into.

Nine crisp business-size white envelopes slid out. I picked one at random and examined it, talking out loud, saying the things that Caleb was surely already aware of. "Typed address label, made out to you, no return contact information, the stamp is a sticker . . . We won't get DNA from this. Looks like it originated in, or was routed through, Boulder. The envelope appears to have been opened with a letter opener."

Caleb nodded. "It was an anniversary gift from Edith. She gave me a letter opener and I gave her a kitchen ice pick. See a theme there?"

"A fondness for sharp objects, apparently." I slipped a folded white piece of paper out of the envelope and asked, "Has she seen these? Your wife?"

"Of course she has." Caleb managed to snort and scowl at the same time. "You try keeping something a secret from that woman. I knew Edith was a pistol when I married her. I just didn't expect her to become a cannon in her middle age."

I smiled, knowing just what he meant. Edith was twenty years his junior, in her midfifties, and the very definition of a spitfire. She was notorious across town for her fiery outbursts, though usually they were done in the spirit of sticking up for the underdog or shaming a merchant for exorbitant prices.

From the other room, I heard Grace and Brody laugh at something. Then their giggles were overpowered by the shriek of a nearby trick-or-treater. As both sounds faded and quiet returned to the room, I was struck once more by the sense of fear, of tension, in the room.

I unfolded the paper and read the four sentences on it. I read the words again, slowly, then slipped the sheet of paper back into the envelope, moving quickly though I knew the futility of trying to put back something evil once it has been unleashed. The images evoked by the letter—Caleb, strung up like a skinned deer set to bleed out, vital organs scattered outside instead of nestled inside—made me sick to my core.

"They're all like this?"

A weary nod from the retired judge.

Reluctantly, I read another of the letters. "This is . . . malignant. Twisted. You should have come to me sooner, Caleb. You know there are protocols for this sort of thing, procedures in place to protect people like you."

"People like me?" He was breathing hard now, rubbing his hands over his eyes as though to wipe out the words on the papers I held.

"You know what I mean. Judges, prosecutors. The threats

come with the territory, but that doesn't mean we don't take them seriously." The clock on the wall chimed seven thirty, and from the other room, I heard Brody clear his throat. It was past Grace's bedtime. She'd be hard to put down tonight, wired from the activities of the evening and the cinnamon doughnut she'd eaten as we strolled Main Street.

"Ah, for Pete's sake. Someone or another has been angry at me my whole life, Gemma. You know the quality of people we deal with in law enforcement, in the courts. Look, I promised Edith I would turn the letters over to you. What you do with them now is your concern."

"You're really not worried?" *Even though the fear in this room is heavy enough to be smothering?*

"I never was in the past and I'm sure as hell not going to start worrying now. You know how many crackpots have threatened me over the years? On both sides of the court, too. Cops and crooks, accuser and accused, it's a fine line that divides them, present company excluded, of course. You're an easy target when you sit in the middle." Caleb stood with a slight groan and rapped definitively on the desk with the knuckles of his right hand. "If someone wants to hurt me, they'll find a way. What am I going to do, spend my sunset days playing golf in a disguise? Hiding out from the boogeyman in my own town? No. Screw 'em, I say."

Caleb's cavalier attitude made me uneasy, especially given that I was certain he was lying. I gathered the white envelopes back into the manila folder and tucked it under my arm. "I'll let you know what I find out."

"Fine." He moved away from the desk, walking with a slight limp to his left leg. I remembered that he'd recently had surgery; knee or hip, I couldn't recall. "You should get that little one home. It's getting late. Nothing but trouble will be out on the streets soon."

In the waiting room, Grace's eyes were nearly shut. Brody glanced at the manila envelope in my arms but didn't say anything other than goodbye to Caleb and the dog. He went ahead of me, taking our sleeping zombie llama back out into the night.

I gave Caleb a pat on the shoulder. "Are you headed home?"

He nodded, turned away toward his office. "In a few minutes. I've got to return Cricket and put a few files away."

"Good night then, Caleb."

"I'll see you around, kid."

*Kid.* I hadn't been called kid in a long time.

"It's Detective now, Caleb," I called after him.

He stopped, turned, and saluted. "Yeah, right. I'll see you around, Detective. And happy Halloween. Watch out for the monsters."


The sky was still violet, though the moon had risen and was now high above us. We walked north, back to the car under the pale yellow orb, the glow of moonlight complementing the evenly spaced puddles of streetlight. As we reached the side road we'd parked on, a pack of teenagers in skeleton costumes rushed past us, pummeling one another with sacks of candy. They turned the corner, the sound of their voices and crazed laughter drifting away.

"Kids," Brody whispered as he strapped Grace into her car seat. "That'll be our baby in just a few short years. Heaven help us."

"I don't even want to think about it."

In the driver's seat, Brody moved away from the curb carefully, mindful of others still running about, and headed west. We'd gotten half a mile or so away when a terrible noise shattered the night. For a moment, I thought the world itself was ending; the noise had sounded as though somewhere a great rock had been torn asunder.

Brody pulled over. We stared at each other, the color draining from our faces. He said, "That was an explosion. A house maybe, or a car. Could be a gas leak."

"You go." My hand was already on the door. "Take Grace home. I'll call as soon as I know anything. There could be people hurt, injuries. I might be able to help."

Brody nodded, knowing it would be a waste of time to argue. His eyes pleaded with mine. "Be careful, Gemma. Listen, hear that? Sirens. The fire department is already on their way. They've got the gear, the training. Don't go inside any structures, even if you think there's someone trapped or hurt. You'll put yourself and the fire personnel at risk."

I nodded. "I love you."

I was out of the car and jogging back toward Main Street by the time the first fire engine sped past me, its lights and sirens piercing the darkness. I watched as it drove by the bulk of the shops and kept going, toward the south end of the street.

Toward Caleb Montgomery's law offices.

I sprinted, cursing the heavy layers I'd worn to keep out the evening's chill. It was a Monday, and with school the next day, many of the families had already called it a night. But a fair number of older teens and adults still roamed the town, the adults taking advantage of the holiday to tuck into a few more drinks at the bars and the teens taking advantage of a one-night-only license to claim Cedar Valley as their own.

Now, though, everyone I passed had stopped, their faces wearing equal masks of horror and confusion, their heads cocked in anticipation of further explosions.

I slowed down as I reached the end of Main Street, then stopped completely, in total disbelief at what I was seeing. Caleb Montgomery's white Mercedes no longer existed. In its place was an inferno of fire and smoke. And all around it, a beehive of activity had commenced; the fire personnel raced to get water on the flames and a set of paramedics stared openmouthed at the site of the blast.

And Caleb himself?

I nearly retched as the realization hit me that his was likely the body in the driver's seat. I looked away though I knew the images— charred skin, a formless shape more mass than human—would stay with me forever.

Flames continued to dance at the edge of my vision and I pressed the heels of my hands to my eyes, willing this to be some kind of terrible, sick practical joke. A gruesome Halloween trick concocted by a madman.

It was an empty wish, of course. This was real, as real as the heat of the fire and the smell of the smoke, the smell of other . . . things burning.

# Chapter Two

I got as close as I could to the scene, then stopped at the insistence of Fire Chief Max Teller. He, too, was on foot, and I vaguely remembered that he had a couple of kids. The devil ears on his head reinforced my belief that he had been on the drag, and that he, like me, had rushed to the scene with the intent of helping anyone who needed it.

But the body in the car was beyond help.

Together, we stood and stared at the carnage. Though we were a good thirty feet away, the heat from the explosion filled the air. I started to wipe at the tears that streamed down my face, then stopped, realizing it was useless.

I knew the tears would be falling for a long time to come.

Beside me, Teller leaned over, tried to catch his breath. He was pushing sixty and, though he was still trim and muscular, twenty years as the chief had left him more accustomed to sitting at a desk than responding, by foot no less, to an emergency callout.

After a few minutes, he straightened up and turned to me. That's when he saw the tears.

"My God, do you know the vic?"

I nodded. "I think . . . it's Caleb Montgomery. That's his car, those are his law offices. I was with him less than twenty minutes ago. I need to help, need to do something . . ."

As I started once more to move toward the burning vehicle, Teller gently grabbed my shoulder. "I can't let you go over there,

Detective. There could be another explosion. Your department can process the scene as soon as we get that fire under control and secure the perimeter."

"There must be something . . ." It was difficult to get the words out; my tongue felt swollen, my throat suddenly parched. I'd sat across from Caleb in a room filled with cold fear and told him that I could help. But he'd come to me too late.

Teller squeezed my shoulder, sympathetic. "My team will go in first. That's the way it's got to be."

Frustrated, I watched as more fire personnel arrived. They moved in what seemed to be slow motion; it was apparent that word had spread: this was one victim who was beyond help. No ambulance would be needed, no sprint to the nearest hospital required. Half of the team set up a perimeter around the car while the other half ran another hose from the engine to put water on the flames. With a final warning that I should stay put, Teller jogged over to join his crew.

Behind the fire personnel came four Cedar Valley Police Department squad cars. It was my team, my second family, and I was immensely relieved to see them. I yanked off the cat ears I'd just realized were still on my head and furiously wiped at my eyes.

By the time Chief of Police Angel Chavez stepped out of the first squad car and met me in the middle of the now closed-off street, I was fully composed.

Chavez was a tall, serious man in a dark, serious suit. Though he dressed more like the president of a bank than a police officer, Chavez was a cop through and through. He was one of the best men I knew and at the moment, there was no one I'd rather see. At his side was our department's new intern, a man a few years older than me, exploring a career change. His name was Jimmy and, though he'd only been with us a short time, he seemed to be working out okay.

And on their heels was my partner, Finn Nowlin. His black hair was slicked back and at the corner of his mouth, three long smears of blood trailed down from his lips into his five o'clock shadow. It was obvious that he, too, had been out enjoying the festivities.

Finn looked ill as he scanned the scene, took in the body and the car. "My God," he muttered. "Explosion like that, there's going to be evidence all over this damn street."

Chavez jammed his hands in his pants pockets. "The car belongs to Caleb Montgomery?"

I nodded. "Yes, sir. My family and I, we visited him tonight. His car was parked in that very spot. It's hard to tell if it's the same car, of course, but it appears to be."

"I'm sorry, I know your families are close." Chavez exhaled, a troubled look in his eyes. "Someone is behind this. Cars don't blow up by themselves."

"You don't know the half of it, Chief. Caleb had been receiving death threats for the last six months." I quoted one of the terrible letters from memory: "'I am coming for you. Gutting you will be the most glorious moment of my life. Death will be a slow dance, you bleeding out, me swaying to the music of your moans. And there will be laughter. So much laughter.'"

"Gruesome." Finn looked at the body again, watched the firefighters douse more water on the now-smoldering flames. "Maybe the person who sent the threats saw you two meet and figured Caleb was spilling the beans, so he took him out."

The chief asked, "Did the threats specifically instruct Caleb not to speak to the police?"

"No, nothing like that. And unless the perp has the law offices bugged, there's no way he could have known what Caleb and I talked about. I arrived with Brody, with Grace. We were in costume." I bent over, a terrible bout of nausea suddenly clenching my stomach. Thoughts of what could have been, what could have happened if we'd left Caleb's office just a few minutes later, made me want to vomit.

My family could have been the ones burnt, melted like wax dolls.

After a moment, I stood, moved past the images darkening my mind.

Chavez said, "That letter, it doesn't sound like fan mail from your average felon. In fact, there's something almost poetic about it."

"I don't think we can assume the threats were sent by someone Caleb put away. They could be from anyone—a felon . . . a peer . . . a rival. Or some crackpot who's become obsessed with Caleb for a reason that has nothing to do with Caleb's career." I thought about the sense of fear I'd experienced in Caleb's office. "I think he knew who sent them."

"A spurned lover, maybe?" Finn offered.

I shook my head. "Caleb and Edith have been happily married for years."

"Word on the street used to be that Caleb liked to have a good time." Finn shrugged. "Maybe there's no truth to it. What do I know."

"I never heard any of that," I said.

"What I don't understand is why Caleb waited so long to bring these threats to our attention. Retired or not, he was still a public figure." The chief rubbed his chin, then added, "And now someone's gotten to him."

I managed a brief nod of agreement as I blinked back another rush of sudden, hot tears. Grief would have to wait; within the next hour or so, the fire department would turn the scene over to us, and I couldn't start an investigation—arguably the most important moments in a case, the first couple of hours—with my head clouded with sadness. For if the explosion was found to be a criminal act, then my interest in the case would be personal as well as professional.

In silence, we waited and watched as the firefighters continued their work. As the last of the flames died down, it was easier to make out more of the car itself. It was a four-door sedan, large pieces of which had been blown to bits. The frame was mostly intact, though warped and twisted by the heat. The exterior was blackened, charred, but a few inches of gleaming white paint shone through brightly against the burnt edges.

In a stroke of luck, two characters on the front license plate were still visible.

Jimmy, showing impressive initiative, offered to run the partial plate and the make and model. It would be the quickest way to confirm that the car was in fact Caleb's and not someone else's. As the intern raced back to the squad car with its laptop and wireless connection, Finn said under his breath, "Teacher's pet."

"Huh?"

"You haven't noticed? Jimmy will do anything for you . . . for the chief . . . even for Moriarty. Me? I'm chopped liver. He barely acknowledges my existence. Not that I care. It's just interesting, is all." Finn shrugged. "Anyway . . . check out that beautiful creature."

I followed his gaze and watched as two of the fire personnel gathered at the driver's side of the car. At their heels was a gorgeous yellow Lab in an orange reflective safety vest.

"The dog? Yeah, beautiful."

We continued watching until finally, one of the fire personnel, a female, stepped away from the car and joined Fire Chief Teller near the perimeter. The dog stayed within a foot of her the whole time. The firefighter removed her breathing apparatus and I quickly walked over, catching the last of her words.

"—body, Chief, burned beyond recognition."

I inched close to the pair. "Excuse me, can you tell if it's a man or woman?"

The firefighter shot me an annoyed look. "Honey, you need to back off. This is a crime scene. Please stay behind the perimeter with the rest of the civilians."

Even the dog gave me a nudge on the knees, as if to reiterate his master's words.

Chief Teller jumped in as I raised my eyebrows, indignation flaring in my chest. "Fire Investigator Olivia Ramirez, meet Detective Gemma Monroe. Gemma, Liv is new in town. And this little guy is her pooch, Fuego."

"Detective? Sorry, no disrespect meant." Ramirez lifted her hands in an appeal. Her words came easy and quickly, though there was still an element of challenge in her eyes, in her tone. She smiled briefly. "Back in L.A., we'd get a lot of civilians, sometimes reporters, messing up our crime scenes. You know how it is. As I was saying, Chief, there's a body. The damage is, uh, extensive. Couldn't tell you if it's a man or woman, though the height would indicate a man."

Ramirez paused, ran a hand over her forehead. She was in her midforties, with bronze skin and intense hazel-green eyes. She was clearly in excellent shape, and while I had five inches on her, she was more muscular, stronger looking.

"We're lucky more people weren't hurt," Ramirez continued. "I'll tell you one thing: whoever did this is sick. Sick, and talented. This took some skills."

"So it *was* an intentional explosion?"

Ramirez shot me another look that I had trouble deciphering. "Yes. This was murder, plain and simple, though it will be up to you, Detective, to prove it."

Chief Chavez was insistent. "Absolutely not. It's a conflict of interest, Gemma. I know how close your family is to the Montgomerys. If the poor bastard in that car is Caleb, you're off the case. Period."

Though my face began to flush with anger and grief, I calmly stood my ground. "Chief, that's the cost of doing business in a town this size. If every cop had to step aside because of the potential for clouded judgments, then we'd have a very small force, wouldn't we? Put me on the case or fire me."

*"Excuse me?"* Chavez stepped closer to me. "Did I hear you give me an ultimatum?"

"I have an idea." Finn moved smoothly between the chief and me. "Monroe has a point, Chief. We all have conflicts, sooner or later. You know she'll be a bulldog on this. How about if I take the lead? If I get the slightest sense that she's going off the rails, I'll put Moriarty on the case in her place."

I started to speak. Finn gently stepped on my foot. With much effort, I bit my lip and swallowed my words. At the moment, if I wanted to stay on the case, he was my only hope.

Chavez exhaled. "Don't make me regret this, Gemma."

"You won't, sir."

He nodded. "All right. Get to it. Talk to that neighbor first, the one with the dog."

*Dog?*

I turned to see a hysterical woman in a pair of overalls and a plumber's tool belt, standing on the front porch of a house two doors down from Caleb's law offices. In her arms was Cricket, still in his bee costume.

Finn and I went to the woman. A uniformed officer was attempting to calm her down, but the woman's breaths came in great, gasping hitches. Cricket, picking up on her distress, was squirming, barking, and struggling to get down.

Speaking quietly, I asked the woman if the officer could hold the dog for a few minutes, maybe take it in the backyard. Something in my voice got through to her because after a moment, she sighed heavily, nodded, and handed Cricket to the officer.

He held the dog close and walked away, and though the woman was still crying, at least I could hear myself think.

"Ma'am? Are you hurt? Were you injured by the blast?" I stood close, lightly grasped her elbow.

"No . . . no. I . . . Mr. Montgomery brought Cricket over and we . . . we stood here and waved to him as he got in his car." With each word, the woman settled down. "Then there was a noise and suddenly . . . the car was in flames."

"You saw Caleb Montgomery enter that car?" I pointed to the wreckage, confirming that we were indeed talking about the same vehicle.

"You see any other burning Mercedes?" The woman fished in the pockets of her overalls, pulled out a pack of cigarettes. She lit one with a shaking hand. "Mr. Montgomery was a nice man."

"Yes, he was. Have you seen anything suspicious in the neighborhood? Noticed any strange vehicles, maybe someone loitering around?" Finn asked, his voice matching the tone and volume of my own. The woman was still very much on the edge; one loud noise or harsh word could send her into hysterics again.

She shook her head. "No, nothing like that. This is a quiet street; at least, this end is."

Finn said, "Okay. I'm going to have my officer take a statement from you—would that be all right? If you think of anything, be sure to give us a call. Here's my card."

The woman took the card, studied it a moment, then nodded and repeated, "He was a nice man."

We left her in the hands of the officer who'd taken Cricket, who had calmed down and was actually nearly asleep in the officer's arms. As we walked to the car, Finn gently took hold of my elbow and leaned in close. "I meant what I said. If I think your judgment is clouded, I'll get Moriarty involved immediately."

I pulled my arm free of his grasp and flashed him a cold grin. Finn was a good cop, a good partner, but the last few months had seen our relationship grow tense and I wasn't sure what was at the root of it. We seemed to have good days and bad days, and it was clear today was turning into a bad day, for a number of reasons.

Some part of me knew this case was the sort to make or break careers. I wondered if there was more to Finn's concern than my emotional investment. In the heat of the moment, grief welling up in me, I snapped. "Don't worry about me. I wouldn't dream of standing between you and New York."

Finn froze and stared at me, his bright blue eyes narrowed in suspicion. "What did you hear about New York?"

"Word gets around. Everyone knows you're suddenly itching to get out of the valley." I took a deep breath and tried to calm down. "Come on, it's no big deal. This town isn't for everyone. You've put in a good stint. I can see how the action in a larger city would appeal to you."

Finn clenched his jaw and resumed walking. I paced myself with his long strides.

"Does the chief know?"

"I don't think so." I didn't add that it was probably a matter of weeks, though, before Chavez heard the rumors. Secrets never last in a town, or a police department, our size.

"Good. Let's keep it that way. There's a lot of unknowns at this time, including a firm job offer." Finn shot me a look, relaxed his jaw. "Have you ever been to New York? Restaurants like you wouldn't believe."

I started to respond, but we'd reached the car and Investigator Ramirez stood there, near the trunk, watching our approach. At her side, Fuego stared at us with big, watchful amber-colored eyes.

I introduced her and Finn.

"First-timers to the party?" she asked us. She noted our confusion and clarified, "First time up close? To a burn vic?"

Finn said, "I worked a homicide a few years back where the perp tried to cover the murder by torching the victim's apartment. It was a mess."

Ramirez sniffed. "Yeah . . . this is probably a little fresher."

"That's my friend in the car that you're talking about." Might as well get everything on the table now, before she said something that really offended me.

Ramirez turned to me. "I'm sorry. You may want to take a minute to prepare yourself. It's . . . well, it's visceral. There's no other way to put it."

"Sure." I took a moment, then moved to the driver's side of the sedan. Leaning down, I stared in at the charred mass in the driver's seat. The smell was indescribable. I tried to breathe slowly, shallowly, through my mouth; tried to maintain a professional composure.

It was no use; I stepped away, turning from what remained of the body of the man who'd been my friend.

A breeze from the south drifted through and I gagged as the stench of still-smoldering human fat blossomed in the air. Beside me, Finn looked equally nauseous. "I don't think I've ever smelled anything so terrible in my life." He turned away and dry-heaved, then spat.

Ramirez leaned in next to me. In a hushed voice, she said, "I did three tours in Iraq as a medic. You never do get used to it. One burnt body's bad enough. Just imagine dozens. It was unbelievable."

Finn straightened. He wiped at his mouth with the back of his hand and cleared his throat. "Where were you stationed?"

"Fallujah, mostly." Ramirez looked away. "Anyway, my hope is that the initial explosion rendered the victim unconscious. At least that way, when the flames got to him, he didn't suffer."

I turned from Caleb's remains and glanced at the crowd gathered on the far side of the street. If this was an intentional act of murder, was the perpetrator somewhere close by? Was he standing there, among the bystanders and witnesses, watching us attempt to start unraveling the damage he'd done?

Someone in the group shifted and I caught a glimpse of a man at the back of the crowd. At least, I thought it was a man. He wore a burlap sack pulled over his head, with two black slits for eyes, and a hooded sweatshirt, worn with the hood pulled up over the top of the sack.

Many in the crowd wore costumes, including a handful dressed as famous dead celebrities, but there was something unsettling, even disturbing about the man's ramrod posture, his body turned in my direction.

The man slowly raised a finger to his mouth in a gesture of silence and shook his head back and forth. Then he turned tail and took off, north along Main Street.

"Finn," I gasped and began pursuit of the individual. Finn stayed on my heels and I shouted to him what I'd seen. Up ahead, we saw the masked man duck right, down a long alley that I knew came to a dead end at a chain-link fence.

We stopped short of the alley. In between deep breaths, I managed to get out, "He's trapped. Unless he's Spider-Man. That fence goes twenty feet high; it backs up to the hospital."

"He's not trapped at all. There's half a dozen doors that open onto the alley." Finn turned around, looked backward. "We need a third man, to cover us."

"We don't have time. You cover the street, don't let him backtrack. I'm going in."

I entered the alley before Finn could say a word. Behind me, ten, now twelve feet, I heard him swear. The alley was dark, the light from the streetlamps barely penetrating the gloomy darkness. Slowly, I pulled my flashlight from my jacket pocket and clicked it on. The light played low on the ground and then I raised it, swiveling the beam in front of and to the sides of me as I moved down the alley. Every couple of feet, I stopped to listen and check the doors; all were locked. Aside from a steady drip of water from a pipe somewhere, and the occasional rumble of a car passing by on Main Street, the alley was quiet.

Too quiet, in fact.

There should have been the rustle of mice, rats maybe, or a breath of wind.

But there was nothing, and finally I stopped, nearly three-quarters of the way down the alley, and turned around. At the entrance, illuminated by a streetlamp, Finn's silhouette provided some, though not much, reassurance. I took a deep breath, turned around, and walked the last twenty feet of the alley and reached the chain-link fence.

Mystified, I ran the beam of my flashlight all over the fence, looking for a cutout, a section where the links had been broken. An escape. Finding none, I sighed. The man, whoever he was, had somehow eluded us.

# Chapter Three

"This guy might really be Spider-Man after all. He must have scaled the fence and dropped down to the other side. Freaking monkey, is what he is." Finn slowed his pace, matching mine, as we made our way back to the scene.

We rejoined Liv Ramirez at Caleb's car.

"You guys took off like the devil was on your heels."

We caught her up on the man with the mask. She asked, "You think this guy might be involved with the explosion?"

"Maybe." I glanced at her, noting how Fuego, the Lab, seemed to mimic his owner's every move. Even now, the two of them were mirror images, each one with one leg forward and one back (in the dog's case, one leg forward and three back) and twin looks of inquisitiveness on their faces. "You said that you were certain this was murder, an intentional act. Was it a car bomb?"

"It's too early in the investigation to know." Ramirez walked to the front of the vehicle, then crouched, peering intently at the melted tires, the ruined undercarriage, and the crater beneath the car. She stood back up. "I won't be certain of anything until we get the vehicle in the lab, run forensics, and hear statements from eyewitnesses."

"Of course." It was obvious that Ramirez was smart. I suspected that in spite of what she'd just said, she already had a working theory. I was curious to hear it. "How about your best guess?"

Ramirez cocked her head, pursed her lips. After a few moments of thought, she sighed. "This is off the record. I think someone laced this car with explosives and then possibly remotely detonated it. That's about the only thing that would cause this kind of damage."

"So it was a car bomb." Finn rolled up his shirtsleeves, then crouched by the side of the car and looked under it. "What kind of explosives were used? Would they have been placed under the carriage? Or in the trunk? How much would it take to do a job like this?"

"Didn't I just say that I won't know anything more until I run some tests?" Ramirez said as Finn stood back up. She punched him lightly on the shoulder, an overly familiar gesture. "You cops are all the same . . . stubborn and aggressive."

He flashed her a dry grin. "You forgot good-looking and charming."

Finn would flirt with a brick wall if it would get him what he was looking for. I cleared my throat. "You said the bomb was remotely detonated. What did you mean by that? A timer?"

Even as I said it, though, I realized just how hard it would have been to pinpoint Caleb's departure from the law offices to an exact time. A timer would have been extremely risky.

Ramirez shook her head. "I don't think a timer was involved. I'm fairly certain that you're looking for a killer with a gun."

"A gun?" I asked in disbelief.

Ramirez asked, "How much do you know about explosives?"

"Not much," Finn and I responded in unison.

"I'll keep things basic, then." The fire investigator thought a moment, blinking her catlike green-gold eyes. "You both know what a detonator is, right? It's the mechanism that triggers the explosive device. A lot of the time, the detonator is a blasting cap containing some kind of compound material. Think of it as a fuse, a sort of first mini bomb that triggers the much larger explosive materials. Anyway, explosives can be set up to detonate in different ways; timers, movement of the car, ignition, et cetera."

"But you think this one was remotely detonated?" I asked again.

"Yes. A few people, including Buddy Holly and Marilyn Monroe over there by the streetlight, said they heard a gunshot blast immediately before the explosion. Buddy Holly, who is an avid hunter, is certain it was a rifle."

Surprised, I asked, "You've already spoken to eyewitnesses?"

"Just a couple." It was Ramirez's turn to grin. Her teeth were small and even and shone brightly against the bronze of her skin. "I guess I can be a little aggressive, too."

"A rifle. That explains the noise the neighbor heard just before the explosion." Finn glanced up at the rooftops of the surrounding buildings. "Maybe it was a bullet that killed Montgomery. He could have been dead by the time the car exploded. It's a clear shot from five or six different rooftops, straight through the front windshield."

Ramirez looked up, then turned in a slow circle, taking in each of the buildings on Main Street. She ended her scan back at Finn. "Yeah, sure, maybe."

I assumed she and I were thinking the same thing: why shoot someone if you've already laced his car with explosives? Ramirez asked the question aloud. "Why go to the effort of a car bomb if you're going to get the same result with a rifle? If this was a remote location, it might make more sense; the fire might cover up the evidence of a gunshot. Enough damage and the ME might even skip a thorough autopsy. But this is a busy, public space. Witnesses heard the gunshot. So no, no I don't think a bullet killed the victim. I think the sniper waited and watched and at the right moment, he pulled the trigger and either hit the detonator or the explosives themselves."

Ramirez pointed across the street at a long-closed restaurant. "And if it was me, if I was going to do it, I'd plant myself up there. It's the cleanest shot to the car. Then I'd clear the hell out in the ensuing chaos."

"There's a lot of assumptions there," Finn replied after a moment of silence. "Something like that would take weeks of planning. How did the gunman know to be here, at this spot, at this exact time?"

I swallowed. "Because the killer's been watching Caleb. He hunted him. We don't deal in coincidences, Finn, not in our line of work. Caleb showed me the threats he's received and a few minutes later, he's dead."

Ramirez stepped away from us to take a call on her radio.

Finn moved closer to me. "Gemma. Think about it, think about the tone of the letter. It expressed glee, excitement at the prospect of watching Montgomery suffer a slow death. A car bomb is quick, dirty, and effective."

Before he could say more, Ramirez ended her call. She moved back to us. "As I was saying, I can't be sure of anything until I get the evidence in the lab. But I stand by my theory, though I'd appreciate it if you kept it to yourselves until I can confirm a few things."

"Have you run across something like this before?" Finn asked. "A bullet used to detonate a car bomb?"

Ramirez nodded. "Sure. I wouldn't say it's common, but it happens." A short burst of sirens pierced the night again, and the crowd parted to let the ME's car through. "Looks like the medical examiner is here. I'll get out of the way, but I'll be in touch as soon as I have anything conclusive for your team."

She left us, Fuego trotting beside her. Even their strides matched, purposeful and deliberate.

"Cool dog." Finn watched them walk away. "Interesting woman."

"Yes. Let's get a team to canvas every building that faces this intersection, including residential properties. Some have security systems, cameras. We might get lucky."

"And every roof as well; there may be trace evidence." Finn stepped away to speak with a patrol officer and wrangle a support team together.

I scanned the crowd again, which was finally starting to disperse, taking it in, all too aware that though we'd collect evidence and take photographs, a crime scene is by its very nature a shifting, changing thing. We'd never again be in this moment, in this place, this close to the actual criminal act. Each moment that ticked past was another moment farther from the event, farther from the killer's last few actions that led to the death.

The beginning of this murder investigation, like most, would start with an ending: the intentional ending of a life. And then the investigation would work backward, but the earth continues to rotate and time moves forward and if you're lucky, you end up somewhere in the middle, at the truth.

"Hell of a day." The scowl on Dr. Ravi Hussen's face deepened at the sight of what remained of Caleb's body. She was already suited and gloved up, with a mask hanging loosely around her neck. Her eyeliner was thick, her hair pulled up in an elaborate twist under her cap. Like Finn, she, too, must have been enjoying the Halloween spirit.

"Hi, Ravi." I was glad to see her. Cool and collected, competent and charming, Ravi was not only an ace medical examiner, she was a dear friend.

Ravi said, "I left Los Angeles to get away from things like this. Thank heavens no one else was hurt. I understand this is likely Caleb Montgomery?"

"Yes. A neighbor observed him enter the vehicle just before the explosion. And as if things weren't complicated enough, we have witnesses who report hearing a gunshot before the explosion."

"I see." Ravi leaned close to the car, peered in for a few moments, then stepped back. A look of deep sadness had entered her eyes. "I testified before Caleb many times. He was one of our own, wasn't he? This one hurts, Gemma. The damage to the body is extensive, but I've worked with worse. If he was shot, I'll find the bullet. The explosion was shortly after seven thirty, correct?"

"Yes. Did you hear it?"

Ravi shook her head, looking pained. "I was trying to get out of a terrible blind date at some terrible Halloween party. The hosts had the stereo on full blast."

Finn approached us, Jimmy hot on his heels. The young intern spoke first, excitedly. "I got a match! It's a Mercedes C-Class sedan registered to Edith and Caleb Montgomery."

My heart sank. Though I'd been certain this was the outcome we were facing, it still hurt to hear confirmation of the car's ownership. A part of me had hoped that the neighbor had been mistaken. "Damn it."

Ravi gestured to her two technicians, twin brothers, both as pale and ghostly as any morgue attendants you'd find in a horror story. They moved to her in tandem, silently, with precision and speed. "Lars, Jeff . . . let's get the body out of here as soon as possible."

As Ravi walked away to gather the tools needed to begin the tricky task of removing the fragile corpse from the burnt shell of the Mercedes, she added with a soft mutter, *"Death, a necessary end, will come when it will come."*

Usually, the Shakespeare quotes Ravi seemed to have an endless supply of were reassuring, timeless. Today, the message felt sinister. It was an ugly reminder that there is rarely the opportunity to stop the Reaper once he's on his way.

The quote also begged the question: *was* this a necessary death? Why had Caleb been targeted? He'd been off the bench for six months . . . but over the years, how many people had he put away or angered?

Hundreds? Thousands?

Of course, it only took one angry man or woman to pull a trigger, detonate a bomb.


Two hours later, Finn and I were ready to leave the scene. We'd watched as the crime scene technicians collected evidence and took photographs, then we'd taken turns interviewing witnesses.

There was the young couple dressed as Buddy Holly and Marilyn Monroe, who confirmed that they heard a sound, similar to a gunshot, immediately before the explosion.

There were others, too, who heard the same noise; some of whom had been sure the shot was a prelude to an active shooter situation.

To my surprise, Judge Gloria Dumont appeared at the edge of the perimeter as I was finishing up with a witness who had dressed as a couch potato. Dumont, who'd been promoted from associate to presiding judge upon Caleb's retirement, stood stockstill, taking in the carnage. With her hands jammed in a thick down jacket, we made eye contact across the street from each other. She gave me the briefest of head nods and I wondered who had called her, who had alerted her to the murder. To my knowledge, she didn't typically monitor the police scanners.

Dumont waited patiently until I wrapped up the interview, then we went to a small park adjacent to the closed restaurant across the street. We sat in the flickering light of a streetlamp, on a metal bench that was hard and cold. Dumont was about forty, with blond hair cut in a precise bob and piercing blue eyes that might have been called cold save for the deep laugh lines at their corners.

Dumont was shaken. She fished a small flask from her purse and removed the cap, then chugged back a large swig. "Gin. It's my emergency stash. Please don't tell anyone."

I considered asking her for a sip myself. "Are you all right?"

"Sure, I'm all right. I'm alive, aren't I? I have a great career, an adoring and younger husband in Nash. And he's the darling of Cedar Valley, after all, just days away from opening the longslumbering Shotgun Playhouse and restoring the old theater to its prime. Like me: I'm in the prime of my life, still young enough to turn heads but old enough not to give a fuck." The judge held up her hand and wiggled her fingers. "This life. Of course I'm all right. Though I'm beginning to believe there's something rotten, as they say, in the state of Denmark. Between the recent museum murders and the killings last winter, I wonder if it isn't time to move to somewhere less violent. Like Chicago."

I had to smile at that. "Why are you here, Judge?"

"I play bunco with Chief Teller's wife. She called me as soon as she heard." Dumont took another swig of the gin. "I had to see it for myself. It's the former prosecutor in me, I suppose. And more importantly, Caleb was a friend, a mentor. I can't believe he's gone."

I nodded, well aware that I was in a precarious situation. On the one hand, Judge Dumont would need to know pertinent details as the investigation progressed, as she or the associate judge would be the ones to sign off on search and arrest warrants. On the other hand, her colleague had been viciously murdered, and as a motive had not yet been established, there remained the possibility that she herself could be a target.

"I'll do whatever I can to help you catch his killer. Whatever it takes. Caleb was a good friend to me over the years," she added.

"Judge Dumont, I'd like you to consider laying low for the next few days. Can you reschedule your cases? Stay out of sight for a while?"

Shock in her eyes. "You think I might be a target?"

Frankly, I was surprised she hadn't considered it. "Possibly. You, or other court personnel. We don't yet know what we're dealing with. At least consider it; talk it over with Nash."

"My husband is many things, but a good listener he is not." Dumont sighed. "Look, you and I don't know each other very well. If we did, you'd know that I don't back down, ever. If it's my time to go, then it's my time to go. Until then, I refuse to be a coward. I have a court to run, cases to rule on. People are counting on me, Detective."

"If I may be so blunt, Judge, that's both commendable and foolish."

She shrugged and took another, albeit smaller, sip from her flask. "I don't know how to be anyone but me. Besides, Caleb had left the bench. I'd look to people who fell outside of his career to find your suspect."

We sat on that, silent, watching as life continued around us. It was late now, past ten o'clock, though the techs were still hard at work collecting evidence. As Finn had thought, the search radius was large and surprisingly high . . . they'd found a piece of bumper from the Mercedes ten feet up in the branches of a pine tree. Though it was incredibly gruesome to think about, it was a wonder that there'd been anything left of Caleb's body at all.

A couple of older boys, maybe fifteen or sixteen, rolled by us on bicycles, their faces obscured by bloodied hockey masks, their handlebars weighted down by bulging bags of candy. One of them let loose with a banshee call and Dumont flinched. She quickly stood. "If there's nothing else? I need to get the hell out of here. I feel as though I'm on the verge of falling down into a very long and very deep rabbit hole, one from which I may never emerge."

"Perhaps we can talk tomorrow more."

The judge nodded, gathered her things, and walked away, her head down but her shoulders squared back. She was a strong woman, but I wondered if she wasn't a little naïve.

I found Finn at the perimeter of the crime scene. As the night had worn on, it had gotten colder and colder. He handed me a knit cap and an extra pair of leather gloves. I slipped them on, grateful.

"I just got off the phone with Ravi. We lucked out; Montgomery had oral surgery a few years ago and his X-rays were in his records at the hospital. She said it won't take long to make a comparison. His, uh, jaw was intact."

Shivering, I nodded.

Finn rested his hand lightly on my back for a moment, then let it drop. "You don't need to do this, you know. Work this particular case. Say the word and we'll sub Moriarty. I didn't mean to be an ass earlier; you know as well as I do that some cases are better handled by others."

"Thanks for the offer, and the apology, but I need to be along for every step of this investigation. I owe it to him, to my family." I stared down, noticed dark streaks of soot on the front of my jacket and black stains on the palms of my hands. I rubbed them on my dark pants but the marks refused to disappear. "This is personal."

"Be careful, Gemma. In this business, we can't afford to let things be personal. You hungry?"

To my surprise, I was. "House of Five Spices?"

"You got it."

We grabbed a couple of bowls of fried rice and Kung Pao chicken from the twenty-four-hour Chinese restaurant near the police station and ate standing at a long white counter under blinking fluorescent lights. I dumped extra sweet-and-sour sauce onto my fried rice and devoured the whole thing in four bites. The Kung Pao chicken took three. A long swallow of lemonade and I was almost feeling back to normal.

Then Finn's phone rang.

He took the call, his face growing more somber with each passing moment. Finally, he hung up, and turned to me. "That was Ravi. Caleb Montgomery's dental X-rays match the body. I'm sorry, Gemma. It's him."

My heart sank. I'd known this moment was coming but it didn't make hearing it any easier.

I pushed the lemonade away, a sour taste rising in my throat. "Come on, we've got work to do."

# Chapter Four

Caleb's last words to me had been a warning to watch out for the monsters. Now Caleb was dead, and it was up to me to break the news to my grandfather Bull and then to Caleb's widow. I was hoping the former would help me with the latter.

And unfortunately, neither could wait until first light.

Caleb was too well known in town; it would be a matter of hours before the news leaked to reporters. The thought of either Bull or Edith Montgomery hearing the worst from the radio or the television was enough to turn the fried rice in my stomach.

From the car, I phoned home and spoke with Brody. He was shocked to hear the news, and sorry that my night seemed to be getting longer by the minute . . . but as he liked to say, he knew what he was getting into when the two of us hooked up six years ago. Once I'd sworn the oath and slipped on the blue, my life was no longer my own; my time, my energy, even my dreams belong in equal parts to both victim and perpetrator.

Brody, and Grace, shared me with the dead.

We managed to make it work. We employed a wonderful young woman, Clementine Major, as a full-time nanny for Grace so that Brody could continue excelling at his job in town. A former geologist, he worked for a consulting company, assisting with international mining contracts and securing business deals. He'd done well for himself and there was talk that he could be appointed a vice president in the coming year. The extra income would be nice, but the promotion would mean more travel for Brody, and I wasn't sure how I felt about that.

A long-ago affair between him and a colleague had left me often unsure of the footing between us; things always seemed to get rockier the longer and more often he was away. Things were . . . easier when he was home.

Less messy, somehow.

Especially now that we were to be married in a few weeks. Things finally felt as though they'd reached a nice, easy state of stability.

I ended the call with a promise to wake him when I arrived home.

By the time I was on the road, it was after eleven. An evening fog had crept into the valley and it hung, a low cloud, over the land. Though the heat ran full blast, my core was numb with cold grief.

On the radio, Warren Zevon sang about werewolves in London. The station was playing all the Halloween hits, had been doing so for the last week. I'd be glad when they switched over to Christmas jingles, which in my experience would happen exactly three seconds after the calendar turned to November 1.

I texted Bull and discovered he was having coffee at a diner that stayed open late near his house. Since we'd moved my grandmother, Julia Weston, into a long-term care center across town, Bull had taken to spending his evenings in a rotation of late-night diners, card games, and double features at the cinema. I found him at a booth near the back, with a full cup of coffee and a half-eaten slice of apple pie.

I gave him a hug, then eyed the pie. "Are you going to eat that?"

"Help yourself. I think it's a little heavy on the cinnamon." Bull sipped his coffee, watched me take a bite.

"It's delicious. I can barely taste the cinnamon. It could have used a pinch more, in my opinion."

He rolled his eyes. "Gemma, out with it. If you're not home with your family, you must be working a case. So, spill. What do you need from me?"

Bull was grumpy these days, though that didn't make him wrong; I was stalling. I took in his shock of white hair, his narrow, lanky frame. He'd lost ten pounds over the last few months, most of it from stress and worry over my grandmother. His angst was understandable. After all, Julia, the woman who had raised me after my parents were killed in a car accident, the woman we both loved, was dying.

Maybe not today, maybe not tomorrow.

But bit by bit, her memory and abilities were being stolen by dementia.

And eventually, the loss of brain function or a secondary infection would kill her.

The last few years had been rough on all of us, but especially on Bull. Though he remained active in the community since retiring as a judge, mostly with his church and the local Boys & Girls Clubs, I worried how he would do once my grandmother did pass. He'd spent the last two years so focused on her health and care that I guessed he'd been neglecting his own.

Bull raised his eyebrows when he saw the serious expression on my face. "This can't be good."

"It's not." I took his hand. The diner was a fifties-themed dive joint, all hot pink and turquoise vinyl. From a jukebox in the corner, a woman whose voice I didn't recognize sang about troubles with her man. It was a strange and surreal setting to deliver the news, but as Ravi had quoted . . . *death comes when it will*. There could be no further delay. "I'm so sorry to tell you this. Caleb Montgomery is dead."

Bull went white. "*Caleb?* That can't be, Gemma. You're mistaken. I just spoke with him yesterday."

"I saw his body, Bull. He's dead. There was an explosion tonight, outside his office on south Main. Caleb's car, it . . . well, it may have been a car bomb. He was inside the vehicle when it caught fire."

Bull's eyes grew damp. "A bomb?"

"The fire department is investigating and, of course, so will we. We'll get the bastard that did this, Bull. I swear it."

"My God. I can't believe this." My grandfather rubbed at his temples, pinched his eyes shut. "Has Edith been notified?"

"No, not yet. I'm hoping you'll come with me. You were Caleb's best friend. I'm sure Edith would appreciate you being there. And, to be honest, it's been months since I've seen her."

"Of course." Bull paused, then added in a weary voice, "They're separated, you know."

"Who, Caleb and Edith?"

"Yes. Caleb moved out of the house in July. He's been living at the Tate Lodge Inn until the divorce was finalized, at which point he planned to buy a condo." Bull looked around the diner, watched as a couple of older women dressed in costumes took up seats at the counter and began chatting to one another loudly.

I had to lean forward to catch what Bull was saying.

"I think he might have been seeing someone on the side. Edith, too, maybe."

"You don't say." I excused myself to call the station and arrange for an officer to secure Caleb's rooms at the hotel until Finn and I got a search warrant. As I ended the call, I bit my lip, thinking. Edith and Caleb Montgomery were wealthy. I'd left the crime scene certain that the same individual who'd sent Caleb the threatening letters had killed him. But divorce can make people do strange things, and if you tossed affairs into the mix . . . I was suddenly forced to confront an unexpected motive, and suspect, in Caleb's death.

As I returned to Bull, I asked, "Were things friendly between them?"

"Well . . . not exactly. The last I heard, most of the conversation was going through the attorneys. They've both got top-notch people representing their interests and I'm sure they've been advised to keep contact to a minimum." Bull saw the look on my face and sat up straight, his eyes darkening. "You can't possibly imagine Edith had anything to do with Caleb's death."

I'd seen too much in my career to put anything out of the

realm of possibility. But at that very moment, I'd actually returned to thinking again about the threats. I described them to my grandfather, quoting what I could remember from the few I'd read. "Why would Caleb wait so long to bring them to our attention?"

Bull thought a moment. "Well, if I had to guess, I'd say that Caleb didn't want to let the sender have the satisfaction of him reporting them. Which of course is all sorts of screwy but Caleb could be an odd duck." He checked his watch and stood, withdrawing a crumpled ten-dollar bill and tossing it on the table. "It's getting late, Gemma. We should go to Edith."

I followed Bull out of the diner. We drove the fifteen-minute trip separately, slowly, through the thickening fog. By the time I parked and met Bull in the driveway of the Montgomery mansion on Fifth Street, it was nearing midnight.

We walked to the house, our shoes crunching on a carpet of fallen leaves, the path ahead illuminated by dozens of ground-level lights. The house was a beautiful rambling manor of redbrick, with a wide wraparound porch and Victorian turrets. It had once belonged to the wealthiest man in Cedar Valley, Stanley Wanamaker James, the town's first silver baron. After the mansion had fallen into disarray in the 1980s, Caleb and Edith had bought it for pennies on the dollar and then sunk thousands into repairing and restoring it.

To my relief, a number of lights still burned in the house's windows. I wouldn't have to rouse Edith from sleep only to then deliver her straight into a nightmare.

Someone, presumably Edith, had placed carved pumpkins on the porch. Next to the gourds, a straw-stuffed scarecrow sat in a rocking chair, a felt hat pulled down low, shading his face. At his feet, a large plastic crow stared at us. All of this, the entire Halloween tableau, was lit up by an orange glow from the hanging porch light.

And on the front door, the wooden silhouette of a witch on a broomstick was carefully hung with a strand of inky black ribbon.

The witch reminded me of something, something I'd forgotten, perhaps even repressed, for years.

The memory came barreling back like a runaway train. I stopped at the first step leading up to the porch and shuddered.

Bull paused at the top of the steps, sensed the fear that had descended over me. "What's wrong?"

It took me a moment to get the words out. "I'd forgotten all about the Halloween party here, when I was six or seven years old. Do you remember it?"

"I'll never forget that night. We thought we'd lost you." Bull shook his head and murmured, "I don't think I've ever been so terrified in my life."

The words tumbled from my mouth as I remembered all the details of that long, strange evening.

Or rather, not all of them.

Not the important ones.

"There were a handful of children here, weren't there? We decided to play hide-and-go-seek in Edith's gardens, at the back of the house. It was warm that year, too warm for Halloween. Then it turned cold. I can still feel the sudden gust of wind, the way the night got darker, like someone had hung a blanket up over the moon and the stars. The sky went black. And then everyone was gone. They must have run inside, but I missed the message. I was alone."

I swallowed the lump in my throat. "It was the most complete loneliness I'd ever felt. I remember walking back toward the house. I was nearly there when a shrub stood up and outstretched its arms. I realized it wasn't a shrub at all but a witch. And out of her head flew a pair of bats, huge, black bats as big as birds. Then a gray mist settled around me. I ran. I ran for what seemed like hours. All I could think about was getting away from the witch."

My mouth was dry and my legs felt like they'd been encased in cement. I forced myself up the stairs until I'd reached the top and joined Bull on the porch.

"Cal always thought there was a cave somewhere around here where the bats hibernated; he'd seen them over the years, too. Anyway, thank goodness we found you." Bull put an arm around my shoulders. "It started snowing, just after we got home and tucked you in bed. Your grandmother couldn't stop crying at the idea of you out there in a snowstorm. Alone, lost."

"Where did you find me?"

Bull paused, his hand about to grasp the door knocker. "You don't remember?"

"No."

"You were in the Old Cabin Woods. We found you inside the ruins, tucked in beside the remains of the chimney. It was a miracle; other than a few scratches and bruises, you were okay."

Bull gripped the door knocker and banged it once, twice, three times. With each knock, the wooden witch jumped on her broom.

Was Bull right? Had I been okay?

The Old Cabin Woods, whose proper name was the Ashley Forest, was the sprawling open space and wilderness that the Montgomery's house butted up against. Its nickname came from the homesteader's cabin that had been the only residential building on the land for years. The cabin, and the homesteader inside it, burned down over a hundred years ago and the ruins were said to be haunted by his ghost. At least, that's what parents told their kids in an effort to keep them from playing in those particular woods. The land was littered with rusted steel animal traps, the kind with sharp teeth that jumped up and snared legs when the trap was stepped on. And under the heavy cover of thick trees, the soil was loose and the many creeks that ran through the forest combined with the soil to create a thick mud, similar to quicksand.

Bull knocked on the front door again as I said, "This property is fenced. How did I get out of the yard? The cabin has to be at least a mile north of here."

Bull drew a hand over his mouth. "We never did figure that out. The back gate was closed. I've always believed one of those kids you liked to pal around with opened the gate and then shut it behind you. A practical joke."

We heard the telltale clack of high heels on wood floors.

I did my best to switch gears, from frightened little girl to confident detective. Edith Montgomery would open the door soon, and when she did, Bull and I would talk to her from two very different places. Murder is never easy; it's ten times harder when the victim is a friend and his soon-to-be ex-wife is also a friend.

And now, possibly a suspect.

No matter what Bull said, a pending divorce is always taken into consideration during a murder investigation. The complications, the emotions . . . and in this case, the immense wealth at stake.

Edith opened the door, a surprised look in her eyes. "Well, well. You're not the trick-or-treaters I expected. Bull, you know that Caleb is staying at the Tate. And Gemma, dear, my goodness. It's been a while. I haven't seen you since Grace was born."

She leaned forward, grasped my shoulders, and gave me a kiss on each cheek. She smelled of tobacco and rose-scented lotion.

"Hello, Edith."

She had aged in the last few months, though still was stunning. Her short silver hair was coiffed, her nails manicured, her cornflower-blue silk bathrobe both tasteful and casual. It was the dark circles under her eyes and the puckering of her lips, as if she'd sucked on a slice of lemon a moment too long, that made her look far older than her fifty-five years. Some of that was her decades-long addiction to cigarettes.

I wondered if the rest of it had to do with the separation. Edith had been very young when she married Caleb. For the first time in her life perhaps, she was living on her own, making decisions of her own accord.

"Edith?" a deep male voice called from somewhere within the depths of the house. "Is everything all right?"

*Or perhaps not.*

"Yes, Tom," Edith said over her shoulder. She turned back to us and frowned. "It's quite late and you still haven't said why you're here. I'm beginning to worry."

"Edie, the thing is . . ." Bull paused, cleared his throat. "Can we come in? We need to talk to you."

Nodding, Edith stepped to the side, then closed and locked the door behind us. We stood in the foyer, a handsome space with antique furniture, potted ferns, and framed portraits on dark-paneled walls. A half-empty bowl of candies sat on a side table, an earmarked paperback next to it. From the adjacent sitting room, a man appeared. He was in his thirties, of average height and weight, remarkably unremarkable save for his twin black eyes and the bandages covering his nose.

Still, something about him was vaguely familiar.

"Thomas Gearhart, at your service." He bowed dramatically, sweeping his blond hair from his forehead where it fell in unruly locks. "You may call me Tom. Please excuse the ghoulish appearance. I had plastic surgery recently. Reconstruction of a broken nose, an accident I sustained on set years ago. I should have fixed it back then, but you know how these things go. Hollywood waits for no man."

"Tom is my younger brother. Half brother, actually, from my father's second marriage. He's an actor and unfortunately, the Los Angeles tabloids are ruthless. He flew to Denver for his surgery and is spending a few weeks here with me as he recovers." Edith gave her brother a pat on the shoulder. "It's been too long since we spent time together."

Bull and I introduced ourselves and Tom shook our hands enthusiastically, even giving me a little bow. "I played a detective once, maybe you saw it? I was Teddy Carmichael in *The Night Is Silent*."

The actor stared at me, then at Bull, hope shining in his swollen eyes.

"Hmm, I *do* think I saw that one," Bull murmured politely.

"Heck of a movie. Edie, darling, can we sit down in the living room? We need to talk and I'm afraid I'm not as young as I once was. Between the dampness of the night and the late hour, these bones are weary."

Edith led us into the living room. She took a seat on a pale pink sofa and I watched as her right hand moved to her throat. She knew it was bad. When a cop knocks on the door at midnight, it's rarely good news. Tom sat in a nearby chair and gripped the arms, his gaze moving from me to Bull to Edith and back again to me. He, too, sensed the worst.

Edith's lips began to twist and pucker. "It's Caleb, isn't it? That's why you're here, something has happened to him."

I took the spot next to her and gripped her left hand. Her skin was cool, her hands bony and free of jewelry. I realized that I'd never seen her before without the enormous engagement ring she wore next to her wedding band. For a moment, I couldn't help wondering what had gone through her mind as she removed the diamond set, after she and Caleb had separated, likely believing she'd never wear them again.

I'd worn my own engagement ring for six months now, and putting it on for the first time had been both exhilarating and ter-rifying. My hands, for so long my own, anonymous and functional, now told the world a story: they were hands that were held.

I was tethered to someone.

"What happened?" Edith asked urgently. She closed her eyes, steeling herself.

Though I'd made notifications to next of kin more times than I liked to count, it never got any easier. Nor should it; it is a mo-ment of profound sadness and despair, absolutely devoid of peace or hope.

I swallowed hard. "Caleb was killed this evening in an explo-sion, in his car. It happened very fast and I don't believe that he suffered."

Edith slumped down on the sofa and began to weep. Tom

jumped up and hurried from the room, returning a moment later with a box of tissues. He handed her a few, then took a seat on the other side of her and placed an arm around her shoulders.

"I can't believe this. I want to see Cal's body." Edith sat up, dabbed at her eyes. "Where is he?"

"I'm afraid that won't be possible. He was badly burned and the medical examiner is performing an autopsy," I said gently.

Tom's brows furrowed. "Is an autopsy really necessary? You said there was an explosion . . . isn't the cause of death obvious? Hasn't my sister suffered enough?"

"It's standard procedure with any suspicious death," I replied. "Edith, it's too early to know what caused the fire. But you should know that I saw Caleb tonight, while Brody and Grace and I were trick-or-treating. In fact, I think I may have been the last person to see him alive. He showed me the threats he's received and I believe there may be a connection."

Silently, moving like a silver-screen actress, Edith rose from the couch and went to the grand piano near the window. Her fingers moved over the keys, filling the space with jarring, discordant notes. After a moment, she sighed and stopped playing. She moved to the window and flicked the curtain to the side.

Staring out into the night, Edith muttered, "Halloween. What a joke. The ghouls are here now, they're always here. As if they'd only come out on one night to play."

From her robe pocket, she withdrew a pack of cigarettes and a lighter. A moment later, she was smoking, moving the cigarette to and from her mouth and exhaling deeply. She turned from the window and faced us. "I begged Caleb to go to the police. He always was a stubborn son of a bitch. He only agreed to go after the noises started up again yesterday."

I asked, "Noises?"

"Yes. At night, there are strange noises and lights coming from the Ashley Forest. You'll think I'm crazy but they seemed to start around the time that the letters began to appear. The noises are incredibly loud thumps, like someone is taking a mallet to a stack of wood. And the lights . . . they're dizzying. Blues and reds and greens, tiny flickering lights. Like lightning bugs, if lightning bugs had nestled into every available nook and cranny in those woods." Edith glanced at me. "I remember that night, you know. The night you got lost out there. Have you been back since?"

I shook my head.

Edith said, "No, of course not. Not after what you went through. Perhaps one of your colleagues could check out the woods, just the area beyond our property. I've asked the neighbors and they haven't seen or heard a thing. Maybe I *am* going crazy."

"You're the least crazy person I know, darling," Tom said, then shuddered. "Death threats . . . noises in the dark . . . My God, Edith, what is going on here? Detective, is my sister in danger? Am *I* in danger? I have a spot in a pilot for a television project in Seattle in two weeks. I absolutely can't miss it."

The man was too much. I swallowed the hysterical, exhausted giggle that threatened to burst from my lips. "Tom, I don't believe you're in any danger, though I'll be honest, I do feel better knowing you're here with Edith."

The actor drew himself up to his full five feet, five inches and puffed out his chest. "I'll stay as long as Edie needs me."

Edith returned to her seat on the couch. I asked, "What can you tell me about the letters?"

She thought a moment, then said, "They started arriving a few months ago, one every couple of weeks or so. It was about the time that Caleb and I first talked about separating. He didn't show them to me until, oh, maybe the fifth or sixth one. I read the first one so many times I ended up memorizing it: *'Time's up, old friend. I will take your eyes and then your tongue, leaving you unable to see or speak. Only then will your lies end. I'm one nightmare you'll never wake up from.'*"

"Good lord," Tom exclaimed. He turned pale and drew his left hand to his bandaged nose. He began to gently prod at it, wincing with each poke. "Are they all like that?"

Edith nodded. "Some are worse, more graphic. They were mailed here, to the house, even after Cal moved out. I found that odd, though reassuring, to be truthful. It seemed to me that if the sender didn't know Caleb had left, then he must not be watching the house."

"Maybe the author wants you to think that, so that you'll let your guard down," Bull murmured.

"You know the kind of people that came before Caleb, the men and women whose fates he, and his juries, decided," Edith said to Bull. "Didn't you ever receive letters like this?"

Bull looked uncomfortable. "Well . . . well, sure. Of course. It comes with the territory of being a judge. But I've reported every letter I ever received, every threatening call ever placed to my house. Edie, I know for a fact that Caleb followed the same protocol in the past. Why did he not do it with these letters? There's something about them that is different. Wouldn't you agree, Gemma?"

I nodded. "Yes, they're disturbing. My partner even called them poetic. There's an obsessive feeling to them as well. Edith, the letter you quoted just now, it mentioned 'lies' and 'old friend.' If I had to guess, I'd say the author was known to Caleb. Caleb might not have been able to name the author, but the familial tone indicates some kind of relationship."

Edith quickly shook her head. "No, I don't think Caleb did know the author. He certainly didn't know what 'lies' were referenced. Well . . . I imagine the threats will stop now. Either the sender killed Caleb or he'll hear about it on the news and that will be the end of it."

"You could be right. Edith, I have to ask . . . why did you and Caleb separate?" I posed the question gently, but inside, my emotions were anything but gentle. The answers I received could point me in any number of directions and motives: lovers, affairs, jealousy, resentment.

Edith sighed deeply. "Lack of attention. I think marriages are like leftovers in the fridge; you stop paying attention and pretty soon you've got mold on what was once a nice meal. Wait too much longer and it's ruined. We were busy, Caleb and I. He had his practice, I'm on a number of boards and do various charity work. Silence over dinner soon became silence at breakfast, then at lunch. I zigged and he zagged. They say opposites attract but they don't tell you that you've got to constantly seek the middle ground. It's the only way we get out of this alive. No pun intended."

Tears began to stream down her pale cheeks. I felt queasy at her words, wondering if I'd been paying enough attention to the "leftovers in the fridge," so to speak, in my own house.

We spoke for a few moments more, explaining the next steps in the process that is an investigation. Eventually, the medical examiner would release Caleb's body to Edith. In the meantime, she could begin planning a funeral, contacting his attorneys, letting them know of his passing. She remained remarkably composed, though I knew grief takes on many forms. Bull and I left when it was obvious that Edith could not take any more. She moved slowly up the stairs in her bare feet, her slippers dangling from her right hand, her left hand hugging the polished banister as though holding on for dear life.

Bull and I spent another few minutes talking outside, at our cars. The fog had lifted, though the night had turned bitterly cold. In the Rockies, autumn often dies a sudden, quick death of her own, her glorious display of color suddenly smothered by a whiteness that will stretch on for miles, for days at a time.

"It bothers me, the fact that the letters continued to be sent to the house and not Caleb's hotel room; his murder, after all, was the work of someone close by, someone mere yards away." I drew my jacket tight. "Could Caleb have known the sender? Perhaps he was protecting someone?"

"Caleb wasn't the type to shelter criminals," Bull said. He started to say more, then his words were swallowed by an immense yawn. My grandfather had aged tonight before my eyes and I knew that before this was over, the death of his friend would take a heavy toll on him.

"Promise me you'll take precautions, too, Bull. You and Caleb were close, and you were the sitting judge before he was. Keep your eyes and ears open."

"Always."

I asked him a final question, one I hadn't been comfortable asking Edith yet: "Why did they really separate? Was that true, what she said? They grew apart?"

Bull gave the smallest of shrugs. "Marriage is hard work, Gemma. I think perhaps Caleb and Edith both got too tired to keep fighting for the union. But at the end of the day, what goes on between a man and a woman is between them."

"Not when one of them is brutally murdered."

"I suppose not. Let's talk more tomorrow, honey."

"I'll call you."

I drove out of town with the radio off, embracing the long minutes of silence and the darkness around me. At home, I stood in the kitchen and drank a glass of ice-cold orange juice. The counters were clean, the day's mail sorted into orderly piles to file, deal with, or recycle. In her high chair, Grace's favorite doll was tucked in, patiently awaiting a meal she couldn't eat. The doll, with its black stitched eyes and sunken crab-apple face, was my least favorite of Grace's toys. It reminded me of something cursed, something from a horror movie.

Even the floor had been swept and the dog's bowls wiped clean.

It was all so normal, such a comforting tableau of home and family and routine.

It could all so easily be taken away.

Upstairs, I checked in on the baby. Grace was fast asleep, her arms and legs tucked in under her body. From the corner of the room, a night-light emitted a soft, warm glow. All was safe, all was secure.

All was at peace, for now at least.

I moved to our bedroom, stripped, and climbed into bed. Beside me, Brody snored softly, and from the floor, cozy in his dog bed, our basset hound, Seamus, grunted. I closed my eyes as moments from the day marched by: the gruesome threats; Caleb's body, burned beyond recognition; the hooded man in the burlap mask.

Was he the one that I would chase in the days to come?

The last thing I remembered before I fell asleep was a witch, and a little girl, running blindly, consumed by fear, headed into a dark and cold night in the Old Cabin Woods.

# Chapter Five

I woke early on Tuesday from a restless sleep with the taste of ashes in my mouth, the lingering aftermath of a dark dream in which I walked among the ruined stalks of a burnt cornfield, an army of crows at my side. I pulled myself out of bed and went to the window and glanced out, not terribly surprised to see a thick layer of frost on the trees and ground.

After a long, hot shower, I dressed in a sweater, dark jeans, and my sturdiest leather boots.

I peeked in on Grace and found the baby on her stomach, still asleep, her face turned to the side. She'd taken to throwing pacifiers out of her crib and I stealthily replaced them, hoping if she woke up, she'd find one, pop it in, and doze back off to sleep. Then I leaned in and gave her the lightest of kisses on her soft cheek. She smelled of deep sleep and baby breath.

She smelled of home.

Downstairs, I made a pot of fresh coffee and reheated a slice of week-old pizza. *Breakfast of champions,* I thought, as I checked the forecast online. I groaned when I saw that temperatures would continue to drop over the week, with another chance of snow by the weekend.

Summer, and now fall, had come and gone too fast.

Footsteps behind me, then flannel-clad arms around my waist. "Morning," Brody murmured into my ear. "I didn't hear you get up. Or come in, for that matter."

"It was late. I didn't want to wake you."

Brody stepped away and went to the windows to open the curtains. "Looks cold out there."

"It'll snow by the weekend."

"I'll check the firewood supply," he said. We had an old iron wood-burning stove in our living room that heated the whole house. I loved the coziness of it, but it was Brody who cut and stored the wood for it. If we were busy, he'd often end up buying wood at the hardware store in town.

He asked, "Did you get any sleep?"

"A couple of hours. I still can't believe Caleb is gone. Bull and I went to Edith last night, broke the news to her." I shut my laptop down and checked my bag, made sure I had my wallet, phone, keys, and snacks. "They were separated; did you know that?"

"Edith and Caleb? Since when?"

"A few months." I poured another half cup of coffee and added a healthy splash of cream. "It must be strange, to be married all those years and then suddenly one or both them decided it was over. Just like that."

Brody shrugged as he poured himself a cup of milk. "I guess. Though I don't think it happens that suddenly. There are always signs."

"I suppose. Anyway, this investigation is going to keep me busy."

"I know the drill, honey. Grace and I will be fine. As long as I get to see your beautiful face at the end of the aisle in four weeks, I'll be a happy man."

*"Four?"* My heart dropped as I went to the wall and flipped the pages on the hanging weekly calendar. "Damn it."

"I remind you that our wedding is in four weeks and you say 'damn it'?" Brody groaned. "Do I need to be worried?"

"No. There's just so much left to do. We need to get the final head count to the caterer, and my dress should be hemmed another inch. I didn't even tell you this yet, but the florist screwed up our order. It won't cost us, but he tried blaming me. How does someone read 'white roses' and walk away thinking I want yellow daisies? In November, of all months?" I asked, still fuming over the way the man had tried to pull a fast one on me. "So . . . maybe we should push the date back again?"

Brody shook his head. "No way. Clementine offered to help us. I'll have her figure out the head count and you can squeeze in a dress fitting in the next few days. We're not pushing our wedding back again. And you know my sisters have plane tickets they've already purchased."

"You're right." I turned away, biting my lip as I rinsed my mug and put it in the dishwasher. We'd originally been scheduled to marry in the middle of September, but I'd postponed things when my grandmother Julia had hit a particularly rough patch and the timing just hadn't felt right. Brody's sisters, all four of them, hadn't been thrilled about changing their travel plans. They were flying in from California and I'd yet to meet any of them.

Rachel, Mary, Naomi, and Sarah . . .

The four furies. Or maybe not. I'm sure they were all lovely women.

"Thank God for Clementine," I muttered. We'd originally thought Brody would take on the role of stay-at-home parent, but that had lasted just a few short months. It wasn't in either of our natures to give up our careers, and to be honest, I knew that being exposed to different people was good for Grace. She and Clementine went to the pool at the rec center, and visited the library, and scheduled play dates with other children in town.

Brody pulled eggs and fruit from the refrigerator. "Would you like an omelet?"

"No, I've got to run. I had the last of the pizza." I gathered the rest of my things. "Love you."

Brody pulled his head from the refrigerator, where he'd been rummaging through the stacks of leftovers and containers of food. "Did you eat the last avocado?"

"Guilty. I didn't think you wanted it."

"I *always* want the avocado."

I laughed. "I'm sorry. I'll make it up to you. Oh, hey, before I forget, on the topic of the wedding . . . the Tate Lodge needs the final deposit for the reception. Can you drop a check in the mail?"

Brody again pulled his head from the fridge and blew me a kiss. "For you, my lady, and for our wedding, I will happily give my hard-earned money away."

Outside, I started the car, turned the heat on full blast, and then began the torturous process of chipping away at the ice-skating rink on my front windshield. Once again I cursed our laziness and wished that we'd taken time over the summer to clear out our garage, so that it could be used for what it was intended for and not as a storage room for camping gear, fishing poles, half a dozen bikes, skis, and ice hockey sticks.

As I got the last of the ice off, Clementine arrived in her beat-up old Ford Bronco. We chatted a few minutes as she gathered her bags from the trunk. She let me know she'd planned to go out of town for a week over the Christmas holiday, to visit an old friend in New York. After a moment of silent panic, I said that was fine, and she agreed to write the dates she'd be gone on the family calendar. A week wasn't too bad; Brody and I could cobble together temporary childcare and each take a few vacation days. I knew he might have an overseas work trip in December, but surely he'd be back by the holidays.

I drove into town on roads that were slick with black ice. It was still early and signs of Halloween remained everywhere: fat, orange pumpkins rested in rows on wide Victorian porches beside giant spiderwebs, Styrofoam tombstones, and, in one terrifying case, a pair of seven-foot-tall lifelike clowns with bloody fangs thrusting out from wide, gaping jaws. Candy wrappers, still-glowing light sticks, and discarded plastic jack-o'-lanterns littered the streets.

As images from the night before began a slow traipse across my mind, I found I was worried about Bull. I couldn't imagine the level of his grief, and while I knew I had to push my own sadness aside, at least until the case was solved, I also knew it wasn't a healthy approach to healing. I decided to pay him a visit, armed with sustenance, so I swung by my favorite café, Four and Twenty Blackbirds. After a few minutes of scanning the pastry display, I decided on a couple of danishes and two hot chai teas.

On my way to Bull's, I made a quick stop at the edge of the Ashley Forest, the section that butted up to the Montgomery mansion. The air was still, the pine trees and aspens dusted with frost. It would have been beautiful but for the darkness that sat within the woods; it was as though it were a primeval forest, never touched by the sun. I shivered and quickly walked a quarter mile in each direction, checking the ground for tire tracks, cigarette stubs, anything to indicate recent visitors.

There was nothing, and I left as fast I could, not sure what Edith had witnessed. The noises could have been anything; the woods settling, trees falling (we had experienced some terrific late-summer thunderstorms, after all), even illegal loggers work-ing under cover of night. But the lights . . . I'd have to come back, perhaps bring a crime scene tech to run some tests on the trees.

I got to Bull's house a few minutes before eight o'clock and found him in the backyard, picking a large twig out of his rake, an exhausted look on his face. He wore heavy-duty gloves, a red plaid flannel jacket, and an old pair of work jeans, the dark denim splattered with paint stains. At his feet was an enormous pile of long-ago fallen leaves, their once-brilliant red and gold shades now a mottled, moldy, and decayed sludge of brown and gray.

"You look tired."

Bull looked at me with eyes that leaked and a nose as red as Rudolph's. He leaned forward and rested on the rake. "That's because I *am* tired. I've been so darn tired for so darn long."

"We can hire someone to do this, Bull. Find a local kid to mow the lawn, rake these leaves. You don't need to carry the whole world on your shoulders. Not anymore."

He brushed off the words with a wave of his hand. "Ah, it's not the physical stuff, Gem. It's all of it. First Frank Bellington, now Caleb. It's hard to be the last man standing."

At one time, Frank Bellington had been one of Bull's closest friends. He'd died the previous fall, but not before a terrible secret he'd been living with had been exposed. I thought at the time that Bull had handled Frank's passing rather stoically, but I wondered now if that had all been an act.

Or if not an act, a numbness.

"I look back at my life, and my friends, and I wonder if I really knew them at all. Caleb was a good man, Gemma—at least I thought he was. But good men aren't stalked and executed in cold blood. Not like this. This was payback. It was revenge for something."

"It's too early to know that, Bull. You're a good man, and look at some of the crackpots you've dealt with over the years. Any one of them could have hurt you, killed you, and you *still* would have been a good man." I gently took the rake from his hands. "If you're tired, stop. Rest. You've earned it. Besides, I brought danishes from the Blackbird. And a chai."

Bull pulled a handkerchief from the front pocket of his jacket and wiped first at his eyes, then his nose. He smiled sadly. "Thanks, sweetheart. I wish I could tell you that life gets easier as you get older, but that would be an outright lie. The Lord has seen fit to teach us lessons not when we're ready to receive them but when we least expect them."

"Well, I don't know anything about the Lord, but you do, and that's good enough for me."

Inside, we shared a pastry and talked about my grandmother Julia. She seemed to be settling in nicely to her new apartment at Carver Estates, the long-term care facility we'd enrolled her in a few months prior.

Then, reluctantly, I left him and headed to work. At my desk, I quickly skimmed my email messages and saw that a meeting had been scheduled later in the day at City Hall with our police team, the mayor, the fire chief, the city manager, and a few other names I didn't recognize. It would be the first meeting of many in the investigation; Caleb's was a high-profile death and everybody, it seemed, wanted to get in on the details.

I sat back, thinking.

I wanted to be able to give Chief Chavez something to report at the meeting, something meaningful. I kept going back to the threatening letters; they might be at the heart of this killing. And somewhere, perhaps buried deep in Caleb's past, might be the key to the sender. Bull himself had said that this was payback, revenge, which implied wrongdoing, either consciously or unconsciously, on Caleb's part.

And Edith had said the very first threat referenced lies.

Lies that Caleb told; or that the sender believed he'd told.

I sighed. Though the case had kicked off with a fiery and explosive bang, I knew a good part of the investigation would be the opposite; it would be conducting research, interviewing witnesses, and identifying patterns. And so I spent the next few hours knee-deep in our legal databases, putting together a list of the cases that Caleb Montgomery had been involved in, first during his time as a prosecuting attorney, then as a judge. The list was long, with some cases dating back to the 1960s, and it was difficult to know where to start.

Theoretically, anyone, even a disgruntled neighbor or an obsessive stranger, could have sent the letters, but I had to start somewhere. The personal tone of the letters, the nature of the violence they promised gave me the sense that the sender was someone Caleb had prosecuted or sentenced. Someone he knew, yet someone Edith—his own wife—could not name or suggest.

I recognized two names that jumped out at me immediately: serial killer Gordon Dillahunt, and John Mark Escher, who'd been responsible for bringing in a devastating wave of methamphetamines into the valley in the 1990s. Dillahunt was currently serving consecutive life sentences in the federal prison in nearby Belle Vista, and Escher had committed suicide after his own young son overdosed on heroin.

I recognized a handful of other names, perps whose cases I'd been involved with in the last few years. While it was possible any one of them could have sent the letters, these were small-time criminals, people whose lives had been overtaken by drink or drugs, addiction or illness. They were people who'd been easily arrested, not criminal masterminds.

I finally stopped, rubbed my eyes, and decided to get the intern, Jimmy, to work on cross-checking names on the list against those still in prison and those now deceased. It would be slow and tedious, but Jimmy was energetic and eager to learn. He was a hard worker, the son of two schoolteachers who'd steered him toward a career in education. After more than a decade working as a teacher in an inner-city school system, Jimmy had realized that his passion lay in law enforcement. He'd moved here, to Cedar Valley, after we'd accepted him as an intern. He was taking a criminal justice course at the community college, then hoped to apply to the academy in Denver.

I found Jimmy in the storage closet.

Well, it had once been a closet. We'd turned it into a temporary office with a narrow desk and a small chair and a laptop. Jimmy loved it. He'd plastered the walls with vintage newspapers and unscrewed the bare bulb that had hung from the mold-splotched ceiling, preferring instead to use a small green banker's lamp set back on his desk.

Jimmy was thrilled to take over my project and promised to get on it right away.

With his unruly cowlick and wide, eager eyes, Jimmy reminded me of another Jimmy: Jimmy Olsen, the erstwhile young photojournalist employed by the *Daily Planet*, friend to Clark Kent and Lois Lane.

Only I was definitely not Lois, or Clark, or Superman, for that matter.

And it would be good for me to remember that Jimmy, for all his enthusiasm, world experience, and helpfulness, was at the end of the day still just an intern. I needed to keep him out of trouble, not whet his appetite for action even more.

Back at my desk, Finn leaned over and said with a dramatic lisp, "Come here. I vant to suck your blood."

"Get in line, pal."

He grinned, his lips twisted around a set of plastic toy fangs. He popped the teeth out and set them next to his computer. "I talked with the manager at the Tate Lodge. He'll have a key to Caleb's suite waiting for us at the front desk. And I've been thinking about the wife. Rich old broad like Edith Montgomery, maybe she doesn't want to air her dirty laundry in court. She and Caleb were headed for a messy and public divorce. So, she hires someone to pack her husband's car with dynamite. I spent some time on the county records site. The Montgomerys used to own stock in a national mining company. Or rather, Edith did. She sold the company for dollars on the penny about thirteen years ago; that's where the bulk of their money came from."

"Mining? What does that have to do with anything?"

"Explosives, Gemma. Every mining company uses some form of them or another. It would be easy for someone with the right connections to get their hands on, say, dynamite." Finn leaned back, tented his fingers, and gazed at me. "By the way, how are you feeling? Late night."

"Fine. Though you're giving me a migraine." I sighed and turned back to the copy of the list of names I'd given Jimmy. "This isn't a Hitchcock thriller. You didn't see Edith last night; she was devastated."

Finn stood up and walked to the wall, where he'd started writing out all the details we knew from Caleb's death. "We need to search the Montgomery house. We'll get a warrant for the law offices, too, of course, but I'd bet there are still files, notes, paper-work at the main residence. He had to have a home office there."

"Let's start with a search of the Tate and *then* think about ap-proaching Judge Dumont for a warrant for the house. She's going to be reluctant to issue it on a grieving widow, especially given that Caleb's been staying at the Tate for the last five months. The Montgomery house was no longer his primary residence."

Finn frowned. "All right, we'll start with the Tate, but I'm tell-ing you, I don't like it. The more time we give the widow to clean things up, the less anything of value we'll collect."

"Take it easy. And stop calling her 'the widow.' If Edith Mont-gomery had anything to do with Caleb's death, she's not going any-where."

A text came in on my phone: *Can you come to the Shotgun? There's been another incident.*

I groaned.

"What is it?" Finn asked.

"Nash Dumont," I replied and shook my head in frustration. "I've been to the theater twice in the last week. Someone's screw-ing with him. The first time he called, it was for a trashed dress-ing room; the second time, it was for a vandalized theater seat. Someone took a knife or scissors and slashed the velvet seat cover to threads."

"Did you interview the cast, the crew?"

I shook my head again. "Nash won't let me. He said it will spook people if they know what's happening. So far, the only people who know are Nash, his wife Gloria, obviously, and the stage manager, some woman named Waverly. I can't wait to see what's happened now."

"Can you get someone else to investigate? We don't have time for this."

"No. I tried that when Nash called the second time; he's so paranoid. Says it has to be me." I thought a moment, then realized I could kill two birds with one stone. I texted Nash back and let him know I'd swing by that evening, then I called the courthouse. When I'd spoken with Judge Gloria Dumont the night before, she'd been understandably shaken, in shock. But she'd had a night to sleep on things now and she could have further thoughts as to who might have targeted Caleb.

I spoke to a deputy court clerk. She said Judge Dumont was tied up in court all day but could meet me that evening at the Shotgun Playhouse.

"Mayor Cabot has bumped up the meeting time at City Hall. Let's go. She's keeping everyone on their toes these days," Chief Chavez announced. He checked his watch and swore. "We're going to be late as it is."

I quickly gathered my purse and jacket. Finn joined me, throwing a tie around his neck, moving awkwardly. He'd been badly hurt by a bullet to the shoulder a few months prior, and every now and then, the old injury acted up. In a low voice, he said, "This murder is going to be politicized. The mayor has been sitting on her ass all these months, twiddling her thumbs, waiting for the perfect opportunity to strike. This is a case she can throw her weight behind, get on top of. It's no secret she's planning to run for governor within the next few years."

"You might be right, though I'm sure the mayor, like all our city leaders, likes to be informed for information's sake," I whispered back. "I do wonder how much sway she's got over Chavez. He seems to be kowtowing a little these days."

"The chief knows how to play the game." Finn was heated now. He hated the bureaucratic slowdown that could happen when elected officials stuck their noses into police business. I did, too, of course, but saw it more as the cost of doing business.

Finn took it personally.

The chief drove the three of us to City Hall in his personal car. It was a short ride, just a couple of minutes, but long enough for me to acquire a small case of nerves. I hadn't yet met the mayor, and in fact still thought of her as "new," though she'd been in office nearly a year. Based on the way the chief's jaw was set and his eyes narrowed, I didn't think we were in for anything good.

We parked, hustled inside, and jogged up the stairs to the city council chambers. Floor-to-ceiling windows looked out over the town, but the stunning view was the last thing on my mind as I took in the people already in the room. Fire Chief Max Teller, Fire Investigator Liv Ramirez, the city manager, and his assistants. A few department heads sat around the table, their expressions glum.

We'd just taken seats when Mayor Betty Cabot stepped into the room. There was a collective tightening up in the shoulders of the group and I wondered at the power this petite woman yielded. Nearly seventy years old, barely five feet tall, and on her fourth marriage, she favored turquoise-colored snakeskin cowboy boots and heavy silver jewelry. She was infamous for carrying four things with her at all times, most often in the enormous purse she lugged around: a wallet brimming with cash; a pistol; a bottle of tequila; and a tiny terrier named Dixie.

Cabot had been overheard saying there wasn't a problem on God's good Earth that couldn't be solved by money, a gun, a dog, or a drink, or some combination thereof.

When I thought about it, I figured she was probably right.

Mayor Cabot nodded to the room and took a seat at the head of the table. At her feet, Dixie let out a mighty bark then settled down. The mayor opened the meeting without preamble. "I understand the body has been identified?"

Chavez took the first question. "Good morning, Mayor. Yes, as we initially suspected, Caleb Montgomery was killed yesterday in the car explosion outside his law offices."

"Well, *shit*." Cabot wasn't one to mince words. "Any suspects?"

Chavez shook his head. "No, Mayor. It's early days yet, though we do have one avenue to investigate. Over the last few months,

Montgomery received a number of threatening letters. We'll look into them, of course. And as I understand it, Chief Teller's team has been working nonstop through the night to put together a preliminary report. Lengthier findings, of course, will take a few days."

"Of course." The mayor swiveled in her chair and stared at Teller. "Chief? What can you tell us?"

Teller cleared his throat and straightened his tie. I began to feel underdressed in my jeans and boots, though I'd had no way of knowing I'd be called into a meeting like this. And besides, I reminded myself, the mayor herself was in cowboy boots.

Turquoise cowboy boots. With crystals on the spurs.

Teller said, "Thank you, ma'am. As Chief Chavez said, my team hasn't stopped working since the explosion. I'd like to introduce Fire Investigator Olivia Ramirez, a top-notch employee. She's prepared to share her initial thoughts. Investigator, if you would, please?"

Ramirez stood, assumed a ramrod posture, and clasped her hands behind her back and pivoted so that she was facing Cabot. "It's a pleasure to make your acquaintance, Mayor. Bomb scene investigations take time, and I don't want to offer any preconceived notions until we have forensic evidence, so I'll be brief. My initial findings are that the blast effects and component fragments found in the deceased indicate a homemade bomb composed of sawdust and nitroglycerin: dynamite. The crater under the vehicle and other trace evidence would seem to confirm this."

"Soldier? At ease. This is not a combat situation, though the city manager might disagree." Cabot winked at the group. "So Montgomery, when he turned the key in the ignition, the dynamite detonated?"

Ramirez relaxed her stance. "Thank you, Mayor. No, I don't believe we'll find that Judge Montgomery was responsible for igniting the detonator. Witnesses in the vicinity of the scene report hearing a gunshot immediately before the explosion. I believe the killer detonated the bomb with a well-placed bullet. He's a professional, whoever he is. I wouldn't be surprised if he's spent time in the military, maybe special operations."

"He or she," Cabot murmured.

Ramirez's brow furrowed. "What?"

"You implied the suspect is a man. That's quite an assumption, considering we don't *have* a suspect yet," Cabot said. She turned to Chavez, in effect dismissing Ramirez. "Chief, what are your thoughts? Do we need to get the Bureau of Alcohol, Tobacco, Firearms and Explosives out here? You can all guess how I feel about the feds, but those boys in black get things done."

Ramirez stepped back, her face flushed, and took her seat. She noticed me watching her and stared back, eyes defiant.

Chavez hemmed and hawed, unusually indecisive. "We've alerted ATF already, of course. The Denver field office is tied up with a large arson investigation in a neighboring suburb, but they thought they could send someone up here in the next day or two. As Investigator Ramirez stated, this investigation will take some time anyway. Based on what I know so far, it sounds as though she and her team are on the right track. The perp may have construction or mining in his or her background. Or, as the investigator suggested, perhaps even military."

The mayor stood up and began to pace at the head of the table, back and forth, back and forth. The room was silent until she spoke again. "You may find this hard to believe, but I myself am a veteran. Lieutenant, United States Navy. While I find Investigator Ramirez's theory solid, here's where I get hung up: dynamite is, as my grandkids like to say about anything born or used before the year 2000, 'old school.' It is a sensitive, easily combustible substance, infrequently used outside of demolition and mining operations these days. In contrast, the military, rightly so, prefers to use explosives that will go off when, and only when, they are supposed to. We like precision with our bombs. So, I'd lean toward a mining contractor over military. And that leaves you with a hell of a lot of places to look. This state was built on the backbones and blood of miners."

"Excellent point, Mayor," Fire Chief Teller said. "I'll tell you where I'm getting stuck. Why use dynamite, or any explosive, at all? If the killer is such an excellent shot, why not just take Montgomery out with a rifle? Is he . . . *or she* . . . sending us a message?"

It was a valid question, and one to which none of us had an answer.

We spent the next half hour listening to the mayor and the city manager stress the importance of a quick collar. As if we didn't know. But we sat there, nodding our heads, smiling politely and looking concerned at all the right moments, until at last we were dismissed.

Chiefs Chavez and Teller walked out ahead of Finn and me, so we hung back a few feet to give them privacy as they talked. As we reached the front entrance of City Hall, Liv Ramirez appeared at my side.

"Well, that was fun," she said. "That old bird handed my ass to me on a platter. I should have known she was Navy, uptight chick like that."

"Sounded to me like she was sold on your findings," I said.

"My findings, sure. It's hard to disagree with facts. But my theory . . . she didn't agree with that," Ramirez said. She sighed and smoothed her hair back from her forehead. "I'm telling you, this reeks of military. Black ops stuff, real deep junk."

Finn scoffed. "Caleb Montgomery, while a hell of a nice guy, was a small-town, two-bit judge. Give me one reason a covert operation would be put together with the intent of assassinating him."

We were outside now, close to the parking lot. City employees and citizens walked by us without a second glance; we were just another couple of cogs in the wheel.

Ramirez stopped walking. "My ride's over there. You asked why someone would put together a covert operation to assassinate a retired judge. You're missing the point. This wasn't covert. If it was, the judge would have been found drowned in his bathtub, or dead of a supposed heart attack. We wouldn't have ever known anyone was here. Bomb like this, while professional, is also crude. And that means it's traceable. No . . . you're not looking for an operation. You're looking for a lone wolf."

# Chapter Six

**The chief ordered a couple of pizzas to be delivered for the team.**
We ate the piping-hot slices from Chevy's Pizzeria standing up,
strategizing our next steps in light of Ramirez's preliminary findings. It was all hands on deck, so Detectives Louis Moriarty and
his partner, Lucas Armstrong, joined us as well. The two Lou's had
a combined seventy years of law enforcement experience between
them. Physically, they were complete opposites: Moriarty was a
beefy red-faced man nearing seventy whose great-grandparents
had arrived at Ellis Island straight from the Emerald Isle. His only
son had been killed years before and he had long ago divorced.

The job was his life.

Armstrong, on the other hand, was a former linebacker from
Alabama. Ten or fifteen years ago, when he'd moved here, his had
been one of three black families in town. Thankfully, Cedar Valley had grown a bit more diverse and his girls were now a couple
of grown women; Maggie was living at home while she studied
for the law school entrance exam, and the younger, Megan, was in
school in Denver but came home every few weeks for a quick visit.
They were a tight-knit family. For Armstrong, law enforcement
had been a calling. He took the job seriously, but it wasn't his be-
all and end-all. That was going home every night to his wife and
daughters in no worse shape than he'd left them in the morning.

Though physically and philosophically opposites, Armstrong
and Moriarty made a solid team. And we could certainly use all

the help we could get. A car bomb was big and the investigation truly would touch a number of departments.

Armstrong spoke first. "So, Chief . . . what do you think the chances are of ATF actually sending someone?"

Chavez leaned forward, careful to avoid getting any pizza grease on his silk tie. "I'd say fifty-fifty. My understanding is that Olivia Ramirez is part of a national task force on bomb scene investigations. They feel like she's probably got things under control."

"How does someone with her background end up here?"

Chavez shrugged. "This is all secondhand, but word on the street is that she's got issues with authority. But she's good, very good, and Chief Teller owed someone a favor. To be honest, she's a coup, a triple win in terms of diversity: female, veteran, Hispanic. It'll be good for the fire department, for the town, to have her on board. Hell, I could see her making deputy someday, if she learns to walk the straight and narrow."

"A rebel after my own heart." Finn wiped his hands on a napkin, then casually asked, "She got any family? Husband, kids?"

For the first time since the pizza arrived, Moriarty took a break from chowing down and said, "Nope. She's unattached and very much looking."

"How do you know all this stuff? An attractive woman shows up and you guys put together a dossier on her? It's disgusting," I said. I paused, fully aware that Moriarty was probably champing at the bit to take my place on the Montgomery case should things get too personal, then added harshly, "She's a colleague. Show some respect."

"Hey!" Moriarty's face flushed. "No disrespect meant. She's renting the apartment above my garage. We share an affinity for a cold beer in the evening. She's told me things. The lady's just trying to make a fresh start, that's all. Her time in the military really messed with her head. She's lonely. To be honest, she could use a friend, Monroe. A *female* friend. A *confidante*."

With that, all eyes in the room swung to me.

"Fine. I'll see if she wants to be pals." I set down my plate and purposely took a step back from the table. There were still two slices of mozzarella with pineapple and pepperoncini in the box, but I knew I'd regret one more bite. "Now can we get back to the case at hand? How do you want to do this?"

We decided that Finn and I would go to the Tate Lodge Inn and search Caleb's rooms, while Moriarty and Armstrong would do Caleb's law office.

Finn and I drove to the Tate and parked near the expansive front lawn. In place of the usual Adirondack chairs and lawn games was a spooky cemetery of cardboard tombs and a few open caskets, their occupants jangly-looking plastic skeletons. The Tate threw an annual adults-only Halloween party, an event that was infamous for both the outrageous costumes and the fistfights that inevitably occurred. Last night's event had been unusually subdued, according to the logs I'd skimmed that morning.

As promised, there was a key waiting for us at the front desk. Even the staff was still in the spirit of things; the man who slipped us the key was dressed as a mummy.

Caleb's rooms were on the fifth floor, the Tate's highest, and were what amounted to a penthouse suite. Housekeeping had been ordered to leave the room as it was, and unless Caleb's killer had crept through here late last night, we were the first to enter the room. We took a quick walk through: two bedrooms, a small kitchenette and living area, and a bathroom. The décor was typical lodge style, with dark wooden furniture, red-and-brown plaid pillows, and heavy quilts in the bedrooms.

"Where do you want to start?" Finn slipped on a pair of gloves and handed me a second pair. "Bathroom?"

"Fine." I examined the items on the cluttered vanity as Finn peered in the cabinets, behind the shower curtain, even in the toilet tank. "Sleeping pills . . . prescription antacids . . . Viagra."

Finn groaned. "Getting old sucks."

"No kidding. There's nothing out of the ordinary here. Let's move on."

We left the bathroom and went to the larger of the two bedrooms. There, the bed remained unmade. A pair of boxer shorts and a crumpled white undershirt hung halfway off the bed. In the nightstand were a couple of paperback novels, a photo album, and a bottle of melatonin.

"Check this out." I held the album up, slowly flipping through the pages. "It's Edith and Caleb's wedding album. Galveston, Texas. Looks like an expensive party. I seem to recall that Edith came from a very wealthy family. Oil money, maybe."

Half of a photograph fell from the album. I picked it up, surprised at what I saw. Or rather, what I didn't see. "Look at this."

It was Caleb, Edith, and a third person standing together under a palm tree. Caleb and Edith were smiling, but it was impossible to know anything about the man other than he wore a heavy silver ring on his hand and a navy-blue suit. The rest of him had been cleanly ripped away.

Finn asked, "Who's the guy and who ripped the photograph?"

"Edith would know." I slipped the photograph into an evidence envelope.

Finn knelt and checked under the beds, feeling around for something—anything—tucked into the mattresses or pillows. "There's nothing here. Why would there be? It's like I said: if there's something to find, we'll find it at the Montgomery house or the law offices."

We were nearly done with the suite when Lucas Armstrong called. "I just got off the phone with Edith Montgomery. The house is ours to search if we want."

"Really? She just offered it up like that?" I relayed the news to Finn and he spun a finger in a circle: *let's go.*

Armstrong said, "Yes. Mrs. Montgomery knows the deal; she knew we'd come knocking sooner or later. So it's easy-peasy and let's not look a gift horse in the mouth. It would have been like pulling teeth to get Judge Dumont to sign off on anything."

"I agree. Okay, we'll wrap things up here and head over there. Did you find anything at the law offices?"

"No. The paralegal met us there, let us in. She was under-standably upset, sobbing the whole time. Anyway, there's this little thing, you might have heard of it, called attorney–client privilege. The warrant spelled it out real clear: we had a very narrow and specific scope of what we could look for."

"Sure." I thought of something and said it out loud: "Why didn't the killer bomb the office itself? Seems less risky than the car. Or rather, more stable. Houses don't move. There's more places to hide the explosives."

Armstrong replied, "I wondered about that, too. Who knows what goes through these idiots' heads?"

*This is no idiot we're chasing,* I thought as I hung up.

We met Armstrong and Moriarty outside the Montgomery mansion on Fifth Street. In the light of day, the witch on the front door didn't seem quite as terrifying, though I was certain she had changed position slightly.

Maybe it was the wind.

Edith's half brother, Tom Gearhart, let us into the house. He explained that Edith was napping in a guest bedroom on the third floor, and asked if we could save that room for last. He avoided any mention of his film career, instead staring at us with baleful eyes still bruised and shadowed from his surgery.

He was different today, more subdued.

Armstrong and Finn took the second floor, while Moriarty and I tackled the first.

We started in the living room. Moriarty gazed at the artwork, the furniture. "Geez, get a load of this place. It's like a museum. Though you've been here a lot, haven't you?"

"Not lately. More when I was a child. Edith used to throw the most incredible parties—Halloween, Christmas. Fourth of July was spectacular; we could see the fireworks on Lookout Mountain from a balcony on their third floor." I lifted the hood of the piano and felt underneath for anything unusual. I wasn't even sure what we might be looking for; a secret diary, perhaps, or the rest of the torn photograph we'd found.

I moved on from the piano to the framed paintings on the wall while Moriarty peeked behind curtains and under sofa cushions. Pulling my hair back into a high ponytail, I added, "Looking back, it was incredibly dangerous; that balcony is nothing more than some wrought-iron posts and a waist-high railing. But we were en-couraged, practically pushed, up there. 'Best seats in the house.'"

"The craziest folks I've ever met are the rich ones. They don't follow the same rules we do, Monroe. It's a different playbook alto-gether," Moriarty said. We moved on from the living room, taking our time in the library, then the kitchen, then the glass-encased solarium, where a beautiful macaw parrot on a wooden swing greeted us. An astonishing array of plants, many of them tropical, filled the room, giving it the look and smell of a secret garden.

Moriarty picked up a blue-and-white vase and whistled. "This is probably worth more than my house."

"Double, I'd say," said a low voice behind us. Tom stepped out of the shadows and gently took the vase from Moriarty's hands and replaced it on the side table. "Best not to drop it. Caleb bought that for Edith in China, on their honeymoon. They left straight after the wedding, flying first class all the way to Beijing."

"Speaking of their wedding . . ." I removed the photograph from my jacket pocket and handed it, still in the clear, protective evidence envelope, to Tom. "Do you know who that might have been? Standing next to Edith?"

Tom gazed at the photograph for a long moment, then shook his head and handed it back to me. "Haven't a clue. I spent most of that night with my head in a punch bowl of champagne. You found it like this, torn?"

"Yes, in Caleb's things at the hotel."

"I see. Well, I'll let you finish. Edith is in the kitchen, with a cup of tea, if you'd like to search the third floor now." Tom slipped back into the shadows of the large plants, and after a moment, we heard a door softly open and shut.

"Creepy little guy." Moriarty made as if to pick up the Chinese vase again, then apparently thought better of it, because he moved away and went to the windows, testing the locks more out of habit than anything else. "What's his story?"

"Tom's a Hollywood actor. You've probably seen a few of his movies; he's usually in the, ah, more supporting roles. Let's head upstairs."

"You know, now that you mention it, he did look familiar. Tom Gearhart, right?" Moriarty chuckled. "Like I said, rich folks are nuts. Who'd have ever thought I'd meet the actor who played Teddy Carmichael in person. *The Night Is Silent* is a classic. 'Teddy! You're an animal!'"

"Whatever you say, Lou."

We joined up with Armstrong and Finn on the third floor. Once more we split up, though we decided for the sake of time we would move through the floor alone rather than in pairs. I ended up with the attic, a long and narrow room that spanned the length of the house. I stood in the doorway, flicked the light switch a few times, not entirely surprised when nothing happened. After a few moments of letting my eyes adjust to the dimness, I found a set of heavy encyclopedias on the floor close to me and used one of them to prop the door open.

"No one's been up here in months," I muttered, noting the thick layer of dust that covered every surface. A couple of dead flies and spiders rounded out the ick factor. When I was a child, the attic was filled with the stuff of hazy daydreams, or perhaps nightmares: mannequin torsos draped in soft velvet clothes; ancient tomes that seemed to hint at spells and incantations; old rocking chairs, their seats occupied by dolls and teddy bears that hadn't been held in decades.

In the years since I'd last been up here, someone had cleaned house. A dozen storage boxes with neatly printed labels, a couple of piles of dated cookbooks, and a dismantled bedframe had re-placed the mannequins, tomes, and rocking chairs. It was more shadows now, less storage.

Less special, somehow.

I moved slowly through the attic toward the one stream of steady light coming into the room: rainbow-hued beams came through the small, though radiant, stained-glass panes set into a single door at the far end of the room. It was this door that led to the balcony, where I'd spent at least six or seven Independence Day holidays watching fireworks set off on Lookout Mountain.

I reached the glass door, my body momentarily imprinted with rays of blue-, green-, and red-tinted sunlight. I gave the dusty knob a halfhearted turn, expecting to find it rusted shut.

To my surprise, it turned easily and the door swung inward an inch, its hinges screeching in protest. A heavy cobweb slipped down, then fell completely, landing at my feet. I swallowed and looked back at the attic door; it was as I'd left it, propped open, bright light from the hall spilling into the space.

And as the balcony door opened wide, more light came in to break up the shadows and the gloom. I checked the knob, clicking off the locking mechanism so that I wouldn't be trapped outside should the door shut, then I stepped out into the cool, crisp air.

The balcony was even scarier than I remembered it. It was nar-row, about three feet wide from the side of the house and seven or eight feet long. The vertical black wrought-iron railings came to my waist, so I imagine as a child it might have been about eye level. The wrought iron was detailed with an intricate floral pat-tern, with no chance of a child falling through it . . . though I sup-pose one could easily climb the thing; a climb that would no doubt result in a long tumble down to the ground below.

A likely deadly tumble.

The view from the balcony, however, was incredible. The Ashley Forest stretched as far as I could see. And directly ahead was Lookout Mountain, where an old fire lookout tower acted as ground zero for the annual holiday fireworks.

For the first time, I wondered why the balcony had been built; it would have made more sense to put one off the master bedroom, or above one of the ground-floor terraces. I shrugged; it didn't matter, really, more just a curious decision on the part of the original homeowners.

As I leaned on the railing and peered out at the forest, a sudden blast of wind blew past me. The gust lifted my hair, swept over my neck and cheeks with an icy chill. From the corner of my eye, I caught sight of the door swinging closed behind me.

It shut with a definitive clicking sound that immediately made me nervous. I lunged for the knob, twisted it this way and that, but it was no use. I must have inadvertently put the knob in a lock mode when I thought I was setting it to unlock.

*Stupid, Gemma, stupid.*

"Okay, don't panic. Just call one of the guys and have them open the door for you." I said the words out loud, feeling better about the situation already. Then I pulled my cell from my pocket and saw that there was no signal.

I punched in Finn's number; nothing. Then Moriarty, Armstrong . . . even the station. Nothing.

Slowly, I put my phone away. Still no need to panic; surely someone would start looking for me when I didn't rejoin the group.

Another gust of wind and I shivered; my thin jacket did little to protect me from the wind this high up. I waited another five minutes with my hands in my pockets to keep them warm, then accepted the fact that it could take a long time before anyone thought to look for me out here. If I was going to take action to rescue myself, I needed to do it soon, before my fingers were too numb to be of any use.

The balcony was narrow, dangerous . . . but the eaves were wide and generous. And there was a good five- or six-inch lip around the outer edge of the balcony that would offer a decent toehold. I took a deep breath, blew on my hands to warm them one last time, then moved quickly, before nerves kept me frozen in my tracks.

Very carefully, I hoisted myself over the railing and made my way to the edge of the eave, where I breathed a sigh of relief. From a distance, the house's exterior brick walls looked smooth, seamless. This close up, though, there were numerous handholds and footholds. I said a silent prayer of thanks to Brody, who had gifted us with a couple of indoor wall-climbing lessons two or three years ago. We'd gotten really into it one summer, then life and other interests had pulled us away.

But the basics had stuck with me, and perhaps now they'd save my butt. Very carefully, I crouched and peered over the side of the eave. There was a wide gutter that ran the length of the house; I could use that to get from the eave down to the brick wall. From there, it would be a relatively straightforward climb down, assuming I could find enough hand and toe grips with sufficient width.

Of course, the last time I'd done this, I'd had chalk on my hands, bouldering shoes, and a safety harness.

By the time I found my colleagues, sitting in the warm kitchen with Edith, each drinking a cup of steaming coffee, I was dirty, dusty, and tired.

And bleeding profusely from both hands.

There was a collective gasp when the group saw me. Edith stood and hurried to the counter, where she grabbed a handful of paper towels and brought them to me. She pressed them to my hands. "What on earth happened?"

"I was in the attic, out on the balcony. The wind pulled the door shut and I was trapped outside. So, I climbed down the side of the house." My hands were killing me. They'd been scraped raw from gripping the bricks, and the paper towels, while catching the blood, did little to help with the pain.

"You what? That's the stupidest thing I've ever heard; you could have called us from your cell," Finn said. He came over and took the paper towels from me and looked at my hands. "Jesus. You need to see a doctor."

"I'll be fine. There was no reception up there. Edith, may I use your sink?" I went to the large basin and filled it with warm, soapy water, then, wincing, plunged my hands in and let the dust and dirt and who knew what else wash away. I tried to remember when my last tetanus shot had been and decided I was okay, that I'd gotten it or a booster while pregnant with Grace.

Finn just shook his head. Armstrong and Moriarty at least had the grace to look impressed. They came to the sink, took an appraising look at my hands, and before leaving, proclaimed me a badass.

After a few more minutes of soaking my hands, I checked them. They still looked terrible, though at least now they were clean. Edith retrieved a roll of white gauze from a medicine cabinet and she carefully began to wrap my palms. I silently cursed; it would be a few days before I'd be able to grip my gun, let alone pull the trigger. Not that I anticipated needing to do that anytime soon, but I tended to get a little twitchy when I knew I didn't have access to my full faculties.

Tom had joined us by then. He took a seat at the kitchen table, cell phone in hand.

As Edith finished wrapping my hands, she held them a minute and said, "I wasn't totally honest with you, Gemma. You asked if I knew what the lies in the threats were about, and I told you I didn't have any idea. But that's not entirely true. I suspect they are related to a trial that came before my husband years ago, twenty, maybe twenty-five years now. Caleb was very protective of me—he sheltered me from a lot of things. I couldn't even tell you which case it was. But he confessed to me in a moment of weakness once, after a bottle of wine, that he'd done a terrible thing. He suspected there was a dirty cop on the case, and he did nothing as it was someone he knew, someone he cared for. He did nothing, and though the defendant deserved to be put away for eternity—in Caleb's words—Caleb still failed his obligation to the court, the law, and the defendant. It broke him."

"But you don't know what case? Which defendant?" Was one of the names on the list I'd compiled the sender of the threats? If a defendant had known there was a dirty cop on his case, perhaps someone who had planted evidence or coerced a witness, and the judge had done nothing about it . . . well, that right there was a hell of a motive for murder.

"No, I never knew. He told me about it years after the fact. I'd say in a strange way that guilt contributed to our separation. There are other reasons, of course, but . . . oh, listen to me blather on. I'm probably making a bigger deal of all this than I should." Edith glanced at her brother. "I'm sorry you have to hear this, Tom. You weren't fond of Caleb to begin with."

From the kitchen table, Tom looked at Edith and shrugged. "It's no secret I despised Caleb, Edie. I'm just sorry you stayed married to the son of a bitch for as long as you did. But I know why you did. Money and power never do lose their appeal."

Edith flinched. "Don't you ever forget that I brought the wealth into the Montgomery family, not the other way around. I loved Caleb."

"Love makes people do strange things," Tom sneered. "Caleb was so smug. Always rubbing it in my face that what he did mattered; that his education and his career somehow made him more of a man. What can I say? I'm a man of the people, not the books. I provide entertainment. It's priceless, really, what I've dedicated my life to doing."

"Still, it must have been hard to be around Caleb," Finn said quietly. He leaned back against the counter, sipped the last of his coffee. "I always thought he was an arrogant man myself."

"Yes, well, I never did have to spend much time with him. I just regret it kept me from seeing more of my sister all these years." Tom checked his phone and stood. "Edie, I'm going upstairs to my rooms to work on this script."

Edith waited until he was out of the room before turning to Finn and me and murmuring, "Tom's always been protective of me. But he was intimidated by Caleb. It made things hard. Holidays, family reunions . . . they inevitably ended in anger and tears, usually on my part."

"Families are complicated," I offered lamely, wincing even as I said it at the triteness of the words. "Edith, I'd like you to look at a picture we found in Caleb's suite at the Tate. It was in your wedding album. It may not be important, but the picture's been ripped and we're not sure who did it, or why."

I slipped the photograph from my pocket and gave it to her. She stared at it, frowning in concentration, then reluctantly handed it back to me.

"I'd guess Caleb tore the photograph, if he had it in his possession, but I couldn't tell you who the man is, the man with his arm around me. It's been too long, and there were so many people there. My parents threw me a hell of a wedding." Edith smiled sadly as tears silently fell from her eyes. "I'm going to miss Caleb. Quite a lot. It's strange; being separated was oddly wonderful. We were still in each other's lives but it wasn't so immediate, so constant. The space did us good."

Outside, in the car, Finn spoke first. "Thoughts?"

"I'm certain Edith didn't pack Caleb's car full of explosives. But . . . you said it yourself a few hours ago, she could have hired someone. What are you thinking?"

"It's weak. She strikes me more as 'Lady of the Manor' than a black widow. The female husband-killer, not the spider," Finn unnecessarily clarified. He shifted in his seat, scratched at a small old stain in his cup holder. "Her brother is something else, though. A guy like that, he's got connections, too. Sure, he seems harmless enough, especially with those ridiculous plastic surgery bandages. But I'm telling you, all those actors and actresses . . . they're all connected. Big, dirty money. Every single one of them. They spend years pretending to be other people on the screen and after a while, it all starts to blend together. Half of them don't know reality from fiction. Everything's an act, a play."

# Chapter Seven

I'm certain that most small towns have a haunted house or two. In Cedar Valley, we were nothing if not overachievers, and we not only had the haunted Old Cabin Woods, we also had a haunted theater.

The Shotgun Playhouse had sat empty for over a hundred years when presiding Judge Gloria Dumont and her husband, stage director Nash Dumont, took possession of it. The historic jewel-box theater, a popular opera house in its past life, was the kind of place that children dared one another to get close to and teenagers illegally entered with the intention of scoring bases and drugs only to leave moments after entering, tears of terror streaming down their cheeks.

There were whispers that the two-story stone structure, with its elegant trompe l'oeil murals, stained-glass windows, and frescoed ceiling, was haunted not only by the ghosts of the various nineteenth-century actors and actresses who'd performed on the stage but also by the German miners who'd built the structure, many of whom had toiled in brutal conditions for pitiful wages only to die in poverty years later.

I'd seen enough of the macabre in my line of work that the idea of a few harmless ghosts didn't bother me too much. It did help, though, that Nash and Gloria Dumont truly had breathed new life into the old building. Since taking ownership two years ago, they'd poured their life savings into restoring the theater. The

grand opening was set to occur the following week, with an evening performance of William Shakespeare's *Macbeth*.

I parked in the adjacent lot then walked in and stood a moment
in the lobby, taking in the changes that had occurred even in the
last few days. Red tapestries hung from the ceiling, and a sparkling-
clean refreshment counter and a row of gleaming tap handles took
up one corner. The box office had new letter boards, and vintage
posters of old Hollywood actors and actresses hung on the walls. As
I moved through the playhouse, my footsteps were muffled by the
plush navy-blue carpet, and the entire lobby smelled of fresh paint.

It was by far the nicest theater I'd ever set foot in.

But I wasn't there for the décor, and Nash Dumont got to me
before I'd taken ten steps.

He was a short, round man with a head like an egg, bald and
smooth, and a Van Dyke beard of black hair. He wore fedoras and
favored tan blazers made of corduroy, paired with dark blue jeans.
He was ten years younger than his wife, about my age, and rumors
around town painted a marriage of convenience.

*The ice queen and her jester,* I'd once heard someone snidely
call them.

The director, as usual, was full of frantic energy, his every
gesture grandiose, his words coming rapid-fire. "Gemma. Thank
goodness you're here. I can't take much more of this bullshit."

"What happened now?"

"It's better if I show you." He turned abruptly on his heel and
strode to a corner of the lobby. Once there, he yanked back a discreet black curtain.

Behind the curtain was a closed door.

After a moment more, I prompted, "There's something behind
the door?"

Dumont nodded and stepped back. "Open it."

With the director now to my rear and side, I was free to roll my
eyes without him seeing. Could the man make a single move with-

out the dramatic gestures, the mysterious showmanship? I gripped the doorknob, turned it, and pulled open the door.

It was a coat closet; or rather, it had been a closet at one point. It was now a water-soaked, smoke-scented, ash-filled chamber of destruction. On the floor was a pile of burnt logs and what appeared to be kerosene-soaked rags.

"My God. This whole place could have burned." I turned to Nash. "This is getting out of hand. Someone's going to get hurt."

Nash shook his head emphatically. "Not until after opening night, Gemma. I will say, it was incredibly lucky that our contractor talked us into automatic ceiling sprinklers. We'll get this closet cleaned; it will be as good as new in no time. But you've got to find out who's doing this."

"How the hell am I supposed to do that, when you won't even allow me to question your actors, your contractors?" I sighed, then stepped closer to the closet and crouched down. Something glittery lay among the ashes. I removed a tissue from my purse and gently dislodged the item from the soot.

"What is it?" Nash asked, a funny look on his face.

"An earring. Looks like real gold," I said and held up the tiny ball in my hand to the light. "Your perp is going to be missing this."

"Your first clue," Nash said with more than a trace of sarcasm.

I ignored him and pocketed the earring, safely wrapped in the tissue. "Look, at the very least, I should speak to Waverly. You said that besides you and Gloria, she's the only person with a key to the theater. And these three 'incidents' have all happened after hours, when the theater is supposedly empty."

Finally, the director relented. "You can talk with Waverly, but not tonight. She's out sick . . . speaking of which, you'll make a perfect witch."

*"Excuse me?"*

Nash looked me up and down. "Your stature, your bearing . . . it's marvelous. My Hecate is out tonight, too, with a touch of the flu and we're running through Act III. It's a critical scene. I need you, Gemma. You must be my Hecate."

"Wait a minute, I'm here to find your vandal and hopefully speak with Gloria about Caleb Montgomery's murder. Don't you have an understudy that can step in?"

"Gloria won't be here for another hour, at least, if she comes at all. She's very disturbed by Caleb's death." Nash shook his head sadly. "And Hecate's understudy is filling in for our third witch. She's out, too; there must be a nasty bug going around. I can only pray everyone is recovered by opening night. Come on, what do you say? It'll be fun. Besides, you owe me."

"I do?"

Nash nodded. "Well, you owe Gloria. Don't you remember? She introduced you to Brody."

Nash was correct, though it had been a long time since I'd thought about the early days in my relationship.

It had been a chance encounter; I'd run into Gloria at the ski shop six years ago. It was the beginning of the season and the place was busy, so we stood making small talk. By the time we reached the front of the line, Gloria had persuaded me to take a friend of hers, an attractive and single geologist, out for a date. I agreed, thinking little of it, but by the next day dinner plans had been arranged.

The rest, as they say, is history.

I sighed. I guess I did owe the Dumonts.

And who knew, maybe after the seriousness of the day, a little levity would do me good. But my throat was already dry and the small laugh that escaped my lips was a weak, nervous cough. "Well, I'm happy to help, but my theater experience is limited to selling tickets in the high school auditorium to our class production of *Little Shop of Horrors*. I'm no actress."

"No, you're certainly not, which makes you perfect. You're relatable. Come on, let's get you the script. Do you know the story?

It's one of Shakespeare's greatest tragedies and, personally, my favorite play," Nash said in a low voice. "For many reasons."

"*Mac—*"

"Egads, shhh, whatever you do, *don't* say the name of the play. You may call it 'the Scottish Play' if you have to reference it."

"Why on earth can't I say *Mac—*"

Dumont practically threw his hands over my mouth. "I'm serious, Gemma. I'll have to ask you to leave if you keep that up."

Was that all I had to do?

He continued, "It's bad luck to say the word inside the theater except as part of an actual rehearsal or production. You could bring terrible disaster down upon us. Already I've got some punk messing with my theater and more than half my cast is under the weather. Oh, and also, do not under any circumstances recite the witches' incantations, except, again, as part of rehearsal." Nash pulled his shirt collar from his neck and exhaled. "Wow, that was a close call. You're worse than my actors, I only had to tell them once. Of course, most of them already know about the curse."

Vague memories from my high school English class came back to me. *Macbeth*, Shakespeare's cursed play . . .

"Do you truly believe in the curse?"

Nash nodded solemnly and pointed skyward. "For me, it's the same as believing in God. If he exists, I'm in the clear! And if he doesn't, well, no big deal."

I thought back to my senior year English class and the semester we spent on Shakespeare. "I read the play in high school. I remember Lady M gets blood on her hands, and of course there are a handful of witches, and some battle scenes. I guess it's obvious that literature wasn't exactly my strong suit."

Nash chuckled. "No kidding. Come on."

I followed him down the corridor and into the theater itself, marveling again as I had the first time I'd seen it. "It really is beautiful. You've done a fantastic job."

Nash nodded, beaming. "She's a beauty, isn't she? I've always wanted to own a theater."

The seats, nearly five hundred of them, had been reupholstered in burgundy velvet. The floors and aisles gleamed with a fresh coat of wax. On the walls, the original trompe l'oeils had been cleaned and were offset with dim lights, built to resemble the theater's original gas lamps. Perhaps most impressive was the gorgeous sparkling chandelier that hung over the house seats. It glowed with what must have been thousands of tiny bulbs, each light reflected in the hundreds of crystals that made up the chandelier.

"It's stunning. You must be thrilled."

"I'm very pleased. Gloria and I sank two million dollars of our own money into this place. Thank God for wealthy Texas oil-baron fathers who love their little girls, am I right? Gloria didn't think I had the tenacity to see this through . . . but just look at this place!" Nash straightened his fedora, then rubbed his hands together. "Right, then. The play. You're on the right track. It's the story of an ambitious, flawed man, whose ascent to the Scottish throne is prophesied by three witches. Along the way, there's murder, deception, even ghosts. I am, of course, simplifying things greatly, but you get the idea."

"Murder, deception . . . sounds like an average day in the office for me."

Nash grinned. "Exactly. Now, imagine being told by powerful witches your twisted fate: that you will one day be king but the children of another—Banquo, your fellow Army captain, no less— will be the future kings of Scotland. Then imagine your wife is even more ambitious than you are and bam, there you have it, the perfect recipe for murder, mayhem, and intrigue."

Nash led me down the aisle to the stage, where the actors, a good-size group of men and women, sat referencing their scripts and talking to one another. Many of them wore pieces of period clothing, or heaps of costume jewelry, perhaps the better to channel their characters. Three of the cast members stood by themselves in a corner, whispering about something.

"Ladies and gentlemen, everyone, please! Listen up a moment, we have a guest joining us tonight. Gemma, meet . . . everyone. We haven't settled on a name for the troupe yet, so we call ourselves Will's Crew for the time being." Nash pointed to each cast member, quickly and exuberantly rattling off their name and character. When he got to the group of three in the corner, he said, "And our stars! Milo Griffith and Maggie Armstrong as the tragic M and Lady M, and Danny Grimes, who plays Banquo, Thane of Lochaber."

"Hello, everyone. Hi, Maggie," I said, relieved to recognize at least one person. Maggie was the daughter of my colleague Lucas Armstrong. She'd graduated from college in the spring and moved back home to study for the law school entrance exam. I remembered she was also working part-time at the courthouse in an administrative assistant role.

I walked onstage to greet her, nearly tripping over the bottom step of the stairs to the stage. An older actor with a heavy British accent caught my elbow. "Watch your step, love."

"Yeah, right. Thanks." I managed to climb the remaining stairs, my cheeks already warm and I hadn't said even a single line yet. I'd read once that public speaking is the most common fear, ranked even higher than death. And at that moment, if I had to choose, I decided I'd probably go with death.

I gave Maggie a hug, careful to avoid her big dangly hoop earrings and heavy sequined choker. She had her father's dark skin and her mother's physique; she moved like a dancer, a natural on stage. I'd been surprised to hear that she had chosen to pursue a law career, as she'd always talked about wanting to be a schoolteacher.

Maggie turned to the man next to her. He was older than me, maybe thirty-five, though he'd been blessed with the sort of skin and bone structure that was ageless. "Gemma, I'd like you to meet

Milo Griffith. Milo, Gemma works with my dad at the police station."

"Nice to meet you," Milo and I said in unison to each other. He had a short crop of brown hair and a smattering of freckles across the bridge of his hawkish nose. He wore a tight, short-sleeved white T-shirt that showed off sleeves of tattoos on both of his muscular arms.

It felt awkward greeting two out of the three actors standing in the small group, so I nodded to the third, Danny Grimes. He was a quiet, serious-looking young man with an American flag tattoo on his forearm and a large hunting knife strapped to the utility belt he wore low on his camo pants.

He saw me eyeing the weapon and said in a dramatic stage whisper, "The knife helps me get into character."

"Hey, whatever works." I turned as Nash approached us. He handed me an earmarked old script, noticing my bandaged hands for the first time.

"Good lord, what happened?"

"Some minor scrapes, it's no big deal."

"If you say so. Okay, we're reading through Act III, beginning with scene five. You're Hecate. Don't worry about being dramatic or overly theatrical," Nash instructed.

"Got it." I nodded and smiled tightly even as the flush on my cheeks deepened. The thought of all the people in the theater, the experienced actors, watching me stumble through an Old English script was horrifying.

Another few moments, then suddenly Nash was glaring at me. "Well, come on, Gemma, let's get to it. Jesus Christ, we haven't got all night. Stand there, right there . . . and ready . . . begin."

A pale young woman in a shroud of black who'd been introduced to me as the First Witch spoke in a pleading voice. "Why, how now, Hecate! You look angerly."

I felt feverish, dry-throated, my knees apt to knock together. I slowly walked to the center of the stage and began reading from the script. "Have I not reason, beldams as you are? Sauce . . . I mean, *saucy* and overbold, how did you dare to trade and traffic with Macbeth in riddles and affairs of death . . ."

My speaking parts were long, though few, and shortly I was able to retreat from the bright stage lights. No one seemed to notice the look of relief in my eyes or the fact that I proceeded to guzzle an entire bottle of water in one long desperate drink. I quickly scanned the theater and was relieved that Judge Gloria Dumont hadn't seen my performance. It was embarrassing enough that Maggie Armstrong had to watch it. I took a seat with the other actors to watch the rest of the rehearsal. The cast was good, surprisingly good for a community theater group that had been pulled together over the last few months.

It was clear, though, why Milo Griffith, Danny Grimes, and Maggie Armstrong were the stars of the show. Each shone with a vitality and confidence that seemed spun of gold; on stage, they could do no wrong. I watched, rapt, as they threw themselves wholly into their roles. When they were finished, I clapped along with the others.

Nash Dumont jumped up and down on the stage with glee. "That was fantastic. You've all nearly got it. I'm wondering, though, Danny, about something. We know Banquo's motives are unclear throughout the play. He suspects M of regicide and yet does nothing. What do you think about showing even a bit more weakness to the character? Really drive his indecisive nature home? Banquo's got to be a true foil to M for us to feel for him. For both of them. And feeling is everything in this play."

Danny swore, loudly. "That's fucking ridiculous. We talked about this, Nash. Banquo's not some patsy. I won't play him if we take things that direction."

Dumont clenched his jaw, an ugly look coming into his eyes. It was so ugly, in fact, that I found myself tensing in anticipation of a coming blow. But just as quickly the moment passed and he smiled tightly. "Sure, Dan. I'm just the director. You're the actor. You inhabit the character however you see fit."

Dumont turned to the rest of the cast and I watched, with curiosity, as the group seemed to sigh a collective sigh of relief that the conversation between Nash Dumont and Danny Grimes was over.

It clearly hadn't been the first instance of tension between them.

"That's a wrap, folks! See you tomorrow. We'll pick up where we left off!" Nash hung back as the actors trickled out of the theater. The cavernous space grew dim as he switched off light after light. We walked together up the narrow, carpeted aisle.

"Promise me you'll find this jerk who's out to get my theater. You must have a list, names, of local punks who get their rocks off by doing these sorts of things." Nash exhaled loudly. "I'm losing sleep over it, Gemma. But hey, listen, you did wonderful tonight. If you ever want a role in one of my plays, just ask. You're a natural."

He looked surprised at my hysterical laughter in response.

"Thank you, but no. That was painful. It was as bad as high school speech class," I said. "I was happy to be of help, though it looks like I missed Gloria. Is that typical of her, to skip rehearsal? Her clerk was certain she would be here. I was hoping to talk with her about a few things related to the case."

Nash adjusted his fedora and shrugged. "Like I said, she's very shaken by Caleb's death. I offered to stay home with her tonight and keep her company, but she knows how much the play means to me, and to the actors. She insisted I come and did express an intent to join me. I haven't even told her yet about the fire in the lobby coat closet. She's got enough on her plate as it is."

As Nash flicked the last light switch and we left the dark theater for the bright lobby, an uneasy feeling settled in around my shoulder blades. We paused a moment while Nash searched his pants pockets for his keys.

I asked, "When was the last time you spoke with Gloria?"

"Oh my God." Nash stared at me, his keys forgotten. "You think she's in danger, don't you? Is she? Damn it. She told me Caleb's murder was unrelated to his judgeship."

Nash dropped the scripts he was carrying and yanked out his cell phone. He stabbed at it with a shaking finger, then jammed it to his ear and listened.

"Come on, come on," he muttered. "Pick up, darling, pick up . . . Gloria? Oh thank God. Where are you? What? . . . I'm at the theater with Detective Gemma Monroe. You may be in danger . . . what? No, I haven't been drinking . . . Oh, for Pete's sake, hang on."

Nash held out the phone to me. "She wants to talk to you."

I took the phone. "Hello, Judge. I was hoping to finish our conversation from yesterday with you tonight, here, at the Shotgun."

"My apologies. This thing with Caleb . . . as soon as I left the courthouse, I went straight home for a soak in the hot tub and a glass of chardonnay." Gloria Dumont cleared her throat. "I can assure you, though, you have my full attention. Is this about the warrants? I've signed what I can but you'll need more for the warrant on the Montgomery house, considering Caleb wasn't living there and Edith is not a suspect."

The judge paused, then added, "Or is she?"

Once more, I got the sense that I should be careful with what I shared with her. "This isn't about the warrants. And you can ignore the request for the residence; Edith invited us to search the house this afternoon. She knows enough of police procedures to know we'd come knocking eventually. I took a look at Caleb's cases, all the way back to when he was a prosecutor. Really just skimming, but nonetheless trying to see if anything jumped out at me. I've got an intern eliminating those who have already passed away, but you worked with Caleb a number of years. Is there anyone who truly stands out as someone we should look at?"

"Well, I've been thinking about that, too, and to tell you the truth, there's no one in recent memory that comes to mind. By the way, how's Bull taking Caleb's death?" Dumont asked.

"He's dealing with it as best he knows how, which is to say likely with equal parts whiskey and prayer."

"Good. Please do keep me informed as the investigation progresses, Detective. This is personal. I want to be kept abreast of things," the judge said. "Caleb was family."

"I understand."

She asked to speak to her husband, so I handed the phone to Nash and took my leave, exiting the lobby of the Shotgun Playhouse through the front glass doors, their bronze handles gleaming in the glow from the outside streetlamps. Most of the cars had left the parking lot, the cast and crew gone off to late dinners or home to their families. As I passed by a blue sedan, I caught a glimpse of a couple fervently making out in the front seats. Not wanting to be nosy, I turned away, but not before catching a glimpse of dark skin and another of a short-sleeved white shirt and an arm, covered with tattoos.

The couple was Maggie Armstrong and Milo Griffith, and from what I saw, they were a lot more than costars.

*Great.*

I got in my own car and turned the key. I was positive that my colleague Lucas Armstrong was not aware of the relationship; I'd have heard by now if his twenty-two-year-old daughter was dating someone at least ten years her senior.

*It's none of your business, Gemma. Leave it alone.*

Yeah, right. Easier said than done, in my experience.

# Chapter Eight

I woke on Wednesday morning to the sound of Grace crying in her crib. It had been a long night; she'd struggled to fall asleep, then had woken every couple of hours. By the fourth time I'd traipsed from my room to hers and back again, I was nearly delirious.

At least in the morning, I could resuscitate myself with a couple cups of coffee. We spent a few minutes snuggling and reading together in the rocking chair in her room, turning the pages of a book about baby animals, over and over. It was cool in her room, and holding her warm body close to mine reminded me once again why I do what I do; why I spend precious time away from her.

It's because at the end of the day, I would do anything to keep her safe, including putting bad guys away and solving ugly crimes. I could only hope that as she got older, she understood my choices, the call I felt to serve the greater good and to keep my community safe. It was a constant push and pull that I struggled with, between the desire to be with her and the need to work my cases.

Grace grew restless, so we headed downstairs and had breakfast with Brody; waffles and bacon for the adults, cereal and a banana for Grace. Brody cooked while I washed and changed the bandages on my hands. He'd been upset to hear how I'd sustained the injuries, but I also caught the tiniest bit of pride in his admonishments.

As we ate, I watched with a full yet heavy heart as Grace fed herself, confident with the baby spoon, an expert already at her sippy cup. It was growing difficult to remember the early days, when she was an infant, as she'd changed so much, especially in the last few months. She was growing opinionated, stubborn, with a hilarious sense of humor and a wide smile that broke my heart with its innocence and joy.

Since having my daughter, time seemed to speed up at incredible rates.

Thinking about time, and the pace at which it was barreling past me, made me realize it had been nearly a week since I'd last visited my grandmother. Since Bull and I had moved Julia into her tiny new apartment at Carver Estates, we'd made a pact that one of us would see her every couple of days, if not more. In fact, Bull had lunch there three times a week. I decided I had time for a quick visit before work. If this case was like most, it could be another couple of weeks before I'd find time to see my grandmother.

At the estates, a manager buzzed me in through the main entrance. I signed into the log book, then made my way up two flights of stairs and down a long, beige hallway to a room at the end. To my surprise, the door was ajar, and then to my delight, I saw Laura, my grandmother's former caretaker, sitting beside her.

"Gemma!" Laura squealed just as I exclaimed, "Laura!"

We hugged, the petite Peruvian woman nearly a foot shorter than me. Laura and Julia had become good friends and I was thrilled to see them together.

From the couch, Julia watched us with amusement. "I don't see what the fuss is all about, it's not like anybody brought margaritas."

"Do you want one, Julia? I'll make it for you." I was teasing but her eyes lit up like it was Christmas.

"Oh boy! Really?"

"Of course not. It's eight o'clock in the morning. Anyway, that stuff will kill you," I said, adding, "Though I'd be happy to take you out for a drink in the evening sometime."

Julia scowled and turned back to Laura, who'd taken a seat next to her. "Everyone sucks around here. They call this help? More like terrorism. I'm not going to tip her."

Laura took Julia's hand in her own and patted it. "Gemma is your granddaughter, sweetheart. She's a very important detective."

Julia gave me a cold once-over. "I don't have any children, or grandchildren, for that matter. Never wanted them. Can't stand the smell of kids."

So it was one of those days, then. I didn't take it personally, not anymore. Mostly what I felt was regret, that Julia and my daughter, Grace, had so little time to get to know each other. My child would never know the woman who'd raised me, and my grandmother would never know her great-grandchild.

If I was truthful with myself, the other emotion I felt heavily these days was anxiety, a sense of being on heightened alert, waiting for the phone call from Carver Estates or from Bull, the phone call that would close this chapter in Julia's life, in all our lives, for good.

Worry, regret, anxiety. How would it happen? Would she slip in the shower and fracture her skull? Pass peacefully in her sleep? Would there be fear and recognition finally at the end, or would her passing occur without much self-awareness, just one moment after another and then nothing?

It wasn't easy being sandwiched between declining grandparents in separate residences and a helpless baby at home.

"Gemma? You look pale. Are you all right?" Laura stood, a concerned look in her eyes. "Sit down a spell, I'll make you some hot tea."

"I'm fine. I can't stay. Julia, I love you very much. I'll be back in a few days." I hurried from the room, embarrassed that my sudden spiral into such dark and personal thoughts had likely been written all over my face.

As I reached my car, I got a text message from Finn. He asked me to meet him in the police station parking lot and to keep my engine running. I did as he requested and after a minute or two of waiting, Finn exited the station's front doors, his hands full with a couple of maps and two coffee cups.

I leaned across the console and opened the passenger side door of my car. Finn slid in.

"The Cathedrals," he said by way of greeting and handed me a to-go cup of coffee. Then he sat back and spread open a map in his lap.

"What about them?" I asked. The Cathedrals were a stretch of the Rockies about fifty miles due north of Cedar Valley, consisting of four distinct peaks and a small town, Bishop. At one time, Bishop was home to one of the world's largest molybdenum mines, though it had been closed since the seventies to allow for environmental cleanup. I'd first learned about the Bishop Mine in the police academy as a trainee, as it had been the site in the 1930s of a homicide that remained unsolved to this day. The nature of the crime—the ax murder and subsequent mutilation of a never-identified John Doe—was ripe with intrigue.

"We're taking a field trip today. That's a cookies-and-cream latte, by the way. Cost me six bucks at the Crimson Café," Finn said. He set his own coffee in one of the car's two cup holders and shook out the map. "I just got off the phone with the general manager at the Bishop Mine. Did you know they're reopening it? Some Japanese billionaire bought it. Anyway, get this: a week ago, someone ripped off a load of dynamite from the mine. We'd have never heard about it, except yours truly put out an APB to be on alert for stolen demolition materials. The sheriff in Cathedral County saw the bulletin and put two and two together. Gemma, there's security footage from the mine. They've got the theft on tape."

I pulled onto the highway in the northbound lane and merged into traffic, excited. "Talk about a lucky break. That's great news. We could have a suspect by the end of the day."

"That would be a miracle. In the Cathedrals." Finn held the map up and peered at it. "Have you ever been to Bishop? There can't be much in the town."

I shook my head. "Nope, I haven't had the pleasure."

"Me neither." Finn leaned back. "Let me know if you want me to drive."

I glanced at him; his eyes were closed. "You're going to sleep?"

"Yes . . . unless you have a different idea?" he asked. "You want to play I Spy?"

"Er, no."

After a moment, he chuckled softly. "Bishop . . . My ex-wife was a bishop."

I nearly spit my coffee out. "Excuse me?"

"Marianne Bishop." Finn folded the map in his lap and stuck it in the door console. "That was her name."

"You were married? When? What happened?"

Finn sipped from his coffee and glanced at me out of the corner of his eye. He smirked. "Aren't we curious."

"Of course I'm curious. I've known you for years. How did I not know you were married? This is shocking. I can't even imagine the woman who would agree to marry you. Are you still in touch with her?"

"I get a Christmas card every year. Does that count?"

I waited to see if he would add anything else. When he didn't, I said, "Well, Finn, the suspense is killing me. Tell me about her."

He glanced at me again. "What do you want to know?"

"Everything. What happened? Who is she? What does she do? Do you have kids that I'm not aware of?"

Finn chuckled. "Not that I'm aware of, either, but it's always a possibility, I suppose. I wasn't exactly careful in my youth and I do wonder if I'll get that knock on the door someday. Christ, I could have a twenty-year-old kid out there . . . Look, Marianne is a very nice woman. She's an eye surgeon and works overseas with Doctors Without Borders. We were high school sweethearts who married young. Then, after college, we decided to go our separate ways."

"When did you last see her?"

"At her father's funeral. Ten or twelve years ago. I flew out for it and met Tad Chester, her current husband. He owns a chain of martial arts schools in Minnesota, a real Jean-Claude Van Damme type. He wears his hair in a bun and calls Marianne 'Doctor.' To her face, as in 'Good morning, Doctor.'" Finn laughed again. "He called me 'Bud' the first time we met. He'd be a good guy if he wasn't such a pretentious asshole."

I was fascinated by this glimpse into a life that Finn usually kept very private. "Was the breakup hard?"

Finn was silent a moment. He scratched at his jaw, then stared out the window at the passing cars. "Devastating. Marianne was the love of my life."

I'd never seen Finn in such a state of vulnerability. It was strangely appealing on him, a stark contrast to his usual arrogance. Then he continued, "Yes, the split was a bitter pill to swallow, but I moved on. I slept with her best friend a week after the breakup. We did it on Marianne's favorite Turkish rug. That helped heal my wounds quite a bit, actually. Come to think of it, I should look her up. She was a gymnast, if I remember correctly. I nearly threw my back out."

I rolled my eyes. "Do you think you'll ever get married again?"

"It will be a cold day in hell." Finn coughed, shifted in his seat. "Enough about me. How about you? Are you going to go through with it?"

"What, the wedding? Of course," I said, glancing at him. "I wouldn't have gotten engaged if I wasn't planning on marrying Brody."

"Sure. Right." Finn grinned. He tapped on my glove compartment box. "You should keep a pair of socks in there. Just in case."

"You think I won't go through with it?"

"Won't . . . or shouldn't."

"Ye of little faith," I responded, getting angry. Finn was the last person who should be doling out advice on matters of the heart. "Just because it didn't work for you doesn't mean it won't for us."

Finn lifted his hands. "Hey, I get it. I wish you two the best of luck. I hope it works out, I really do. You have a kid together, responsibilities."

We fell silent after that, me thinking about the reasons behind my delay in accepting Brody's proposal, Finn thinking about who knew what. We reached Bishop in less than an hour. It was a tiny town, dusty and forgotten-looking. Though the narrow main street had a number of old houses and stores, they all had the same sad veneer of abandonment and disrepair. The only places open for business were the absolute necessities: a grocery store, a liquor mart, a couple of gas stations, and a church, its siding badly in need of a paint job. In an overgrown lot between the church and the liquor store, a scrawny dog took a break from licking its nether regions to watch us roll by.

Aside from the dog, and a young blond boy standing motionless in the doorway of the grocery store, there were few signs of life. "Exciting place," Finn muttered as he stared out the window. "What a dump. This town dried up years ago. Gives me the creeps."

"No kidding. Check out the houses." I pointed at the twenty or so houses spaced far apart on the low hills all around us. Their windows looked down on the town, and us, as though they were watchful, sentient beings. "There's no schools, no industry . . . Who sticks around a place like this?"

"Folks that don't have anywhere else to go." Finn shrugged. "Don't forget, the Bishop Mine is back up and running. The town will see a boom over the next few years, though it will be nothing compared to the mine's heyday. Slow down, there's the turnoff."

I took a right. After a mile or so, a small parking lot appeared, adjacent to a trailer that had a sign in the window that read FRONT OFFICE. As Finn and I exited the car, we stretched our legs, noting the county sheriff's vehicle parked nearby. A dozen yards west of the trailer was a stop point, complete with a manned guard station and a lowered gate.

An enormously tall man came out of the trailer. He had a black beard that grazed his belt and dusty boots with spurs the size of half-dollars. He spit a stream of brown tobacco juice on the ground, then raised a massive hand in greeting.

"Detective Nowlin?" the man called out around the mouthful of chewing tobacco. "I'm Frank Poe, we spoke on the phone. I'm the general manager for the mine."

"Yes. This is my partner, Detective Gemma Monroe," Finn replied. We walked over to Poe and shook hands all around.

Poe gestured to the trailer behind him. "Let's talk in here."

We followed him inside to a dark and cool room. There was a desk, a few tables and chairs, a number of filing cabinets, and maps—underground surveys and mining maps, some of them quite old. In the far corner, an older woman sat reading a newspaper. She wore the county sheriff's department uniform and when she lowered the paper, I saw first her face, then her badge, and recognized her immediately.

Sheriff Rose Underhill.

She'd run for sheriff of Cathedral County the year before, going up against an incumbent who had a reputation for being as dirty as they come. She'd won in a landslide and I'd been curious ever since to meet her. The county was large, and word on the street was that Underhill ran a tight ship, that she was taking names and cleaning house. A petite woman, she wore her curly gray hair cut short, pinned back from her pale green eyes with a number of bobby pins. Her nails were trimmed and neat, her hands free of jewelry.

The sheriff set aside her newspaper and stood. "Rose Underhill. I don't believe I've had the pleasure. Though I'd recognize the two of you any day. Your department has had some fine collars the last few years. How's my old friend Angel Chavez doing?"

"The chief is busy," I replied. "We're running on all four cylinders to try to catch Judge Caleb Montgomery's killer."

"It's a horrible thing," Underhill said with a frown. "I knew Monty, as we used to call him, many years ago. He and I go way back. Got any leads yet?"

I shook my head. "Nothing solid. I'm hoping the video you all have might point us in the right direction. I'm sure you can imagine, this is hitting everyone hard, myself included. My grandfather Bull and Caleb were best friends."

"Bull?" The sheriff started, then narrowed her pale eyes and stared at me appraisingly. "Well, I'll be a monkey's uncle. That must make you Buford Weston's granddaughter. Talk about a small world. Old Bull and I shared many a whiskey together under a full moon. He was a gentleman and a cowboy, like someone in an old Western where it's obvious who the bad guys are and who the good guys are. Those were the easy days, in many ways." She smiled tightly. "Yes, Bull and Caleb and I all go way back. Someday, ask Bull about Red Dalton."

"Red Dalton?"

She nodded. "He'll know what I mean. Though make damn sure he's in a good mood when you ask him."

Frank Poe cleared his throat. "Please, have a seat," he said as he went to the other side of the desk and sat down. Underhill remained standing as Finn and I pulled chairs up to the desk.

"Bishop's a grim little town," Finn said. "Are you expecting things to pick up now that the mine is running again?"

"That's unlikely." Poe stroked his long black beard and leaned back in his chair. "Most of the mine employees are living in Eagle's Run. They commute in; the Kenzi Corporation—the mine's new owner—pays for buses to shuttle them back and forth. You'd stay in Eagle's Run, too, if you were in their shoes; Kenzi built a row of fancy new condominiums and invested in a couple of amenities like a grocery store and a state-of-the-art gym. Plus, the county seat is in Eagle's Run; the town hall and Sheriff's Department share a building. Ironic, isn't it? The head honchos could have sunk all that money into Bishop, where the goddamn mine is actually located."

"That must be frustrating," I said. "You mentioned most of the mine employees are in Eagle's Run, but not all of them?"

The mine manager nodded. "Correct. There's a handful of us who are partial to Bishop. My wife and I bought a house on the hill just above the church. And most of the security staff are hunkered down here, on site, in a couple of rentals. My wife, she's in charge of local accounts for the mine. Kenzi lets her work out of the house. We got it for a steal. It's a gorgeous property, turn of the century, with original—"

"Frank, these folks aren't interested in architecture. They're here about the theft. Tell them what you told me this morning." Underhill adjusted her badge, a six-point star, on her right breast. "Didn't I tell you that reopening the mine would bring trouble? I sure as hell told the city council . . . and the voters. No one listened to me, though, did they? And now who's going to pay?"

"Has there been other trouble?" I asked. "Other incidents, besides the dynamite theft?"

Poe wearily spit tobacco juice into a soda can and wiped his lips. "Hell, I don't know. We've had a few things happen. Fistfights, drunken brawls, a couple of minor accidents. Nothing out of the ordinary, though. The mine's been closed for nearly forty years, see; there's a lot of old ghosts coming up out of the ground."

"I don't know much about ghosts, Mr. Poe. What about the dynamite? When exactly did you notice it was missing?" Finn asked.

"According to the time stamp on our security footage, it was stolen a week ago, last Monday. I reported the theft to Sheriff Underhill. She came out to investigate with a couple deputies, then my security team performed an internal investigation as well. We've purposely kept it quiet; the other employees know nothing about the theft. It's a rather, uh, strange situation," Poe said. He slid open a creaky desk drawer and withdrew a small flash drive. "You'll see what I mean when we review the film."

Finn and I leaned forward as Poe inserted the drive into the laptop on his desk. He swiveled the monitor so that we could see the screen. From behind us, still standing, Underhill sighed and said, "Wait until you get a load of this. Why do all the nut jobs come out this time of year?"

Frank hit a few keys on the laptop. "We store the dynamite in a secure building near the back of the mines. As you may expect, we have fairly high security measures in place—guards, cameras, that sort of thing. You have to understand that the Kenzi Corporation has invested millions into the mine, and Mr. Hayashi, the chairman, intends to keep this place safe."

We watched as the computer screen went from black to gray to an eerie green. It was night; the time stamp read close to midnight. The camera was pointed at the door of a large warehouse. In the corner of the screen, a fat white rabbit moved in and out of the camera's view. Then the animal disappeared. After a long moment, a person appeared where the rabbit had been. It was hard to tell if it was a man or woman, as a hooded sweatshirt was pulled over his or her face. What was clear was that it was a large man or woman, nearly obese. The individual stood stock-still, taking in the night, then went directly to the door of the warehouse.

Finn groaned. "Let me guess, you don't have any visuals of their face."

"Nope." Rose Underhill rolled up her newspaper and swatted at a couple of flies that had begun to buzz noisily over our heads. "And start practicing some patience, young grasshopper. Just watch the damn tape."

There was something lithe and deliberate, almost catlike, about the thief's movements. He cocked his head to the side, as though thinking or listening, then bent forward. Because of the camera angle, it was impossible to see what he was doing, though I had a pretty good guess. Within a minute, the thief tossed something small over his shoulder and opened the door.

Poe sighed and spit another stream of tobacco juice into his can. "He picked the lock. With a couple of hairpins, if you can believe it. We found them on the ground, a few feet away. You better believe my security team got their butts handed to them when I saw that they'd put such cheap and flimsy locks on the doors. Anything to save a buck. Though once inside, the thief would have found the dynamite locked behind a secure inner door. Somehow, he broke the code and gained access."

"I can't tell from the footage if he's wearing gloves," I said. "Sheriff, did you recover prints from the pins?"

"Nope," Underhill muttered. "Frank, you need to do something about these flies—lay some sticky paper down or get one of those fly-eating plants. These buggers are the size of sheep testicles."

The video rolled another minute, then faded to black.

Full of questions, I asked, "Where's the rest of the tape? How long was he in the warehouse? Is there an interior camera? Do you have footage of him actually leaving with dynamite?"

"No, no, and no." Poe ejected the flash drive and shrugged. "I'm afraid that's all we've got. The film is on a loop, though it shouldn't have reset until six in the morning. Theoretically, we should have captured footage of him leaving with the explosives. But something happened with the camera; we're not sure what."

"So there's no evidence he actually did steal the dynamite." Finn raked a hand through his hair, frustrated. "Could he have tampered with the system?"

"No." Poe shook his head emphatically. "We're certain—okay, fairly certain—that he didn't sabotage the security system. Also, we found tracks on an old dirt road just north of the mine; my security team, and Sheriff Underhill, determined this guy came in on that road. There are sensors back there, along the edge of the property, but he evaded them. It's clear to me that he's a pro. There's more. You saw that rabbit at the beginning of the tape?"

I nodded, not sure I wanted to hear more.

"We found him next to the hairpins, dead. Poor guy's neck was broken."

I bit my lip, thinking of the moments when both rabbit and thief were offscreen.

Finn asked, "How much dynamite was stolen?"

"About twenty pounds, plus a dozen detonators," Poe said. "We were lucky even to have that much on hand. We keep some on reserve, but these days we tend to stick with aboveground pit mining practices. It's cheaper; less manpower required. Hell of a lot safer, too. Most operators around here just aren't using dynamite anymore."

"That's the second time I've heard dynamite referred to, at least in a roundabout way, as an out-of-date explosive," I said. "Why is that?"

Poe scratched his head. "Well, it comes down to the fact that there's product with better control out there. Used to be dynamite was all there was. Now, our techniques are much more sophisticated, our explosives higher quality. Refinement is the name of the game."

Sheriff Underhill slammed her newspaper down on the desk and we all jumped.

"Got it!" She lifted the paper and exposed the remains of an enormous blackfly, now just another mark on the scarred and messy desk. "So, Detectives, what do you think? Is twenty pounds of dynamite enough to blow up a car? My research tells me it is more than enough. In fact, I'd bet your bomber didn't use all of it. If he had, a couple of houses would have come down, too."

Poe nodded in agreement. "That, ladies and gentlemen, should be the scariest thing of all . . . you could be looking at a second explosion soon, another victim."

A mad bomber? Finn and I exchanged looks. If Caleb's murder had been random and unconnected to the threats he'd received, then finding the perp would be that much harder.

My gut continued to tell me the opposite was true, though; that Caleb's murder *was* deliberate, his death very much foreshadowed in the letters he'd received.

Poe handed us a stack of printouts. "Well, here are the screen shots from the video footage. I'll email you a copy of the file, if you like."

"Thanks." I flipped through the images, once more struck by the professionalism of the thief. The way he evaded getting his face on camera; his ease at accessing the dynamite.

And the hooded sweatshirt he wore.

Finn read my mind. "The sweatshirt looks the same, but this guy has a hundred pounds on the man we chased in the alley."

"We could be looking for two suspects. Let's get back to Cedar Valley."

As Finn and I drove away, Frank Poe and Sheriff Rose Underhill stood on the steps of the trailer, their arms raised in two identical waves. In town, the boy in the grocery store door and the dog in the church lot were both gone. My car's wheels left dust and dirt clouds behind us that trailed up into the air and then disappeared.

Suddenly an enormous turkey vulture set down in the road ahead of us, pecking at a splatter of roadkill. I slowed down and honked. After another few nibbles, the bird flew off with a ferocious beating of its wings, the intestines of a squirrel hanging from its talons.

"Hell of a town," Finn muttered.

I stepped on the gas. "Hell of a town."

# Chapter Nine

It was early afternoon by the time we arrived back in Cedar Valley. We grabbed lunch from a Greek deli and ate it in the station, at our desks. I barely tasted the pungent feta cheese and olives in my Greek salad; a ticking clock had perched itself on my shoulder and though I couldn't explain it, I knew with every fiber in my being that we hadn't seen the last of the bomber.

It was more than the fact that the thief stole more dynamite than was used in Caleb's death. It was the sense that we were standing at the edge of a dark chasm, just beginning to see tiny pinpricks of light, of understanding, at the bottom.

We had a long way to go.

"He's going to strike again, Finn," I said around a mouthful of tomatoes. "He, or they, didn't do all of this, the theft, the extensive planning it took to kill Caleb, only to disappear."

Finn finished chewing his sandwich. "But when? And where? And what's his objective? We should go back to the threats Caleb received. See if there's anything there."

"Maybe Jimmy has narrowed down the list of names I gave him." I paged the intern and he appeared a few minutes later, a thick stack of reports under his arm.

"It's like a tomb in that closet; I never see the sun. I love it but I'm turning into a vampire, I swear. So . . . I take it you want to know what I've found out so far?" Jimmy pulled up a chair and crossed his long, gangly legs. "There are some messed-up people in the world, are you aware of that? Yeah, yeah . . . 'course you are. I checked all the names of defendants that went before Judge Caleb Montgomery during his tenure. I started with the county death records first and was able to eliminate maybe twenty percent. Then I looked at prison records; there's another forty percent or so still incarcerated."

"So . . . about forty percent of the men and women Caleb saw in his courtroom are both alive and out of prison?" I asked, thinking about the hundreds of names on my initial list.

"Well, it's probably less, when you really think about it. I only checked Colorado state prisons and county records," Jimmy replied.

"Of course. Which doesn't tell us much." Finn groaned. "If Joe Smith got arrested in Florida or died in Texas, we wouldn't necessarily know about it."

"Correct." Jimmy nodded. "Unless you want me to run the names through the DOJ database. It will take some time . . . but it could shorten your list significantly. A lot of these guys, they don't stay out of prison long."

"Yes, please do, though I suppose the threats could have been mailed from anywhere, then routed through Boulder. Knowing Joe Smith is in a Florida jail doesn't mean we can eliminate him," I said.

Jimmy scowled. "It's worse than that. What about family members? Just because Joe Smith is dead, maybe his son or wife sent those letters."

I rubbed my eyes. "Good point. What if we're on the right track and Caleb's death is just the beginning? Think about how many people intersect with a single case during the investigation, trial, and sentencing: the arresting officer, other police personnel, the victims and their families, the judge, the court employees, the prison guards, even probation officers."

"Until the killer strikes again, we'll be searching for the proverbial needle in a haystack. Let's put aside Montgomery's former

cases for a moment and do the same with his current legal practice." Finn rolled his shoulders, exhaled. "We've been assuming the
threats he received were related to his career, but let's look at the
man *personally*. What were his hobbies? Was he seeing someone?
How did he spend his time?"

"If anyone knows, it's Bull." I called my grandfather, explained
what we were interested in, and put him on speakerphone. Jimmy
and Finn crowded in. "Okay, we're all here."

Bull cleared his throat. "What exactly do you want to know?"

I asked him the same questions Finn had posed. Bull was
silent a long time, then finally said, "Well, let's see. Caleb loved his
work, he really did. He loved the law, loved the logic and the purity
of it. I know that sounds strange, but he felt in this crazy world we
live in, the law was steadfast, made up of principles a man could
count on."

Jimmy rolled his eyes and I remembered hearing he'd done
a semester of law school at some point. The intern asked impatiently, "What about outside of work?"

"Caleb was a true outdoorsman. Fly-fishing was his great love,
though he enjoyed hiking, playing cards, or settling in with a good
British spy novel and a bottle of scotch," Bull said. "Is that the sort
of thing you mean? I'm not sure what else I can tell you."

Bull sounded as though he were reciting the obituary of a beloved uncle. It was all true, but none of it helped our case.

"This is good stuff. But we're looking for a motive for murder.
You told me on the night Caleb died that you believed he was seeing someone." I held my breath and crossed my fingers. "Do you
know who?"

On the other end of the line, Bull sighed. "I don't know. I may
have been wrong, Gem. There was a spring in his step, if you know
what I mean, the last month or so. Someone, or something, was
making him smile."

I thought a moment, then asked, "Could it have been a case?
We've been unable to get into his current files. His paralegal is

protecting attorney–client privilege. She's offered to review them, see if anything jumps out, but to be honest, they sound like run-of-the-mill small-town issues. Contentious divorces, disputed wills, that sort of thing."

"We rarely discussed work." Bull's voice sounded weary, frustrated. "I wish I could help you, but I don't know anything else. For as close as I thought Caleb and I were, there's a lot he kept private."

"I understand. You've been helpful, Bull. I'll talk to you later." I ended the call and sat back, stared at Jimmy and Finn. "Well? What do you think?"

Jimmy tapped a pen against his chin, leaving a small blue dot of ink behind. "There's a woman. There's got to be, I'm certain of it."

I said, "Okay. I'll play. Why do you think that?"

"Look, people kill for three reasons, right? Greed, passion, and power. That's it. Let's look at greed first. Who benefits financially from Montgomery's death? His wife. But she's already got the house and she doesn't seem the type. Plus, from the sounds of it, the family money comes from her side, anyways. Let's skip passion for a moment and examine power: again, who gains power from Montgomery's death? The paralegal? One of his clients?" Jimmy paused a moment, looked at us for an answer, then quickly moved on. "I don't think so; both the paralegal and his clients stand to lose the most, in fact, with his death. It would be a different story if Montgomery hadn't retired; if that was the case, then I'd say a big red circle needs to go around Judge Gloria Dumont. But he *was* retired, and Dumont *is* on the bench, so she as well gains nothing from his death. Which leaves us with passion. He's been messing around with the wrong woman. Maybe he wouldn't marry her. Or he was going to end it. She stewed for a while, growing angrier and angrier. Finally, she couldn't take it anymore. She loved the judge, but if she couldn't have him, no one could. So she arranged the hit."

The intern paused again. He stared at me, then at Finn. "Well? How did I do?"

"I think I saw the movie. You should have stuck with law

school; you spin a fine story," Finn said, a patronizing look in his eyes. "Gemma, you want to take the first stab?"

I shrugged. "Why not. Here's the thing, Jimmy. Passion can be born of love or hate. If Caleb was seeing someone, maybe the woman's husband took him out. Or perhaps, as we've considered, this was an act of revenge, a killing born from absolute all-consuming hatred. Greed . . . with the right businesses in place, the potential property value on the south end of Main Street could be worth millions. There are developers who have been harassing homeowners and businesses for years, trying to get them to sell. Caleb and Edith Montgomery bought the house he used for his legal offices fifteen years ago as an investment property. And power? It's the stickiest of your three motives. Power comes in many different shapes and colors, Jimmy, not the least of which is knowledge. What if Caleb was killed for something he knew? Some secret he's protected all these years?"

Jimmy blushed and hung his head. I leaned over and patted his knee. "Hey . . . it's a great start. And I agree, it sounds as though there might be a woman involved in this. But one of the things we have to do as detectives is keep our eyes open. Going into a case with only three motives in mind blinds us to other possibilities. Do you want to take a shot and see if you can track down Caleb's possible lover? I'd start with the paralegal. Support staff know everything that goes in their bosses' lives; she could tell you if he had frequent off-site lunches, or late meetings."

The color faded from Jimmy's cheeks and he sat up straighter. After a moment, he grinned and said, "Sure. I can do that. I would like to say, though, for the record, that all motives for murder really can be tied back to the three I listed. Just like there are only six core stories that make up all the literature in the world. We like to make things complex but at the end of the day, humans aren't that complicated."

Jimmy stood and ambled off to his closet. Finn smirked. "Where did we find this guy?"

I shrugged. "Where do we find any of our interns? They appear out of the blue and sell Chavez a story he can't refuse. Our chief has the heart of a nun, Finn. He's like Sister Maria from *The Sound of Music* with thousand-dollar loafers and fifteen rounds in a Glock 22."

Finn burst out laughing. "Now there's an image I'm not likely to forget for some time. But seriously, you really think a woman could be behind this murder? I know I threw Edith Montgomery's name out there, but a car bomb detonated by a sniper's rifle seems a bit out of character for the fairer sex."

"You're as bad as Jimmy. Talk about a narrow perspective. Women can be just as vicious, just as violent as men. Ever hear of Lizzie Borden?"

"Borden was acquitted."

I tipped my head. "Still, she remains the prime suspect in the case. My point is yes, forensic psychologists have put together profiles that show significant differences between male and female killers. But there are always outliers, Finn. Always."


Restless, I decided to go for a run. Between the long car ride to Bishop and back, and the fact that I'd been sitting in front of a computer for too long, I needed to move my body and get some fresh air.

I thought about what Moriarty had said, about Liv Ramirez needing a friend. He had given me her number and I sent her a text, asking if she was interested in joining me at a local trail. A few minutes later, her response came back: *I'm in. Where?*

I chose the path at the base of Lookout Mountain. It was a four-mile loop with a gradual incline, not too strenuous but enough to get the heart pumping and blood flowing. We agreed to meet there in thirty minutes. I changed in the station gym, swapping my jeans, sweater, and boots for black tights, a dark jersey, and running shoes.

Ramirez was already at the trailhead by the time I arrived and parked. She was warming up with a series of stretches and jumping jacks. Fuego sat patiently near a log, shooting excited glances every few seconds in the direction of the trail.

Ramirez laughed when she saw me: we wore identical outfits, even down to the bright red stripes on our shoes. "Thanks for the invitation. I haven't spent nearly enough time out here as I'd like to."

"Sure. I could use the exercise."

She glanced at my bandaged hands. "What happened?"

"An unexpected half hour on a roof. It's a long story. This is a loop; do you have a preference for starting east or west?"

The fire investigator glanced up at the sky, noting where the sun was. "East."

The trail was wide enough to allow us to run side by side. After a few minutes, Ramirez gasped, "The altitude is crap."

I huffed alongside her, my own breath coming in hitches. I noticed Fuego didn't seem to have any problems whatsoever; he kept pace with us just fine. I couldn't imagine my own dog, chubby Seamus with his squat legs, even attempting such a feat. He'd take one look at the trail and turn tail to head back home.

Another shallow breath. It really had been too long since I'd done this; trail running was vastly different than jogging on the station's treadmill. "You get used to it, but it never gets easier."

Ramirez glanced sideways at me, taking in my labored breathing. "No kidding. So what's the story on your partner?"

"Finn? He's an arrogant man with a heart of gold and a mouth that runs faster than his brain sometimes. A ladies' man through and through." I remembered what he'd said about marriage earlier and added, "From what I understand, he's not looking for anything serious."

"Who is? So you two, you're not . . . ?"

I snorted. "No. Definitely not. I'm getting married in a few weeks. Finn and I are strictly work partners. That's all."

We came to a bend where the trail narrowed and a momentary spurt of competitiveness shot through me. I sprinted ahead of Ramirez, catching her by surprise. I went through the narrows first, then slowed until she caught back up with me, Fuego a few feet behind her.

"Hundred meter?"

I shook my head. "No, cross-country. I was a speedy little kid, but I didn't enjoy it. I like taking in the scenery. That's why I love working on cases. Fast answers are great for closing investigations, but I enjoy the hunt. Putting the clues together, finding and eliminating suspects."

"High jump was my baby. I like heights. I never did enjoy playing it safe."

Two miles in, we caught up to an older couple using walking sticks to carefully pick their way amongst the boulders, rocks, and muddy crevices. They heard us coming and moved to the side. As we ran past with a thanks and wave, I heard the woman mutter, "Crazy girls."

Another twenty minutes and we were almost done when Ramirez suddenly gasped. She darted to the edge of the trail and looked down at a steep, rocky embankment. A narrow sliver of icy water flowed over the rocks and came to a stop a hundred feet down in a small, nearly frozen pond.

"It's beautiful," she whispered. "It's sights like this I missed when I was in the desert. Ice . . . ponds. Forests."

Fuego whined and gave Ramirez's pants leg a quick tug. She laughed. "Am I too close to the edge, buddy? You big worrywart." Instead of stepping back, she leaned forward, her toes on the very edge of the ravine.

Even I was uncomfortable with how close she was. "Liv . . ."

"Shhhh. Do you hear that? It's the sound of adventure, Detective." Another step closer, her toes now totally off the edge. She closed her eyes and inhaled. I waited, my own breath caught in my throat.

Finally, Ramirez stepped back, opened her eyes, and smiled. "Ready?"

I nodded. I wasn't sure what I'd just witnessed, if there was a daredevil side to the fire investigator or if she literally just liked to live life on the edge. We finished the run and came to an easy, gradual stop at the trailhead. Ramirez walked in tight circles while I leaned forward and rested my hands on my thighs, careful not to put too much pressure on the wounds on my palms. Even Fuego walked in small, tight circles, shaking off the last of his adrenaline.

"Man, that felt good. I needed some speed today." Ramirez threw a leg up on the fender of her truck and stretched forward. "Thanks again for the invitation."

"You're welcome. We should do it again sometime. To be honest, I've been a little reluctant to hit the trails by myself lately. There was a mountain lion attack a few months ago. The hiker survived, but Fish and Game was never able to track the cat." I grabbed a water bottle from my trunk and chugged it down. "Something about knowing he's out there gives me the spooks."

"Not me. I'd rather deal with a wild animal than a human any day of the week," Ramirez said. She peeled off her sweat-soaked jersey, exposing a tanned and toned stomach, and replaced it with a fleece sweatshirt. Shivering, she yanked the hood up over her head and whistled for Fuego to jump in the truck. She climbed in after him and rolled down the window. "Next time let's get a beer after, okay?"

"It's a deal." I followed her out of the parking lot, then we went in different directions, me headed up the canyon, Liv headed south to her rental above Lou Moriarty's garage.

As I walked in the front door of my house, I smelled jerk chicken. I found Brody and Grace in the backyard, Brody grilling the chicken alongside corn on the cob and slices of squash, and the baby, bundled up in a warm jacket and hat, playing in her sandbox. It was that magical time of day, dusk, when the sky is soft and the blackness of night not yet fallen.

"I thought we'd get in one more barbecue before the weather changes for good," Brody said. "I picked up a six-pack of that hard pear cider you like. And I dropped the deposit off at the Tate. So don't get cold feet, or you'll cost me a thousand bucks."

"No cold feet here." I picked up the baby and squeezed her tight. Her cheeks were rosy and cool to the touch. "Did Grace eat?"

"Yes. She's ready for her bath, I'll keep dinner warm until she's in bed."

I nodded. "Thanks. Come on, sweet pea, ready for a bath?"

"Ya," Grace replied in that funny little voice of hers.

I let Grace play in the tub longer than usual, enjoying the sight of her smashing bubbles and throwing the assortment of colorful plastic toys around in the water. After, I dressed her in footed fleece pajamas and turned the thermostat up a few degrees. There are not many things sweeter than a clean baby, scrubbed pink, in a pair of footed fleece pajamas. We lingered over bedtime stories and a cup of warm milk, then I reluctantly put her down for the night.

As I crept out and gently closed her door, I was grateful to have this precious time with her. Already she was quick to change her mind about affection, sometimes leaning in for cuddles, other times asserting her independence. I choked back unexpected tears at it struck me again just how fast this was all going. Though Grace had been a surprise, she'd had our hearts since the moment we first saw her on the ultrasound, and motherhood was quickly becoming my most favorite role.

Though night had fallen and the air was again chilly, Brody and I added a few more layers, then ate outside at the picnic table on the back porch, a couple of candles illuminating the darkness. It was romantic, like camping, and I wondered why we didn't do it more often.

Content, Brody sipped his cider and leaned back. "Want to watch a scary movie? TMC is still showing horror movies, twenty-four hours a day."

"You hate horror movies."

He shrugged. "They're kind of fun. I bought caramel corn . . . and roasted tamari pumpkin seeds . . ."

I sighed. "You realize I have a wedding dress I need to fit into in less than a month, don't you?"

"You're perfect. Come on, it'll be fun."

We watched *Friday the 13th* and though it was nice to snuggle up, my mind was a million miles away. By the time the movie ended, though, I was surprised to find myself more than a little spooked. As we dragged ourselves up the stairs to bed, my eyes saw masked men in every shadow, their only goal to stab at me, over and over again, until I was no more.

# Chapter Ten

By the time Finn walked into the station at nine a.m. on Thursday, I was nearly done with my third cup of coffee and my nerves were on edge. I took a break from the gruesome material I'd been reading and went to the window and cracked it open. Outside, a brisk wind rattled a trio of aspens. The trees were harbingers of the fate we'd all meet someday: bare, exposed, skeletal.

Vulnerable.

No, not vulnerable. Armored. Stripped down to their barest form, ready to face the snow and sleet and ice and wind. Ready to survive.

Finn joined me at the window, a cup of coffee in his hands, dressed in dark jeans and a navy wool sweater that turned his baby blues into twin ponds of dark, moody water. "You look like you've already put in a half day's work. What time did you get in?"

"Early. I couldn't sleep. I've been reviewing the list of names Jimmy narrowed down. It's an ugly list; Montgomery met a lot of nasty people." I returned to my desk, sat down. "Including Gordon Dillahunt."

Finn paused, his mug halfway to his lips. He slowly lowered the coffee and cleared his throat. "Now there's a name that no one around here is likely to forget."

I shrugged. "It was before our time. I didn't know if you knew . . ."

"I doubt there's a cop in this state, hell, in the *region* that isn't familiar with Dillahunt. You know that Chief Chavez was the one who finally caught up with him, right? Of course, the bastard managed to kill three more men before Chavez finally arrested him in Montana."

I quickly did the math in my head. "The chief would have been young, just a few years out of the academy."

"Yes." Finn lowered his voice. "There are some that say the Dillahunt collar paved the way for the chief to quickly move up the ranks. Without that arrest, there's a good chance we could be reporting to Moriarty."

"The horror. I guess we should consider ourselves lucky, then. I made some calls this morning. Gordon Dillahunt is serving multiple life sentences at the penitentiary in Belle Vista. He hasn't had visitors in years; he's difficult to work with and dismisses attorneys left and right. Then all of a sudden, sometime last year, a law student from Boulder made contact with Dillahunt. Since then, she makes the drive down to Belle Vista twice a month. Her name is Colleen Holden."

"Is this one of those sick stories where you tell me they've fallen in love? Prison pen pals turned beloved?" Finn asked.

"No, not at all. Holden is researching case law in hopes of getting Dillahunt an appeal."

"Why would anyone in their right mind want that lunatic out on the street?" Finn pinched the bridge of his nose. "Dillahunt goes through attorneys like used tissues, but he's okay with a *student*? That doesn't even begin to make sense."

I shrugged. "They've developed some kind of rapport. Anyway, she visits every other Friday. She's due to be there, at the prison, tomorrow. I'm going to be there, too, see if she'll meet with me."

"Wait a minute. What do you think is going on? Dillahunt persuaded this woman to do his dirty work? You believe a Boulder law student assassinated Judge Montgomery?" Finn rubbed his eyes. "I must be dreaming, still asleep."

"I know it sounds crazy. Just hear me out. Belle Vista Penitentiary is only a two-hour drive from Cedar Valley. After Dillahunt was sentenced, he pointed at Montgomery, then at the prosecutor's team, and finally at his own attorney. Dillahunt said that he would be coming for them, each of them, in their dreams. Then he added, 'You'll wake and find it wasn't a dream. I'll be there, in your bedroom. I'll be the last thing you ever see.'"

"What a psychopath," Finn muttered.

"You haven't heard the best part. Colleen Holden is not some naïve young idealist. After college, she enlisted in the army. Holden went on to spend the next six years in Virginia, teaching and training EOD specialists."

"EOD . . . what is that?"

I waited a beat, then smiled. "Explosive Ordnance Disposal."

"No shit." Finn's eyes lit up. "You're on fire this morning. Where did you get all this intel?"

"Dillahunt's trial transcripts include his threats, ones that sound similar to the threats Caleb received. Caleb even told me that there was something familiar about them. I'm certain it was Dillahunt's courtroom threat that Caleb was remembering. As for how I got the information about Holden . . . well . . . I talked to the Squirrel."

Finn blanched. "What did you have to promise old Stinky Nuts in exchange?"

"Nothing. He was happy to share. He doesn't like Colleen Holden very much." In fact, Richard Nuts, the parole officer with the overbite and an unfortunate propensity to forget deodorant, had used words so unflattering toward Holden I wasn't comfortable repeating them even to Finn. "I talked to the warden, too. He'll let me meet with Dillahunt tomorrow, assuming Dillahunt himself is willing and interested."

"Great," Finn said and rubbed his hands together in anticipation. "What time are we leaving?"

"You're not coming. Dillahunt refuses to see male visitors. And I need him cooperative and calm, if I'm going to learn anything."

"Like hell you're going alone to see this crackpot. Besides, what if you're onto something? You could be in serious danger."

"Holden's hardly going to attack me in full view of an army of prison guards. I'll be fine. As for Dillahunt . . . all of his victims were male. He's intrigued by women, entranced by them."

Finn stood up and began pacing. "Have you talked to Chavez yet?"

"No. I'm hoping you can help pave the way. At the moment, this is the best lead we have."

"You're right." Finn kicked at the small metal wastebasket next to his desk. "But I don't like it."

We found the chief in his office. After Finn explained what we wanted to do, Chavez leaned back and tented his fingers. He stared at us for a long moment, his eyes growing dark. "There's a reason people in this valley don't talk about Gordon Dillahunt. He's garbage, trash. Dillahunt is the stuff of nightmares, the real boogeyman. I should have killed him when I had the chance."

"Why didn't you?" Finn asked, quickly adding, "I'm not second-guessing things. I'm just curious how it all went down."

Chief Chavez was silent a moment, then he exhaled. "A lot of this is common knowledge. We had Dillahunt cornered in a little rental home on a couple of acres near Marble Pond. At least, we thought we did. He'd killed four men by then. 'The Jawbreaker,' we called him, before we knew Dillahunt's identity and profession. He . . . did things to the mouths of the victims, disfigured them after death. Once we learned he was a dentist, the techniques and tools he used made sense."

"Is that how he found his victims?" Finn asked. "They were his patients?"

Chavez tipped his head in acknowledgment. "Single, white, professional middle-aged men. Dillahunt never did share what made him choose one victim or another; there were dozens of men who visited his practice that fit that description, dozens of potential victims."

I asked, "All men . . . was it a sex thing?"

"No." Chavez shook his head. "No, to my knowledge, Dillahunt is straight. Profiles done on him suggest his rage toward these types of men stemmed from seeing his stepfather, an insurance broker, abuse his mother."

Finn, always impatient with backstory, said, "So you were at the rental home . . ."

"There were seven of us, plus another half dozen men in the woods. We weren't taking any chances. What we missed, what we somehow goddamn missed, was that he had a hostage. Keep in mind that this was twenty-five years ago, and things were different back then. Tactical operations, protocols . . . he got away. He got away. We found the hostage at the Wyoming border, dead, of course; Dillahunt had been purposeful about where he dropped the body, knowing jurisdictional conflicts would slow us down. After a few weeks, most of the rest of the team dropped off. They gave up, other cases cropped up. But my partner and I, we stuck with it. I guess we both felt like we had something to prove; me a young tough Hispanic kid new to town, her an itty-bitty female cop. Anyway, Dillahunt took down two more men before we caught up with him in Montana. We found him in a candy store, of all places, if you can believe it. The store owner was a big tabloid reader and she recognized Dillahunt's picture."

Finn sat back. "God, what a collar. What a story."

"In the end, the arrest was simple and straightforward. Dillahunt was unarmed and we took him without a struggle."

Finn was right; it was quite a story. Something bothered me, though. There had been no mention of a female officer in the trial transcript.

"Chief? What became of your partner, the woman?"

Chavez looked down at his desk, his face sliding into something that looked an awful lot like regret. "She wasn't involved in the actual arrest. Our chief at the time, a relic from the Jurassic Age, held her back. He refused to let her come with me to Montana. She quit shortly after and moved away. Though she's done okay for herself, came back to the state and started fresh after years in

Nevada. In fact, I just caught up on your daily logs. You all met her the other day. Sheriff Underhill."

Rose Underhill, the woman who'd indicated a long history with both Caleb Montgomery and my grandfather, had been Chief Angel Chavez's partner twenty-five years ago on the case that would make Chavez's career.

Life was full of interesting coincidences. I found myself back at the dark chasm, staring down as another pinprick of light appeared at the bottom of the pit.

Before returning to my desk, I made a fresh pot of coffee and ate the last chocolate chip cookie from a bowl on the counter in the break room. It was stale and did little to settle my nerves. Then I went to my desk and found in my in-box a progress report from forensics. I scanned the contents and settled in to read the full report. While Liv Ramirez was still working on the bomb analysis, the crime scene team had managed to collect a great deal of evidence.

I'd learned years before at the academy that, contrary to popular belief, a bomb doesn't destroy evidence; more often, the explosion scatters it. The team had scooped up anything and everything that might be relevant: leaves, soil samples, cigarette butts, and other trash from the nearby rooftops. One of the paragraphs in the report referenced a comic book found on the roof of the abandoned restaurant directly across the street from Caleb's law offices. It was described as a vintage pamphlet in perfect condition, dating to the 1980s, chronicling the adventures of one Ghost Boy.

I paused from my reading and did a quick search online. Ghost Boy was a supervillain, born in Japan and skilled in martial arts, a superstar in the comic world. He first appeared in a March 1982 edition.

I glanced back at the forensics report. The comic had been found encased in a plastic sheath, tucked under a brick, sheltered in a corner of the roof. A most unusual place, and yet obvious to anyone searching the place.

The team had been unable to lift fingerprints from either the comic or the plastic envelope, though they did find a single black human hair in the envelope. Tests had determined the hair was from an individual of mixed racial ancestry.

I thought about what I knew about that particular restaurant; it had been abandoned for roughly four months, ever since the massively-in-debt owner ran off in the middle of the night. Since then, the front windows had been boarded and the doors locked, though there was an old fire escape ladder bolted to the back of the building that provided rooftop access. We'd busted a couple of teenagers for loitering up there, but the novelty of the abandoned place had passed, and to my knowledge, no one had been up there for a while.

Except clearly, someone had.

Someone who enjoyed the adventures of Ghost Boy.

Was it connected to the case? It was impossible to say yet and at the same time, it was highly suspicious. But what did an old comic book have to do with the murder of a recently retired judge?

I moved on to the rest of the report, questions continuing to churn in my mind.

Why a car bomb? What was the significance of killing Caleb that way? Was it meant to send a message to the town, as some had suggested?

Or was some other factor at play, something we weren't aware of yet?

And if a gunman had truly detonated the dynamite with an incredibly well-placed bullet, why not just kill Caleb that way and save himself the dangerous effort of gaining access to Caleb's car, packing it full of dynamite, and determining his schedule such as to be in the right place at the right time?

After all, Caleb could have opened his trunk to stow groceries or retrieve a spare jacket. If the dynamite had been placed in there, say, he would have discovered it.

When I sat back and really thought through it, imagined each and every step the killer must have taken, the whole thing seemed incredibly risky.

There are a hell of a lot of easier ways to kill a man.

My thoughts were interrupted by a call from Gloria Dumont, asking if I could meet her at the Shotgun Playhouse. She'd bring dinner; she ate there often, she said, to enjoy the peace and quiet before Nash arrived with his cast for rehearsals. We decided to meet at five, which gave me time to put together a rough plan for my visit to Belle Vista Penitentiary the next day.

Everything I'd read about Gordon Dillahunt indicated the man would appreciate, and perhaps respond better to, a direct approach. Even more important, I didn't have the luxury of time. The drive there and back would take up half the day, and in all likelihood, I'd only get fifteen or twenty minutes with him. Every word would need to count.

If I was honest with myself, I was more than a little nervous about the visit. While I'd come face-to-face with killers before, Dillahunt was a different caliber. And no matter how many cases I worked, how closely I stared death in the eyes, the day I became comfortable chatting with murderers was the day I quit the force.

The parking lot at the Playhouse was empty, save for a red luxury sedan. Judge Dumont met me at the locked front door, and once in, led me into the theater. We sat on the stage, staring out at the empty seats, a platter of sandwiches and a couple of sparkling juices between us.

Dumont sighed. "I love this place, don't you?"

"It's beautiful, Judge. You and Nash have done a wonderful job restoring it."

"He deserves all the credit, and please, call me Gloria." She sipped her juice, sighed again. "Lately, this is the only place I feel at home."

After a few minutes of silence as we ate our sandwiches, she asked, "Can you keep a secret?"

I hesitated, then shrugged and said, "Sure, unless you're about to confess to something horrible."

"Depends who you ask. My secret is this: I hate the law. I hated being an attorney and I despise being a judge. I'd give anything to be sixteen again, working at the local ice cream shop in the small town in Texas where I grew up." Gloria laughed, a bitter sound that set my nerves on edge. She tucked a strand of short blond hair behind her ear. "I was something then, cocky and bullheaded and sure of my place in the world."

"Can I ask the obvious?"

"Why I'd go into law? It was my daddy's idea. He was an oilman, a millionaire by the time he was thirty and I came along. Momma couldn't have kids, so they adopted me, and a few years later, a little boy. Daddy was rich and he was street-smart, but he was uneducated. He'd gotten lucky, knew some people in oil and gas and made some wise choices. But he never wanted my brother and me to feel stupid, the way he did in business meetings, with his attorneys. So I was pushed into law and my brother into medicine. Daddy paid for everything: school, my wedding to Nash, even the capital to get this place up and running." Gloria paused, toyed with the emerald-and-diamond set on her necklace. "If there's anything better than bacon and Brie, I haven't found it yet."

"Why are you telling me all this?" I asked, interested but failing to see a connection to my case.

I should have known, though, that the connection would be there.

"Because family is everything, and children are always trying to live up to the people their parents hope they will be. Caleb gave me this when I took his seat on the bench." Gloria reached into her bag, pulled out a photograph, and handed it to me. "It's Caleb, and his father, Henry."

Though in the picture Caleb was a boy, no more than five or six, he would grow into the spitting image of his father. It was physically painful to see the young and the old, both now gone.

"His father was a judge in Cedar Valley, too?" I asked, noting the somber robes and familiar courthouse in the background.

"Yes. On Caleb's last day of work, about six months ago, he gave me that picture and said he'd failed. He said he'd spent years trying to atone for his father's sins, but in the end, he'd followed him down the same path. Caleb wouldn't say anything more, just told me to keep the picture safe and to try to be fair and always, always side with the law. 'It's the only ace an honest judge has got in his robe,' he said."

Gloria stood, brushed crumbs from her lap. "And now I give the picture to you. I have no idea if it will help with your case, but it's not doing me any good. It's too painful to keep. If you can't use it, give it to Edith or Bull. They loved Caleb; they should see the boy that became the man, and the man that influenced the boy far more than we'll ever know, I think."

There was something in her voice, a slight tremor, that gave me pause. "Did you love him, too?"

"I thought I could. I might as well tell you, you'll figure it out sooner or later. We saw each other a few times, over the last couple of months. I could never be with a married man, but once Cal and Edith separated . . . we thought we'd give it a try. I was at a low point in my own marriage, desperately unhappy with Nash. Cal was attractive, with the most brilliant mind I've ever encountered."

"But?"

Gloria wiped at her eye, though it was a piece of lint she came away with, not a tear. "The idea of it was better than the reality. As soon as we'd been intimate, I knew it was a mistake. But Cal refused to listen to reason. He was convinced I was to be his muse, his goddess. He said life without me would be colorless, devoid of meaning. He was utterly ridiculous and I told him as much."

I bit my lip, thinking. "When did you end things with Caleb?"

"A few weeks ago. We had dinner at Luigi's. The next day, I received a dozen roses and a note from Cal, begging me not to break his heart over a plate of spaghetti. I phoned him immediately and told him to stay away." Gloria sighed. "I promised to expose him if he didn't back off. Tell his wife, my husband, even the newspaper."

"Would you have gone through with that?"

She shrugged. "I don't know. Possibly. It never came to that. Caleb got the message. He left me alone. The last time I saw him was a week ago. We ran into each other at the liquor store. He needed a bottle of dry white wine for a lentil dish and I had a strange craving for sherry."

"Did you speak to one another?"

Gloria nodded. "Caleb showed me the recipe on his phone and explained that his doctor had encouraged a more plant-based diet. I asked him to recommend a good sherry. That was it."

"That sounds so civil after what sounds like a difficult breakup."

"Gemma, you're young but you're no spring chicken. I'm sure you're aware that time and distance put things in perspective. Caleb and I were two adults who tried something that didn't work. That's all. I'm so sorry he's dead. I will miss running into him around town. I'll miss his wit and his mind." Gloria paused, then put a finger to her lips as voices from the lobby carried into the theater.

She whispered, "Nash doesn't know. I see no reason why you need to tell him."

Before I could respond, the director was inside the theater, bounding up the stage steps to embrace his wife in a big bear hug. After a long moment, he released her and she excused herself to use the restroom.

Nash watched her walk away, then adjusted his fedora and turned to me. "Well? Any progress on the punk who's messing with my theater?"

"No. As you can imagine, I've been rather tied up with a murder investigation. Is your stage manager here? I could talk to her. What's her name? Weather?"

"Her name is Waverly and yes, she's here. Gemma, this is not good. Opening night is a week away. You've got to find this guy." Nash scowled, an anxious expression suddenly rising in his eyes. "You didn't say anything to Gloria, did you? About the fire?"

"She doesn't know? Nash . . . she's your business partner. Your wife. She has a right to know what's going on." I shook my head, annoyed to find myself being asked to keep yet another secret. "Maybe Waverly's already told her."

"No." Nash's voice was a hiss now, as more people began to fill the theater. "Waverly knows which way the winds of fortune blow. That's her, with the red sweater. Talk to her all you want but don't you dare say a word to Gloria."

Before I could ask him anything further, Gloria returned. Nash said quickly, "My Hecate is still out sick . . . Gemma? Would you like to give it another spin?"

I gathered up the trash from our dinner, using the opportunity to hide the sudden flush in my face. "Nash, I wish I could help, but I need to be going. I'm sure you can persuade someone else to take up the mantle. Your wife, perhaps?"

Gloria laughed. "There's not room enough in our marriage for two dramatics. My role is to clap for the actors and sign the checks."

Nash turned away, but not before I saw an angry look in his eyes. He muttered, "I contribute what I can. You fell in love with the starving artist, remember? You liked that I was the opposite of your dad. You liked that I didn't have money to buy my way in the world."

Gloria reached out to take hold of Nash's arm, but he brushed her aside. "I have to get my cast ready. Stay or don't stay, I don't care. I'll see you later."

Nash stormed off and Gloria turned to me, a blush high on her cheeks. "Sorry about that; he's worried about opening night. The damn curse has him on edge. It's consumed him; he's half-convinced something terrible will happen—the chandelier will come crashing down on the audience or the lead actors will succumb to food poisoning."

If she only knew what terrible things had already begun.

"Well, let's hope nothing like that happens. Gloria, thank you for trusting me with your story and this photograph. I'll take good care of them both. And if it makes you feel better, sometimes I hate my job, too."

As I left her, she was debating whether to stay or not.

Waverly, the stage manager, was a young woman in her early twenties with a nose ring and beautiful red hair piled high in a ponytail. To my surprise, she knew who I was.

"Clementine is my best friend. I know all about you, and Brody, and baby Grace. Clem tells me everything," Waverly said with a bright smile. Her eyes flickered around the room, though, and it was hard to tell if the smile was sincere. But, if she was good enough for Clementine, she was good enough for me.

Though I did wonder what she meant by *everything*.

"Can we sit in the back, up in the rear of the theater, and talk for a few minutes?" I asked, though my tone suggested it was a polite command and not really a question.

"Sure." The stage manager set her clipboard down and followed me up the narrow aisle. We took seats in the back row; from that distance, the actors on stage were small and diminished, as though they were mere atoms experiencing half-life.

"So what's up?" Waverly popped a red jawbreaker into her mouth and moved it back and forth, the tiny ball protruding from first one cheek and then the other. Red seemed to be her color: her hair, her sweater, her lipstick, and now even her candy. As she spoke, the scent of cinnamon filled the air and I noticed that she wore red earrings, heart-shaped rubies, in her earlobes.

I was tempted to ask if she'd ever considered changing her name to Scarlet.

"Nash has asked me to investigate the vandalism occurring in the theater. As I understand, only you, he, and Gloria Dumont have keys to the building. Can you tell me anything?" I kept my voice low, as actors and crew members continued to travel between the theater and the lobby. "Maybe you've seen or heard something suspicious? Or come in after hours and noticed things were amiss?"

Waverly's big blue eyes grew even wider. "Wow, I can't believe Nash talked to you. I've been begging him to go to the cops for a week. He must really trust you. I wish I could help . . . but I haven't seen anything. I was home sick when the fire in the lobby closet happened. And honestly, I'd *just* finished cleaning that dressing room the day it was vandalized. I was so pissed when I saw it."

"Can you think of anyone who'd want to hurt the Dumonts, or the theater?"

Waverly started to answer, then stopped as a middle-aged woman approached us. Her eyes were downcast behind thick eyeglasses, her hair long and limp around her moonlike face.

Waverly sighed in exasperation. "Yes, Freya?"

Freya's entire being spoke of someone who'd lived her whole life in a painful state of shyness. "I heard Mr. Dumont say that there are still some actors out sick. I was wondering if I could read the part of one of them? Just for tonight?"

Waverly scrunched up her face, put a finger to her lips as though deep in thought. It was so obviously a charade that I was embarrassed for both women. Waverly dragged out the suspense for a good minute, then said brusquely, "We've talked about this before. We need you to run sounds and lights. That's what you're good at, Freya. And for the love of everything holy, you have got to stop calling Nash Mr. Dumont. He hates it."

Freya blushed, her pale orb of a face turning a strange shade of orange.

Waverly softened her tone. "Sounds and lights, Freya. It's what you're good at."

The woman nodded and moved away, her head down. Waverly sighed again. "Where were we? Oh yes . . . suspects who enjoy slashing velvet-backed chairs and arson. I haven't a clue."

"Is there any chance someone borrowed your key? Perhaps a boyfriend, a roommate?"

Waverly crunched down on her cinnamon jawbreaker as she glanced out at the theater. "No. I live alone and I'm kind of like Nash—I'm paranoid. I keep my stuff with me at all times."

I glanced down at her empty arms, the single script in her lap. "All the time? What about now? Where's your purse, your key ring?"

I wasn't trying to trick her, but the stage manager was insulted by my question. She swallowed the last of her candy and said in a snotty tone, "My keys are in my locker. In one of the dressing rooms. I keep the key to the locker on this." She pulled a red (of course) key ring wrist coil from her back pocket, a single key on it. "Satisfied?"

"Not really. Anyone with internet access and some time on their hands can learn how to pick a lock."

I wasn't sure what to make of Waverly. On the one hand, I trusted Clementine wholeheartedly, and if this was her best friend, the young woman must have some redeeming qualities. But thus far, I'd seen her be rude to a colleague, dismissive of my questions, and frankly, cavalier about serious issues in her theater.

Waverly suddenly stood up. "I've got to go; Nash is starting rehearsal in ten minutes. He'll have my head on a silver platter if I'm not down there with him. He's such a child sometimes. Helpless as a baby seal on a drifting piece of ice."

There wasn't much left for me to work with at that point, so I walked out alone as a few remaining actors were walking in. They were wrapped up in their phones, or each other, barely noticing me, the stumbling, blushing cop who'd pretended to be one of their own for a moment days ago. It wasn't until I was nearly to my car that I saw Maggie Armstrong and Milo Griffith once more entangled in each other's arms. This time, instead of in a car, they were in a thicket of trees just off the parking lot.

Maggie and I saw each other at the same time. She instantly pushed off from Milo and straightened her shirt. It would have been too awkward to ignore them, or worse, to wave. I slowed my steps and pretended to look in my purse for my keys, and let Maggie decide how she wanted this to play out.

After a moment, the young woman and her older beau moved toward me.

"Hi, Gemma," Maggie mumbled. "Um, you remember Milo?"

"Of course, nice to see you both," I said, adopting a stiff, formal voice that instantly had me feeling twice my age. I forced myself to relax; I'd known Maggie for years. There was nothing wrong with their behavior. "How's the play coming along?"

"Oh, fine. Milo, why don't I meet you inside?" Maggie shooed him off, then turned to me. "You can't say a word to my father. I'm still trying to figure out how to break the news to him."

I bit my lip. "Maggie, I see your father every day at work. Lucas sits two desks down from me. You're asking me to lie for you, to a fellow cop, when you know in our profession we have to be able to trust one another. Your father would never forgive me."

"I'm not asking you to lie, just be silent. The topic should never come up; don't ask him how I'm doing, what I'm up to. Avoid talking about anything personal with him, just for a few more days, pretty please? Until I can talk with him. He's going to have a coronary as it is. White boy, ten years my senior. My dad's progressive, but he's not *that* progressive. Not when it comes to his little girl," Maggie said. She was breathless now, fully begging. "I'll do anything; you want a free babysitter? I'll walk your dog. I'll clean your car."

"Why do I have a feeling that I'm going to regret this?" I sighed. "Do you love Milo?"

Maggie grinned. "More than anything. Thank you. I owe you, big-time." She scampered off.

*Hell.*

I was definitely, surely, for certain going to regret this.

# Chapter Eleven

Belle Vista was a recreation destination, a playground for mountain bikers and water enthusiasts. There were cabdrivers with doctorate degrees in chemistry and baristas who'd once been CEOs. People didn't move to Belle Vista for careers, they came to play. They skied in the winter and hiked in the spring, rafted in the summer and hunted in the fall. Sunk in a shallow basin, surrounded by hills, and with the expansive Johnson River running through it, Belle Vista was like Neverland: live here, and you'll never have to grow up.

Or rather, it would have been like Neverland, if Neverland had a high-security prison on its outskirts that housed thugs, rapists, and murderers. Captain Hook's quarters. It was ironic: many of the prisoners inside would spend the rest of their days mere miles out of reach of paradise. And the residents themselves could never forget what loomed over their town, high on a neighboring bluff; there were signs everywhere warning drivers not to pick up hitchhikers.

I'd left Cedar Valley at seven in the morning on Friday, but not before casually mentioning to Clementine that I'd run into her best friend, Waverly, the night before. Clementine had blanched when I said the woman's name, and explained that while they'd been close a few months before, Waverly had started showing obsessive behavior that Clementine wasn't comfortable with. Things like jealousy when Clem didn't return Waverly's texts soon enough, or showing up unexpectedly after Clem had already declined an invitation to hang out.

I didn't tell Clem that I was relieved to hear that the two weren't so close anymore; I'd had a strange feeling about Waverly since meeting her the night before. She wasn't suspicious, not exactly, but she was unsettling.

And now, driving away from the sanctity of my home and toward Neverland's underworld twin, my nerves were shot. The two-hour drive should have been pleasant, but all I could think about was coming face-to-face with Gordon Dillahunt. The meadows and peaks I passed were lost on me, the songs coming from the radio all toneless.

I'd faced down killers before, but Dillahunt was different. He was, as Chief Chavez had said, the boogeyman. In photographs, the dentist was a small, unassuming man with pale arms and freckled hands. He wore his black hair short and neatly combed, with a razor-straight center part. Thick eyeglasses over a hooked nose and a tiny, almost feminine, mouth.

Of course, those were the press photographs, the ones that were printed for the public to gawk over, the ones published by the newspapers.

That was Dr. Dillahunt's public persona, and his appearance was what he based most of his defense on, as his victims were men twice his size: muscular, strong men.

But to truly understand Dillahunt, or at least try to, as I didn't know that I could ever truly understand that breed of evil, I had to study the private photographs, the photographs taken at the crime scenes. I'd seen the damage Dillahunt had inflicted on his victims, their broken faces and unhinged jaws. I knew how this man, with his small pouty mouth and flat eyes, killed.

He incapacitated his victims with chloroform, then viciously, without hesitation, stabbed them through the heart with a thin stiletto knife.

Then he moved on to their faces.

I followed the signs for the Belle Vista Penitentiary, leaving the town proper and curving up a winding road to a compound set high on a bluff. A series of guard stations required me to repeatedly slow down, stop, and show my identification. At the last station before entering the parking lot, the guard searched my trunk and ran an inspection mirror under the body of my car.

"This feels like visiting the CIA," I joked with him.

The guard didn't match my smile. "Standard procedure, Detective. We've had a couple of serious threats over the last few months. We can't be too careful. Drive on through. I'd park close to the handicap spots, that'll put you near the entrance. The warden's expecting you."

I did as the guard instructed and shortly found myself in a pristine white concrete-walled lobby devoid of any wall hangings or decorations. There wasn't even a water fountain. I was given a set of paperwork to complete and a visitor's badge, then told to sit on the bench that was bolted to the wall.

Ten minutes later, a thick, muscular man with a gray crew cut and beady eyes set into a fleshy face appeared at my side. "Detective? I'm Warden Cash Harrison. Come with me, please."

"I appreciate your time, Warden." We walked through a series of locked doors; at each one, Harrison would first scan his badge, then shield the keypad and enter a code.

"I'm happy to help my colleagues. Though from what you explained on the phone, I believe you're wasting your time. Dillahunt is one crazy son of a bitch," Harrison muttered. "I think that law student that's been working with him is making things worse, though I'd have the ACLU up my butt if I dared tried to restrict her visits."

"Colleen Holden, right?" I asked. We'd come to a set of stairs and began to make our way up them.

"Correct. I understand you've been in contact with Field Parole Officer Richard Nuts? He's had a few run-ins with Holden. She's been reaching out to his parolees, interviewing them, trying to dig up intelligence on alleged prison abuses. Detective, I have no patience for that kind of nonsense," the warden said. "I can't speak for other facilities, but I run a tight ship here. I have to, or people get hurt. Killed, even."

Another few flights of stairs, then I asked, "How many floors is the prison? I couldn't tell from the drive in—the compound is deceiving, the way it's situated on the bluff."

"We do that on purpose, helps to muddy the waters if anyone's trying to collect intel on our floor plans. This building, Unit A, is six stories. We have a visitor room here on this floor that you can use, though rest assured, Dillahunt will stay restrained the entire time. It's sometimes easier that way than carting the prisoners back and forth on the stairs or elevators. Too much can go wrong. Here we go, we're at the top. Dillahunt is at the end of the corridor. Penthouse suite." The warden laughed mirthlessly. "More like the sky suite. That's all the view his window affords: nothing but sky for miles and miles. The architect of Belle Vista Penitentiary, a sadistic old fart from the East Coast, purposely angled the windows so that they only look up. At the time, it was to prevent the inmates from seeing citizens on the ground, or signals from nearby peaks."

"Why hasn't anyone changed them?" I asked. We'd stopped before a door, where two black prison guards waited, their faces devoid of all expression.

"You got a couple million dollars to spend on window treatments for inmates? I didn't think so. Well, this is where I get off the bus. Dillahunt doesn't appreciate seeing me, and I'd hate to sour him off before you get what you need. Santiago and Lofland will take it from here." Harrison ran a hand through his short gray hair and for a moment, his beady eyes widened in what I understood to be a look of pity. "Listen, I wish you luck. If you've got an appetite after your visit, there's a great little Indian restaurant on South Street in Belle Vista. You can sit on the patio, soak up the scenery, and all of this will melt away like a bad dream."

As Santiago and Lofland let me through the door, Warden Harrison strolled away. He began to whistle "Pop Goes the Weasel." He turned a corner and disappeared down another corridor, the sound of his song and his footsteps echoing in my ears long after he was gone.

The guards left me in a windowless room while they fetched Dillahunt. I sat on a cold metal chair bolted to the ground, on the far side of a cold metal table, also bolted down. Like the lobby, the space was devoid of any wall hangings or other accoutrements. After a few minutes of waiting in the silence, I'd nearly picked the skin clean from the cuticle on my thumb. I forced myself to sit up, take a deep breath, and get a grip.

Dillahunt, though evil, was just a man.

Wasn't he?

Quickly, too quickly it seemed, Lofland and Santiago were back. They escorted the petite, meek-looking man into the room and sat him in the chair opposite me, bolting his handcuffs to the steel ring set into the middle of the table. Then the guards stepped back and stood by the door, arms crossed, eyes on the back of Dillahunt's head.

Dillahunt stared at me, his flat dark eyes magnified behind thick black-rimmed spectacles. When he spoke, his voice was high-pitched with the faintest trace of a Boston accent. "Who are you?"

"Mr. Dillahunt, my name is Gemma Monroe. I'm a detective with the Cedar Valley Police Department." I stopped there, considering again what I wanted my next words to be.

On the table, Dillahunt's fingers began to tap a steady beat. "Cedar Valley? You're a long way from home, Detective."

I nodded. "Yes. As are you."

The tapping intensified. "Why are you here?"

"I'd like to talk to you about Caleb Montgomery."

His eyes widened. "Oh? Do tell. I haven't seen Old Monty in many, many years."

"The judge has been receiving some nasty threats. I wonder if you could tell me anything about them."

"Nasty how? What do they say?" Dillahunt's voice was full of curiosity but his eyes remained flat, dark, unaffected.

I shook my head. "The content wasn't memorable enough to quote, Mr. Dillahunt. What I'd like to know is if you had anything to do with sending them. I've read your trial transcripts. The words you use, the threats you've issued in the past . . . the letters Caleb received are similar in tone."

"*Caleb*? So he's a friend of yours, is he? Lovers? Is he your *mentor*?"

I remained silent, cursing myself for giving the killer the smallest glimpse into my personal life.

Dillahunt smirked. "No, not lovers. But you care for him. Did he ask you to harass me?"

"No. I came on my own."

Dillahunt licked his lips. His tongue was quick, darting in and out of his small mouth like that of a snake. "Tell me, why else do you think I'm the ink slinger?"

"More than one of the letters accuses Caleb Montgomery of lying, perhaps in the courtroom."

Dillahunt glowered. "Of course he's a liar. I never should have been found guilty, at least not on the charges that the district attorney brought forward. Old Monty knew the evidence was dirty and he turned a blind eye. He turned a blind eye to it all and lied, there, in that courtroom, from his high horse. I hope he rots in hell."

I sat back, thinking. Dillahunt wasn't making any sense. Dirty evidence doesn't come from judges or prosecutors; it originates with cops. I followed that thought and landed, with a sinking feeling in the pit of my stomach, right back at the Cedar Valley Police Station.

Dillahunt was smug. "You've read my case, seen my work. Chavez and Underhill were a couple of dogs on my ass but I was too good for them, too . . . clean. They planted evidence and it was that evidence, and *only* that evidence, that is the reason I sit here today."

I shook my head. "No. You're a serial killer, Dillahunt. You'd have landed here sooner or later. No way you were going free."

Dillahunt licked his lips again. "I hope the letters make Monty very uncomfortable."

I tensed, aware that the investigation was likely to turn on its head with the answer to my next question. "You haven't heard? It's been all over the news."

"What has? I lost my media privileges a week ago." The killer mimicked chewing. "I took a small bite out of Santiago. He's a tasty piece."

My eyes slid over to Santiago, and the bandage wrapped around his arm. He stared back at me with a blank expression on his face. I gripped my hands in my lap; I'd removed my own bandages that very morning. My hands, while still pink and raw, seemed to be on the mend.

As Dillahunt opened his mouth again, I saw that his teeth were perfectly white, even, nearly sparkling. Once a dentist, always a dentist, I supposed. He asked, impatient now, "So, what have I missed?"

"Caleb Montgomery is dead."

"No!" Dillahunt lost all color in his face. He let out a tortured moan and began to shake his head vigorously. "No! No, this can't be true."

Lofland, the larger of the two prison guards, stepped forward and laid a hand gently on Dillahunt's shoulder. "Settle down."

Dillahunt flinched. "Get your mitts off me, Lofland. Detective, please, tell me. What happened? Did the old fuck choke on a chicken wing? Swallow a piece of glass? Fall down the stairs and break his neck?"

Dillahunt's reaction was too pure, too honest, to be staged. He was truly surprised. I saw in that moment that he didn't have anything to do with the murder.

"He died in a car explosion, outside his law offices, on Halloween."

Across the table, Dillahunt began to sob. With his hands bound to the table, he was unable to wipe his face, and the tears mingled with great gobs of snot. "He got off too easy! Look at me. How the hell am I supposed to survive another thirty years here? Montgomery issued my death sentence. I didn't deserve it."

"You killed seven men, brutally, then shattered their faces. You, no one else. You deserve everything that you have coming to you," I replied, starting to understand Dillahunt's game. "You sent the letters."

The killer nodded. "The idea came to me a few months ago. It was something to pass the time, something I could do to get at Montgomery, get inside his head like he's been in mine all these years."

"Mail's monitored. How did you get the letters to Cedar Valley?"

With lightning speed, Dillahunt stopped crying and moved into rage, pure rage. "Screw you. You come here and deliver that kind of news to me, then expect me to answer your questions? Forget it. Guards! I'm done here."

"Wait, please. Chavez and Underhill . . . the evidence you think they planted . . . what was it?"

Dillahunt screamed, "Guards! Get me the fuck out of here!"

Santiago unbolted Dillahunt from the table, then he and Lofland each took hold of one of Dillahunt's arms. As they began to escort him out, the serial killer stopped screaming and looked back over his shoulder. "I like your smile, Detective. I hope to see more of you. Maybe in your dreams?"

I ran from the small cold room as soon as they left, desperate for fresh air and strong sunshine. In the lobby, I nearly crashed headfirst into a slim woman who was hurrying along, sunglasses holding her dark hair back, her face buried in her phone.

"Excuse me, sorry about that."

The woman looked up at my apology. I recognized her immediately and blurted out, "Colleen Holden?"

She was twitchy, surly. "Yeah? Who are you?"

"My name is Gemma Monroe. I'm a detective in Cedar Valley. Can we talk a moment?"

Holden checked her phone again. "This isn't a good time—I'm late for an appointment with my client."

"Yes, Gordon Dillahunt. Only he's not your client; you haven't passed the bar yet. I don't know what game you're playing here, Ms. Holden, but knowingly aiding and abetting a felon to send death threats through the United States Postal Service is a crime."

The young law student went white. "What do you want?"

"Like I said, a moment of your time."

We found seats at a wooden picnic table near the prison parking lot, under the shade of a dying maple tree. Holden spoke first, having recovered her wits on the short walk from the lobby to the table. "I don't have to tell you anything."

I nodded. "That's true. So how about I talk first while you shut up and listen. Judge Caleb Montgomery was killed Monday night in a car bomb. You're familiar with Dillahunt's trial, so you know Montgomery was the presiding judge. Not only that, he was a close friend of my family, so please understand, I'm serious when I say this is all very personal to me. And I'm mad as hell right now."

Holden nodded slowly, her eyes never leaving my face.

I continued. "Turns out Montgomery's been receiving death threats for the last five months. They started just about the time you and Dillahunt got friendly. And guess what? Dillahunt admitted to writing them, just now."

Holden gasped. "You spoke with him?"

"Yes. You'll find him a little brokenhearted, actually. Seems writing those letters was keeping his mind off his very long prison sentence."

The young law student exhaled. "So that's what they were. I didn't know, I swear."

"Bullshit."

"No, I promise! I didn't know!"

"You'd better start from the beginning."

"I first heard about Gordon Dillahunt my freshman year of college. I grew up here, in Belle Vista, and have always been fascinated with true crime. What motivates people to kill, that sort of thing. Anyway, I had to choose a research subject this year in law school and I chose Dillahunt. I was thrilled when he actually agreed to speak with me in person. We met, and he took an interest in me. No, not like that, it's not sexual. He considers me a . . . a friend, I suppose. Anyway, at the end of our first meeting, Dillahunt promised I could continue to visit on one condition. I had to mail a letter for him, anytime he asked, from my post office in Boulder." Holden paused, sniffed. "Look, I'm not an idiot. I knew where the letters were going, saw who they were addressed to."

"And yet?"

Holden exhaled. She slid her sunglasses off her head and began to play with them in her hands. "I need high marks on this project. I need Dillahunt. It was the only way he'd agree to meet with me on a regular basis. I didn't know what was in the letters. Dillahunt used me to bypass mail-room searches and to be honest, I didn't see what the big deal was. I could tell by their feel and weight that they were just papers."

"What do you and Dillahunt talk about when you meet? May I remind you, you're not bound by attorney–client privileges."

Holden took a deep breath. She stared up at the dying maple's leaves above us. "He's told me a lot about his trial. There was definitely something fishy with the evidence that finally convicted him. Someone was dirty, and I think Montgomery knew who it was. But the judge kept his mouth shut, and Dillahunt went away for life."

"And you think that was the wrong call?"

"Yes. Dillahunt may be a monster, a terrible person. But he's still a person. He deserved a fair trial. This is America, after all."

I stood up. "You're naïve, Colleen. I hope it doesn't hinder your career."

"You're not going to report me?" She tucked her hair behind her ears and chewed her lower lip, tears welling in her eyes. "I didn't know."

"But you should have." I looked to the prison walls and decided that sometimes, a sentence of remorse can be harder than time in a cell. Holden regretted her actions, that much was clear. What she would now do with that remorse was in her hands; I had a killer to catch and to do that, I needed to get back to Cedar Valley and look at everything from the beginning.

The answers were there, not here.

I gently patted Holden on the shoulder. "Consider our conversation a harsh lesson from my side of the street. Don't ever enter into a bargain with the devil again. He'll get your soul, every damn time."

# Chapter Twelve

I did as Warden Harrison had suggested and stopped for lunch in downtown Belle Vista. I found the Indian restaurant he mentioned and enjoyed a generous platter of rice, lamb, and vegetables. Sitting outside in the brisk breeze, the sun shining down on me, it was easy to forget that just a few miles away, some of the state's most notorious criminals whiled away their time.

The trip hadn't been a total waste of time, as it was a relief to know that the death threats Caleb had received were themselves a dead end. The timing of him bringing them to my attention, and then being killed mere minutes later, seemed to be a terrible coincidence.

It had only been twenty minutes since I'd sat down, but once again I was struck with the urgent sense that I needed to head back to Cedar Valley. Reluctantly, I paid my bill and gathered the remaining half plate of food into a take-out box. As I left the restaurant, I bumped into the warden.

"I told you this place was good, didn't I? I eat here nearly every week." Harrison shook his head ruefully. "You've sure stirred up a hornet's nest, Detective. Gordon Dillahunt had to be sedated after you left. He about near ripped off Santiago's ear. As it is, I'm going to have to reassign Santiago to another floor. He's refusing to get anywhere near Dillahunt."

I was surprised and said as much. I'd had no idea my visit would set off such a reaction.

Harrison ran a hand over his close-cropped hair. "We're accustomed to drama at the prison, Detective. Nothing shocks me anymore. But Dillahunt . . . well, he's a creepy little weasel. He sets people on edge in a way that the other prisoners don't. He's like a worm and once he gets in you, he's there for good. Best you don't come back for a while."

"You can count on it."

I drove out of Belle Vista with the windows down and the radio turned up high, fifteen miles over the speed limit, desperately trying to shake images of Dillahunt's crime scene photographs from my mind. Slowly, with each mile I put between us, my time with the serial killer seemed less reality and more nightmare.

I made it back to the station in record time. Inside, I found Finn at his desk, Liv Ramirez at his side. The two of them sat close together, huddled over something on her phone, laughing. I fought the urge to roll my eyes. People are allowed to cut loose every once in a while. Who was I to begrudge a few laughs? Even Moriarty and Armstrong were in on it, chuckling every time Finn and Ramirez erupted with another set of giggles.

"Ahem," I said by way of greeting, setting my stuff down.

"Have you seen this? This video where the cat is dressed as a pirate with a wooden leg?" Finn sat back and wiped tears from his eyes. "I could watch that all day."

"I'm sure. Liv, how's the investigation into the car bomb going?"

Ramirez smiled at me. "It's done. I brought copies of my findings. Can we talk through them?"

I held an arm out to the side. "Be my guest. Let's go in the conference room."

As we walked down the hall, Finn asked in a low voice, "How was Belle Vista?"

"Dead end. Dillahunt wrote the threats. Colleen Holden smuggled them out for him and mailed them from her house in Boulder. But, Dillahunt's devastated about Caleb's death. He didn't have anything to do with the bomb. His hate for Caleb was about the only thing keeping him going."

Finn exhaled. "At least it's an avenue we can close off for the time being."

We reached the conference room and took seats around the table. Ramirez slid a thick, spiral-bound notebook across the table to each of us.

"Caleb Montgomery was murdered, plain and simple," Ramirez stated. She held up a hand. "Yes . . . we've known that since Monday. However, my report will show it without doubt."

I flipped through the pages, pausing a moment on the photographs, nearly able to smell the scene once again. No matter what sins he may have committed, or believed he committed, from his seat in court, Caleb Montgomery didn't deserve the death he got. "Can you give us the highlights?"

"Of course." Ramirez sat up and folded her hands in front of her. "Caleb Montgomery's Mercedes was packed with dynamite. It was placed in the trunk, along with a small detonator, tucked just behind the right taillight. The killer fired a bullet that pierced the light and detonated the explosives. It was a professional job."

"Professional how?" Finn set aside the report and rubbed his jaw. "You mentioned black ops a few days ago."

"Yes. I stand by my initial thoughts; you're looking for someone with a military background. If it was just the dynamite, I'd lean to a suspect who's worked in construction, or mining. Someone comfortable with explosives." Ramirez paused, considering her next words. "When you add in the sniper shot . . . and it was a sniper shot, I'd stake my life on it. The angle of the car was such that the shot had to have come from the roof of the restaurant across the street. I checked it out and ran a few scenarios. Look, you two are the detectives, but this is simple math. Explosives plus sniper equals military."

It was an easy conclusion to draw, and one that may have been right.

But I could think of a few other scenarios. "What about a contractor who likes to hunt? Or a cop, with an affinity for blowing things up? Point is, I think you're probably right. It *feels* right and instinct is ninety percent of this game. But as you said, we're the detectives. We've got to keep an open mind and open eyes until we're positive."

"Yeah, sure." Ramirez bent over and flipped through her own copy of the report, taking what seemed like a long time to find what she was looking for. When she looked back up, there were high spots of color on her cheeks. "Like I said, I did some trajectory analyses. The killer had to have been watching Montgomery for some time, had to know that was his typical parking spot. Anywhere else on the street, there wouldn't have been a clear shot. Too many trees, streetlights."

Finn leaned back and crossed his legs. "We watched footage of an obese man steal dynamite from a mine fifty miles from here. Different guy than the man we chased in the alley the night of Caleb's murder, so maybe there are two killers: one who set up the bomb, the other who detonated it with a rifle."

"Let's not make it more complicated than it already is," Ramirez said with a groan.

"We've got to go back to character and motive on this one. Our suspect is a planner; he's not impulsive. This was a killing that intended to send a message, to us, to the community, or to some unknown person or persons." I sat back, thinking. "And yet, at the same time, it *was* a risky killing; as Liv says, had Caleb parked anywhere else on Main, there would not have been a clear shot from the roof of the restaurant."

"And why Halloween night?" Finn asked. He flipped through Liv's report again, stopping, as I had, on the crime scene photographs. "Was there something special about killing Montgomery on that night, of all nights?"

We fell silent, each thinking.

Finn spoke. "Everyone was in costume. The killer could have been anywhere on the street, disguised, and we'd not have known it. Think about the man, the hooded man, in the alley. Halloween is a night of intrigue, mystery. A thrill-a-minute kind of evening. If you want to make a dramatic statement, blowing up a car with dozens of trick-or-treaters a few blocks away will do it."

"We need to keep those two things at the forefront of this case: the method of killing and the night. There's something important, something telling, about both." I leaned forward, rested my head in my hands.

Ramirez checked her watch. "You guys want to continue this conversation at a bar? Preferably somewhere with greasy burgers and generous pours? First round is on me."

"I'm in. Gem?" Finn stood up. I nodded in agreement and sent a quick text to Brody that he should go ahead and give Grace dinner, and I'd bring him some takeout.

We agreed to drive separately and meet at O'Toole's, a dimly lit pub on Fifth Street where we'd be guaranteed privacy amidst the pool tables and the mixed crowd of hip young professionals and wizened older men.

Within minutes of the server taking our order, she appeared with a frosty pitcher of light beer, two ice-cold mugs, and a sparkling water for me. I stared longingly at the beer but images of my wedding dress kept dancing in front of me. It would do me good to watch what I ate for the next few weeks.

Or more realistically, what I drank, as I never could say no to a good meal.

We sat and drank in silence, letting the cool, dark bar numb the edges of the day. It wasn't until our food arrived, cheeseburgers heaped with lettuce and tomatoes, fries and spicy pickle slices piled high on the side, that we began to talk.

Ramirez went first. "I dreamed of food like this when I was overseas. Chow-hall meals have nothing on a beef patty slung in some grease on a skillet by a guy who's been cooking the same burgers for thirty years."

As if on cue, a hunched man with deep grooves in his skin and gray curls peeking out from a hairnet glanced through the open window in the kitchen, taking in the crowd. Ramirez flashed him a thumbs-up and the man grinned, his toothless mouth gaping with pride.

"Did you like it, being over there?" I asked.

Ramirez shrugged. "Iraq was . . . hard. I was a medic and saw some terrible, terrible things. My last tour, I treated troops at a military field hospital outside Fallujah. The insurgents had control of the city for a long time; they had time to prepare to inflict the most damage possible. We saw a lot of shrapnel, close-explosion injuries. The human body can only take so much. We're more fragile than we like to believe."

"You said you did three tours, though?" Finn asked. He'd finished his first beer and was pouring another. "There must have been something about it you enjoyed."

"Pour me another, too, would you? I liked the camaraderie. My parents adopted me when I was a little girl, and I grew up an only child. My mom split when I was four, and my dad tried the best he knew how, but I was a hard kid. Always in trouble, always on the offense. Easier than being on the defense. I never knew who my birth family was until I was eighteen and tracked them down. They'd dealt with their own shit for years and weren't too excited to see me. By then, my adopted dad had passed. I didn't have anyone. The military gave me a second family." Ramirez took a long swallow from her second beer, taking down half of it. "Damn, that's good. Look, I'm not justifying the killer's actions . . . but if he's military, a veteran . . . he may be dealing with some dark things. Some of us come back with more baggage than others . . . but we all come back with something. Anyway, enough about me. Talking about Iraq is depressing. What about you two? How'd you end up wearing the blue?"

I shifted in my chair. "My parents died when I was a little kid. My grandparents raised me. My grandfather was a judge, and I was always fascinated by the law. I liked the rules, the structure of it, but I wasn't a great student. Law school never seemed like a possibility for me. Then, at a career fair my senior year, I listened to a female detective from Denver talk about her job and I was smitten. I haven't looked back since."

Ramirez nodded. "So you're an orphan, too."

She slipped off her jacket and I was surprised to see she had full sleeve tattoos on both muscular arms. I was about to ask her how long it had taken to get the ink done when she turned to Finn and said, "How about you, Francis?"

"Francis?" Finn blinked in surprise.

"Yeah, Ol' Blue Eyes. You got Frank Sinatra peepers," Ramirez said with a wink and tucked back into her burger.

Finn grinned. "No one's ever said that to me. I went to school at Florida State on a golf scholarship and got a criminal justice degree along the way. My folks live in a condo in Miami. I've got a couple of brothers that I see every year at Christmas. No skeletons in my closet; nothing terrible happened to me as a child. I thought I'd work for the feds but I got tired of the local news, tired of seeing crime in my own backyard. Thought I could do more service in my own community than pushing papers in some office in DC."

"And how'd you find yourself in Cedar Valley, Colorado? It's not exactly excitement central," Ramirez said with a smirk. Then she looked at me. "No offense."

I shrugged. "None taken. Yes, Finn . . . how did you end up here?"

I knew the answer—he'd followed a love interest from Miami— but I was curious to see if he'd share it with Ramirez.

He didn't and instead simply lifted his glass and said, "To second chances."

"To second chances," Ramirez and I muttered in unison.

We stopped talking then, and concentrated on finishing our food. The crowd had picked up and I noticed a particularly rough-looking trio in the corner. They'd been eyeing our table since they came in. Ramirez saw where I was looking. She stared at the men a moment, taking in their greasy shoulder-length hair, ball caps set low on their foreheads.

"You know those guys?"

I shook my head. "No. They're probably truckers, passing through. Finn?"

He took a look as the server dropped our bill on the table. "Never seen them before in my life. Hey, this one's on me. I feel guilty; between my sweet pastel-wearing parents and college years on the golf course, I've got nothing on the two of you."

We walked out single file, headed toward the table of truckers on our way to the door. Finn was in front, followed by Ramirez, while I brought up the rear. As we passed by the table, one of the truckers, a short florid man with a dirty bandanna around his neck, quickly shot out his hand and firmly squeezed Ramirez's buttock. Before I could even register what had happened, Ramirez had flipped around and had the man in a stranglehold, her right arm around his neck, her left hand with a pocketknife to his throat.

The man arched his back, kicked at the table, but Ramirez's grip was sure.

And she didn't appear ready to let go anytime soon.

As the man's face turned red and he gargled, the two other truckers slowly lifted their hands from the table and raised them up to shoulder height.

The bar had fallen silent. No one in the room moved.

"Liv." I said it quietly, my voice barely above a whisper. "Liv, he can't breathe."

She looked over at me and smiled. "That's the whole point. This prick here needs to learn to keep his hands to himself."

"Got that? Keep your hands to yourself," she hissed into the man's ear. Then she released him and he sagged forward, his hat falling to the ground, his hair hanging in limp strings.

"Gonna . . . kill . . . you," the trucker managed to gasp out.

I yanked my handcuffs from the back of my pants and pulled the man's hands behind his back. As I slapped the cuffs on, I said, "You damn idiot. You should have kept your mouth shut. I'm placing you under arrest for harassment. Lucky for you, it's Friday night. You'll have a nice long weekend to think about your behavior before you appear in front of Judge Dumont on Monday morning."

At my side, Liv gave the men a triumphant grin. I turned to her and said in a low voice, "Put that knife away. Are you crazy? You want to end up in the cell next to him for assault with a deadly weapon? You're reckless, Ramirez. Reckless and shortsighted."

The grin fell from Liv's face and she quickly snapped the knife shut. It disappeared into her purse and she stepped back, looked down at the ground. After a moment, one of the man's buddies stood up, an angry look on his face.

Finn pointed at him and said, "Sit down and shut up."

The trucker did as he was instructed; then he raised his hand and waited patiently until Finn exhaled and asked, "What?"

"We're due in Omaha tomorrow morning, the three of us and our rigs. We're not going to make our payload if you throw Ronnie in jail. Can't you give us a break? He didn't hardly do anything. It was just a piece of ass."

Rage coursed through me and I started to respond when Ramirez put a hand on my shoulder and whispered, "Let me."

She turned to the table and spoke in a voice loud enough for everyone in the bar to hear. "How would you enjoy having your privates squeezed by some stranger? Or walking to your car late at night, always on alert for footsteps behind you? How about scanning a crowd as you enter any space, any room, making sure you feel comfortable with the folks in the room before taking another step forward? Pigs like you have made our lives hell for centuries. You have no idea what it's like to be a woman. You have mothers? Sisters? Wives? I feel sorry for them. You should be ashamed of yourselves. Oh, and one more thing. I served this country for six years in Iraq. This *piece of ass* risked her life for the freedoms you enjoy, to drive a truck across the country and sit in a nice bar. You three are pathetic."

The entire bar erupted in cheering, with the young women in the crowd adding whoops and hollers. As we carted Ronnie out of the bar, his two buddies threw down a couple of bills and hustled outside through a side door, their faces beet red. We stood by Finn's car and called in a uniformed officer on patrol to come by and pick up Ronnie. Though I hadn't had anything to drink, it was better if an on-duty cop took him in for booking and processing.

The trucker stared at us with baleful eyes, his cheeks still florid. After a moment, he muttered something under his breath.

I took a step closer. "What was that? I didn't quite hear you."

Ronnie spit in Ramirez's direction, then stared at the ground. "I said, we don't need her kind here."

"You're not even from here, you jerk." Finn calmly scratched at the back of his neck, staring down at Ronnie. "If you were, we'd have met by now. I know all the local trash."

"Figures." Ronnie spit again. This time, his aim was off and a wad dropped down onto his dirty bandanna. I didn't even want to think about how disgusting the skin on his neck must have been. "Well, we don't need her kind where I'm from, either."

Ramirez stepped forward. She pulled the knife from her purse and began to flick it open and shut, open and shut, in her left hand. "Oh yeah? What kind would that be? Hispanic? Soldier? Woman?"

Ronnie finally looked up and said with a sneer, "Lesbian."

"In your dreams, pal." Ramirez moved away, already bored. She slid into her truck and sat there, gazing out at the night sky through her window.

After what felt like long minutes, two officers arrived and took Ronnie into custody. Finn and I walked to Ramirez's truck. Before I could reprimand her again for the risk she took pulling a stunt like that, Finn gave her an admiring look and said, "That was impressive. Where did you learn moves like that?"

Ramirez smiled grimly. "I'm a black belt in martial arts. Comes in handy from time to time. Well, it's been real. Thanks for having my back in there. I'll see you guys around."

She started her engine and drove away, a small cloud of dust shooting up behind her.

Finn whistled low under his breath. "Interesting woman. She was pretty quick with that knife back there . . . Do you think she has anger issues?"

"Anger issues?" I sighed and moved to my car, ready for the day to be over. "No more than any woman who's ever lived. She was right, Finn. You men, all of you, you have no idea. Guys like that are a dime a dozen, our whole lives."

# Chapter Thirteen

In life, Caleb Montgomery hadn't been a man of religion; as such, his memorial service on Saturday morning was secular, and, not surprisingly, rather subdued and in keeping with my opinion that violent death rarely lends itself to anything but serious funerals. The people attending were quiet, their conversations hushed and held in small groups not larger than three or four. Most gripped mugs of coffee or tea, the hot beverages serving to ward off the chill of both City Hall, where the reception was held, and the topic at hand.

Photographs of Caleb at various stages in his life were displayed on stands and in frames all over the lobby. I found it hard to see pictures of victims of violence in their younger days. As a boy, Caleb had a bright, wide smile that spoke of wonder and innocence, with no idea what his future held.

I'd arrived at the same time as Bull and Julia. My grandparents were a handsome couple, her with her chic bob and high cheekbones, him with his thick white hair and commanding presence. They knew everyone at the service, or at least it seemed that way. Caleb Montgomery was of their generation, after all, and he and Bull had run in many of the same circles. And, as I found myself saying more and more these days, it was a small town. It was hard to tell how much Julia was actually processing, though. As I watched her with Bull, I saw she did very little of the talking.

When I'd arrived, Edith Montgomery and her brother Tom

were perched on a low sofa in the foyer, occasionally standing to receive a hug or words of condolence. After I gave them both my regards, I stepped away. A few minutes later, I watched as Tom weaved through the crowd to the elevator, his phone in his hand, a sickly expression on his face. Edith watched him go, worry in her eyes. I wondered where he was headed. In the basement, there were restrooms and an exit to the parking lot. And on the second level, another foyer, much like this one; more restrooms; a vending machine; and offices.

Curious, I went to Edith. She shook her head at my concern and explained that Tom was weaning himself off the pain medication he'd been prescribed for his surgery, and it was causing him nausea. He needed the restroom and a few minutes of fresh air. Then an elderly couple joined us and I moved away, giving the trio space and privacy.

As it was Saturday, the building was closed to the public, the service by invitation only. I found myself watching the guests, wondering if Caleb's killer was among us. It would be insane if he were; insane, but not unusual. If the killer had done it for the sensationalism, for the attention, then he would likely be here, here or somewhere nearby.

Maybe it was the man in the corner, the guy with the red tie who'd been staring at his phone for the last twenty minutes and not talking to a single person. Or perhaps the server, stationed behind the coffee and dessert table, who kept making eye contact with me, then quickly looking away.

"These things always give me the creeps." The voice came out of nowhere, speaking soft, low words directly into my right ear. I stepped back, regaining my personal space, then turned.

Liv Ramirez lowered her voice even more. "Please tell me I'm not the only one?"

"What, who's bothered by memorial services?" I shrugged. "Actually, I think they're kind of nice. Sad, of course, but lovely to see people gathered and paying their respects."

Ramirez laughed. "Paying their respects? That's a good one. They're doing nothing of the sort. They're gossiping, and congratulating one another on not being the body in the box. Trust me, I've been here an hour and I've heard a lot of conversations in that time."

"Anything important?"

She stared at me shrewdly. "Important to your investigation? No, no, I don't think so. It's mostly petty gossip along the theme of what it must be like to be burned alive. Or killed by a bomb. Et cetera. Old people with nothing better to do than sensationalize what was in all likelihood a mercifully quick death."

"Do you really believe that, that Caleb died quickly?"

Ramirez shrugged. "It's better than thinking the alternative, isn't it?"

"I suppose. How are you feeling after last night's activities?"

The fire investigator laughed. "You should have seen the looks on your faces when I pulled the knife. It was priceless. I'm fine. I've dealt with a lot worse. Those guys, they're big and mean . . . but they're also dumb. Put an alpha in front of them, even an alpha female like myself, and they usually fall in line. They want to be led; they don't want to think for themselves too much."

"Still, it could have turned ugly. One of them could have pulled a gun. The bar was packed. It wouldn't have been good." I sipped my coffee, once again watching the crowd. "You'd be the idiot literally bringing a knife to a gunfight."

Ramirez laughed. "That's why I like you, Gemma. You tell it like it is. I don't know that I've ever been called an idiot this early in the morning."

After a moment, she turned serious. "It's the one thing I don't like about small towns like this, though. You all are a closed-off bunch to newcomers. And if it's someone a little different? Someone 'not from around these here parts'?" She whistled. "Then watch out. You should see the stares I get at the grocery store."

Before I could respond, my cell phone buzzed. It was Finn.

"Excuse me, I've got to take this." I stepped away from Ramirez and answered. "Monroe. I'm at Caleb's service. What's up?"

"I'm at the First Pillar Bank and Trust. Get your ass down here, we've got a robbery with shots fired and a security guard, badly injured."

By the time I arrived on the scene, the first responders had established a perimeter with yellow tape and traffic cones. I parked as an ambulance pulled away from the curb, lights flashing, sirens screaming. Inside my car, I threw on a dark blazer over the black funeral dress I wore and clipped my badge to the lapel. Crowds milled about in front of the shops on either side of the bank—a yoga studio to the north, a natural foods store to the south. Many of the bystanders had cell phones out and were recording the scene.

Finn stood at the bank entrance, under a green-and-white-striped awning, fuming. "There's got to be seventy-five people on the street at this very moment and no one saw a thing. Not a goddamn thing."

His estimate of the crowds felt right. It was obvious that a packed Saturday-morning yoga class was just letting out, and at the grocery store, ads in the front windows advertised rock-bottom sale prices on seasonal goods. It would have been crowded at both places.

"Nothing? Not even the perp's getaway?"

Finn shook his head. "He fled on foot, the bank teller is sure of it. After that, things get fuzzy. He could have ducked into any one of these stores and exited the street through a back door. If he had a partner with a car, waiting, or even a parked car somewhere close by, he could have been on the highway in less than ten minutes."

"Maybe we'll get lucky. Maybe someone saw something and will come forward." We walked into the lobby, careful to avoid the small plastic flags that the crime scene techs were already laying down. The flags were like game pieces against the rose-colored marble floor, as though we'd stumbled into a life-size world-conquering board game. My heels clacked against the tiles, each step taking me farther into the belly of this new, fresh hell.

I asked, "What do we know so far?"

"The Saturday shift is minimal: two tellers, a manager, and an unarmed security guard, Michael Esposito. Four people in total. The perp timed it perfectly. He entered the building at one minute to noon, just after the manager and one of the tellers had left for their break. No customers. The man approached the front counter and demanded all of the cash in the till. When the teller, a sweet old broad named Dee Bullock, hesitated, he pulled the gun."

Finn paused, surveying the lobby, then pointed to an overturned stool in the corner, near the front entrance. "Esposito, the guard, was seated there, on the stool. As Bullock gathered the cash, the perp aimed the gun at Esposito and instructed him to lie facedown, on the ground. By this time, it's about two minutes after noon and both Bullock and Esposito are following bank protocol for this sort of situation."

"Don't resist, the money's insured?"

"Yes, exactly," Finn said. "But then things go off script: according to Bullock, as the perp is exiting the bank, ten grand in hand, he stops, bends down, whispers something, then shoots Esposito in the back. Twice. I don't know if he's going to make it, Gem."

"But the guard wasn't a threat . . ." I stared at the pool of blood congealing on the marble floor. The scarlet blood and pink tiles made me think, strangely, of Valentine's Day.

Bullet wounds. Bleeding hearts.

Finn said, "You're correct. Esposito was unarmed and did not put up a fight."

"Could the robbery be a cover-up? Maybe Esposito was the target all along and the money grab just a distraction, a way to get to the guard."

"We'll look into it, of course. It's a strange place to do something like that, though. Busy, public place like this . . ." Finn trailed off.

"Bullock said the perp whispered something to Esposito. Do we know what?"

"No idea. The paramedics whisked him away, unconscious, as I arrived. You think this is a strange case so far, just wait." Finn pointed to an area behind the overturned stool. "Check it out."

I walked over and looked down at the object that lay there. It was still and silent and deadly: a long-barreled pistol that vaguely resembled a semiautomatic Luger.

Surprised again, I glanced at Finn. "The perp left the weapon?"

"It's not Esposito's gun, that's for sure."

We crouched by the gun, careful not to touch anything.

"Why on earth would he leave the gun? Look, see that writing on the rear of the receiver? Does it look like a series of Japanese characters to you? Serial number, perhaps?"

Finn agreed. "Ballistics should be able to tell us what the symbols mean."

I summoned a nearby officer, a burly sour-faced man with hands the size of ham hocks. The officer bagged the gun and added it to a box of other evidence already collected. The pistol was now part of the crime scene, and would be examined for fingerprints and other trace evidence. Finally, it would make its way to ballistics, where an expert would examine the firearm and ammunition, if any remained in the weapon.

Before he left us, the officer stared down at the blood and shook his head. "I play softball with Esposito. I hope he makes it. I heard the bastard who shot him was too much of a coward to show his face. That right?"

Finn nodded. "He wore a mask."

The officer leaned over as if to spit, then thought better of it. This was a crime scene, after all. "Shoot. Well, I'll get this evidence over to forensics right quick. Hope you catch the son of a bitch soon."

Finn and I made our way to the far wall of the bank, where a long service counter held three teller stations. I asked, "A mask? Like a Halloween mask?"

"Not exactly. It was a gas mask. Bullock said it looked like something out of a history museum. You know the kind? With the large, dark bug eyes and a long snout. It sounds almost worse than a Halloween mask, in my opinion. A little too close to reality."

A Japanese pistol and a gas mask . . . like something out of a movie . . . I tried to connect the dots but came up empty, though something niggled at the back of my mind, something I'd seen or heard.

I realized we hadn't talked about the bank teller yet. "Any chance Bullock was a part of this?"

Finn snorted. "Doubtful. That's her in the photo right there, holding a jar of her three-time prize-winning apple butter. Don't look at me that way, I heard all about it before she, too, was whisked away by the paramedics. Something about her heart, palpitations maybe."

I went to the framed photograph on the wall and held back a giggle. It was hard to imagine Dee Bullock orchestrating or aiding an operation such as this one. The frame read "Employee of the Month," and the woman in the portrait must have been nearly eighty years old. She smiled beatifically at the camera, her white curls tight against her scalp, her large round eyeglasses last popular in the 1980s.

In her hand was a jar, and in her lap an enormous cat snoozed.

Finn said, "Bullock's been with the bank for thirty-two years. She has eighteen grandchildren and runs a nonprofit out of her house. Rescue cats."

"Cats, huh?" Already moving on, I scanned the lobby and wondered what we were missing.

Ten thousand dollars was nothing to laugh at, but this was a small bank branch, with few customers. Had the perp hit one of the larger branches up the street, he'd have walked away with at least double the cash, if not more.

This was too clean of a job, too well organized, for an amateur. But it was risky; a robbery in the middle of the day, even timed perfectly, had the potential to become a disaster, very quickly.

This was bold; like Caleb Montgomery's murder, it made a statement.

It was curious to think about Caleb's death now; the two crimes were obviously unrelated, but there were subtle similarities there, lurking beneath the surface.

"How about the manager or the other teller?"

Finn pointed to the street. "I've got an officer interviewing them in the coffee shop across the street. Nothing there that screams they're involved. They, like Bullock, are longtime employees. Both married, each with a couple of kids. Steady folks."

I nodded and glanced up at the three cameras set high in the ceiling, each with a different view of the bank. "Tell me we got lucky."

"We might have. A tech is checking footage." Finn rubbed the back of his neck, uneasy. "I've got to say, I don't like this one bit. Esposito was on the ground, vulnerable. Whoever shot him has a violent streak. And he might be out there now, on our streets. Just like the bastard who killed Caleb Montgomery."

"Hey, Detectives?" The voice belonged to a crime scene tech, a young woman who at that moment leaned out into the hallway from a door a few feet away. She had an excited look on her face. "You better come take a look."

We joined her in the small, cramped room. It was little more than a closet, with a low wooden table that held a computer and two monitors. Dozens of cables ran from the computer to terminals on the floor, then continued up to the ceiling. I assumed they were linked to the cameras on the other side of the wall.

The tech pecked at the keyboard, then hit Enter as a "play video" icon appeared. A strong sense of déjà vu swept over me. It had only been a few days since Finn and I had traveled to the Cathedrals and watched the mine manager, Frank Poe, hit Play on a similar video.

A similar video, of a similarly strange crime.

The recording offered a clear view of the muscular man who entered the bank, though his head was tilted and it was impossible to see his face. The images were in black-and-white. We watched in silence as the man slipped a gas mask on, then stood where he could train his gun first on Esposito, then on Bullock. My earlier thought had been correct; it did look like something out of a movie. I half expected military troops to start storming the bank or B-52 bombers to pepper the sky with their loud engines.

On the screen, Esposito lay down and placed his hands over his head. Across the bank lobby, Dee Bullock moved slowly from one till to the next, pulling cash out of each drawer and stuffing it into the bag the perp handed her. Her mouth opened and shut, over and over, though it was hard to tell if she was speaking or simply moving her lips and jaws in shock, like a fish caught suddenly out of water.

"Is there sound?" I asked.

"No," the tech responded.

The man grabbed the bag of cash from Bullock's hands before she was finished. Maybe he'd gotten frustrated by her slow movements, or by her talking, if that was in fact what she'd been doing. Then he bent over, fiddling with something on the counter, while Bullock threw her hands over her face and covered her eyes, unable to take any more.

The gunman moved on to Esposito. For a moment, it appeared as though he were going to step over the security guard and walk out, but then he paused. I watched in horror as he leaned down, put his mouth to Esposito's ear, then stepped back and shot the guard in the back twice, with absolutely no hesitation between shots.

Finn, the tech, and I all flinched as Esposito's body twitched in response, then went deathly still.

"Gas Mask Guy leaves at this point." The tech lightly touched the screen. "Watch, you can see Bullock lean down a bit to hit the panic button. Then she makes her way to Esposito."

On the screen, Bullock reached the security guard and rolled him over. The bullet had gone through him and blood began to spill forth. Bullock removed her cardigan and pressed it against his chest, trying to stem the flow, but it was a losing battle. The cardigan quickly turned dark. Finally, paramedics and uniformed officers entered the building and attended to the employees.

Something bothered me about the video. "Play it again, please."

Finn asked if I'd seen something.

"Maybe." I watched as on the screen, the scene unfolded again. "He's slipping something under the counter, did you see?"

I stepped out of the closet and quickly made my way to the front of the lobby, my heels beating a rapid staccato on the floor. I peered under the customer counter, between the wood shelf and the granite top. Something was there, something clear and plastic.

"What is it?" Finn asked. He and the tech had followed me.

"I'm not sure," I said, and ran a gloved hand under the counter.

Finn gripped my arm, holding it in place. "Are you sure you should do that? It could be a trap."

He was right, but I was too close at that point, too committed and too curious. I tugged at the plastic until I felt it pop loose, then pulled it out.

"Oh my God," I breathed when I saw what it was.

Confused, the tech asked, "Is that a . . . comic book?"

"Not just any comic book. It's *Ghost Boy*."

# Chapter Fourteen

We were already tossing theories back and forth by the time we got to the police station.

"What's the connection?" Finn's voice was animated; the way it got when things started coming together. "Gas Mask Guy leaves the same comic book at the bank that our team found on the roof where we think Montgomery's sniper holed up. But Gas Mask Guy doesn't look anything like the dynamite thief, who's likely the sniper. Gas Mask Guy is trim, muscular. The dynamite thief was grossly overweight."

We parked and exited the car. I was anxious, shaken by what I'd found. Finn held the door, then followed me into the station and back to our desks in the squad room, still talking. "None of it makes sense. There's the question of motive, to start. Why would someone murder a retired judge and a week later, rob a bank and shoot a guard? First Pillar's been on the decline for years. The guy made off with ten grand, nothing to laugh at, but honestly, hardly worth the effort. Especially if he could then be linked back to a murder charge in an earlier crime."

"There's got to be a connection between Montgomery and the bank. Or maybe the connection is between Montgomery and Esposito. There could be a hit out on both of them." I was thinking out loud, trying to make sense of the seemingly senseless. "Could that be it? The bomb that killed Montgomery was a professional job. Did you see the way the gunman shot Esposito? No hesitation, just a cold, quick double tap to the back. Expert techniques in both cases."

Finn sat down, rubbed his eyes. "Jesus, you're talking hit men, Mafia-type killers. In Cedar Valley."

"It wouldn't be the first time."

My phone rang. It was one of our officers, who'd followed the paramedics to the hospital.

"Bad news, Monroe. Esposito passed away. The doctors did everything they could to save him, but the injury was too grave. One bullet pierced his lung, the other his heart."

"Damn it. Did he ever regain consciousness? I'd like to have known what the suspect said to Esposito before he shot him."

"No, the poor guy never came around. Whatever the gunman said to him, Esposito will take it to the grave. I did request that the doctors try to retrieve the bullets from him, and they were able to do that. I'll take them to the lab now."

"Great, thank you. Tell them it's the highest priority." That was one nice thing about being a detective in a small town that had years ago budgeted for a state-of-the-art lab. While we saw violence, we didn't see enough of it to run into the backlogs and delays that some of the bigger cities did. As a result, every request was treated as a priority.

Finn walked to the wall and added to the notes already there. "We started the Montgomery homicide investigation thinking there was a link either to the threatening letters he'd received or to Edith Montgomery herself, on account of the pending divorce. Based on your conversations with Colleen Holden and Gordon Dillahunt, we can safely eliminate them. Edith . . . I'm undecided. But I am certain that the First Pillar bank robbery has nothing to do with the Montgomery homicide. Totally different MO's and motives."

I snorted. "Aside from a vintage comic book placed at or near each crime scene."

"Hey, guys."

I turned to see Jimmy standing behind me, his eyes gleaming

with interest. "Detective Moriarty said I should hang out with you two for today."

"Jimmy, it's Saturday. Go home." Finn reached into his back pocket and slipped out his wallet. "I'll give you twenty bucks to go see a movie, take a lady friend out for a root beer float."

Jimmy rolled his eyes. "Okay, Dad, whatever you say. Listen, I'm bored at home. I want to be here. I want to help. Moriarty said you two caught another case. So . . . tell me the haps."

The intern wouldn't be deterred, and to be honest, he was actually turning out to be rather helpful. I explained what had happened that morning, watching as Jimmy's eyes got wider and wider. After I finished, I said, "Look at what Finn's written. Do you see any patterns, any connections?"

The intern scanned the board. "Why were these victims targeted? Is it random or purposeful? Judge Montgomery, while his killing was obviously planned, could have been chosen randomly. Was Esposito? A public place, in the middle of the day. The tolerance for risk seems high. And the comic book . . . what the hell is that all about? Did you read it? Maybe there's a message inside. So far, that's the only thing these murders have in common."

"The comic book I found at the bank is with evidence. I'll let forensics have the first crack at it. But we should look at the comic that was discovered on the restaurant roof. I know it's already been processed. Jimmy, would you get it from the lab?"

He nodded and jogged from the room, practically tripping over his shoes in his eagerness to be helpful. While we waited, Lucas Armstrong stood up from his desk and joined us, a strange expression on his face. He held his cell phone out to me, the screen showing a television station. "Did you see this?"

The three of us watched in silence as the redheaded weekend reporter brushed hair from her eyes. She stood outside on the windy plateau of the Belle Vista Penitentiary and spoke, her voice grave. "Yes, Jerry, as I was saying, Gordon Dillahunt had been serving consecutive life sentences for the Jawbreaker murders, a killing spree that claimed victims from New Mexico to Montana. Let's hope his death brings some measure of peace to the families of the victims. Back to you in the studio, Jerry."

"Dillahunt's dead?" I sank slowly into my desk chair, numb. "What happened?"

Armstrong perched on the edge of the desk and drew a hand over his face. "They're not reporting it on the news, but I heard that Dillahunt used one of his bedsheets."

"He hung himself?"

Armstrong grimaced. "No. He shoved the fabric down his throat, blocking his own airway, then wound it around his head, covering his nose. He suffocated. Hell of a way to go."

I thought about the small man with the perfectly even, white teeth. I'd seen him yesterday. Could the news of Montgomery's death have been so devastating it drove him to suicide?

Armstrong was asking me something.

"What did you say?" I tried to clear my head of the fog that had suddenly descended.

"What does this do to your case?"

I was at a loss. "I don't know. I don't believe Caleb's murder is tied to Dillahunt and yet Dillahunt truly believed Caleb had turned a blind eye to planted evidence, corrupt cops. Edith herself said Caleb lived with the guilt of something he'd done, years ago, in the courtroom."

Armstrong shrugged. "Maybe one of those cops decided to do some housecleaning. Take out Montgomery and no one's the wiser."

I lowered my voice. "The problem is, the two cops that secured Dillahunt's arrest are Chief Chavez and Sheriff Rose Underhill. Digging into their pasts is a hornet's nest that I don't believe we can kick at the moment. Not with Esposito's death, not now. Especially given that there simply can't be a connection between Esposito's killing and the Dillahunt trial."

My phone rang again. It was the ballistics lab, and the tech, a young guy from Chicago named Rusty, was excited. His words came quickly, tumbling out of his mouth. "Man, I'm sorry about the dude who got shot, but you made my freaking day. It's not often I get to handle a Nambu pistol. Awesome."

"A what?"

"A Nambu. The gun you recovered at the bank scene is a pre–World War II Type 14 Nambu pistol. Gorgeous. It's in most excellent condition. You know these things are collector's items, right?"

"Really?" My mind was racing. There were a hell of a lot of gun enthusiasts in the region. A Nambu pistol might be rare enough that its provenance could be traced.

"Really. I kid you not. I know what you're thinking. How does a thing of beauty like this end up thousands of miles from home? Well, I can answer that for you. Or at least try to. If I had to guess, it was purchased and then brought back from Japan by a returning serviceman. You know, after World War II?"

"A souvenir?" I turned to my computer and entered the gun name into the search engine. "I'm looking at it online right now. That's definitely the same gun we pulled from the scene."

Rusty snorted into the phone. "Of course it is. They don't pay me to make mistakes. And yes, exactly like a souvenir. The guys brought back all sorts of deadly, dangerous things; guns, binoculars, daggers. Bayonets. Wives."

"Wives?"

"*Wives*." Rusty paused and I heard the tab of a soda can pop open. The tech was notorious for his addiction to diet cola. He took a noisy sip, then continued, "So, I'm about to make your day. Do you remember seeing a couple of tiny symbols on the pistol?"

"Yes. Are they serial numbers?"

"What, are you trying to do my job for me? Of course they're serial numbers. That first symbol, the circle with the smaller circles within it, that's from the Nagoya Arsenal. Give me a couple of days and I can tell you exactly when and where the gun was manufactured."

"You're kidding. The records go back that far?"

"Gemma, there are two things I never joke about: ballistics and doughnuts. And my mom. I guess I don't really joke about my mom."

"Got it. Listen, Mike Esposito died. The doctors were able to retrieve the bullets. They're on their way to you right now."

Rusty sighed deeply. "Poor bastard. He was a hell of a short-stop. Made some damn fine home brew, too." More background noise as Rusty murmured to someone else in the lab. "The bullets are here. I got to go, Gemma. I'll be in touch soon."

"Thanks. I owe you big-time."

"Nah, this one's on me. Like I said, it's not every day I get to see something so cool. Freaking awesome."

We ended the call. I shared with Finn what I'd learned. He added the new information to the notes we'd already written on the wall, then stepped back and rubbed his hands together. "This is getting stranger and stranger. Why slip on a vintage gas mask and then kill someone using a pistol from the same era? What's the message there? It's like with Caleb's death . . . the drama of it all. Maybe that's the point . . . to distract us with these flashy methods—a car bomb, a souvenir pistol—so that we don't see what's right in front of us. Did Montgomery serve in the war?"

I did some quick math in my head. "No, he missed it by about twenty years, I think."

"And Mike Esposito was definitely too young," Finn murmured. "We should look at their relatives. Montgomery's father, maybe Esposito's grandfather. These killings could be revenge for something that occurred during the war."

"Sounds a bit far-fetched to me." I tilted my head, thinking about the bank robbery. "What if Esposito *was* in on it? We've seen it before; one guy supplies all the information and the second does the robbery. How did the perp know what time to hit the bank? How did he know there'd only be two people there? There had to be an inside man or woman."

Jimmy returned from the lab, a bag of pastries tucked under his left arm and the comic book under his right. "I took a detour," he proudly announced, and dropped the pastries on my desk. "I know you love these."

Although a part of me wondered why he was buttering me up, a larger part smelled the cinnamon and sugar. Reluctantly, I set aside the treats until after I had a look at the comic book.

I slipped on a fresh pair of gloves and cut open the top of the evidence bag with a pair of scissors. Inside, the comic was still encased in the protective sleeve it had been found in. I opened that, too, and held the thin, light comic in my hands. I flipped through the pages, reading the bubble captions and studying the sketches.

The comic mirrored what I'd found online; the Ghost Boy character was a skilled martial artist and a double agent for Japan whose own mother had been a KGB officer. It was a violent comic; every other page seemed to depict another bloody match between the villain, Ghost Boy, and a less-skilled and therefore quickly killed U.S. soldier or marine.

I handed it to Finn, who skimmed it, then passed it off to Jimmy.

It was Jimmy who, a number of minutes later, finally spoke up. "What if the comic itself is the message?"

I lifted an eyebrow. "Go on."

He lifted his cell phone into the air and waved it back and forth. "You've only seen two issues in the series. But Ghost Boy's whole story is here, online. It was a thirteen-issue series that ran between 1982 and 1983 and then mysteriously and abruptly ended. Fans were devastated. Riots nearly broke out."

I raised the other eyebrow. "Over a *comic* book?"

"Okay, I exaggerate. But seriously, people were pissed off. They wanted some kind of resolution. The most popular comic book fan site online pushes the theory that the author was himself a double agent and was killed in action." Jimmy lowered his phone, held up the comic book. "Look at the author and illustrator's name: anonymous. That's extremely unusual in the comic world."

Finn took the book from Jimmy. "You learned all that in the last ten minutes from your phone?"

The intern nodded. "Dude. Ever hear of this little thing called Google?"

"'Dude' me one more time and I'll make sure you spend the next week fetching coffee and filing reports," Finn responded. He added grudgingly, "You've got skills, son, but that attitude of yours is going to get you in trouble. How about a little respect for your elders?"

"Sure thing, boss. Sir. Although you know I'm only like seven or eight years younger than you, right? It's not like we're a generation apart. So, in the original comics, Ghost Boy is killed. But then years later, he's resurrected by a cult devoted to spreading mayhem across the globe. Or at least, sort of resurrected. They're only halfway successful and Ghost Boy comes back to life as a zombie general. He travels around the world, leading armies of evil." Jimmy paused, set down the comic.

I asked, "If the comic *is* the message, then does our killer fancy himself an evil half-dead double agent?"

Jimmy shrugged as Finn rolled his eyes. I didn't blame either one of them.

It was both confusing and ridiculous.

I continued. "Say the killer models himself after Ghost Boy. Cedar Valley is hardly the headquarters of an evil army. And I certainly can't think of any martial arts experts who've also spent time in the KGB or the CIA or MI6 or any other spy agency. An antique gas mask, a Japanese military pistol . . . dynamite . . . Ghost Boy . . . There's something else going on here. It's as though ghosts from the past have touched down in Cedar Valley, returning to old familiar haunts."

"Gemma, ghosts didn't kill Caleb Montgomery and Mike Esposito. The killer or killers can't stay hidden forever; sooner or later, masks will come off and we'll get them. Jimmy, do you have any sense of how easy it is to get ahold of these comics? Is this something we could track to a single seller?"

Jimmy shook his head. "That was the first thing I thought of, but no. Each volume is pricy but not so rare as to be traced to, say, a specific store in New York. I saw dozens of copies for sale online in the couple of minutes I just spent browsing. I can take the time if you like to put some feelers out there? See if anyone's been aggressively scooping up issues?"

I shook my head. "I don't think it's worth the time, to be honest. These comics are personal to the killer; I'd be shocked if they were recent purchases. My gut is that the books have belonged to the killer for years."

"Then why leave them behind?" Finn asked.

None of us had an answer for that, though I finally offered, "Maybe the killer's evolving. Shedding his Ghost Boy persona as he turns into something else. Something worse."

Finn pushed up from the desk. "We should get a start on Mike Esposito's background. Who he was, what he liked to do, and what he and a retired judge might have in common."

As we strategized next steps, something unsettling occurred to me. I realized I did in fact know someone who was a martial arts expert, and while she hadn't spent time in a spy agency, she'd sure done her share of time in the military: Fire Investigator Liv Ramirez.

# Chapter Fifteen

A few hours later, I had a more complete picture of Michael Esposito's life. While Finn had worked the crime scene notes and the list of evidence collected, Jimmy and I tried to peel back the curtain on Michael Esposito. If there was anything, anything at all that linked Esposito to Montgomery, it could break our cases wide open.

We reconvened in the small conference room, with the last of Jimmy's pastries and a fresh pot of coffee to sustain us.

I went first. "Michael Esposito was thirty-seven years old at the time of his death. He lived alone in the basement of a Victorian on the north side of town. No pets, no living relatives. His landlord, who lived above him in the main house, said he was a perfect tenant. Never any trouble, though he was gone for long stretches of time. Curiously, she thinks he either had a girlfriend in another town or was a spy for the CIA. Anyway, I've got a couple of officers searching his apartment. He owned a rather valuable vintage motorcycle and honestly, that's about it for assets. Oh, and he played on the local softball team. His buddies are devastated and are holding a wake for him tonight at the Stop Sign."

"Interesting choice for a wake." Finn smirked. The Stop Sign was a topless bar on the outskirts of town, sandwiched between a gas station and a pawn shop. It was far from a high-end establishment, and in fact, rumor had it that the owner wouldn't hire any staff who had all their teeth. It was a badge of honor at that place, to be missing a few pearly whites.

Finn gave a mock shudder and added, "If I go out before you, Monroe, please don't let any of my buddies plan my funeral. What else do you have? Any local relatives?"

"As far as family, Esposito didn't have much. Both parents are deceased, and I didn't find any record of siblings or even cousins. He appeared in town about seven years ago and worked a few odd jobs here and there until he was hired on at the bank." I paused, reviewed my notes. "According to the manager, who is very shaken up, Esposito's performance there has been steady. Usual absences, illnesses. Takes two weeks of vacation a year. The tellers and customers all love him. He's especially popular with the older ladies; a number of them make weekly visits to the bank simply to bring him cookies. Jimmy? What'd you find?"

The intern smiled like the cat who'd caught the canary. He opened his notebook, waited a moment, then smiled even wider. "I found a connection between Caleb Montgomery and Michael Esposito. Actually, two connections. And they're big ones, guys. Like, *big*."

"Jimmy?" Finn asked.

"Yeah?"

"What the hell are you waiting for? Speak, man."

"Okay, okay. So, four years ago, Caleb Montgomery sold a parcel of land to Mike Esposito. It's an acre on the north side of town that includes a small cabin. I spoke with the realtor who handled the sale; apparently Caleb was looking to rid himself of the property and Esposito made him a good offer. The deal went through and that would seem to be the end of it. Except six months later, Edith Montgomery rear-ended Esposito on a deserted country road in Belle Vista."

"Belle Vista?" I was surprised and my first thought was the penitentiary. "They were both there on the same day?"

Jimmy nodded. "Now, don't get too excited. It was the last evening of the tri-county summer fair. Edith Montgomery served on the planning board. Any guesses why Esposito was there?"

Finn snapped his fingers. "The softball championship. The Cedar Valley Starfighters always play the Belle Vista Belly Rubbers at the fair."

"Exactly." Jimmy smiled. "It's a great matchup."

"Wait just a minute. Our softball team is the *Starfighters*? And theirs is the *Belly Rubbers*?"

Finn gave me a look of pity. "What did you expect? The Red Sox?"

I rolled my eyes. "Jimmy, what came about from the accident?"

The intern closed his notebook with a resounding clap. "Edith Montgomery was convicted of a misdemeanor. DUI. Turns out she'd had one too many glasses of champagne that day. She was sentenced to community service and lost her position on the board. Apparently it was quite the scandal. There were quite a few other boards and commissions she was a part of, and all of them, every last one of them, kicked her off. Edith, of course, blamed Esposito. She testified that he had all of a sudden swerved, then stopped dead in the middle of the road."

I tried to think back to three and a half years ago, tried to recall a time when Edith was suddenly ostracized from the community for one mistake. She'd done so much good for the town over the years, poured thousands of dollars, and hours of time, into countless charity events.

Bull often said it was a long hike up to heaven and a quick tumble down to hell, and I thought I understood what he meant.

Edith's fall from grace had been quick and likely very unpleasant.

It had also been quiet. I hadn't been aware of it, couldn't remember Bull or Julia breathing a word of it. Then again, it wasn't my social circle, not exactly. They'd have known, though.

And, I was sure, Edith had slowly been making that climb back up over the last few years. She was involved in a great many number of local organizations and it had been clear at Caleb's memorial service that her standing had been restored.

But had her pride?

Had she simply been biding her time, waiting for the right moment to take out both Caleb and the man whom she blamed for her ruin?

I thought about her claim of strange noises, odd lights in the Old Cabin Woods . . . I'd found nothing at the edge of the forest, but maybe there had been nothing there to find. Maybe that was all just another distraction.

Finn said, "If Edith had anything to do with the murders, she's not working alone. She was at Caleb's memorial service at the time Esposito was shot. And we all saw the video footage; a man pulled the trigger. I suppose it could have been a woman but the build sure looked like a man."

"Tom Gearhart, her brother?" Jimmy suggested.

I shook my head. "No, Tom was by her side during the service. Although . . . oh no."

Finn sat up, leaned forward, his eyes on mine. "What?"

"He stepped away. Maybe fifteen, twenty minutes before you called me, Gearhart entered the elevators. I don't know where he went; Edith said he was ill. Gearhart could have taken the elevator to the basement, exited the building, cut across that alley, and been at the bank three minutes later. Add a minute or two in the basement to swap his suit for the casual clothes and there would have been plenty of time." I exhaled, thinking through things. "We know Caleb and Tom didn't like each other. And Tom seems to worship the ground Edith walks on."

Jimmy jumped in. "You said the dynamite thief was fat, but moved like a dancer, right? It could have been a disguise. And Gearhart's an actor! He knows how to change his walk, throw on a costume, and become someone else. *It all fits.*"

"Everything except *Ghost Boy.* What does the comic book have to do with it?" Finn stood, scratched at his back. A few of the hairs at his temples had started to lighten from black to silver. Another couple of months, a year maybe, and more hairs would have turned. For a moment, I saw Finn as an older man, with more salt than pepper in his hair. He'd be retired somewhere on the coast, living the good life on a boat, a pail of shrimp at his feet and a frosty beer in his hands.

For now, though, Finn was a forty-year-old cop with a rumpled suit and a look of confusion in his eyes. "Look, let's stay on Esposito for a minute. His landlady said he'd be gone for days at a time, right? We know he's got a cabin somewhere. That's a likely place to start looking for signs that he spends time there."

I called the officers who were searching Esposito's apartment and gave them the address of his cabin. If there was anything of interest there, Finn and I could check it out after the officers. But they called me back an hour later with not much to report. One of the officers added, "Unless you count skin flicks, in which case there are a few dozen here. Nothing unusual, just your standard naked ladies and so-so plots. Frankly, I'm not surprised one bit. We met Esposito's landlady at his apartment in town; she's about a hundred years old and nosy as hell. If I had to guess, this place is Esposito's hidey-hole, his man cave."

I hung up, dejected. I'd been hoping for a little more discovery at the second residence to help fill in the picture. So far there was nothing to indicate Esposito lived a life out of the ordinary. There was nothing to indicate that he'd be a target for a crazed killer.

Finn checked his watch. "It's late. Let's break and get back on this on Monday. We've been working nonstop, going in circles. Everyone could use a day to regroup. We hit this hard, first thing Monday morning."

That night, at home, after Grace was in bed, Brody and I went over the final head count for the wedding. There would be close to a hundred guests, mostly friends and work colleagues, some family. We sat on the floor in the den, a pencil sketch of the dining hall at the Tate Lodge between us. It was the most tedious puzzle I'd ever done in my life, and I wasn't shy about telling Brody that; figuring out who should sit next to whom, and at what table, made me feel as though my soul was slowly seeping out of my body.

"Make a game out of it, Gemma." Brody poured us each another glass of wine, his spirits high. He loved this sort of thing. "Okay, table ten. It's closest to the dance floor, but farthest from the buffet. Do we know anyone who's trying to lose weight?"

I rolled my eyes. "I'm not having a dieter's table at my wedding. Let's put your sisters there, and a couple of eligible bachelors from your work. Maybe we can make a love connection."

Brody stared at the diagram, his lips pursed in concentration. "I suppose that could work . . . though Sarah has very sensitive hearing. If she's too close to the DJ, she'll get upset. And I don't think Jeff Junior is going to like sitting there, either. The kid is growing like a weed, he'll want to be near the food."

Jeff Junior was the son of Brody's second youngest sister, Naomi. Jeff Junior, as everyone called him, was twelve and, if Naomi's frequent Facebook posts could be believed, had the appetite of a linebacker in the NFL. Jeff Senior, Junior's father, was himself a generously stout man with a belly that shook in two counties when he laughed.

"Yeah, let's put Jeff Junior, Jeff Senior, and Naomi near the buffet." This was giving me a headache. "You're so much better at this than me, honey. Couldn't you go a lot faster if I stepped out?"

Brody shook his head, carefully penciling in names on the sketch. "It's too entertaining to watch you sit there and squirm. I realized yesterday that we've done most of the wedding planning separately. This is good for us to do together."

"That's not true!" I protested. "We agreed on the Tate together . . . although I guess we toured it at different times, didn't we . . . well, the DJ. We picked him out together."

"No. He was recommended to me from a buddy at work. You spoke with him on the phone and gave him a deposit before I could even think about a playlist."

I exhaled and hugged the pillow in my lap tighter. "Is that what you're mad about? The DJ? We can find someone else."

Brody looked up at me, laughter in his eyes. "I'm not mad about any of it, Gemma. I'd just like to do some of this with the woman who is about to become my bride. Okay?"

I nodded and took a large swallow of wine. "Okay."

One long hour later, we were done and Brody released me from the room with a steamy kiss and a sincere thank-you. Feeling good about my generosity in the face of such soul-numbing labor, I decided to spend some time on real, actual, meaningful work.

I went online. Though I had extensive training in modern firearms, my historical knowledge was weak. I started by reading up on matchlock guns and flintlocks, muskets common in the seventeenth-century American colonies. Then on to revolvers. To my surprise, though I may have known it at one point and forgotten, it wasn't until 1835 that the Colt revolver appeared. That was a pivotal moment in mankind's history, for with the appearance of the Colt revolver, guns entered the world of mass production. They became cheaper, more accessible to the common man. Deadlier, too. With each new model came better accuracy and ease of use.

There was a lot of information as well about the various Nambu models. I scanned the websites for anything that seemed relevant to our case, but there was little connection I could make between the historical weaponry and our small town in Colorado until I stumbled onto a footnote on a website that referenced an Aimee Corn in Avondale, Colorado.

Avondale was one town over from Cedar Valley.

I did another search. Aimee Corn. She was a published military historian and sometime college professor. According to the biography on her website, Corn's research was specifically focused around Camp Amache, also known as the Granada Relocation Center. The internment camp in southeast Colorado had housed thousands of Japanese-Americans during World War II.

"What the hell, it's worth a shot." I found her email, then

logged into the police server and sent her a quick message from my official work address. I didn't expect much. Corn wasn't a weapons expert. But maybe, just maybe, she could provide some context to the investigation. To my surprise, as it was quite late, a reply came just fifteen minutes later. Corn wrote that she'd love to meet with me, in Avondale, and was I free tomorrow on Sunday? She listed her address and a suggested time, and asked that I confirm.

I sent her a response back and then went to bed, falling asleep quickly with the knowledge that the next day might help bring some answers.

# Chapter Sixteen

*Some towns are pretty and some towns are gritty...*

The refrain, lyrics from a popular song by the Beetdiggers, a local band, ran through my mind, over and over. The words felt appropriate as I drove from Cedar Valley to the more remote, less colorful Avondale. It wasn't hard to compare the two towns and have Avondale always come up short.

Cedar Valley had the ski resort, the picturesque Main Street. We had unique shops with actual artisan products, instead of the typical plastic tourist trinkets. Our restaurants were locally owned, and the town had been built up, organically, house by house, business by business, over the course of nearly two hundred years.

It was a town full of character, with great natural beauty.

Avondale, on the other hand, had been hastily developed in the late 1960s. Its buildings were low and squat, ugly concrete structures that sat like hulking sulky monsters around a monotone downtown that was more strip mall than main street.

As I slowed and entered the town limits, I took in just how bad Avondale had been hit by the recent recession. Letters on the town's movie theater marquee hung crooked, advertising a blockbuster that had been popular six months before. A couple of older men shuffled along the sidewalk, shooting me dirty looks as I drove past. Two women, perhaps the men's wives, sat huddled together against the wind in a nearby bus stop shelter, where vandals and the weather had taken turns etching and pitting the plastic windows.

As I left the strip and headed into the country, I acknowledged that Avondale had a few things going for it. One of the largest freight railroad networks in North America ran directly through the center of town. A small museum had been built next to the original train station, and the collection was world-class. In addition, the woods-product industry had been revived over the last decade, with beetle-killed wood turned into usable, beautiful lumber at a recently reopened sawmill. There was a cider brewery and some lovely trails, but at the end of the day, the town had never taken off the same way Cedar Valley had.

And so, fair or not, Avondale sat, rural and somewhat sad, in the shadow of Cedar Valley.

Aimee Corn's house was therefore a pleasant surprise. It sat on a couple of acres of land, her drive framed by a series of pine trees. In addition to the bright yellow farmhouse, there was a red barn, a couple of sheds, and a small greenhouse with nearly transparent polycarbonate siding.

As I parked and got out of the car, two young girls ran by on the heels of three clucking, frantic-looking chickens. The girls, in brightly patterned rain boots, indigo jeans, and matching yellow sweaters, cornered the birds near one of the small sheds and laughed as the hens squawked loudly.

At the house, the front door banged open. A woman stepped out, drying her hands on a dish towel, and yelled, "Emma! Rebecca! Don't you scare those chickens! I'll set Brutus on you."

The girls stopped running. They stared at each other with wide eyes, their mouths falling open. Then, ignoring me completely, they skipped away from the chickens and disappeared into the woods behind the house, maniacal laughter trailing behind them.

I joined the woman on the front porch. She had reddish-brown hair, piercing green eyes, and an infectious, charming grin. Her sweatshirt had all the stains of a busy morning in the kitchen.

She extended a hand. "You must be Gemma. I'm Aimee. Those two hellions are my daughters."

"And Brutus?"

Aimee winked at me. "Brutus is our rooster. He's a mean son of a bitch; I rescued him from a cockfighting operation two years ago. Of course, I'd never really set him on the girls. I'm not a monster, after all. Emma and Rebecca would scare the poor gent to death. Come on in. Watch out for the pig."

*Pig?*

I stepped into the house and set my bag down on a narrow bench. The room was small but warmly decorated. Potted plants, books, and craft projects seemed to compete for every available surface space, and on the floor were hooked rugs and more piles of books.

A timid snort at my feet caused me to look down and watch as an adorable pink pig, the size of a small dog, scampered by.

"That's Pliny. He rules around here," Aimee said. "Coffee? Tea? Hot cocoa?"

"Coffee sounds great, thank you. Brutus . . . Pliny. I sense a theme here."

"You're good; usually it's not until folks meet Socrates that they get it. My undergraduate degree is in philosophy and I spent a few years in Italy and Greece," Aimee replied. "Make yourself at home, I'll be right back."

The pig had disappeared, but an enormous gray-and-white-striped cat with three legs sauntered in. I stepped over it and made my way to the bookshelves. They were crammed with books about military history, philosophy, and homesteading. Looking closer, I saw that a number of them listed Aimee Corn as the author.

She appeared behind me. "Here you go; I took the liberty of adding cream and sugar. I hope that's all right? It's my opinion that black coffee is tar. Let's sit down. Watch, Archimedes will be in my lap in less than a minute."

Aimee moved to the couch, while I chose a seat in an armchair facing her. The three-legged cat, who must have been Archimedes, bounced up from the floor and curled next to Aimee. She stroked its head as she sipped her tea, and the cat began to purr loudly.

I was curious as to Aimee's background. "What got you interested in military history?"

"You could say the military is in my blood. My grandfather served in World War II. He met my grandmother overseas, who was working for the Resistance in France. Their son, my dad, is a Vietnam veteran." Aimee paused, sipped her tea. "The Corn family has been serving this country for generations. Thomas Corn, my great-great-great-grandfather, was a soldier for the Union Army . . . Ansel Corn, his cousin, was a drummer boy for the Confederacy. Incredibly, both Ansel and Thomas passed on September 17, 1862, at the Battle of Antietam. Ansel was twelve years old; Thomas, nineteen, with a wife at home. They were just boys."

"That's awful. How have you managed to trace your family tree back so far?"

Aimee shrugged. "It's not so hard anymore, so much history is available through the internet now. In fact, even the teaching I do these days is mostly online. That, plus the history books I write, keep the old homestead lights burning. Speaking of online . . . Gemma, I know we've just met, but I can sense you are the kind of woman who appreciates bluntness. After I received your message last night, I spent some time on research. And I think you should be worried. Very worried, in fact."

"Oh?" I leaned forward and set my tea down. "What did you find?"

"Are you familiar with a man named Josiah Black?"

I racked my brain, coming up empty. "No." I started to say more when the front door banged open with a tremendous boom. Aimee and I both jumped and the cat let out an angry hiss. One of the Aimee's daughters ran into the room, panting, out of breath. She was followed shortly thereafter by the second daughter.

The taller of the two shouted, "Momma, Momma, we saw the witch! She was in the barn again!"

"Emma, calm down. I told you, Mrs. McCready is storing a few things in the empty horse stalls for the winter," Aimee said in a patient yet firm voice. "She won't hurt you. Why don't you two monkeys play down by the old orchard? I bet we missed a few apples when we went searching yesterday."

The girls scampered off and Aimee called after them, "Watch the water, Emma. Keep your little sister away from the pond."

Aimee turned back to me. "Sorry about that. Old Widow Mc-Cready is the bane of Emma's existence. McCready is a sourpuss, and she certainly can be a bitch on wheels, but she's no witch. Though she does mutter a lot and dead frogs are always turning up in her yard. Actually, now that I think about it . . ."

From outside came loud shrieking and then muted laughter. The sound of the girls faded away as Aimee pointed to a plain manila folder laying atop a stack of books in the middle of the coffee table. "That folder is for you. In it is everything I found on Josiah Black, though I'm sure there's much more information out there. You can access the trial notes, the murder reports more quickly; if I did it, I'd need to file a request with the county. And then there would be a record and I'd prefer not to have my name associated with any of this."

I opened the folder, feeling a momentary sense of dizziness as I did so, as though it were somehow a door to a strange and different universe. A portal. And in a way, it was; it was a door to the past.

The first item in the folder was a piece of paper, obviously printed from a website. It showed a young man, handcuffed, maybe thirty years old, in the process of being escorted out of a courthouse by half a dozen men in uniforms. In the background, a mob of people watched the prisoner, their faces twisted in angry grimaces.

The picture was black-and-white; judging by the clothes and cars in the images, the photograph had originally been taken in the 1940s or '50s. Most disturbing was the handful of small children in the mob, their tiny hands raised to mimic their parents.

"Anything look familiar?" Aimee asked softly.

I started to shake my head no, then peered at the courthouse. "This is Cedar Valley."

"Yes. October 1949," Aimee said. "The man in handcuffs is Josiah Black, aged twenty-seven, husband, father, and veteran of the Second World War."

"What was he charged with?" I asked as a sudden gust of wind shook the windowpanes. Aimee glanced over her shoulder, watched for a moment as more clouds moved in. She sighed. "I hate this time of year. Everything seems to turn dark, to die."

"Aimee? What was Josiah Black's crime?"

"Murder, multiple counts. Black returned to the States from a tour in the Pacific with what we would nowadays diagnose as post-traumatic stress disorder. PTSD. You're familiar with the condition?" Aimee asked.

I nodded. "I'm no expert, but I did take a few psych courses in college and at the police academy. I'm aware of the basics."

"Black came back to Cedar Valley a changed man. The things he'd experienced and the things he'd seen . . . They say war makes men out of boys. I don't believe that's true. I think war devastates boys and the men who emerge from the wreckage have wounds that go far deeper than we'll ever know. Black came home and for a few years, things were okay. He got a job at a local grocery, and worked up to manager. Along the way, he married his high school sweetheart. Her name was Amelia. Life was good. Then, in October of 1948, a madman struck." Aimee's voice grew quiet. "At first, the cops couldn't connect the dots. His crimes seemed random, unconnected."

A veteran. A series of random, unconnected crimes. My flesh broke out in goose bumps. "What did Black do?"

Aimee was grim now, all trace of joviality gone. "I'll tell you, and you'll see why I think you should be worried. The first thing he did was lace a truck with explosives. A local doctor, on his way to dinner, was blown to bits in the middle of Main Street. On Halloween.

Five days later, Black slipped on a gas mask and robbed a bank. Though no one resisted, he shot the guard in the chest, twice, killing him almost instantly."

"My God," I breathed. Sour acid rose in the back of my throat as I realized the full scope of what we were dealing with. "We've got a copycat killer."

Aimee nodded. "Unfortunately, it gets worse. Less than a week after the man robbed the bank, he barricaded the front doors of a popular tavern and set fire to it. Twelve people died. Josiah Black was eventually arrested, tried, and convicted of the crimes. He received the death sentence but maintained his innocence throughout the trial and after. Appeals kept him alive for years."

I skimmed the first couple of pages of the trial transcript, coming to a dead stop when I saw the presiding judge's name.

Henry Montgomery.

Caleb Montgomery's father.

What had Gloria Dumont said? That Caleb had tried to atone for the sins of his father. Had Henry Montgomery put an innocent man away?

"Can I take this research? I've got to get back to town, now. Right now. I have to inform my chief." I was unsure how to adequately thank this woman who'd just given me the key to hopefully not just solving two murders, but to preventing a massacre as well.

Aimee moved the cat from her lap and stood, her eyes still deeply troubled. "Yes, please, take the file—it's yours. I'm only sorry I couldn't find out more information for you. I'm a wiz with the national military databases, but when it comes to parolees, I'm dead in the water."

"Parolee?" I froze. "Black was released? I thought he was sentenced to die."

"He was, but he was freed in 1995. He was seventy-three years old. He was released on a technicality after some hotshot law student writing an article for his law review discovered the error. Incredibly, the student graduated, passed the bar, and then spent the next three years working pro bono to get Black released. And he succeeded. But as I said, the trail grows cold with his release."

I did the math. "Black would be in his late nineties if he were still living. I've seen footage of the man who robbed the Bishop Mine and footage of the man who shot Mike Esposito; there is no way that either man is nearly a hundred years old."

I was left with the terrible thought that someone had resurrected a ghost and brought him back to life to kill, again and again.

I got two miles outside of Avondale before I had to pull over to the side of the road. My hands were shaking, my heart racing. If my suspicion was correct, there would be a terrible act of violence in my town in mere days.

But where would the killer strike?

There were seven bars and more than a dozen restaurants in Cedar Valley, not to mention the movie theater, the Shotgun Playhouse, and all the other public places like the hospital, the schools, the parks.

We were a small police force; we'd never be able to cover them all.

I balled my hands into fists and squeezed until they stopped shaking, ignoring the pain this caused my still-healing palms. Then I fished my cell phone out of my bag and dialed Chief Chavez's cell. I reached him at home, the sound of a radio and his kids in the background.

"Come on by, we're carving the last of the pumpkins. I could use the break; I don't know why the hell my kids think Halloween is a monthlong holiday," Chavez said. "We can talk outside."

"I'm on my way."

Chavez, his wife, and their four young children lived in a newer subdivision on the eastern edge of Cedar Valley. I made good time, quickly putting distance between the mist-shrouded town of Avondale and myself.

I parked in his driveway and realized I'd never been there at this time of year. With the trees bare, I could turn to the north and see the edge of the Ashley Forest, the Old Cabin Woods. Funny how I hadn't been in the woods in years, and now, everywhere I turned, they seemed to be right there.

Chavez must have heard my car. He stepped out of the large, two-story house with a can of beer in one hand and a screwdriver in the other. It was disconcerting to see him in jeans and a casual sweater.

"Come on in," Chavez said. "Want a beer? Coffee?"

"No, thanks."

Inside, the house was warm, decorated in the bright colors of Lydia Chavez's birth country, Jamaica. I followed the chief into the kitchen, where I kissed Lydia on the cheek and said hello to each of the kids. All of them ignored me, intent on carving their pumpkins. Spooky Halloween sound effects were blaring from a set of speakers set high on the wall. The kids worked at the kitchen table; there were seeds and pumpkin innards splattered everywhere. Fake cobwebs, plastic spiders, and rubber rats completed the tableau.

As the chief and I stepped out onto the porch, Lydia pulled a tray of chocolate chip cookies from the oven, the smell wafting across the room and nearly drawing me back into the pumpkin-carving circus.

Lydia grinned at the conflicted look on my face. "I'll save you a few."

Though the backyard was fenced, it was the fencing that was popular in so many subdivisions: low, open slats, so that the fence was more a token of boundary lines and not necessarily designated to keep things in . . . or out.

The yard had recently been raked. Mottled leaves that had once been the color of flames in a fireplace sat in three tidy piles. The trees were bare and there was a sense of weight in the air, of something soon arriving, or something recently left.

We stood against the railing, resting our arms on it, leaning forward.

"Terry Bellington is dying," Chavez said. He finished his beer and crushed the can, then tossed it at the closest pile of leaves. "Cancer."

"I'm sorry to hear that." Terence Bellington was the former mayor of Cedar Valley and one of Chavez's best friends. The year before, though, his family had been involved in a murder investigation, the ripples of which tore apart both family and friendships. "Have the two of you stayed in touch?"

"No, not really," Chavez said, "In fact, until yesterday, we hadn't spoken in ages. He's on hospice care now, at his home. The cancer came back four months ago. It sounds as though Terry's made peace with it."

"Will you see him?"

"I don't know. He didn't ask for me to come. Do you think I should? What would I say?"

I shrugged. "You two were close once, for a long time. Dying shouldn't be lonely, Chief. If the situation was reversed, what would you want?"

At my side, Chavez was silent. I studied him out of the corner of my eye, the pockmarked skin on his face, the receding hairline, the way his ears seemed too big for his face. These descriptions sound like petty things, but in a society where first impressions are everything, his features marked the chief as plain, average. Some might even say ugly.

Chavez was one of the best men I knew, with a razor-sharp intellect and a heart of gold. His beauty lay on the inside, in his heart, his character.

After a moment, he said in a low voice, "I'd want to see him. Everything that happened last fall . . . you know none of that was Terry's fault. He lost everything, including his whole family, and why? Because of other people's choices, other people's decisions. He's a broken man. A broken, dying man."

"Go to him, Chief."

"I will. Enough melancholy. What's going on, Gemma? When we spoke earlier, I heard fear in your voice."

I pushed off the fence and turned to the north, looking out at the Old Cabin Woods. Though the sun was still high in the sky, and clouds were few and far between, the woods remained dark, under shadows of their own. "The truth is, I *am* scared. Have you ever heard of a man named Josiah Black?"

"Sounds vaguely familiar . . ." Chavez thought a moment. I knew that after he moved to Cedar Valley, when he first started on the force, he took it upon himself to learn as much history as he could. Finally, he shook his head. "I can't pinpoint it."

I summarized what I'd learned from my visit with Aimee Corn. Hearing it all again, watching the way the words fell on Chief Chavez, was disturbing. By the time I finished with a couple of suggestions on what to do next, his face was pale and his eyes haunted.

"Gemma, we can't close the whole town. What you're talking about, mandatory curfews, officer patrols . . . we can't go down that road based on a potential threat. For one, Mayor Cabot would never approve it. For two, can you imagine the fear that would create?"

"Chief, we know this guy is going to strike again. We have less than five days to find him."

"Exactly." Chavez nodded. "If you're right, you've got about three and a half days, Gemma. Start with Josiah Black. I want to know everything about this son of a bitch, what happened to him before, during, and after his trial; his family; his friends. The case must have been a huge publicity generator. The story of the crimes, and the trial, likely sold thousands of newspapers all over the state. If we truly do have a copycat killer, he's probably doing it for the fame, the attention."

I nodded, then added, "Or revenge."

"Look into the Black family, any living friends. If it's revenge . . . why now? What's changed in the last seventy years?"

"Seventy years is a long time. From what Aimee told me, the family's long dead. Whatever secrets they had, they took them to the grave. If someone is doing this for revenge, maybe it's an outsider."

Before we left the backyard, the chief said, "You know this town, Gemma. You know that secrets never stay buried forever. Someone knows something."

# Chapter Seventeen

From Chief Chavez's house, I headed to the public library. The unassuming redbrick building, built low to the ground, hid the fact that a cavernous basement held thousands, if not hundreds of thousands, of archival materials. Most of it was in the process of being moved to the History Museum, where a second-story floor would offer better protection in case of flooding. But the museum was closed on Sundays, and I seemed to remember that they were starting with the older things first, so if there was material on Josiah Black, it should still be at the library.

I entered the building as a Halloween-themed story time was letting out. Witches, ghosts, goblins, and unicorns, all of them no more than four feet tall, swarmed around my legs and then they were gone, moving to the next room. The library always did like to stretch out the holidays.

At a reference desk in the middle of the first floor, I found the woman I was looking for. Her name was Tilly Jane Krinkle, and she was that most underappreciated of all superheroes: a reference librarian. She was nearly eighty years old, with bright orange hair, a penchant for red high-top sneakers, and a stuffed parrot that accompanied her when the mood struck.

Most people in town simply called Tilly the Bird Lady.

She looked up and harrumphed when she saw me. "When are you fools going to deputize me? I swear, every time I turn around, you all need me for something. Don't you know I'm dying? Can't you leave me in peace?"

I leaned down and kissed her on the cheek. She smelled of cinnamon and cloves and I guessed she hadn't quit smoking, even with a terminal diagnosis of cancer. "You're not dead yet, Tilly. I'm here about—"

The Bird Lady cut me off before I could say anything more. "Josiah Black. I know."

"How the hell do you do that?" I was shocked and yet strangely, not surprised. The first time I'd met Tilly had been during the course of an investigation. I'd come here, to this exact spot, and been about to launch into a long explanation of what I needed when she'd done the same thing she'd done just now: known why I was there, and what I needed, seemingly before I even knew.

A sly look in her eyes, Tilly shrugged. "I've been doing this job going on fifty years. Not much gets past me. I've got a mind like a steel trap and a memory like an elephant. After that young security guard was shot at the bank yesterday, an old feeling started scratching something fierce at the back of my mind.

"And then it finally hit me early this morning." Tilly gestured for me to follow her across the main reading room, to the locked door that I knew led down the steps to the shadowy basement. "Josiah Black's crimes, and his subsequent trial, were sensational news in town, heck, even in the state. We have a great deal of stuff about him, some of which I've come across in town history books over the years."

She unlocked the door. The smell of dust and untouched papers and something else, mold or mildew, floated up the wide stairs and out the open door.

It was the smell of old stories and long-buried secrets.

I followed the librarian down the stairs and saw that she'd pulled a number of things together for me and left them at a long study table near the bottom of the stairs. I was grateful I wouldn't have to wander through the labyrinthine aisles; the basement had lights tied to motion sensors, and if you dawdled or stopped, chances were good the lights would shut off behind you. I'd once been trapped down here in the dark with a killer; it was an experience I didn't care to repeat.

"Why didn't you call me? Once you made the connection?" I asked.

Tilly shrugged. "First off, I knew you or Trouble would come by soon. And second, I know what people in town call me. 'Bird Lady.' What kind of a name is that? They think I'm a kook, an odd duck. Insane. I'm nothing of the sort."

"I think you're one of the sanest people I know, Tilly. Who's 'Trouble'?"

"That handsome partner of yours with the dark hair and the sapphire eyes. In my day, if it looked like trouble and acted like trouble, it *was* trouble. Anyways, here's what you need." She motioned to the things she'd collected. "Most of this is articles from the *Valley Voice*. Also some memorabilia, such as Black's report cards from elementary school, a baseball card collection he had, that sort of thing."

"How did the library end up with his personal effects?"

Tilly grew sad. She said in a low voice, "After Black's trial, his parents disowned him. They packed up all his belongings from his childhood and teen years and dumped them at the church for the rubbish sale. My predecessor was a wise woman; she went through all the boxes and took what she thought might be of interest to future generations. Isn't that sad? A life reduced to tabloid headlines and some cardboard boxes."

"The whole thing is tragic." I picked up the top box, opened it, and stared down at Black's elementary school report cards. Young Josiah had been a good student, it seemed, in English and math . . . in Latin, not so much.

Tilly sighed. "I'll leave you to it, then. I should get back upstairs. Let me know when you're done and I'll get one of our aides to put all this stuff away. One of these days, you are all going to learn that you should just leave the past well enough alone. Why anyone would want to drag up these old hurts is beyond me."

It was beyond me, as well, but more important, none of this had been up to me. A vision of Caleb's killer drifted before my eyes and then he was gone; like the comic book character Ghost Boy, our killer seemed impossible to grab hold of.

Ghost Boy was responsible. He was the bad guy in all this.

I sat at the table and read an article written by a reporter who had been attending Black's trial since day one, quickly becoming fascinated with the norms of the late 1940s lifestyles that I was reading about. This particular article relayed testimony from Amelia Black. She recounted for the court the terrible dreams Josiah suffered from on a nightly basis and his obsessive habit of checking the locks on every door and window before turning in for the night. She spoke of his increased moodiness and alcohol use, the way he'd veer between indecision and impulsiveness. Amelia also shared his deep love and affection for her, his parents, and his hometown; the civic pride he took in raising the flag each morning on their front lawn and entertaining neighborhood children with handmade puppets.

By the time I finished the article, I felt incredible sympathy for Josiah and Amelia. He hadn't asked to be sent off to a strange land where he was instructed to kill or be killed. And she hadn't asked to live with the man who'd returned, a stranger in so many ways.

It was clear from her testimony that Amelia herself was conflicted as to Josiah's guilt. She couldn't provide an alibi for his whereabouts at the times of any of the killings, though Josiah had insisted he was home with her. But she also couldn't believe that her husband would hurt anyone in town.

Amelia's testimony was followed by that of a medical doctor called in from Denver who had not treated Josiah Black but was

considered an expert on combat stress reaction. The doctor testified that it was his expert opinion that Josiah Black had returned
from the war a changed man; that he suffered from psychological
and behavioral concerns stemming from repeated exposure to ex-
treme stress in combat situations. The doctor was sympathetic to
the defense; he explained that there were methods and medicines
available to treat veterans like Josiah Black.

In response, the prosecution brought in witness after witness,
all local Cedar Valley folks, who each swore up and down they'd
seen Josiah at or near the scene of each crime. The first witness,
the deputy police chief, testified he'd heard Josiah threaten one of
the victims just a week prior to the first killing. The testimonies
for the prosecution were each brutal and telling in their own way; it
truly had been a mob mentality that had overtaken the town. They
were out for blood and Josiah Black was in the water, defenseless,
bleeding like a stuck pig.

On rebuttal, the defense called a young man named Ives
Farmington. Farmington had been classmates with Josiah Black,
and in fact, the two had been stationed together in the Pacific.
After the war, they'd both made their way home to Cedar Valley.
Ironically, Farmington had joined the local police force and was
one of Black's arresting officers.

But Farmington had not agreed with the evidence and, by the
time of the trial, had himself nearly been ostracized from the force
because of his dogged, fervent belief of Black's innocence.

Fascinated, I read on. The defense attorney was a man named
Rogers, and he seemed to thrive on the courtroom drama.

*Farmington:* The evidence that has placed Josiah Black in
this courtroom is circumstantial, plain and simple.

*Rogers:* Are you telling me that the prosecution's claims of
deceit and intrigue, spy skills picked up in the war, all of
that is untrue?

*Farmington:* Correct. Josiah Black is innocent of the charges.

*Rogers:* Mr. Farmington, have you personally suffered as a result of this trial?

*Farmington:* Yes, sir, I have. As of this morning, I resigned my position as a lieutenant with the Cedar Valley Police Force. My life has been threatened, my parents subjected to verbal abuse and late-night calls. I don't have a friend left in this town and still . . . still I tell you, Josiah Black is innocent. I respect my former colleagues, my former chief. But sir, they're wrong. They're dead wrong. The evidence doesn't match up. The timelines, they don't work. And at the end of the day, I know Josiah Black. I know the horrors he saw during the war, because I saw them, too. I know the nightmares he greets every night, because I greet them, too. The things we live with, sir, they're horrible. I wouldn't wish war on anyone. Someone else did these terrible crimes.

*Rogers:* Who, Mr. Farmington, who? Who murdered more than a dozen people in cold blood?

*Farmington:* I can't tell you that, sir. Not yet, at least. I need more time.

I turned the page, only to find that Farmington's testimony ended there. I wondered for a moment if pages were deliberately missing; if Ghost Boy had come before me and taken what I needed. Then I found another set of records and realized that no, Farmington never took the stand again. A few more testimonies and Black was convicted; things wrapped up fairly quickly.

Too quickly.

Though what I'd read had been brief, it had been damning. Rarely does someone in Farmington's position risk their livelihood unless their conviction is so strong, their belief so powerful, that to not stand up and tell what they believe to be the truth would bring them to their knees in shame and ruin.

I moved on to the stack of later articles, stopping at a clipping from a national paper from 1956. It was an op-ed piece, written by a young law student, laying out each and every mistake that Judge Montgomery and the prosecution had made during Black's trial. The piece insisted that guilty or not, Josiah Black should be released from prison immediately and granted a new trial. The student was passionate, but was he right? He spoke of circumstantial evidence and a biased judge hell-bent on punishing someone, anyone, for the killings in his town.

It was this piece that must have sparked another young lawyer's interest, all those years later, to fight for Black's release.

I spent another few hours at the library and then had to leave. I couldn't absorb any more pain, any more hurt. By the time I got home, my eyes were bleary, my head hurt, and I didn't know what to believe anymore.

Had Josiah Black killed more than a dozen people? Was he truly the monster that his former friends and family seemed to think he was?

Or was he a scapegoat, an easy target? Was there some other killer lurking in the shadows, never seen, never caught?

It was a chilling thought.

Like the Gordon Dillahunt trial, there were cracks in the case: allegations of misconduct, inadequate defenses. I'd seen a news program recently about the Innocence Project, out of New York, and to date they'd exonerated more than three hundred people through DNA.

Three hundred men and women, falsely imprisoned for years. They'd lost jobs, spouses, families, and friends along the way. And why? Because something went wrong, plain and simple. Had it been the same for Josiah Black? Was that why the Ghost Boy was now re-creating Black's crimes, to avenge him?

At home, I found the baby bathed and fed. She and Brody sat in the family room, playing with a couple of stuffed animals. Brody lifted a small orange lion and made an enormous roaring noise. Grace shrieked with laughter.

I smiled. At least here, in my home, all remained well.

That feeling of contentment lasted approximately until midnight, when Grace woke in her crib, crying softly and sweating. I went to her, took her temperature, gasped when I saw how high it was, and immediately woke Brody. He called a twenty-four-hour pharmacy advice line while I gave her Infants' Tylenol and a cup of diluted apple juice and then paced, rocking her on my shoulder, between the family room and kitchen.

I'd never felt her tiny body so warm.

Brody hung up. "It may be an ear infection. Let's see if the Tylenol reduces the fever; we can take her temperature again in an hour. Urgent care can see us first thing in the morning."

I felt Grace's forehead; it was still burning up. "Not tonight?"

"Honey, the only thing that's open is the emergency room and that will be a significant co-pay for what in all likelihood will pass. Let's monitor her for the next hour and if her fever hasn't gone down, we'll take her in." Brody rubbed at his eyes. He always did take a while to wake from sleep.

We were opposites in that way; it had been years since I had slept anywhere but on the edge of wakefulness.

On my shoulder, Grace had fallen asleep.

*Crib?* I mouthed to Brody. He thought a moment, then whispered back, "Chair?"

I nodded and crept back upstairs to Grace's room. At her rocking chair, I awkwardly tried to sink down without disturbing her, then pulled a thin blanket over us. Her breathing had become relaxed and deep, and after a while, I checked her forehead again. It was cooler, though still much warmer than normal, and I sighed a breath of relief.

I couldn't remember ever feeling so helpless.

Even with the baby for the moment at rest, it was hard to get comfortable in the wooden chair. I thought about asking Brody to spell me, then decided it wasn't worth risking waking Grace. As gently as I could, I shifted around in the chair until I'd gotten my legs up on the edge of a nearby bookshelf. Then I closed my eyes and tried to sleep.

But the day had brought too much for sleep to come easy.

We had two people dead. How many more would die before we found the answers we needed to bring Ghost Boy to justice?

# Chapter Eighteen

After the restless night, I woke Monday morning with a crick in my neck and toes that were nearly frozen. The blanket I'd draped over us had slipped to the floor at some point. Thankfully, Grace seemed to have slept well and stayed warm, snuggled close to my body. When I took her temperature, it was lower than it had been, though still not back to normal. Brody met up with us in the kitchen and it was agreed that he'd take Grace to urgent care, then bring her back home to spend the day with Clementine.

After they left, and before Clem showed up, I stood at the front window and tried to finish my coffee. A thick band of clouds filled the sky and the sun struggled to peek through. The horizon had taken on a greenish cast, as though the heavens themselves were ill.

It was an ominous sky, one that spoke of strange and fearsome things to come, and I dumped the last third of my coffee in the sink, my stomach already clenching with nerves and anxiety.

I spent a few minutes talking with Clementine after she arrived, explaining our plan for Grace and reviewing with her where all the infant medicine was kept in the master bath.

"We'll be fine. It's probably just an ear infection. Kids get them all the time." Our nanny pulled a bottle of blue nail polish from her bag and began to touch up her nails. "If her eustachian tube is blocked, fluid may have gotten trapped behind her middle ear. Has she been exposed to cigarette smoke lately?"

"Of course not. And when did you get your medical degree?"

Clementine burst out laughing. "Come on, don't you watch television? Or pick up a health magazine every once in a while? There's a whole world of knowledge out there, Gemma. It's not just bad guys and dead bodies."

"I know that. But eustachian tubes? Seriously?"

"I'm telling you. Fifty bucks says it's an ear infection." Clementine put her nail polish away. "You got any chamomile tea? Just in case it's not an ear infection and is something worse."

My heart dropped. "Worse? Like what? Don't you dare say plague."

Clementine rolled her eyes. "Plague? Seriously? Maybe if we had a prairie dog colony nearby. I meant the common cold. Or flu. You should probably get to work now. You're going to be late."

"Gladly. Good luck; let me know immediately if Grace gets worse." I left Clementine rummaging through our pantry, looking for tea. It was a painfully slow drive to the station, long-forgotten images of bubonic plague victims from my old school history books dancing before my eyes.

At my desk, a tiny skeleton cookie entombed in plastic waited for me. I picked up the bag of bones and flipped it over, reading from the short list: "Sugar, flour, butter, eggs . . . Perfect. Just what I need."

"I thought you might like that. The bakery down the street is still selling Día de los Muertos cookies. You know what's strange? It's called Day of the Dead but the lady selling the cookies explained to me the festival is actually celebrated over the course of two days, November first and second." Finn opened a skeleton of his own and bit off the head. "Strange, isn't it . . . Why not just call it *Days* of the Dead?"

I shrugged and set my papers down. I had so much to tell him. I launched right in, starting with my drive to Avondale and ending with my conversation with Chief Chavez. "His last words to me were a reminder that in this town, secrets never stay buried forever."

By the time I was finished, Finn had gone pale. His first question was the most important, and one that we desperately needed to answer if we had any hopes of preventing further loss of life: "How did Josiah Black pick his victims?"

I recalled what I'd read. "The prosecution claimed that Black targeted the doctor—his first victim—because the man refused to treat Black's psychoses. The medical community was of course aware of the horrible stresses that those in the military suffered from, but PTSD hadn't yet been identified as a treatable disorder. Back then it was called battle fatigue, or combat stress reaction. Anyway, the doctor, a general family physician, didn't have the necessary tools and training to fix Black, so, according to the prosecution, Black took revenge."

Finn rubbed his jaw, thinking. "And the guard at the bank? What was the motive there?"

"The guard was a man named Alfred Dietrich. The prosecution argued that Black shot Dietrich because of the man's German ancestry." I opened a soda can and took a long swallow, secretly wishing that it was a glass of wine. "I know . . . it's weak. But you haven't seen the newspapers; the town was out for blood by the time of the trial. The prosecution could have been grasping at straws and they'd probably have stuck."

"Mob mentality like that, Black never had a chance." Finn scratched at the back of his neck. "And the massacre at the tavern?"

"The Sinker was a popular bar owned by a Swedish couple, Lois and John Sven. John Sven signed Black's enlistment papers a few months after the attack on Pearl Harbor. Black may have blamed Sven for his subsequent time overseas." I shrugged and finished my soda. "The more I read about it, the more far-fetched it all becomes. But to prove Black was innocent, or feel comfortable with the guilty verdict that was handed down on him, we need to look at everything. All the answers to the Montgomery and Esposito murders lie with him."

I thought a moment, then added, "I'll start with his parole

records. I doubt he stuck around Belle Vista once he was released from prison, but it's as good a starting place as anywhere else."

Finn nodded. He looked uncomfortable.

"What is it?"

My partner sighed. "I went out with Liv last night. You know, on a date." I raised an eyebrow and waited for him to continue. Finally, he said, "She's a cool chick, but she's got some issues, Gemma. Anger. A lot of resentment, toward a lot of people. She's ex-military and a karate master. She's the female version of Ghost Boy. She's Ghost Girl."

"I thought the same thing. But what possible connection could she have to Josiah Black?" The hum of the building's old heating system kicked on. It was notorious for running too hot, too long. "Maybe she's got a partner. Did Ramirez say anything specific that's giving you heartburn?"

Finn's eyes narrowed. "She talked a lot about her family, her birth family. She was eighteen when she tracked her mom down to a trailer park outside of New Orleans. Mom was living with a boyfriend, a real gentleman with prison tats and track marks up and down his arms. Mom was using, too. She wasn't too happy to see her long-ago abandoned daughter on the front steps of her trailer. Liv stuck around long enough to get a good picture of the family history and then hightailed it out of there."

"Let me guess. Mom and the boyfriend met in prison? Or perhaps he was her pimp?"

Finn exhaled. "Something like that. It's a sad story; sounds as though the mom never really had a chance. Her own father was a small-town criminal, and her boyfriend, Liv's birth father, left town as soon as Liv was born. After giving Liv up for adoption, the mom didn't have many options. And as we both know all too well, a life of crime is for some people their only shot at survival."

I said, "Ramirez's spotty family tree can't be the only thing that's got you worried."

Finn stood suddenly. "You know, you're right. I'm overthinking this. I'm going to read through Josiah Black's case and trial records. There might be something there that can help us, something you didn't get to or was missed."

I watched him stroll away in the direction of the restrooms, his hands casually jammed in his pants pockets. There was something he wasn't telling me.

I checked in at home; Grace's fever had for the moment passed. Clementine gave me the scoop, via Brody, from the morning's hospital visit. A harried nurse had given Grace a cursory exam, then sent them home with instructions to let the illness, whatever it was, run its course. Clementine was working to keep her hydrated, quiet, and resting. Once more, I found myself thanking the powers that be for putting Clem in our family. I knew we were lucky to afford the in-home care; there was no way a day care would have let Grace come in ill, and it would have been hard for either Brody or I to stay home.

Less than an hour later, though, Clementine called me back, her voice panicked. "Gemma, I just took Grace's temperature and it's over 104 degrees. She's not acting like herself. And Brody is in a day-long meeting; he said you should take Grace back to the hospital."

*104 degrees.* My heart stopped. "I'll be right there."

I made it home in twenty minutes. Clem met me at the door, her face worried, her eyes scared. Grace was in her arms, limp and lethargic.

"The fever's gone up slightly. She won't take any liquids and I can't get her to play." Clem's eyes welled up with tears. "Sorry, I don't mean to be a worry but this is so unlike her."

I took my daughter from her arms and hurried back to my car. "Lock up, will you? I'm taking her to the emergency room."

My hands were shaking as I buckled Grace into her car seat. Her eyes were glazed, her cheeks bright red. I couldn't remember ever being so scared in my life.

"It's probably an ear infection, it's probably an ear infection," I whispered to myself the whole way back down the canyon and across town to the hospital. The words did little to calm me.

I parked in the first spot I could find at the hospital and raced inside. My heart sank as I took in the seven people already sitting in the olive-and-beige chairs. A nurse at the check-in handed me a clipboard, instructed me to fill it out, then take a seat.

"I don't have time for this. My daughter is really sick." I tried to hand the clipboard back but the nurse looked at me with steely eyes, then at Grace.

"High fever and lethargy, you said? And she's a year? Ear infection. Fill out the form and take a seat. We'll call you as soon as we can. The doc is a little tied up at the moment." The nurse went back to her computer screen. I restrained from chucking the clipboard at her head and instead found a seat in the back corner, as far away as possible from a woman hacking up her lung and a man whose open facial sores looked like something out of a horror movie.

I filled out the lengthy form, returned it to the nurse, then took the seat again. In my arms, Grace had fallen asleep. I slipped off her sweater and shoes, trying desperately to cool her down.

And then I waited.

Bull was the first to call. "Gemma, are you busy? I saw my family practitioner this morning and he thinks I should be on Prozac. Can you believe this nonsense? He said I've slipped into a depression since we moved your grandmother. I need you to call him and talk some sense into him. It's my prostate he should be worried about, not my mental state."

"Well, to be honest, you have seemed a touch morose the last few weeks. Anyway, I'm at the ER with Grace. She's sick," I replied in a low voice. The baby was still asleep and the last thing I wanted to do was wake her. "I think you should take your doctor's advice."

"The baby's sick? Her age, it's probably an ear infection. I'll take pills over my dead body. You know what's in them? Might as well just go find a loony bin and check myself in."

I closed my eyes and focused on breathing in and out. "Bull, that's totally ridiculous and frankly irresponsible. Antidepressants have saved countless lives. There's nothing wrong with taking medicine when you are sick. And if your doctor, who's known you for thirty years, thinks you are sick, then you probably are. So take the damn pills and make it easier for the rest of us to be around you." The words were out of my mouth before I could stop them and I winced. "I didn't mean that, Bull. This isn't a good time. I'll call you tonight."

For the first time in my life, he hung up on me.

Finn was the next to call. "How's the baby?"

I told him where we were, how horrible it was to sit in this sterile-smelling room with sick people all around us.

"Sounds rough. Listen, uh, I know you're a little preoccupied, but is there any way you can come back this afternoon? Like, leave the kid with the nanny or with Brody? Chavez wants an update and I've been thinking. About the masks, the hooded sweatshirts, the costumes. Why does the perp disguise himself? There's only one reason. He's well known. He must be someone we'd recognize."

"Finn, I have no freaking clue what time we'll be seeing the doctor, let alone when we'll get out of here. And when we are released, I'm not leaving Grace's side. I'll be in tomorrow." This time, I did the hanging up. Had Finn never been sick, never been to the emergency room?

What did he think this was, a drive-through?

A couple came into the waiting room, a young woman pushing an older man in a wheelchair. The man was nose-deep in a Tolstoy novel, the woman preoccupied with maneuvering his chair through an aisle crowded with dangling legs and crossed ankles. I watched them for a bit, trying to determine if she was his daughter, his caretaker, or his wife.

My phone rang again. "Hi, Gemma, I mean, Detective. It's Jimmy, you know, the intern? I was just wondering if there's anything you need help with."

I nearly snapped at him, then calmed down. Ives Farmington's testimony had been bothering me since I'd left the library the day before. "Actually, there is something you could do for me. Take down this name. Ives Farmington. He was a local cop back in the 1940s. He's probably long since passed away, but there may be relatives still around. If there are, set up a meeting with them as soon as possible."

"You got it."

Call waiting beeped through. *You've got to be kidding me.* It was my grandmother, Julia, calling from her cell phone.

"Jimmy, I'll talk to you later. I have to take this call." I switched over to Julia. "Hi. What are you doing?"

My grandmother's voice was shaky, fearful. She sounded as though she'd been weeping. "Who is this, please?"

"It's Gemma, Julia. Your granddaughter. Are you all right?"

"I don't know where I am. I'm in a locked room and the people here won't let me out. I want to go home." Julia began to sob quietly. "I want to go back to my house, my things. Can you help me? I don't know who else to call."

My heart nearly split into two. A terribly sick baby in my arms, a frightened grandmother on the phone, and me, stuck in a waiting room, unable to help either one of them. Just then, Grace began to stir.

I thought quickly; no sense telling Julia that she *was* home.

"Julia, I can't help you. I'm so sorry, but my daughter, Grace, she's sick. I'm going to text Laura and see if she can come see you. Would that be all right?"

I waited a minute for a response that never came. "Julia, are you there?"

Then a click, and in the space of twenty minutes, I'd been hung up on twice. I fired off a quick group text to both Bull and Laura and then silenced my phone. I couldn't handle any more calls. Grace was awake now, cranky. I managed to get her to sip from my water bottle. Then she wanted to play with it and that seemed to make her happy.

Across the aisle, the young woman and the older man she'd wheeled in had taken seats. She smiled at me. "How old?"

"Almost a year. Do you have kids?"

"Two. One about that age, the other is four. Both boys. It's hard, when they're sick." She waved at Grace. "She's beautiful, by the way."

"Thanks. She's never been this sick before." I glared at the wall clock. "And I can't believe how long this is taking. You'd think they would prioritize babies and children. I'm going to write a letter to whoever is in charge of this operation."

The young woman rolled her eyes. "Tell me about it. I'm here with my dad nearly every week. We make a whole day out of it. Do you live around here?"

"Up the canyon. You?"

"In town, near the elementary school. We're in that lilac Victorian just south of the park." She rummaged in her bag, pulled out a cream-colored card lined with blue and pink hearts. "Here. I'm the mob president. You should join us."

I blinked and rearranged Grace in my lap. She'd moved from my water bottle to my car keys. "I'm sorry, did you just say you work for the mob?"

She laughed. "Not that mob, although it can be just as cutthroat. M-O-B. Mothers of Babies. It's a local mom's group. We have play-dates at the library, bake sales. Lots of potlucks. You're not vegetarian, are you? We had one of those once. I swear, I've never eaten so much cauliflower in my life."

I stared down at the card in my hand, traced the heart in the middle. The woman's name was Jewel, and at the bottom of the card, in tiny script, was what must have been the MOB's slogan: *Moms, getting dirty since day one.*

I nearly broke out in hysterical laughter at the idea of casually standing around the sure-to-be perfectly styled dining room table in Jewel's sophisticated refurbished Victorian mansion, munching on Brie amidst designer diaper discussions. I wondered how the

MOBs would feel about car bombs and dead bank guards? How they'd react if I told them I marched in my dreams alongside both the dead and the dealers of death?

I tucked the card in my purse and smiled brightly at Jewel. "Thanks, I'd love that. I'll call you."

She nodded and smoothed back her hair. To my relief, a man in a white jacket and a harried look on his face appeared in the doorway and called Grace's name. I said my goodbye to Jewel and hurried to the man. He got us settled into a curtained room.

"So sorry about the wait. Let's take a look at Grace, shall we?" The doctor took her temperature, checked her mouth, and then examined both ears. "Yep. She's got a raging bilateral ear infection. You can pick up a course of antibiotics at the pharmacy. She'll be feeling better by this time tomorrow."

"That's it? An ear infection?"

"Oh, they can be quite serious if not treated. Or if they're recurrent. But Grace will be fine. Give her some Infants' Tylenol or Motrin tonight if she seems especially uncomfortable and put her to bed early. You'll see a marked difference by the morning." The doctor wrote something illegible on his prescription pad and tore it off with a flourish. He handed it to me and asked, "Anything else?"

I thought of everything I had on my plate, all the balls that were being juggled, the tasks left undone.

"You don't plan weddings, too, do you?"

"'Fraid not. Have a great day." The doctor left, moving on to some other patient, some other hurt person. I took Grace to the pharmacy, where we waited another twenty minutes to get her prescription filled.

Finally, both tired, hungry, and cranky, we were in the car and headed home. It was late afternoon by then and I felt as though I'd run a marathon. Every muscle and bone in my body ached. The emotionally draining day and uncomfortable night in the rocking chair were manifesting in actual, physical soreness in my body. I started a fire in the fireplace, then made us a couple of yogurt and fruit smoothies. Grace and I sat together on the couch, staring numbly at the fire, occasionally sipping our beverages. After a while, Seamus heaved his long, wide, basset hound body up on the couch and curled up next to us.

We were still there when Brody got home, though by then two of the three of us had fallen asleep. The third had gotten too warm and launched himself back to the floor, where he lay on his dog bed and kept watch over us.

Brody took the baby up to bed while I emptied the delicious-smelling bags he'd brought in. Cartons of egg rolls, wonton soup, sesame chicken, and fried rice overtook the kitchen counter. I leaned over, rested my head next to the food, and said a lengthy and sincere prayer of thanks to Brody. The man knew that the way to my heart was through my stomach.

And it had been a very rough day, I told myself, justifying two servings of each dish. Actually, it was three servings of the fried rice, but that was hardly worth mentioning. Rice wasn't that bad for you. Plus, it had eggs and vegetables in it. The whole thing was practically an omelet.

As I waited for Brody, I checked my phone and saw I had two missed calls from Nash Dumont and a couple of texts. The vandal had struck again; incredibly, Nash had arrived at the theater to find the lobby crawling with ants. Every bottle of sticky simple syrup behind the bar had been poured over the counter.

I couldn't see the connection. A trashed dressing room, a slashed chair, a fire, and now this. Ants marching on Broadway. I shot Nash a quick text and told him I'd try to come by the theater the next day to start interviewing every actor and crew member. Then I flipped over my phone, not really caring what his response might be.

After Brody came down, I caught him up on everything that had happened.

"I'm so sorry I couldn't get away today. I know you're incredibly busy with your cases." Brody put together a much more restrained plate for himself. He joined me at the table and apologized again.

"It's fine. Grace is a thousand times more important than any case could ever be. I'm allowed to take a break from work when I need to. It's just in the past, I never felt like I had a good enough reason to do so. But things are different now. Family comes first." I tucked into the soup first, before it turned cold. "I swear, they put crack in this stuff. How can it be so good, every time?"

"It's the best. Listen, I've been thinking."

"Uh-oh. I never like anything that anyone ever says following that statement." I paused over my soup. "Are you about to spoil my dinner?"

"Hear me out. There're no kids in the canyon, sweetheart. And the elementary school has been slipping the last few years in comparison to its peers across the state. I've talked to a few friends with kids; they're pulling them out and enrolling them in the new wing at the Valley Academy." Brody chewed an egg roll thoughtfully, watching my reaction. "It's preschool through fifth grade."

He had to be joking, so I laughed. "We can't afford private school, let alone the VA. It's got to be what, six or seven grand a year."

"Nine, plus expenses." Brody moved on to his rice. "And you're right, we can't afford private school. Which gets me to my point. Don't we want Grace to grow up near other kids? Go to a good, solid public school?"

I set my spoon down, worried now. "What are you saying?"

"I think we should look at moving. If I get this promotion, I can work anywhere. You could easily get a job with the police in another town, maybe one with better pay and better benefits. You should be in a leadership position, Gemma. And Chavez isn't going anywhere." Brody reached across the table, gripped my hand. He paused at the dark look in my eyes, released my hand, then said, "Just think about it, honey. We don't have to decide right now. But we've got busy lives. Sooner or later, Grace will have friends. Are we going to drive up and down the canyon every weekend to parties, activities? Are we truly comfortable with the quality of education she'll get at CV Elementary?"

"Brody, these are huge, life-altering decisions. You can't just drop them in front of me over Chinese food and expect a quick answer. I mean, my God, you're talking about uprooting our whole lives. I can't leave Julia and Bull here to fend for themselves. We have responsibilities. I like where I work. I like my colleagues. I like this town, warts and all." I pushed my fork around my food, moodily stabbed a piece of chicken. "Of course I want what's best for Grace. I'm not oblivious; I always knew we'd have to move sooner or later to be close to a school, people her own age. But leave town? Where would we go?"

Brody shrugged. It was obvious he was disappointed that I wasn't as excited as he was. "Anywhere. Minnesota, Wisconsin. We could get a house half the cost of this one and three times the size. Better schools, lower crime. And we can take your grandparents with us. Of course we wouldn't leave them here."

I dropped my fork and buried my head in my hands. *"Minnesota?"*

"Okay, not the Midwest. How about Arizona? Or Utah?" Brody reached over again and patted my arm. "Eat up, honey. This was a bad time to bring this up. We can talk about it more later."

*We have to talk about this again??*

I sat up. "It's been a very long and draining day. You're right; let's talk later. And you eat up, too."

We went to bed shortly thereafter. In our bathroom, I washed and dried my face and brushed my teeth. Then I slipped a bare foot out of my house clog and gingerly touched the tile with my big toe. The floor was freezing and I quickly jammed my foot back into the warmth of the wool slipper. I'd bet a thousand dollars the floors in Minnesota were a hell of a lot colder.

# Chapter Nineteen

"Suzanne and Eleanor." Jimmy grinned as he repeated the names.

It was Tuesday, and early; I thought I was the first one in, but Jimmy beat me. He looked fresh as a daisy. I on the other hand felt heavy with fatigue and bloated from too much Chinese food. Luckily, Grace had already seemed markedly better and I felt comfortable leaving her with Clementine for the day.

"And they are?" I slipped off my coat and put my things away.

"Ives Farmington's two daughters. They're in their sixties, neither of them ever married. They live together, just a few blocks from here. They said you're welcome to stop by anytime." Jimmy paused, added, "They also invited me. I hate to intrude but I sort of feel like I should go with you. You know, since I tracked them down and made the initial contact?"

I was already pulling my jacket back on. "Come on. Maybe they're up and about."

The two Farmington sisters were not only up and about, but they were just starting in on a feast of a breakfast. Eggs, biscuits, gravy, bacon, and fresh fruit, along with hazelnut coffee and a pitcher of ice-cold orange juice, were laid out on an enormous dining room table, alongside elegantly patterned china, heavy silverware, and sparkling crystal goblets.

Suzanne, the elder sister, a tall, stately woman with white hair neatly pinned back, invited us to join them. Jimmy grinned. "You don't have to ask us twice. I bet Gemma could eat you both under the table. A spread like this is right up her alley."

"A skinny thing like you?" Eleanor reached over and pinched my arm, harder than I would have liked. Her eyes were huge behind the thick glasses she wore. She was half the height of her sister and three times as wide. Unruly gray curls sprung from her head in every direction. "I don't believe it. In fact, I've got some sweet rolls in the freezer. I should put them in the oven; they're just the thing to fatten you up."

"Please, we're fine. This will be plenty," I said, rubbing my arm and shooting a discreet but definitive glare in Jimmy's direction. "We'd like to ask you about your dad, Ives."

Suzanne smiled. "Now there was a one-of-a-kind guy. Talk about a hero; they just don't make them like that anymore. What specifically did you want to know?"

I set down my cup of coffee. "Did he ever talk about a man named Josiah Black?"

Eleanor coughed. She and her older sister stared at one other, some unspoken thought moving between them. Finally, Eleanor nodded to Suzanne, who responded with a deep sigh and a brief nod of her own.

Suzanne turned to me. "Dad died fifteen years ago from cancer. At that time, he said his greatest regret in life was not proving Josiah Black's innocence. *Of course* he talked about that man. In some ways, that was all he talked about. I exaggerate, but at least once a week, usually on Saturday evenings after he'd had a few beers, Daddy would get to talking about the war, and our mother, who passed away when we were just girls. He'd take these long strolls down memory lane and inevitably, the Black family name would come up."

"He felt just terrible about how Josiah and Millie had been treated," Eleanor added. "He said she'd been run out of town like a wolf who'd been in the sheep's pasture, but she was as much a sheep as anyone else in town. And Josiah had been the subject of a witch hunt, just like all those years ago in Salem."

"Why was your father so convinced Josiah was innocent?" I asked. "Was it just because they'd been friendly in school and then served together?"

Suzanne laughed and added another few slices of bacon to her plate. "Oh, heavens, no. In fact, it was the opposite. They hated each other. They were rivals, not friends. Sports, women, music . . . They were the two best-looking boys in town, the most athletic, the most popular. Cocaptains on the baseball team."

"So what was it, then?" Jimmy asked impatiently. He tore a biscuit in two and shoved half in his mouth. "These are delicious, by the way."

"Thank you, we make them from scratch. Dad was a good cop. He loved police work. Resigning from the force was the hardest thing he ever had to do. But he couldn't stay in a place that he felt had covered things up. He was convinced the targeting of the victims had nothing to do with the war and everything to do with corruption in Cedar Valley. All three of the victims—the doctor, the bank guard, and John Sven, the pub owner—had at one time or another been the subject of police investigations into illegal dealings. After the war, things here were like the Wild West. Widows were taken advantage of, financially and otherwise; businesses suffered."

I sat back, thinking. "And Ives believed the victims were killed by someone bent on revenge."

"Someone or some people. Dad never thought there was a single killer operating alone. He thought it more likely that a couple of men got together and decided to take matters into their own hands." Eleanor picked up the carafe. "More coffee?"

We declined. Jimmy said, "John Sven wasn't the only person killed at the pub that night. Eleven other people died, including his wife and brother. That's a lot of collateral damage."

Suzanne agreed. "The pub was closed to the public that night, as it always was on Mondays. But John Sven held a weekly private poker night in the back room for his friends. The killer must not have known about that."

"Tell her about the other thing," Eleanor prompted. "The 'incident.'"

"Something happened when Josiah and Dad were overseas. Dad said the two of them witnessed a commanding officer interrogating a Japanese prisoner of war. Things turned rough and after, when Josiah and Dad were back at their camp, Josiah was terribly ill, vomiting repeatedly." Suzanne paused, smoothed back an errant strand of hair. "Dad assumed it was a stomach virus, until Josiah explained that he abhorred violence, couldn't stand the sight of someone being hurt. Being involved with the war was slowly killing him, he said. Dad said it was that look in Josiah's eyes, more than anything, that convinced him all those years later that Josiah couldn't be a killer."

A few hours later, I hung up the phone and pushed back from my desk, my eyes bleary. I had a stack of notes, a lot of questions and fewer answers. On the screen in front of me was a map of Utah, specifically the border region and the canyon lands the state shared with Arizona, zoomed in to one small town in Utah: Harvey.

I'd spent the last thirty minutes on the phone with a feisty city clerk in Harvey and now I called Finn over to share what I'd learned. He looked relieved at the opportunity to step away from his own computer.

Jimmy, once again smelling blood in the water, meandered into the room and pulled up a chair behind me. The intern had a small bag of corn nuts in his hand and every few minutes, another terrific crack of his teeth against a nut had me cringing. I couldn't believe he was hungry; even I was still full from brunch with the Farmington sisters.

"Josiah Black was released from prison in 1995. He was

seventy-three years old, in relatively good health. He bummed around Cedar Valley for a few months, then made his way to Utah. Specifically, this tiny border town of Harvey." I pointed at the map on the monitor.

"Why Utah?" Jimmy asked. He cracked another nut on his molars and I resisted the strong urge to turn around and slap the bag from his hands.

"Josiah was trying to find his wife, Amelia. Millie. It appears that she fled Cedar Valley shortly after Black's trial and made her way southwest. She spent a number of years in Harvey, but the city clerk's files show that by 1970, she'd left town. The trail grows cold, but the clerk said she'd reach out to the post office and see if their records indicate a forwarding address." I checked my notes, doing the math. "So Amelia had been gone from Harvey for twenty-five years by the time Josiah Black arrived. Josiah must have run out of money then, or close to it, because he rented an apartment and took up employment at a gas station. He was only there a few months. This is how small Harvey is: the city clerk that I just spoke to was Josiah's landlord in the nineties. She remembers him well; he reminded her of her grandfather. Josiah talked a lot about his wife, the clerk said, and how he hoped to find her someday."

"So he stayed and worked long enough to earn funds to keep tracking Amelia and then he left?" Finn asked.

"No. Black died while hiking in the desert. He was caught in a flash flood, in a place called the Blue Rose Canyon; he drowned."

"Pretty name for a place to die," Jimmy said with another crunch and crack. "This is all fascinating, but how does knowing any of it help us catch Ghost Boy?"

I wasn't the only one who'd nicknamed the killer, it seemed. "I haven't told you the best part. The city clerk boxed up all of Josiah's belongings after his death. She's kept them in her storage unit all these years. She said she's always hoped someone would come asking about Josiah. She's going to get the box, call me back, and open it while I'm on the line."

"Great work, Gemma," Finn said and held up a sheaf of papers. "We've got wheels turning on the Mike Esposito murder as well; turns out old Mikey was quite busy, between his job, his softball league, and the marijuana grow house he kept on the north end of town."

I was surprised; the insertion of drugs into an investigation has the tendency to get nasty, fast. "Marijuana? How'd you discover that?"

"Moriarty got a tip. He's headed there now with a couple of officers. Depending on how much Esposito was growing, we could be looking at a drug deal gone bad. It's big business these days. Maybe Esposito's killer got word of the comic book left at the Montgomery scene and decided to throw us off the scent by planting a similar one at the bank," Finn replied. He shrugged. "Or maybe the house will turn out to be nothing. Couple of plants, a home hobby. But . . . if we find ties between a drug dealer and Judge Montgomery, well . . . heads are going to roll."

Jimmy smirked. "I've got friends that found jobs in Denver in the marijuana tourism industry. Some of them are making six figures. *And* they get free weed." He noticed our looks and quickly added, "Not that marijuana is my thing. Can't stand the smell. Never touched it. I told all my students to just say no."

I was about to respond when Renee, the city clerk in Harvey, called me back. I put her on speaker. She spoke slowly, knowing that I was taking notes. "There wasn't much in Josiah's box. A couple of paperback novels, and this funky old blue-and-white glass vase. He said his wife had made it for him and it was one of the few things he had left of her. The day he died, he'd left his wallet at home, so I've got that, too. There's a driver's license and some photographs inside. I donated his clothes to charity, hope you don't mind that. I did empty his pockets first but he was orderly; that must have been from his time overseas."

I paused in my note-taking to ask, "Did he talk much about his years in the service?"

"Oh, here and there it would come up. He never went into too many details, though; it seemed to make him sad. Okay, so, books, wallet, vase. Oh, he liked to collect arrowheads. He had about twenty or thirty. I've got them in the storage box, too. Someone might pay a few bucks for the collection."

"Renee, tell me about the photographs in his wallet. Can you take them out and describe them one at a time, please?"

"You bet. Okay, the first photograph is of a young woman and a man. The man is definitely Josiah, though he hardly looks older than twenty. This is a wedding portrait, so the woman must be Amelia."

I jotted down a few things. "Renee, is there a date on the photograph?"

"No, though judging by the fashion of their clothes, this was early 1940s."

"Great. How about the next photograph?" I asked.

The city clerk gasped. "Oh boy. Or . . . girl. I can't tell."

"What? What are you looking at?"

She was excited and spoke quickly, eager to aid in my investigation and put together the pieces of the life of the man she'd briefly known. "Well, there's a child. Amelia is holding a toddler! And there's a date on the back of this photograph; it says 1950. Well, I'll be. The baby must have been Josiah's. He never talked about a child, though he'd had to have known. He had the baby's picture in his wallet, after all."

I exhaled and sat back, feeling as though the wind had been knocked out of me.

Josiah and Amelia had a child together, born sometime after his trial. I thought back to the articles I'd read; the trial had been quick, his sentencing immediate. It was entirely possible that Amelia had been newly pregnant at the time of Josiah's arrest.

Then, after the trial, after a few more months of trying to live with the constant wrath of her neighbors, Amelia fled in search of peace and safety for herself and her unborn child.

I did the math; that child would now be in his or her late sixties. On the other end of the line, from somewhere deep in the
deserts of Utah, Renee was thinking the same thing. She muttered, "Little tyke would be a senior citizen now. Imagine that. Say,
you don't think the child has anything to do with your investigation, do you?"

"At this point, nothing is out of the realm of possibility."

"Oh!" Renee sounded as though she'd been electrocuted.
"Well, would you look at that. For heaven's sakes, there's another
baby!"

I sat up. "There were *two* babies? *Twins?*"

"No, no. The last photograph in Josiah's wallet is a picture
of a much older Amelia, a young woman, and a toddler on the
woman's lap. They're standing in front of an amusement park ride.
The young woman is the spitting image of Amelia. The back of the
photograph reads 'Christmas Eve, 1983. Grandma Millie, Debbie,
and Casey's first time to Disneyland.'"

So Josiah Black not only had a daughter, he had a grandchild
as well.

I glanced at Finn and Jimmy; the huge grins on their faces
must have matched mine. "You've struck gold, Renee. This is an
incredible break in our case."

"This is so exciting! I love a good mystery. Oh, I hear a fax coming in. That might be Amelia's last will and testament. I haven't
even told you about that yet. I tracked Amelia down to an itty-
bitty town in Texas on the coast. Poor dear, she died in the early
1990s; but bless her heart, she filed paperwork with the county a
few years before. I sweet-talked the clerk into faxing it over to me,"
Renee said.

"You are an angel, Renee."

"Okay, here we go . . . last will and testament, blah, blah, blah,
legalese, more legal speak. Ah-ha! Amelia Black left everything to
her only living child, one Debbie Jo Black of Seaport, Texas. Looks
like the whole family relocated there."

"This is wonderful, Renee. I can't thank you enough."

"As I said, it's my pleasure. I'll get this will, and the photographs, scanned and emailed to you. I know you're hot on the trail."

I hung up slowly, certain that what I'd expressed earlier was true: we were chasing down ghosts.

# Chapter Twenty

Finn, Jimmy, and I spent the next hour digging deep. I put Jimmy on tracking down Debbie Black, while Finn and I tossed around ideas. The thing was, not only were Debbie and Casey Black the only known connections we had to Josiah Black, they were also both potential suspects in the recent killings. Debbie would be in her late sixties; if Casey had been a toddler or infant in 1983, that would put him or her in their mid-to-late thirties.

Just a few years older than me.

*Debbie and Casey Black.*

Finn tossed a rubber stress ball up in the air and caught it, over and over, from the chair at his desk. "Josiah Black testified during his trial. But instead of focusing on an alibi or excuses, he used his time to talk about the suffering Amelia Black had endured since the moment he was arrested."

"Yes. That's why she fled town; she was practically chased out by crazed neighbors with pitchforks and torches. Can you imagine what kind of stories Debbie and then Casey grew up with? What resentments they might harbor toward this town?" I flipped to a section in Black's trial notes that I'd earmarked and read aloud: "'My wife has done nothing wrong. And yet she can no longer go to the market, or walk with her parents in the park. Perhaps worst of all, she has been let go from her position at the elementary school. Her life has been ruined.'"

Finn threw the ball in the air one last time, then caught it and slipped it in a drawer. "I feel for her, but Josiah, her husband . . . he caused all of this. He brought this down on the family himself. No matter what Ives Farmington believed, Black was the only suspect. Any pain that his actions caused his family rest with him."

"But Amelia didn't do anything."

Finn shrugged. "Collateral damage. Gemma, we see it all the time. Dad or Mom is incarcerated and generations suffer."

I started to respond when Louis Moriarty and Lucas Armstrong arrived. Moriarty slipped his jacket off and wiped his brow. "Why can't this shit ever be easy? Mike Esposito's grow house wasn't a house at all—it was an old Quonset hut that was locked from here to eternity. Took us an hour just to get the front door open. Not only that, but the house was a quarter-mile walk in off the main road. Need an ATV to get in there. Did we have an ATV with us? Of course not. So we hoofed it in, then back to get the bolt cutters, then back to the house, and so on. My feet are killing me."

Jimmy, still deep in his research on Debbie Black, said in a low voice, "Maybe you should think about retiring."

What Jimmy hadn't yet learned was that Moriarty's hearing was excellent, the best on the squad. The older cop turned a black eye to Jimmy and said in a low voice, "Maybe you should think about keeping that big mouth of yours shut, kid."

Jimmy's head snapped back to his computer, his eyes wide.

"What Lou is saying is true. Hell of a mess getting in. But, once we were inside . . . Esposito was supplying someone, some-where, with a heck of a lot of weed. He wasn't dealing himself; town this size, we'd have known about it. It was a slick operation; generators for power, top-of-the-line lighting system. There's a lot of money in cannabis growing. I heard wholesale can get up to four grand a pound." Armstrong slipped off his own jacket, loosened his collar. Half-moons of sweat stained the armpits of his otherwise immaculate white dress shirt. "Esposito's murder might have been a hit after all."

I shook my head. "That doesn't explain the comic book connection. And we know that Josiah Black also targeted First Pillar for his second crime."

Moriarty and Armstrong wore identical looks of confusion. I started the whole story over again, beginning with my email to Aimee Corn and ending with the latest: that while Josiah's wife had passed, there was a chance both their child and grandchild were still living.

Armstrong went to the board and tapped first the photograph of Caleb Montgomery's burned body, then the photograph of the pool of scarlet blood on the pink marbled floor of First Pillar Bank and Trust. "You're telling me this has been done before?"

At that moment, Maggie Armstrong enter the squad room. "Hey, Dad."

Armstrong moved quickly, hoping to intercept her before she got too close to our murder board, but he wasn't quite quick enough. She gaped at the crime scene photographs, fixating on the bloody holes in Mike Esposito's back.

"Ah, Mags, you should have waited up front." Armstrong put his hand on her shoulder, tried to turn her away from the gruesome images, but she was rooted in place.

"I had to use the restroom," she said in a low voice. "These are . . . horrible. What kind of a monster could do this to another human being?"

Armstrong yanked at the curtains that hung from the ceiling, in place specifically for this reason, but the fabric got stuck on the rod, and did little to cover our notes.

"No, don't try to protect me. If I'm going to go into law, these are the sorts of things I have to get used to seeing." Maggie's big brown eyes widened. "How do you live with it, all of it?"

She looked around at us, stopping at me. "How?"

I thought about the cases I'd worked over the years, the victims and their families, their friends. The loved ones left behind. I swallowed and gave her the only answer I had. "One day at a time, Maggie. One day at a time."

On the way home, I decided to pay another visit to Bull. I owed him an update on the case and it would be good to get his insight on the Josiah Black angle. I found him in his study, sipping from a tumbler of whiskey, an old black-and-white murder mystery on the television, a photo album in his lap.

He was happy to see me, though the room had an air of melancholy about it and I knew we weren't alone. Bull was sitting amongst the ghosts of old friends. Maybe he was on his way to becoming one himself; his eyes were tired, his face pale in the reflection of the television.

I told him about the Josiah Black crimes, the robbery and killing at First Pillar. My sense that somehow, an evil presence had been summoned to our town.

Bull sighed. "Perhaps it never left. There's something wrong with Cedar Valley, Gemma. I think most people know it; they just don't like to dwell on it. Much easier to turn a blind eye and go about the day, never acknowledging the terrors that run beneath our feet like sewer water."

"Isn't it like that in most places? All the towns in the valley were built by greed and heartache; pillage and murder. I've heard it said that as the buildings on Main Street went up, the blood of miners and builders ran down the streets like so much rainwater. And all the while, the founders, those old men we've all so quaintly taken to calling the Silver Foxes, smiled and counted their coin." I sat back, took a sip of Bull's whiskey. "Anyway. How are you holding up? I didn't get to talk to you very much at Caleb's memorial service."

Bull shrugged and drew his thin red cardigan tighter against his chest. "I've been thinking about France."

"France? As in Paris, France?"

"Provence, specifically. After your grandmother passes, which

God willing won't be for many more years, I think it would be a good idea to get out of the country. I've always wanted to visit Provence, ever since I was a little boy and read about it in a history book. There won't be much keeping me here at that point, Gemma. Oh, I know, you and Brody and Grace are here. But you're busy with your own lives. You don't need to spend your precious free time entertaining an old coot." Bull paused, finished his whiskey, glanced at me. "I didn't even offer you a drink."

"Don't change the subject. Bull, this is the first I've heard of your plans. We enjoy seeing you. I'd like Grace to grow up knowing you." Though I tried to hide it, I was shaken. My grandparents had been the grounding force in my life for years. As a child and teenager, it was them I'd always aimed to please; it was their smiles and praises I'd loved to earn.

And as an adult, it was to them that I went for wisdom and advice, for reassuring hugs no matter how bad it got, how gravely I messed up. The thought of Bull and Julia no longer being nearby was deeply unsettling.

They were both still here and I was already grieving.

I thought of something important. "You hate foreign food. You'll starve to death in France."

Bull chuckled. "I'm fairly certain that if push came to shove, I could survive on bread and cheese and wine. You know, you could come visit. All of you. I've been looking online at rentals; they've got these gorgeous old farmhouses for pennies on the dollar. Grace would love the lavender fields."

"You're really serious, aren't you? I can't deal with this right now. Listen, there's something else I wanted to ask you about. I met Rose Underhill the other day." I paused, watching for his reaction. To my surprise, he went pale.

"Now there's a name I haven't heard in a long time."

"She insinuated that at one time, you two were quite close."

Bull massaged the back of his neck. "I suppose you could say that. We were . . . friends."

"The sheriff said I should ask you about Red Dalton."

Bull suddenly stood, the photo album in his lap falling to the ground with a sharp thump. "What else did she say?"

Startled, I leaned back. A look of fury, and something else, something that appeared to be panic, had risen in his eyes. "Nothing. That was it. She had sort of a funny smile on her face and just said to ask you about it."

Bull sighed and clicked off the movie. He moved slowly to the study door. "I'm tired, sweetheart. I think I'll lie down for a while. I haven't been sleeping well."

"That's it? That's all I get?"

He gave me a brief, sad smile. "Good night, sweetheart. Drive safely. And if you see Rose Underhill again, please, don't trust a word she says."

# Chapter Twenty-One

**Wednesday dawned and with it, the unsettling sense that I'd never** see the sun again. In my mind, the coming darkness of winter, with its short days and longer nights, seemed to stretch on to the end of time. As I made breakfast and fed Grace, I tried to shake the unease that had settled over me. I knew some of it stemmed from the fact that we were rapidly approaching the seventy-year anniversary of the terrible fire at John Sven's pub, and that a copy-cat killer aimed to somehow re-create the massacre. I was also still unsettled by my visit with Bull. The man I thought of as an open book appeared to have secrets of his own.

A gentle snow fell as I drove down the canyon. The powdery flakes should have been comforting, cleansing. Instead the snow seemed to smother all that it touched, as though winter could only exist once everything around it had died.

At the station, Finn intercepted me in the lobby. "I just asked Liv to come in for an interview."

"Right now? Okay. Let me put my things down." I headed to my desk, Finn at my side. "Has something happened?"

"Not exactly. Well, yes." Finn looked at the ground, the ceiling, anywhere but at me. "I slept with her last night."

"I need to know this?"

"We stayed at her house. I felt like a damn teenager, sneaking up Moriarty's garage steps to her rental. Anyway, afterwards, she fell asleep. I was up late, watched some shows. But she's got all these books around her living room, journals and sketch pads." Finn rubbed his face. "Personal things."

"Please don't tell me you took a look at them."

"I took a look at them."

Groaning, I sat down. "What were you thinking? You shouldn't be poking around her things. If she's innocent, it's a disgusting invasion of privacy. And if she's guilty, anything you found will be inadmissible in court."

"You think I don't know all that? Jesus."

I let him stew another minute, then asked, "What did you find?"

Finn pulled his phone from his back pocket and pulled up a series of photos. "Liv is an artist. She sketches, mostly pencil, some ink. Look at these drawings."

I took in the art. It was incredibly detailed; detailed and creative. Ramirez had taken various comic book superheroes and placed them, as older individuals, into scenes of everyday life, where their superpowers had little or no importance.

She'd drawn Batman with a welding mask on, lifted to reveal a sweat-soaked brow, a broken-down Batmobile at his side. In another scene, a pregnant Wonder Woman stood in line at a grocery store, a couple of babies in her shopping cart and another pulling at her lasso. She flicked through a tabloid, the look on her face equal parts boredom and grief. A third sketch showed Superman on the floor, a limp dog in his arms, tears streaking down his face. Standing above the sobbing superhero was a veterinarian, a long syringe in his hands, a sympathetic look in his eyes.

They went on like that, dozens of sketches. Each seemed to ask and say the same thing: *How did I get here? What happened to my life? I was a big deal once.*

Finn put his phone away slowly. "See what I mean?"

"You did the right thing, calling her in."

He was quiet a moment. "I like her, Gemma. I like her quite a bit." He started to say more, but the desk sergeant rang, announcing her arrival.

Finn smiled grimly. "Showtime."

We sat with her in a small room used for interviews and interrogations. Ramirez refused to look at Finn and was frosty, cold, even, with me. She wore a black turtleneck sweater and dark jeans, with steel-toed boots. With her hair down, loose around her shoulders, and her green-gold eyes flashing with anger, she looked like a softer, more vulnerable version of herself. She'd brought Fuego, and the dog lay at her feet, softly whining.

"Why am I here?"

"We need to ask you a few questions. About the Caleb Montgomery and Mike Esposito killings." I opened my notebook and turned to a fresh page. Ramirez watched me with disdain in her eyes, though I noticed her hands were tightly wound together as if to keep from shaking. "As our investigation has progressed, as you know, we've narrowed our suspect list down to someone with military experience, especially sniper and explosives work. We now believe the killer or killers are re-creating the crimes of a man named Josiah Black, who was convicted of multiple murders in the 1940s. In addition, we believe the killer models him or herself after Ghost Boy."

"Who?" Ramirez asked, a confused look on her face.

"Ghost Boy is a comic book supervillain, a double agent who is skilled in martial arts."

She sat back, a disgusted look on her face. Still not acknowledging Finn's presence in the room, she said, "Last night, I made the tremendous mistake of having sex with a colleague. Finn Nowlin. I believe you know him? When I woke this morning, it was obvious he'd gone through my things. He's sloppy in more ways than one. That's really why I'm here, isn't it? He saw my art, my *private* art, and now you guys think I'm a maniac killer."

"Then help us. Help us understand these connections you have to our case," Finn pleaded. I'd never seen the look in his eyes before; it was one of humble penitence. "I'm truly sorry for what I did. It wasn't right and you have every reason to hate me. But you have to understand, we're trying to prevent a massacre."

"I don't have to understand anything. Also? You're terrible in bed." Ramirez turned away, stared at the wall. Under the table, I kicked Finn. When he looked at me, I mouthed, *Get out of here*.

He sighed quietly and left, closing the door gently behind him.

"Liv? Finn's gone. It's just the two of us. Please. I know you didn't kill Caleb Montgomery or Michael Esposito. Is there someone, perhaps from your past, that could be involved? A partner, a former soldier you knew overseas?" My questions were cautious, stated calmly. Liv Ramirez was giving off every signal in the book that any minute now, she, too, would bolt from the room.

"Liv? Talk to me. The sooner you do, the sooner you can go."

Finally, she turned and met my gaze. She sighed deeply, unclenched her hands. "I was really tired when I arrived in Cedar Valley. I'd driven all night from Las Vegas, just Fuego and I, a couple of suitcases and my art supplies in the trunk of my car. As my chief in Vegas explained, Max Teller owed him a favor and if I wanted it, there was a job in Colorado with my name on it. I liked Vegas, I truly did, until I didn't."

"What happened in Vegas?"

Fuego whined again. Ramirez leaned down, scratched his head. "A couple of buddies of mine from Iraq were passing through. We met up at a bar after my shift ended. I knew them well, or at least I thought I did. But they'd brought some other friends, guys I didn't know. Anyway, by midnight, there were five of them. I was careful, watching how much I drank. Someone, I don't know who, slipped something into my margarita when I stepped away to use the restroom. I woke up the next morning, covered in bruises, in some shitty hotel room off the strip."

"You'd been raped?"

Ramirez nodded. "Raped, beaten, and robbed. The assholes stole three hundred dollars from my purse. The worst part was it wasn't the first time. I'd been attacked, twice before, in Iraq. Each time I reported it to my commanding officer and each time, nothing was done. You'd be surprised at the 'boys will be boys' mentality still entrenched in the military. Or maybe not. Maybe you've experienced it yourself."

I met her stare. "Nothing like that. Did you report the crimes in Vegas?"

Ramirez nodded. "Yes. The guys were long gone by then. I don't know how seriously the Vegas cops looked for them. I took a day off from work, then went in hot and furious. I was pissed at the world. I wanted someone else to hurt as badly as I did. I let it get to me and I did something stupid."

She paused, took another deep breath, and smiled. "His name was John Dervy. We called him Pervy Dervy because he was a fat old pig of an engineer on our crew, always leering at women, making disgusting jokes. We were at a simulation and I got my hands on the fire hose. I turned it on Dervy full blast, right in the nuts. He went down screaming. It took four guys to get that hose away from me. God, it felt good."

I had to smile, too. Although I rarely advocated violence, it was satisfying to hear Ramirez kick at the establishment, one perv at a time.

She continued. "After that, my chief wasn't too happy with me. I think he was mostly pissed because I was a good, solid team player, but he couldn't keep both Dervy and me on. And Dervy had seniority while I was the hothead busted with a hose in my hand. So a week later, I was here, tired and exhausted and about ready to throw in the towel." Ramirez straightened up, her eyes blazing with emotion. "Then things started happening; good things. I found a sweet little rental. Fire Chief Teller turned out to be awesome. And this town is beautiful. I'd never spent so much time in the mountains. I always thought of myself as a beach gal, but these peaks, they're something else. Why would I risk all of that to copy the crimes of some old guy I've never even heard of?"

She was right, of course. Absolutely nothing she'd done to this point was indicative of a murderer. I took a deep breath and said, "I'm so sorry, about all of it. The last thing I want to do is make you feel even more persecuted than you've been."

Ramirez said, "I served in the military, with honor. You will *never* understand the sacrifices our troops make so that you can live in the land of the free. And yes, I've earned a black belt after hours, hours, of practice and further sacrifice. As for the comic books? I had a learning disability when I was younger. I struggled with reading. A librarian at my elementary school introduced me to comic books. She taught me how to enjoy books; she saved my life that way. How do you think I survived Iraq? Fiction. Stories. Comics. Drawing. I poured my anxiety and my pain and my anger into those things. And now you're holding all of that against me."

My face was on fire by the time she finished; I couldn't remember being more embarrassed in my professional life than at that moment. Finn's reckless actions had put me into a baseless confrontation with not a superhero, but an ordinary woman who was using every tool at her disposal to simply get through the day. She was a thousand times more impressive than any superhero.

Lamely, I tried to appeal my case. "You're an investigator; you know the drill. I had to ask."

"Not like this, you didn't. I shouldn't have expected that we might be friends." Ramirez leaned back and stared at the table, a scornful expression on her face.

I was sorely disappointed. If we hadn't questioned her, we wouldn't have been doing our jobs, and yet she was right; it didn't have to go down like this. I was sorry she'd had to relive her trauma; sorry she'd had to lay bare her past in order for me to understand her present. And sorry that in all likelihood, I wouldn't be part of her future. In the short time I'd gotten to know her, I too had thought we could become friends. Maybe even good friends. And that was something I was missing in my life: strong female friends that I could both respect and learn from.

Ramirez pushed back from the table. "Are we done here?"

I nodded. "You've done a great job with the investigation. I respect your skills tremendously."

"Yeah, sure. Fuego, come." The dog followed his master out of the room, with me trailing behind them. In the hallway, Finn straightened up from the wall where he'd been leaning. Ramirez paused in front of him.

Fuego looked up at Finn and pulled his lips back in an angry snarl, then let out a short, quick bark.

My God, even the dog hated him.

Ramirez stared Finn in the eyes. "Was any of it real? Or did you just use me for your investigation?"

Before he could answer, she slapped him, hard, against the cheek. "See you around, Francis."

She walked away, her long dark hair swinging behind her, matching her angry strides.

I said to Finn in a low voice, "Consider yourself lucky. She could have knocked your head against that wall and I, for one, wouldn't have stopped her."

But my partner ignored me, instead staring after Liv Ramirez, a hangdog look in his eyes and a bright red palm print on the side of his face.


Finn and I sat with the team and went over everything, from the beginning: the death threats Caleb had received and his murder; our trips to Bishop and Belle Vista; the robbery and killing at First Pillar; all of it. On the conference room table were copies of the investigative reports into Josiah Black; his arrest and trial records; copies of newspaper articles covering the crimes; and finally, all the paperwork, photographs included, that Renee, the clerk in Utah, had faxed to me.

Also on the table was a red-and-white-striped box of doughnut holes. Someone else had brought in a bag of clementine oranges. The fruit sat untouched as the doughnut holes dwindled, though

I knew if we were in here long enough, eventually one of us would cave and then we'd all follow suit.

Occasionally someone would pick up a transcript, or stare at a photograph, praying that something new would jump out. But nothing did, and the collective mood was glum and anxious. Only Jimmy maintained a steady level of excitement, and I had to admit I knew what he was feeling; it was akin to being in the air mid-dive, feet off the ground, body high up, not yet in the water. It was the same feeling I got when I was deep in the belly of a twisting, complicated case.

But this case, this one, it was too personal, too twisty. I felt nothing but a sense of despair in my chest.

Moriarty leaned forward and rested his forearms on the table. "What about the father? Casey Black's dad?"

"We have no idea who he is. Jimmy tracked down a birth certificate and the name of the father was left blank. I think we can assume that Casey, who is male, by the way, was born out of wedlock." I reached for the last doughnut in the box. It was chocolate, with orange sprinkles, and I quickly popped it in my mouth before anyone could object. "Jimmy did great; he stayed late and found out quite a bit. Jimmy, why don't you share the rest?"

The intern stood and slipped his hands into the pockets of his camo-patterned jacket. "In 1990, just before her mother, Amelia, died, Debbie Black rented a house in Seaport, Texas. She worked days at a dry cleaner and nights at a bar. And she enrolled Casey Black in the local school system. But Debbie wasn't happy. She'd spent too many years looking for a home of her own, listening to Amelia spill poison about Cedar Valley, telling her to never trust anyone. A lot of this is conjecture, by the way, but I think it's close to accurate. Bottom line is that Debbie took her own life during Casey's senior year of high school."

As we sat back and absorbed the tragic story, Armstrong caved first and pulled a clementine from the bag. As he peeled the fruit, the smell of citrus began to fill the room and I found myself wondering if oranges were grown in Texas. Had Debbie Black stood at her kitchen sink, morning after morning, washing dishes and looking out at citrus groves?

Or was Seaport actually on the coast? Had her view been one of blue on blue, sky on ocean?

Had that been the last thing she'd seen on the day she died?

I couldn't fathom taking my own life, especially now that I had a child . . . but my tragedies, my losses, were different than those of Amelia and Debbie Black. Though I'd grown up without parents, I'd been raised with love, in a loving home. This was my home, my town; it grounded and centered me.

Amelia, and Debbie by proxy, must have felt like refugees; forced to leave their home to escape persecution, never to go back.

"How did Debbie kill herself?" Armstrong asked.

"She rented a small boat and took it out in the harbor. When night fell, she still hadn't returned. It was two days before they found the boat, drifting out at sea. Inside, they found ropes and bricks. They never did find Debbie's body." Jimmy paused, swallowed. "Cops didn't suspect foul play; Debbie went out on the water alone, the harbormaster and the manager at the rental company both swore to that. A couple of days later, they found a suicide note in Debbie's personal effects."

The thought of Debbie Black picking up brick after brick and tying them to her body, then slipping from the boat down into the dark, cold depths of the Gulf waters was too gruesome to bear.

"And Casey?" Chief Chavez asked. "What happened to him?"

Jimmy continued. "Casey soon graduated high school and enlisted in the military the next day. This morning, Gemma sent an urgent request to the National Personnel Records Center in St. Louis. Turnaround time could be two days, though they're going to try to get it to us sooner."

"Get what? His military records?" Moriarty asked.

I nodded. "The trail goes cold after Seaport. We've been unable to locate a Casey Black with that birthdate and Social Security number anywhere in the U.S. But if we can determine where Casey was sent, if he was deployed overseas or stationed in another state, we're that much closer to tracking him down."

Chief Chavez rubbed at his jaw. "And we're sure that's where we should be expending our energy?"

"Yes," Finn said. We'd spent a long time talking about this. "These are the facts: someone is re-creating Josiah Black's crimes. That someone is comfortable with explosives and weapons. He didn't flinch when he shot Mike Esposito. Now we discover Black's grandson has military experience. The kid's mom took her own life. He has all the reason in the world to hate this town. He's our best, and only, suspect."

Jimmy jumped back in. "And the comic book is the icing on the cake. The Ghost Boy character debuted the year Casey Black was born. At his core, Ghost Boy is a soldier who believes the world owes him something. He's a big baby, really . . . his dramatic allegiances to evil armies, his disguises. A real man would come out, show himself, and fight an honorable fight. But our killer, like Ghost Boy, slinks around in costumes. The comics he leaves behind are his calling card."

"Do we have a photograph of Casey?" Moriarty asked. He too went for a clementine, though he bit into it and peeled it with his teeth. "Might help if we knew what the kid looked like."

"I'm hoping the military records can provide one. We've left a message with the DMV in Seaport; they may have a copy of his driver's license photo still on file. We also tried the high school. Tragically, it burned to the ground a few days after Casey graduated, taking with it all the archived yearbooks. We've sent a request to the principal; perhaps there's a teacher or administrator still around with yearbooks of their own. At this point, anything would help. All we've got is the picture of Casey with his mother and grandmother at Disneyland, and all *that* tells us is that Casey is Caucasian with brown eyes." I paused, looked over the room. "In other words, Josiah Black's grandchild, who is now an adult, could be anyone . . . anywhere."

Finn added, "There are signs the fire at Casey's school was a deliberate act of arson. He's been comfortable with flames, with fire, for a long time."

Chief Chavez sighed and leaned forward. "Talk to us about the 1948 crimes. Who got hurt and why."

Finn stood up, began pacing the room. "The first target was the doctor, then the bank guard, then the people in the tavern, specifically the owner. In all three instances, the prosecution argued that Josiah Black's victims were people he blamed for the suffering he'd endured during World War II."

Moriarty ran a hand through his thick white hair. "So the next hit is a bar."

I said, "Not necessarily. Our modern killer didn't target a doctor. Instead, he killed the son of the judge who presided over Josiah Black's trial. The location of the killing was off by about a half mile. In this instance, the victim was more important than the absolute re-creation of the original killing. However, with Mike Esposito's death, it's the opposite; the location becomes the driving factor: First Pillar Bank and Trust. The victim doesn't matter, as long as it's a guard."

"So what Gemma's saying is that the third attack, which we believe to be imminent, could be either victim-based or location-based. Not only that, but this town's roots go deep. There are folks here, our neighbors, friends, whose relatives are the people pictured in the angry mob outside Josiah Black's trial." Finn paused, took a deep breath. "What I'm saying is that for all we do know, we have no way of knowing where the killer will strike next."

After a moment, Moriarty quietly asked, "And the theater?"

I looked at him. "What about it?"

"Oh, come on. The Shotgun Playhouse will open its doors tomorrow night to the public, for the first time in over a hundred

years. It's a sold-out crowd. Doesn't that seem like an obvious target for the creep?" Moriarty sat back, crossed his legs, and folded
his arms. "You're friendly with Nash Dumont, Gemma. Get him to
reschedule the grand opening."

"I'm hardly friendly with him. I know him and his wife very
superficially. He's not going to budge. Opening night, the play . . .
his reputation is at stake."

Moriarty turned to Armstrong. "Lucas, your own daughter will
be on that stage. You're okay with that?"

"No, I'm not." Armstrong shook his head, troubled. "But Maggie's
an adult. I can't lock her in her room. Besides, if the theater is the
target, pushing back opening night won't make any difference. The
killer will simply wait until the later date, then strike. I think a better approach is to get every available cop in this valley on board. All
hands on deck, Chief. We run patrols at the theater, do bag and
purse checks. We can move in metal detectors. There's no way this
punk gets through us."

Jimmy said, "However . . . thus far, the killer has stuck to
Black's schedule, with attacks roughly five days apart. If the theater is the target and we keep its doors closed, the killer may move
on to another location anyway, to stick with his timetable. He
won't want to delay."

"So is it the date or the location that's important?" Moriarty
groaned. "This is like playing poker with the three blind mice.
All bets are good; all bets are bad. Doesn't matter what the cards
show; there's no one around to see them."

I bit my lip. "If we direct our efforts on the theater, and we're
wrong, then we risk leaving the rest of the town defenseless. And
I just don't think the theater is the target. The Shotgun Playhouse
closed its doors well before Josiah Black's time. There's no connection to him, no link to his crimes or his personal life."

We fell silent after that. Long minutes later, Chief Chavez
said, "What I don't understand, and what I think is critical *to* understand, is why now? What's happened to bring this son of a bitch

forward? Sure, we're at the seventy-year anniversary of the original crimes. But his crimes, they're history."

"No. Not to the killer, they're not." I looked around the room, briefly stopping at each person on the team. "To him, they're personal. They're everything."

We broke after that. Moriarty and Armstrong decided to pore through Black's records and the articles on him once more, this time looking for any mention of something or someplace that might be especially personal to Black, someplace that could be a potential target. In the meantime, Finn and Jimmy would check the names in the same articles and records, to see if there was anyone still in town that might be a relation to, say, the arresting officer or jury members.

I would have joined them, but Edith Montgomery called and asked me for an update on the case. I reached her house in the late afternoon, once more parking on the street and walking down the driveway, now clear of the leaves that had been there the week before. The snow had stopped falling, although the air remained frigid.

"We can talk in the library; I've got a fire going." She gestured for me to follow her and I did, our footsteps echoing on the floor. "It's as though frost has settled in my bones. Maybe it's in my soul."

"Where's Tom?"

She said in a low voice, "He's around here somewhere. I think he's having a midlife crisis. Our mother always did coddle him. I think it made him soft, if you know what I mean. Truth be told, I'm looking forward to him leaving soon. He can be a bit . . . dramatic. It's wearing on me."

Inside the library, a fire roared. Edith offered me a brandy, which I declined. She shrugged. "Suit yourself." She poured herself a generous amount, neat, into a crystal snifter.

We took seats in two plush armchairs that were set back a

comfortable distance from the fireplace. Edith had left the ceiling lights off, preferring instead to turn on only a few side table lamps. Though the fire was bright, and Edith pleasant, the room felt heavy with gloom.

Gloom, and regret.

"Are you making progress on finding my husband's killer? It's been over a week. Surely you've found something."

"Yes." I told Edith what I could, watching as her face registered shock and horror as I recounted Josiah Black's crimes. She gasped when I explained that Henry Montgomery had been the judge at Josiah Black's trail. "You're saying that's why Caleb was killed? Because of something that crazy old man did?"

"I take it you weren't a fan."

Edith nodded emphatically. "Henry Montgomery was a punitive son of a bitch who made life hell for Caleb. Henry even went so far as to proposition me on my wedding night; he asked why I was content to be with the boy when I could have the man. Can you imagine? He was disgusting. I was thrilled when he dropped dead of a massive stroke. And though he'd never admit it, I know Caleb was happier after his father was gone."

From my purse, I pulled out the photograph that Gloria Dumont had given me, of a young Caleb and his father, Judge Henry Montgomery. Silently, I handed it to Edith and watched as her eyes filled with tears.

She stroked Caleb's face. "Where did you find this?"

"Caleb gave it to Gloria Dumont when he retired. He wanted her to have it, said she should have it as a reminder to always keep the law on her side. He also mentioned something about wanting to atone for the sins of his father." I paused, thinking about everything I'd read on the Josiah Black trial. "It's not obvious that Black was guilty. Could Henry Montgomery have done something to ensure a conviction?"

Edith set the photograph in her lap and wiped her eyes. After a moment, she nodded. "As I understand it, there was a lot of corruption back in those days. In many ways, Cedar Valley was the Wild, Wild West. From what I've read and heard, it was like that all over the country. You had these young, and older, men and some women who'd been away during the war. Then they returned, changed. Scarred by their time in the service, by the things they'd seen and had to do. It's my belief that some people, even those too old to enlist, those who'd remained behind, like Henry Montgomery, were changed by the war. We're all part of one big quilt, Gemma. A few loose threads here, a small tear there, we might not notice it. Not right away. But eventually, we all feel it."

I wasn't totally following Edith. She'd finished the brandy by then and in her eyes, an amber glow seemed to burn. It was the haze of someone on the edge of tipsy.

Then she perked back up. "Oh! Do you remember, you were asking about that torn photograph you found in Caleb's hotel room?"

I nodded, and she went to a nearby bookshelf and returned with an album. I flipped through it, once more taking in the images of the expensive Southern wedding. I paused a moment on a picture of the beaming bride and happy groom with their parents, noting Henry Montgomery's predatory gaze at his son's new bride.

I moved on, finally coming to the last picture in the album. It was Edith, a young Tom Gearhart, and Caleb. Tom's arm was draped around their shoulders, a heavy ring visible on his hand.

Tom was the person who'd been ripped out of the photograph.

Even more surprising was the fact that Tom, who could not have been older than twenty or twenty-one years in the picture, was in Marine Corps dress blues.

"Tom served?"

Edith nodded. "Oh yes. He was in the Middle East for a spell, then was injured in a roadside bombing. He was brokenhearted about it, but I suppose everything happens for a reason. He made his way to Hollywood after that and well, the rest is history."

I swallowed, aware of how quiet the house suddenly seemed. "Can you call him? Ask him to join us for a moment?"

Edith looked surprised but nodded. "Of course." She went to a sideboard, where a discreet house phone was set into the corner. She picked up the phone, murmured a few words into it, then hung up.

She returned to me and poured herself another brandy. "Tom will be down in a moment."

I sat with my hands in my lap, my heart thudding. Had we been completely thrown off track by learning of Josiah Black? Was there something else going on here? Why hadn't Finn and I questioned Edith and Tom after we'd learned of her run-in with Michael Esposito in Belle Vista?

Moving silently, Tom appeared in the doorway. He slunk into the room and made his way to the brandy. His mood was surly, his only acknowledgment of me a brief nod. Gone was the showman, the bright actor. In his place was a hungover man who smelled of stale cigarette smoke.

I walked the album over to him and flipped it open to the photograph in question. He stared down at it, then looked up at me. "Yeah?"

"Were you Marine Corps?"

"First Battalion, Third Marines. I was stationed in Afghanistan," Tom stammered. A faint blush bloomed across his throat. "I was discharged, honorably, of course, for an injury I sustained in the course of duty."

"What kind of work did you do over there?"

"A little bit of this, a little of that. Look, why are you asking me about my time in the service? What does that have to do with the price of tea in China? Why haven't you caught Caleb's killer yet?"

I decided to take a chance. "Tom, we're looking for a killer with a military background. Possibly a man about your age. Someone who had access to Caleb; knew his habits, his routine. Someone who is comfortable with costumes, disguises."

A log in the fireplace fell and the three of us jumped. The flames leaped up and out, then resettled. Tom paled. "You can't think . . . It's impossible. I didn't have anything to do with Caleb's death." He turned to Edith, who wore an equally shocked look on her face, the color high in her cheeks.

She took a step toward us, her hands balled into fists.

"What did you do?" she hissed and shot a glance toward the fireplace, where a set of brass pokers rested against the brick.

"Edith, stop right there. Please don't take another step." I held an arm up, willing her to freeze. Then I turned back to Tom. His face was full of confusion. But he wasn't looking at me. He was staring at his older sister.

"Edie, my God, how could you think I had anything to do with your husband's murder? Look, I wasn't in the Marine Corps, okay? They wouldn't take me. I made the whole thing up. I moved to Charleston when I was nineteen and faked letters home. You could say it was the start of my acting career." Tom seemed to veer between embarrassment and pride. "It was a rather clever and crafty scheme."

Edith swayed with disbelief. "Thomas. How could you? Your mother and our dad were so proud."

"And that's exactly why I had to keep the lie going. You were the golden child. You could never do anything wrong. Do you know, the first time Dad ever said he was proud to call me his son was after I told him I enlisted." Tom went to Edith, but she moved away and perched on the edge of an armchair, shakily pulling a pack of cigarettes from her jacket pocket.

"How did you keep the lie going for so long?" she demanded. "I have letters from you, postmarked from the Middle East."

"Oh, that was easy. I had so many friends there. I'd send them packages that included sealed letters I asked them to send back for me. No one questioned it." Tom shrugged. "After a while, the lie just became a part of who I was."

I was frustrated to once again find myself with a possible lead only to have it dashed to pieces. "So just to be clear, Tom, you don't have *any* military experience?"

He shook his head vigorously. "No. Though I have played a number of soldiers on the big screen. I was the sergeant who appeared as a witness for the defense in *The Glorious Fall* . . . You may have seen it?"

"No, I missed that one."

I left Edith and Tom still bickering in the library and let myself out.

It was dark by then and I walked with the moonlight my only illumination. As I approached my car, I suddenly stopped. I was ten feet away. The driver's side door was ajar, and a man sat in my seat, hunched over, doing something with, or under, the steering wheel. I saw by the dome light that he was a decent size and weight, solid, with a dark hooded sweatshirt pulled up over his head.

Slowly, silently, I withdrew my weapon from the harness on my hip. With the utmost care and stealth, I clicked the safety off and took a wide-legged stance, both hands painfully gripped around the gun; hands that were still healing, tender to the touch.

I said a silent prayer as I exhaled that they were hands that still knew how to do the job, if it came to that.

"Freeze! Put your hands on your head, now, now!" I shouted. Inside the car, the man flinched and then went very still. "Hands on your head, do it, right now!"

Still the man refused to move. We were at an impasse. I could hardly shoot a man in the back simply for breaking into my car, and yet the longer he went without obeying my command, the closer we got to a dangerous point.

I tried again, shouting louder. "This is the Cedar Valley Police Department. Move your ass, right now."

Slowly, the man lifted first his left hand and then his right. He placed them on the top of his head and backed out of the car.

"Turn around."

The man turned and I gasped when I saw his face. Under the

hood, he wore a latex mask of a stitched face. Sutures in neat X's crossed his eyes, and his mouth was sewn shut by a dozen more. Around the sutures, bruises competed with dried blood.

I swallowed, hard. "Take off the mask."

The man shook his head and I lowered the gun so that it pointed dead center on his chest. "Take off the goddamn mask. Slowly."

With a reluctant nod, he put his right hand on the left side of his face and began to tug the rubber from his skin. I loosened my grip and then, impossibly, an enormous brown bat flew down in front of me, close enough for me to feel the beat of its leathery wings against the cold night air. It shrieked and darted around my face. Startled, I stepped back with a cry and swung at the air with my hands, gun still firmly gripped in both.

From the corner of my eye, I saw the man bolt. By the time I'd stepped away from the bat and made it into the street, he was gone. I turned in a slow circle, gun raised again, my heart thudding a million miles in my chest, but it was no use.

The street was empty and I was alone, a shaken cop standing under the light of a blinking streetlamp, furious at myself and at the man in the mask.

Back at my car, I called Finn and a mechanic, Mac Neal, whom I trusted implicitly. They arrived at the same time and as I told Finn what had happened, Neal inspected every inch of my car. Finally, he stood and pronounced it hunky-dory.

"If I had to guess, kiddo, I think you interrupted the creep just as he was getting started. Looks like he was going for the brake lines." Mac stroked his long salt-and-pepper beard, his eyes heavy with worry. "Driving up the canyon, late at night like this, all it would take is a deer crossing the road and bam, you'd be up shit's creek if you didn't have your brakes."

"Thanks for the mental picture, Mac. What do I owe you?"

He shook his head. "This one's on the house. You've given me a lot of business over the years."

After he left, Finn and I spent a few minutes talking. Finn thought we should go after the man in the mask immediately.

"How? I have no idea what direction he went, or what he looks like. Take off the hoodie and the mask and he could be anyone. I think we take this as a good sign, Finn. We're on the right track with our investigation." I slid into my car and sniffed. It smelled of Mac's auto shop and heavy, male sweat. Quickly rolling down the window, I smiled up at Finn. "We're on the right track."

He leaned down, rested his forearms on my windowsill. "A bat, huh?"

"They're hibernating somewhere close by. This one must have been sick, or maybe hungry. Maybe it just needed a breath of fresh air. You ever smelled guano? It's horrific." I turned the ignition and started the car. Nothing unusual happened and I exhaled shakily. "The thing was three feet across, at least. Probably a vampire bat."

"Uh-huh. Drive safe. I'll see you tomorrow."

I drove away from Edith's house and headed home under the light of a pale, rising moon. It moved slowly across the indigo sky, traveling as though it didn't have a care in the world. What a life, I thought, to meander among the stars, crossing the universe one evening at a time. If there was a man in the moon, sitting up there since the dawn of time, the sheer number of things he'd seen in his existence was staggering.

As I drove, my heart was heavy with anticipation and dread. Every few seconds, I checked the rearview mirror for the head-lights of someone following me, but I had the roads to myself. I remembered a scary story my girlfriends and I used to tell every Halloween when we were young, about the woman driving home alone who looks in her rearview mirror and, to her horror, sees a man with an axe slowly rising from the backseat.

I shivered, hoping I'd soon forget the mask the man in my own car had worn, with its crude stitches and bloody, battered eyes and mouth.

Instead, I tried to focus on the fact that I didn't know what the next day would bring, what fresh horror might find us. The worst part of all was the voice in my ear, constantly whispering to me, that the town itself had somehow summoned its own version of Ghost Boy back to life for one final act of terror.

# Chapter Twenty-Two

**Thursday.**

Time was up.

The phrase ran on repeat in my mind, as I rose and showered. I made a bowl of oatmeal for Grace, too nerve-struck to eat myself. It felt as though every fiber in my being were clenched in anticipation.

Time's up.

When I'd gotten home the night before, I'd woken Brody and told him everything I could about the investigation, ending with my run-in with Stitched Face at the Montgomery house. Brody was concerned, but we both knew I'd been in much worse situations. To be honest, other than worry, there wasn't much either of us could do.

I was a cop, through and through, and we knew what that meant; that there would be times, now and in the future, when I'd find myself face-to-face with truly bad people.

When I pulled back the curtains in the kitchen windows, I saw it had snowed again. In fact, it was still snowing. The sky was white, and the whole world appeared bleary, tired. I poured a second cup of coffee and sipped it as I spooned oatmeal into Grace's mouth. She babbled and cooed and laughed as Seamus waited anxiously at her feet for a dropped morsel. It was a magical moment of peace and domestic bliss, until Grace decided to upend the bowl of oatmeal onto Seamus's head.

The dog howled, the baby cried, and I felt like breaking into tears myself.

But, by the time Brody woke and joined us, I'd gotten both dog and floor cleaned. Grace was content to crawl around with a couple of empty containers. As she played, Brody and I talked. The night before, we'd decided that he would take a few days off and stay home with Grace. I didn't want him going into town, to work, and I wanted Grace at home, safe. We didn't know where the killer would strike. What if he went for a commercial building, an office structure, instead of a tavern? Or the library or rec center?

Clementine was happy to take a couple of days off as well. I told her to stay out of heavily populated buildings, and she made me feel crazy but I wouldn't let her off the phone until she agreed.

Then she wanted to know all the gory details, and I couldn't end the call fast enough.

As I drove through town, it was still early. Yellow light from front porch bulbs flickered weakly against the gently falling snow.

At the station, I reviewed my notes and the murder board, willing something to jump out at me. I was frustrated and anxious, though, unable to concentrate. Finally, I went to Chief Chavez's office. Inside, I was surprised to find Sheriff Rose Underhill stretched out on the chief's couch, reading a copy of Josiah Black's arrest record.

Underhill lowered the report and stared at me. "You've got a real doozy on your hands." Sighing, the sheriff sat up and fluffed her hair. "I hate this time of year. Every November, I think I'll move to Miami or Los Angeles, but I never do. You know what keeps me here?"

I shook my head.

"Sheer laziness. Sounds like a real bitch to pack up and move. Much easier to stay put and complain."

"What are you doing here?"

"My old pal Angel Chavez sent up the Bat-Signal, so here I am, at your disposal. Though to be honest, this town has become a bit of a snooze, hasn't it?"

"Compared to Bishop?" I asked in surprise.

Underhill let out a guffaw. "Good point. Listen, we've got rein-forcements coming from all four corners of this state and then some. We'll find your perp, this 'Ghost Boy,' make no bones about it."

The sheriff stood up and stretched and I saw that she wore a revolver on her belt, instead of the semiautomatic pistol favored by most law enforcement officers.

She noticed me looking.

"It's an antique, a relic from another era. It belonged to my father. He was a marshal in Nebraska, a real mean son of a bitch. He died of emphysema twenty years ago, and on his deathbed, he asked for one thing: to be buried with his revolver." Underhill pulled the gun from her belt, gave the cylinder a spin, and then slipped the gun back into the belt with a toothy grin and a slow wink. "Mama gave me the gun after his funeral. I expect the bas-tard is still rolling in his grave, looking for it."

Chief Chavez came in. "Ah, good, you're here. I want to go over the plan for today. Everyone's gathering in the conference room in ten minutes."

I took a deep breath. There was something that had been bothering me for days, since my visit to Dillahunt at the Belle Vista Penitentiary. I didn't know when I would get an opportunity to have both Chief Chavez and Sheriff Underhill to myself again and I had to know.

I had to be absolutely certain that Dillahunt, his letters, Col-leen Holden . . . that none of it was related to my cases.

Chavez waited, his hand on the doorknob, staring back at me with an inquisitive look in his dark eyes. "Something on your mind, Detective?"

"Yes. I want to know about Gordon Dillahunt and why he in-sisted, to the day he died, that the two of you were dirty cops." The words were out of my mouth before I could think of a gentler way to say them. Chavez colored, though Sheriff Underhill merely sat back down on the couch, an unreadable expression on her face.

"You've been to see him? Dillahunt?" the sheriff asked, her voice as cold and crisp as January frost.

"Yes. Last Friday. The day before he killed himself. He said you two planted the evidence that led to his arrest."

Another big breath. I was in it deep now. "I'm sorry, Chief, but I have to know the whole story. Dillahunt's dead . . . Caleb Montgomery's dead . . . there can't be any harm in telling me now. I have to be sure Ghost Boy is not somehow connected to Dillahunt; that Montgomery's and Esposito's deaths have everything to do with Josiah Black and nothing to do with Dillahunt."

After a moment of silence that felt heavy with meaning, Chavez took a seat at his desk. I remained standing, leaning against the far wall, my hands tucked behind my back, trying to be as unassuming as possible.

Sheriff Rose Underhill spoke first. "I don't have to tell either of you that it's hard to be a minority—female, Hispanic, black, whatever—in this field. I've been trying to prove myself my whole life. The Dillahunt case was big. Angel, you remember those days? We were like a pair of bloodhounds on a coon's trail. We tracked him to that shitty little cabin. Only we didn't know he had the hostage."

Chavez exhaled. "It has always bothered me *how* we tracked him there, Rosie. We had our suspicions that it was Dillahunt all along but we couldn't get a search warrant for his business or his home. He was too wily, he covered his tracks too well. It wasn't until we found that blood splatter, remember, that we were finally able to get Montgomery to sign off on a warrant."

"Blood splatter?" I asked.

Chavez nodded. "We went to Dillahunt's home, his main residence. It was November, twilight. Cold as heck. We were hoping he'd be there, that we could have a chat with him, try to whittle away at the inconsistencies in the previous interviews he'd given us. But he didn't answer when we knocked. Rose decided to go around to the rear of the house, try knocking on the back door.

And that's when she found it. An enormous puddle of frozen blood, saturating the back porch, seeping out from under the door. And that was all we needed."

Sheriff Underhill smiled faintly. "We called in the troops and lit that shack up like it was the Fourth of July. Goddamn. Inside were photographs and maps. Lots of maps. We figured out pretty quickly where he was holed up."

Chief Chavez scratched at his face, uncomfortable. "It was the oddest thing, though. We had the blood analyzed, to see if it matched any of the known victims. Turned out to be deer blood."

I shrugged. "You didn't know. November is prime hunting season."

"Gordon Dillahunt wasn't a hunter." Chavez leaned forward, elbows on his knees, head in his hands. "We'd fucked up, but no one said a word. After all, our little screwup ultimately led to the capture of the most wanted man in the valley. No one cared, especially not Walt Johnson, the Neanderthal who was running this department at the time."

"But Dillahunt knew, didn't he? He was brilliant and would have known immediately that someone planted the blood on his porch. Someone with a vested interest in getting into his house when all other *legal* methods had failed." I shook my head, marveling at the thought of the planning that would have gone into it. "Of course no one said anything. But people knew."

Rose Underhill held up her right hand and cocked her fingers like a pistol at me. "You're a sharp cookie, Gemma. Of course Dillahunt knew. Chief Johnson did, too. He may have been a prick, but he was a smart prick, sharp as a tack. And boy, did he punish me. My career in Cedar Valley was over. There are times I think he punished me because he was jealous I'd thought of it myself."

Chavez started, understanding finally dawning on him. "It was you that put the deer blood there?"

"Of course it was. You knew I'd spent my whole life hunting. You just didn't want to connect the damn dots. You've been blind to a lot of things in your life, Angel, because you don't understand that most people will leap, if they're pushed hard enough." Underhill sighed and weariness settled in around her eyes. "I'm not proud, but I don't regret it, not any of it. Gordon Dillahunt was a monster and he needed to be put down. And it was never going to happen unless we helped things along. I was desperate." She turned to me. "You'd have done the same thing."

Would I? I didn't know. I liked to think I wouldn't, but there are some people out there who are so bad, so vicious, so inhumane, that your vision gets a little blurry just thinking about them.

These are the shadows that cops live with; we catch glimpses of them behind us in the bathroom mirror, out of the corners of our eyes. They are dark, shifting things that mimic humans; things we don't like to spend too much time thinking on.

Underhill was still staring at me, a haunted look in her eyes now. "I know that when I go to meet my maker, my conscience will be clear. Everything I've ever done, all the things that others might judge me for, they've all happened in the name of putting garbage away for the long haul. News flash, folks . . . we're not cops. We're trash collectors, rat chasers."

It was quiet in the office after that, the slow, steady tick of the clock on Chavez's desk the only note in the somber air.

Finally, Chief Chavez stood. He placed his hands on his desk and stared at Rose, his onetime partner and now peer. He spoke in a low voice. "Sheriff, I don't think you're wrong, not exactly. Dillahunt was guilty as sin. But if we break the law to prove it, we inch that much closer to that which we detest. Where does the line go? It starts to fade, to twist. And if we're not walking the straight and narrow, well, then I think we're all damned."

Underhill stood, too, and winked at Chavez. "Angel, hell is the one place we won't see each other. You, as your name implies, are destined for much loftier places. Now listen, don't we have a killer to catch? Haven't we had enough chitchat for one day?"

I slipped out of the office then, having gotten what I needed.

I felt hollow inside. A lot of cops were dirty. The fact that it was common didn't make it any easier to swallow, but most of the ones I'd met personally, or heard of, were rank and file. Rose Underhill was an elected official, sheriff to all of Cathedral County.

And she'd just implied there had been other transgressions, other things she'd done to make sure, as she put it, the trash got collected.

I went to the restroom, splashed cool water on my face. Then I stared at my reflection for a good long while, taking in the wavy, dark hair that fell past my shoulders. The green eyes, set a smidge too close, the average nose and mouth. The thin scar that wrapped itself around my neck.

I didn't know what I was looking for; reassurance, perhaps, that I was on the right side of the line dividing honor from dishonor, order from chaos. And if I was firmly planted there, would I stay? Or might there come a day when I'd find myself toeing the line, even crossing over?

The door behind me opened and Sheriff Underhill paused. "Am I interrupting?"

I shook my head. "I'm done." As I moved to go past her, she gripped my elbow. I stared at her.

"Don't judge me, Detective. We all have our demons."

"Sure. Just keep yours out of my case."

She released me, nodded once. "Your case, your demons. I'm just here to help."

I found the others already in the conference room. Another few minutes and Underhill joined us. Staring at the notes and diagrams on the whiteboards, it seemed as though the killer was close and yet remained so far out of reach.

"Where's he going to hit, folks?" Chief Chavez asked. He sat at the head of the table, Sheriff Underhill to his left. "Have we made any progress since yesterday?"

"Sir, if I may?" Jimmy asked tentatively. "Casey Black's military records came through. It's bad."

The chief nodded, the scowl on his face deepening. "By all means, Jimmy, please illuminate us with your knowledge."

"I'll stick with the highlights. Or rather, the lowlights. In 2006, Black was part of an elite Navy SEAL team in Afghanistan that was tasked with hunting down Taliban members. This was often down and dirty, face-to-face, bloody combat. Some nights, the raids netted ten or fifteen kills. After a while, rumors began to spread. The troops were enjoying the hunts a little too much. In fact, they enjoyed it so much that several SEALs were subsequently investigated for war crimes. Black was said to be one of the ringleaders in the, ah, activities." Jimmy paused, then held up a photograph. "Exhibit A."

"Jesus," Moriarty muttered. The rest of us were silent, having already turned away from the image of the mutilated corpse in the sand, his or her body desecrated beyond recognition. "Casey Black did that? He's a psychopath."

Jimmy shrugged. "From what I can tell, Black never went before a court. He was suddenly dishonorably discharged, which if you ask me is a hell of a lot better than being tried and sentenced for war crimes. Anyway, if you read between the lines, it's clear there was some kind of a cover-up, high on the chain of command. We'll likely never get to the bottom of it."

Chavez tapped a pen on the table. "Someone somewhere knows something. Josiah Black, he wasn't accused of war crimes, was he?"

"No, Chief. His military records are clear," I answered. "And just so we're all on the same page on this . . . there's a fair chance that Josiah Black was innocent of all the charges brought against him. I'm afraid that a man who served his country at its darkest hour, with honor, was wrongfully persecuted."

"So noted. If you're right, then shame on us and this town. But it's clear to me that Casey Black is a vicious son of a bitch. How does this help us figure out where he is?" Sheriff Underhill asked. She stared around the room, looking at each of us in turn. "We need butts on the streets."

Moriarty sighed heavily. "I'm telling you, Black is going to target the theater. Think about it; it will be like shooting fish in a barrel. All he has to do is create some kind of scare, and *bam!* He'll cause a stampede and it will be a bloodbath the likes of which this town has never seen."

My phone rang. I looked down at the caller ID and saw it was Nash Dumont. "Speaking of the theater . . .

"Nash, this isn't a good—"

He interrupted me, his voice shaky. "Milo Griffith is missing. We open in nine hours. Seven o'clock sharp. What the fuck am I going to do?"

"What do you mean, he's missing?" I said, pinching the bridge of my nose. I didn't have time for this. "You've tried his cell?"

"Of course I've tried his goddamn cell. Damn it. If he doesn't show up, we're screwed," Nash yelled. "God. All this work, all this planning . . . I'll have to cancel the show."

"Canceling seems rather drastic, Nash. What about Milo's understudy, is he available?"

"Ezra? Ezra can't act his way out of a paper bag. But yes, of course . . . If I use Ezra, I can still open the doors. And if the play is a flop, he'll be the one to blame, not me." Nash was calmer now, talking more clearly. "Still, Milo is a director's dream, a natural. You have to find him."

"I'm sure he'll turn up. I'll swing by the theater. Is Maggie Armstrong there? I'll talk to her, see if she has any ideas where Milo may have gone. I know the two of them are . . . close."

"Yes. Come as quick as you can. I must get ahold of Ezra in the meantime—he's going to have a coronary when I tell him he's our lead tonight," the director said. "And Maggie is not here yet, but I expect her any minute. She's always very punctual."

I hung up, excused myself, and drove over to the Shotgun Playhouse. Two posters, both as new and fresh as if they'd been printed that morning, hung on either side of the front doors, advertising the one-week-only run of William Shakespeare's tragedy *Macbeth*, starring the Cedar Valley Theater Troupe. I was glad to see that they'd settled on a name. I parked and hurried in, nearly running into Danny Grimes in the lobby. He had a nervous look on his face and a sword dangling in his left hand.

"Are you here about Milo? Nash is throwing a fit. At this rate, it's probably safer if Milo doesn't show. This whole thing's about to blow up in our faces."

"I'm sure he'll turn up," I said.

"Well, if Nash doesn't kill him, I'm going to. We've worked so hard and this is so typical. Milo is a real prima donna. He's probably off with Maggie somewhere, getting lucky, while the rest of us assholes twiddle our thumbs and pray he shows up. No, screw that. We're a troupe, we're more than any one individual." Danny swung his sword in a practiced arc, then stepped back and held it out, ready to parry.

"Exactly. I've seen you rehearse, you're all wonderful. The show will go on, isn't that what they say?"

"Sure," Danny muttered. He lifted his arm to wipe his brow with sleeve of his shirt and I saw two more tattoos in addition to the flag on his forearm: the letters USMC and a skull.

"Marine Corps?"

Danny straightened up and saluted. "Yes, ma'am. I did four years and then left while I was still in one piece. Some of my buddies, they weren't so lucky. Proud to serve, glad to be out."

"I'll bet." I began to move away. "I'd better find Nash."

Danny was still talking, more to himself than me. "Yeah, you want to hear some real horror stories, talk to Milo when you find him."

I froze, then slowly turned around. "Milo was in the Corps as well?"

"Nah. That dude is a badass. He was a Navy SEAL sniper, special ops. I think he's actually killed people." Danny swung his sword again, the blade slicing through the air with a sharp hiss.

My heart pounded as pieces of the puzzle began to drop into place. I didn't have the whole picture, not yet, but I could feel with every fiber of my being that I was inching that much closer to Ghost Boy.

To Casey Black.

Danny added in a low voice, "Yes, I think old Milo has killed quite a few people."

*You have no idea.* I thought of the fuzzy picture that had come in over the fax with Casey Black's military records. Change the hair color, tweak the eyebrows, add some facial hair . . . It was all so obvious now that I knew who to look for.

I found the director in the theater, pacing on the stage, his face an ugly shade of purple. He practically clawed at me as I approached, a man barely treading water. This was the nasty side of Nash Dumont, and it was on full display.

"Have you found him?"

"No, not yet. How about Maggie, is she here?" My voice had a new urgency in it, and Nash noticed.

He stepped back and paled. "Oh my God, is she missing, too? What's going on?"

"I'm not sure yet. Do you have a home address for Milo?"

Nash nodded. "Of course, I've got it here in my phone. I was thinking of driving over there myself, but there's no time! We are absolutely out of fucking time!"

He calmed down enough to pull up Milo's information and read it to me slowly. By the time he was finished, I'd texted it to Finn and told him to meet me there as quickly as possible. Then I left a near-hysterical Nash with the promise that I'd be in touch the moment I had any news. I gently suggested that he also call in Maggie Armstrong's understudy and he about fell over.

Then I raced across town.

The address Nash had given me was in a run-down neighborhood on the south side, where stone-cold dead appliances compete with children's toys in yards that are defined by low chain-link fences and, more usually than not, a barking dog tethered to some sort of small wooden structure or discarded trailer tire.

Milo's rental was at the end of a side street that had no name, simply numbers. I parked across the road, taking in the scene. His house was a small one-story ranch-style abode, with dying grass in front and thankfully, as far as I could tell, no accompanying dog. There was no garage, only a tin-roofed carport, empty save for a red gasoline can, tipped on its side, and a couple of days' worth of newspapers.

The place had a feel of emptiness to it, and yet the flowers in a wooden box by the front door were fresh, and the fall leaves swept into a tidy pile. Someone had been here; how recently, though, was the question.

As Finn pulled up, I thought of something and called the fire department. After a couple of transfers and a few minutes on hold, the fire investigator answered. "Ramirez."

"It's Gemma. I'm at the property of a suspect in the Montgomery and Esposito killings. He's a former Navy SEAL, a sniper. Obviously experienced with explosives. Can we get some support here? I'm not about to walk into his house without knowing if it's rigged to explode. And there's a time factor; his girlfriend, my colleague's daughter, is missing."

Ramirez was silent. I knew she was still upset that we'd considered her a suspect.

"Liv, I'm sorry for the way things went down at the police station. I don't . . . I don't have a lot of female friends. It's a job hazard, I suppose. I get the feeling you may be in the same boat. We should try to be allies, not enemies." I waited another beat, then said more urgently, "There's a woman's life at stake. She's young, ambitious. Wants to be an attorney and fight the good fight."

Ramirez sighed. "There are no good fights anymore, Gemma. Just bad ones and worse ones. I'll bring Fuego and a couple of medics. You made the right call; do not enter the building under any circumstances. Don't even get close. What's the location?"

From the other end of the line, I heard Ramirez rummage for a pen and paper. I gave her the address and again reiterated the need to hurry, ending the call as Finn leaned in my open window. I quickly caught him up to speed.

Though Finn had never met Milo Griffith, he was shocked that a local actor, dating Armstrong's daughter, was Casey Black. "Is Lucas aware of the situation?"

"Not yet. I want to wait until we know more. It all makes sense, Finn. I read or heard that Amelia Black went by Millie. Millie . . . Milo. When Casey changed his name, he chose something in tribute to his beloved grandmother." I stepped out of my car. "And dating the daughter of a local cop is the perfect foil. He'd have had instant access to whatever Maggie knew. It's the perfect cover."

I gave Finn a stern look. "Also, Ramirez is on her way. Try to behave."

Finn frowned. "Is she still pissed we brought her in for questioning?"

"Yes. But I think she's coming around. She knows why we did it."

Finn rubbed his jaw, looking out over the property. "This is going to be tight. We've got a neighbor ten yards down on the east side, another fifteen yards to the south. Let's get these houses cleared."

We were in luck—both of Griffith's immediate neighbors didn't appear to be home; at least, they weren't answering their doors. We saw a group of middle-school kids playing in the road one street down, and scared them off with promises of truancy charges. It was the middle of the day, after all, and they should have been in school.

At one point, Finn took a phone call. He stepped away, his back to me. The conversation was short and when he returned, he had the strangest look of both disappointment and excitement in his eyes.

"What's up?"

Finn slipped his phone into the back pocket of his jeans. "I have an interview in New York in December."

"Congratulations." I meant it, though the thought of Finn leaving Cedar Valley left me feeling hollow. "That could be an amazing opportunity."

He shrugged. "We'll see. The more I talk to my buddies who are there, the less appealing it sounds. It's expensive as hell. Maybe my folks have it right; get a little place in Florida and commute to the beach instead of to the concrete jungle."

Ramirez pulled up. Finn watched as she parked her truck and added, "And there might just be enough excitement in town to keep me here another few years."

*Not if you don't make some serious amends, my friend,* I thought.

The rest of Ramirez's team was on-site within minutes. She and Fuego leaped from her truck, both ready and eager to get to work. The ever-faithful yellow Lab waited patiently, though, while Ramirez retrieved protective gear for them both from the cab. Meanwhile, the two paramedics she'd brought stood by, awaiting orders of their own.

I hoped they wouldn't be needed, that we'd find the house empty and abandoned.

Ramirez joined us. "We'll do the perimeter first, then move inside. If this guy is as much a pro as you say, he'll have made the bomb that killed Montgomery somewhere else and we won't pick up any trace. But I won't take any chances. Fuego and I will enter the house only after I'm certain the outside is clear and that the place hasn't been rigged. And get someone stationed at the end of the road, a street worker, someone with a big truck who can block off the entrance. I don't want to be caught with my pants down when Griffith comes home."

It was a great idea. Finn made the call to utilities while I phoned Chief Chavez and let him know where things stood. I reluctantly told him that Maggie Armstrong was known to date Milo Griffith, and she, too, was missing. I heard his sharp intake of breath and winced; Lucas Armstrong's reaction was apt to be ten times as bad.

Our calls over, Finn and I joined the paramedics. Together, we watched in silence as Ramirez and Fuego walked the perimeter. They spent a good deal of time behind the house, out of sight, long enough to make me nervous.

I pulled out my radio and switched to the frequency we'd agreed upon. "Ramirez? Do you copy?"

A few moments of static, then, "Copy. I've cleared the perimeter and am moving into the house through an unlocked back door."

"Copy."

At the end of the street, a large city truck parked at a diagonal, barring anyone from exiting or entering the area. As the driver hopped out and proceeded to set up cones, a dark blue sedan approached. It slowed down, way down, as it passed, then sped up and was gone. I turned around to mention it to Finn when Ramirez's voice, shaky and rushed, jumped back at me through the radio.

"Get in here, right now. Bring the medics. And you're going to want to call in your crime scene techs. You've got a live one, kids, in more ways than one."

We entered through the unlocked front door and found ourselves in a narrow foyer. A single denim jacket hung on a hook behind the door, next to a box intended for keys, a wallet. The house smelled of burnt toast and something else, like sweat but muskier.

"Back here," Ramirez called. We followed the sound of her voice to a bedroom at the rear of the house. Fuego sat just outside the room, keeping watch. Inside, we found Ramirez smoothing hair back from Maggie Armstrong's forehead. The young woman lay on her side, on an unmade bed. Her eyes were closed, her feet covered with loose blankets. Her hands had been tied together, then laced through the bed's frame. The left side of her face was bruised and swollen.

"Oh my God." I dropped to my knees beside Ramirez. Behind me, I heard Finn swear and pound his fist into the wall in anger. "Is she . . . ?"

"She's alive. She's breathing, but drifting in and out of consciousness. I haven't been able to rouse her. If the guy you're chasing did this to her, he's a monster. Anyone who beats a woman should get a Taser in his nuts." Ramirez stepped back and turned to the medics, who'd followed us into the room. "Her pulse is low. I think he gave her something, a sedative maybe. Get her to the ER."

There wasn't anything more that we could do for Maggie, other than step aside and let the medics do their job. The four of us, Ramirez, Fuego, Finn, and I, gathered in the kitchen. It, like the rest of the house, was small and neat, with a few feminine touches that I was certain had come from Maggie.

I called the department and spoke with the desk sergeant on duty. I asked him to pull up the car registration for one Milo Griffith, currently residing at the present address. I held while he did so, a sinking feeling in my heart. After a minute, the sergeant was back on the line. He read me the license plate number, then said, "It's a four-door sedan, dark blue 2012 Honda Accord."

"Thanks, Dave." I hung up and turned back to the group. "Damn it. Griffith drove past us just as the city truck was getting into place. He knows we're onto him."

"So that's good, right?" Ramirez asked. "He can't possibly move forward with his plans now that his cover's blown."

"Don't be too sure. He's a pro. I bet he's got a backup nest somewhere. We haven't seen the last of him," Finn said. At his side, Fuego took a seat and looked up adoringly. While his master may not yet have forgiven Finn, it was clear the dog had.

Finn sighed and scratched the animal's ears. "Good boy. Good pup."

I watched as the medics carried Maggie out on a stretcher. As they maneuvered through the narrow hallway, her arm flopped off the edge and hung there, her hand outstretched. I heard a low moan come from her and a wave of nausea rolled over me.

"We can't let Griffith hurt anyone else. He's done enough damage in this town for a lifetime." I rubbed my eyes, willing some fresh life into my suddenly weary bones. "Ramirez, did you find anything?"

She shook her head. "No, though Fuego picked up trace evidence. I can tell you Griffith handled materials, but not here. I think Finn's right; Griffith's got a hidey-hole somewhere. It's got to be secluded, private. Off the beaten path. But, I did find something you should see. Come on, it's in the other bedroom."

We entered what appeared to be Griffith's master bedroom. A framed photograph of Maggie and him cuddling was on the dresser and I felt like picking it up and throwing it through the window. Maggie didn't deserve what had happened to her, no woman did, and I knew it was a trauma from which it would take a long time to heal. The physical scars would fade but the emotional ones, the loss of trust and innocence, might last for years.

Ramirez pointed to a door at the back of the bedroom. "I checked it—it's clear of wires, timers, and traps. But it is locked."

"Not for long," Finn muttered angrily. He stepped back and gave the door a mighty kick. It flew open, revealing a surprisingly large walk-in closet that appeared to have been converted to a tiny study. A table in the center took up most of the room.

We stepped in, crowding around the table, and looked around.

"Holy shit," I breathed.

Ramirez glanced around, then immediately stepped out. "I don't do small spaces, let alone psychopathic shrines. You've all got one seriously screwed-up dude on your hands."


Ramirez had been right; the room was a shrine of sorts. Plastered to the walls were old newspapers from across the nation, each with a different headline on the same topic: the infamous Josiah Black of Cedar Valley, Colorado. It was disconcerting to see pictures of my small hometown on the cover of all the major papers stretching from Los Angeles to New York.

There were also home photographs, some of Josiah and Millie, some of Millie and Debbie, and quite a few of Debbie and Casey. The pictures of Josiah and Millie had been altered; the backgrounds were heavily scratched out, some hard enough to poke holes through the photo paper.

"He's taking his rage out on the town. Think about it, every picture of Josiah and Millie together had to have been taken before his arrest. They were taken here, in Cedar Valley." Finn pointed to a small Polaroid picture of a young Casey on a trampoline, his face split by a grin that stretched ear to ear. "What happened to this kid? How do you cross the line to killer?"

I shrugged. "One step at a time, I suppose." It was unsettling to see the photographs, as they told the story of the rest of the Black family; what happened in the years after Josiah Black went away for his crimes.

On the table, next to a blank notepad and a couple of pens, was a stack of comic books. *Ghost Boy*, to be specific. "Bingo," I whispered.

"What's with the maps?" Ramirez asked from her place in the doorway.

I hadn't noticed, but scattered among the photographs and newspaper clippings were area maps. They were old maps, though, vintage renderings likely sixty or seventy years old. I went to them, tracing with the tip of my finger the roads and trails that still existed. The maps themselves were untouched, save for a single red dot on one of them. Unfortunately, it was a map without words, without familiar landmarks.

Finn tapped it. "Where is this?"

I started to shake my head, unsure, then stopped. I peered more closely. "This is the creek, isn't it? And this here, that must be the pond out on Jack Welch's old farm. I'd heard there was once a pond there, but it's been dried up for years. So if that is the creek . . . and that's the Welch property . . ."

I felt myself go pale as Finn and I realized what the red dot represented.

*"What?"* Ramirez asked, coming in close behind us in spite of herself.

I answered her, my voice trembling. "It's the Playhouse. Moriarty's been right all along; Milo Griffith is going to hit the theater. For the last two hours, I've been racking my brain to figure out why Griffith got himself cast in a community play. Don't you see? It was the perfect way to both woo Maggie and to learn the ins and outs of the theater. He's probably already put his plan into motion. He can't show his face; he's supposed to be on stage tonight. So he'll have had to set things up ahead of time."

I yanked my phone from my jacket pocket. Three rings and then Chavez picked up. "Chief, I don't have time to explain. We think Griffith has rigged the Shotgun Playhouse, either to blow or somehow catch fire. If that happens, there will be hundreds of people trapped inside. You've got to send every available unit over there. I'm with Ramirez and her dog right now; they're on their way there. If there are explosives, they'll find them."

"Copy that. What else do you need?"

I thought a moment, then said, "Send a team of officers to this address; we need the house thoroughly searched. We think Griffith might have a nest somewhere, a secret room or house. Maybe a cabin. Somewhere that he uses to prepare his explosives."

"Where will you be?"

"At the hospital." I explained to him that we'd found Maggie Armstrong, how she might hold the key to Griffith's whole story. "Finn and I will try to get what we can from her."

"Okay. I'll let Lucas Armstrong know what's going on. A man's got a right to know when someone has hurt his family." As the chief ended the call, I heard him say, "Especially when it's his child."

I put my phone away and stared at Ramirez and Finn. "We don't have much time."

Ramirez and Fuego left first. Finn and I took a final look around the shrine.

"Are we sure on this? It's the Playhouse?"

I'd been staring at one photograph in particular, an image of Josiah Black being led into the courthouse the day his trial started. In profile, it was easy to see a resemblance between Milo Griffith and his grandfather. I turned away. "It has to be. He's had weeks to get to know the place. He's kicked things up a notch from his grandfather. The masks, the dramatic gestures. There will be no bigger target in Cedar Valley than the Playhouse, not tonight."

Finn's eyes were dark. "Then that's where we'll be."

# Chapter Twenty-Three

By the time we arrived at the hospital, Lucas Armstrong was already there. He sat in Maggie's room, his hands wrapped in hers. To my immense relief, Maggie's eyes were open. Lucas saw Finn and I hovering in the doorway and stood up to meet us. We stepped back into the hall as he gently closed the door behind him.

Then he turned and I saw the full force of a father's rage in his eyes.

"This guy is dead meat."

"We'll get him, Lucas. Is Sonya here?"

Armstrong shook his head. "No, thank God. This would break her. She's with Megan; they went to visit Sonya's folks in Atlanta for a few days. I'll give her a call once I understand more."

That was one blessing; having Maggie's mother and little sister on-site would have made it difficult for Finn and I to have a straightforward conversation with her. It was going to be hard enough to do it with her father in the room, but I held no illusions that he'd let us do it without him.

"Have the doctors evaluated Maggie yet?" I asked gently.

Armstrong nodded. "There's no concussion. The bastard gave her some kind of sedative, then popped her in the face for good measure. When I get my hands on him . . ."

Finn gave Armstrong's back a solid thump. "We're all feeling it, Luke. Has Maggie said anything?"

Armstrong gritted his teeth and straightened up to his full six and a half feet. "She started to, and I asked her to stop; I told her to wait until you all arrived so she'd only have to go through it once. You know what kills me? Her first words were, 'Daddy, I'm sorry.' My baby didn't do a damn thing wrong and she's already blaming herself. Well, let's get to it. As I understand it, we're on a tight time frame here."

I sat in the room's only chair and pulled it close to Maggie. My heart broke for her; the bruises and swelling on her face, combined with the thin hospital blanket, made her look even younger and more scared than she already was.

Armstrong and Finn stood in opposite corners of the room, each discreetly fading into the background as well as they could, given the circumstances. They knew Maggie might talk more that way, if she felt as though she were only speaking with me.

Maggie looked at me with wide, fearful eyes. She whispered, "Why did he do this?"

"Milo is ill, Maggie. We need to find him so we can get him the help he needs." I spoke softly, gently. "What can you tell us?"

She closed her eyes; tears leaked out. "It was my fault. Milo told me never to open the closet door in his room. He said he kept his service weapon and memorabilia from his time in the Navy SEALs in there, and he wasn't comfortable with anyone seeing it. I didn't care about any of that, I was just looking for an extra towel."

Her eyes, open now, cut over to her father and then away. "I'd stayed the night there, for the first time. Milo went to the store to get bagels and fruit and I wanted to shower while he was gone. We were supposed to be at the theater early today for final rehearsal. Poor Nash. Is he terribly upset?"

"No, Maggie, he's just worried about you. Don't think about the play right now, it will all be fine."

She bit her lip and nodded.

I prompted, "So you needed a towel . . ."

"Yes, and there's no linen closet in the house. Milo must have forgotten to lock the closet door; I wasn't even thinking, I just opened it and that's when I saw it. All of it. At first it didn't make sense, why Milo would have all these old newspapers taped up. And those creepy comic books. But then I started reading the articles, and saw the photographs, and suddenly everything made sense. I remembered the murder board at the station, knew you had found similar comics at the crime scenes." Maggie laughed bitterly. "Even him dating me, that made sense. I'm such a fool. I thought he loved me, and all this time, he wanted to be with me because of who my father is."

"I know it hurts, Maggie. What happened then?"

Fear clouded her face and her voice began to shake. "He came home. I didn't hear him, though. All of a sudden I felt someone behind me and I turned and there he was. The look in his eyes . . . I've never been so scared in my life. He slapped me and pushed me out of the room. I fell on the bed. Then he started laughing, but it was this awful crying laugh."

From the corner of my eye, I could see Armstrong physically trying to restrain himself from racing out the door, finding Griffith, and tearing his head off.

Maggie continued. "Milo told me everything. For as long as he could remember, his grandmother Millie talked about her hatred for Cedar Valley. Millie said the town had robbed her of her husband. She'd been tormented and harassed by people for so long that she finally had it and left town in the middle of the night. Pregnant, alone. She moved around a lot, raising her daughter, Debbie, in town after town, never daring to get close to anyone, ever. And then Debbie grew up and fell in love with a businessman and had his child, Casey. But when Casey was just a toddler, the man died. A few years later, Millie passed. And when Casey was eighteen, nearly about to graduate high school, Debbie killed herself. Too much had been taken from her. He changed his name to Milo and enlisted."

I nodded slowly; Maggie's words jibed with the theory that we'd been toying with, that the killer was not only re-creating Josiah Black's crimes but also enacting an act of revenge on the town that had shaped his family all those years ago and continued to shape it, even now.

"Did Griffith tell you what his plan was? There are similarities with his grandfather's crimes, but differences, too. Important differences, like locations and victims. As far as we can figure, we think Griffith might target the Playhouse for his final attack."

Maggie started crying again. This time, Armstrong left his space in the corner. He came and held his daughter's hand, tight. She said, sobbing through her words, "You might be right. Milo said that after tonight, we wouldn't be able to be together . . . and then he said he'd rather see me dead than not be with me. I honestly thought he might kill me. He gave me a shot of something, in the arm, then said I had to stay away from the theater tonight. Gemma, I think he might hurt himself."

"We're going to find him before that can happen." I didn't bother telling her that we would do whatever it took to prevent a massacre, even if that meant stopping Griffith with force. Deadly force, if necessary.

"He's not a bad man," Maggie said, her voice choked with emotion. "I think he's sick. He . . . gets angry easily. Shuts me out. Then he's apologetic, upset with himself."

"Did he talk about his years as a SEAL?"

She nodded. "Yes, though he'd told me most of it when we first started dating. It wasn't some big secret. He joined the Navy when he was eighteen. Within a few years, he was recruited for the SEALs. He loved it, really thought that was where he'd spend the rest of his days. Milo liked the idea of serving his country, like the grandfather he'd never met. But then he was involved in an accident. He wouldn't go into details, but he said the military forced him to resign. Milo was lost after that. He had no degree, no real home, no ambition to do anything but be a SEAL. And that was taken away from him. And he started thinking it was an awful lot like what had happened to his family; everything they loved was taken from them one by one. And he had an idea about something that might make him feel better."

"Take revenge on the town that started it all."

Maggie tipped her head in acknowledgment. Her eyelids fluttered, and for a moment it appeared as though she might pass out. Telling the story, reliving Milo's pain, was taking a toll on her.

But we were too far in to stop now.

"Maggie, what else can you tell us?" I asked her urgently.

Armstrong had been watching his daughter. Now he turned to me and shook his head. He whispered, "She's had enough. I'll stay with her; if she remembers anything more, I'll call you. You and Finn should get to the Playhouse."

By the time we arrived at the theater, it was nearly four o'clock. Doors would open in three hours and Nash Dumont was fit to be tied. He, and his crew, had been sequestered across the street in a pancake joint that had been cleared of all other customers, a sign hung in the door that read "Temporarily Closed."

Dumont and the actors had been told that there was a possible gas leak, and the source of it needed to be found before anyone could reenter the theater. It was a weak excuse, but at the end of the day, no one wants to die from a gas explosion, and so the whole lot of them went, in their medieval costumes, and picked at blueberry pancakes.

Everyone except Nash Dumont.

The director stood resolutely in the front window of the restaurant, his stage manager, Waverly, by his side, watching as yet another emergency service vehicle pulled up. She was dressed in gold from head to toe, a shimmery turtleneck sweater atop gold-toned jeans, bangles at her neck and wrist. I realized it wasn't red she preferred at all, but monochrome dressing. The gold reminded me of something, but before I could put my finger on it, Nash

Dumont broke free from the pancake place and intercepted me in the street.

"Goddamn it, Gemma, tell me what the hell is going on. I am supposed to open my beautiful theater to a sold-out crowd in three hours, and no one will tell me a damn thing about what is happening. Where are my lead actors? Do they have anything to do with this bullshit about a gas leak?" His face was practically the same shade of purple as his shirt, and it was painful to watch as he threw an adult-size tantrum. When he actually stomped his feet, it was hard not to giggle.

But there was nothing to giggle about, in all of it.

He was also married to the town's judge and I knew he deserved to know the truth, at least part of it. I took a deep breath. "Milo Griffith attacked Maggie Armstrong. She's in the hospital. We have people looking for Milo, but we currently believe the biggest threat is to the theater itself. So, we are doing our due diligence and checking things out."

The director went completely pale. His hand went to his chest and for a moment, I thought he was having a heart attack. He managed to gasp out, "What . . . are . . . you talking about?"

Finn cut in and as usual, got right to the point. "There's a good chance your play is going to be canceled tonight, by order of the Cedar Valley Police Department. And I'd find yourself a couple of new lead actors."

Dumont staggered backward and not without some grace sank dramatically down to the street curb, where he sat, head in hands, and wept.

Ramirez and Fuego emerged from the theater. She gestured for Finn and me to join her, off to the side, in privacy. She wiped sweat from her forehead, and for a moment I had a terrible sense of déjà vu. This was how I'd first seen her, wiping at her brow, standing by the body of a burned man.

"There's nothing."

I stared at her. "Nothing?"

She shook her head and squatted to pour water from her bottle into a collapsible bowl for Fuego. The dog lapped it up, then lay down. "There's not a trace of explosives in the theater. Nothing. The place is cleaner than a whore on Sunday . . . Well, let's just say it's clean."

"That doesn't mean Milo couldn't still be planning to hit the Playhouse. He could lock everyone in and set fire to the building from the outside. Throw a couple of Molotov cocktails through a window and whoosh, the whole place would go up." My imagination was running down a dozen scenarios. We were missing something, but what? The Shotgun Playhouse fit with everything we knew about Milo Griffith. "We can't let the play go on tonight."

"The hell you can't," a low but insistent voice said from behind me. I recognized it immediately and made a face at Finn and Ramirez for not warning me that Mayor Cabot had crept up.

I turned around and faced her. "Excuse me?"

She smiled coldly. "Detective, over my dead body will the opening night of this play be canceled. Gloria and Nash Dumont are upstanding citizens of our fine town and they've sunk a lot of money into this theater. I'll be damned if we don't open on account of a little theory of yours. Yes, Chief Chavez filled me in. Decades-old crimes, comic books . . . you've got a fancy imagination in that pretty little head of yours."

"But Mayor—"

"No." She wagged a finger in my face and hoisted her shoulder bag up higher. From within the depths of it, her terrier, Dixie, let out a growl. "No. You can station cops wherever the hell you want. But these doors will open on time or you'll find yourself out of a job. Understand?"

She didn't wait for a reply, at least not one from Finn, Ramirez, or me. Instead, she went to Nash Dumont and leaned down close, whispered something in his ear. Dumont's face lit up. He shot me a look of triumph.

"Damn it," I muttered underneath my breath. "Can she do that?"

Finn had an equal look of dismay. "I think she just did."

Dumont sprang up from the curb, his fedora askew, and raced across the street to the pancake house. Within a minute, the whole troupe of cast and crew was running back into the theater, their medieval costumes gathering modern dirt and grime at the hems.

Finn and I spent a few moments conferring, realizing we needed to change our game plan. Finally, we decided that if this was really going to happen, if the doors would open come hell or high water, then we'd have to cover every exit and entry point. I called Moriarty and asked him to join us, and to bring another couple of officers. Meanwhile, Finn called the chief and recommended that he position all other available personnel, including Sheriff Underhill and anyone else from out of town, in strategic places across town.

As soon as Moriarty arrived with two officers, I politely requested that Nash Dumont lead the seven of us, including Ramirez and Fuego, on a complete tour of the theater. Dumont agreed, though remained snooty throughout, muttering the whole time that Fuego better not dirty the carpets.

After Ramirez finally muttered back that her dog was better behaved than he was, Dumont shut up.

I was already familiar with the soaring lobby, and the beautiful theater itself, with its burgundy seats and polished-to-a-sheen banisters. The enormous chandelier shone brighter than I'd seen before, throwing down thousands of sparkly beams of light. Tucked discreetly behind a gold, shimmery curtain about halfway down the aisle was an emergency exit. I tested it, noticed no alarms went off when I found it unlocked and pushed it open. I also noticed there was no knob or handle on the outside; the door could only open from the inside.

Then a deep whirring noise drew our attention to the stage, where the curtains were slowly parting. I gasped when I saw the set. I could practically smell the open fires of the military camp and feel the chilly night air of the gathering storm. In the forefront, to the side, was the courtyard of a gray stone castle.

"What play is this?" Finn asked in a low voice. *"Hamlet?"*

"No, it's *Mac—*"

Quicker than I could breathe, Nash Dumont had swirled around, a raised finger practically up my nose. He shouted, "Do not say that word!"

Then he turned around and continued to walk us down the aisle and backstage. Finn looked at me, his eyebrows lifted high. I shrugged and said, "It's a long story. The play is cursed. You're not supposed to say M-A-C-B-E-T-H."

Ahead of us, Dumont stopped suddenly. "There are three dressing rooms on the right, three on the left. It's what you'd expect, where we do our costume changes and apply stage makeup and in general take a break from the spotlight."

"How are they separated? By gender?"

Dumont rolled his eyes at Moriarty. "This is the *theater*, pal. Nothing shocks us. No, the rooms are used by whoever needs them, whenever. There're no prima donnas in my cast."

I stepped into the closest dressing room. It was the size of a bedroom, the walls lined with counters and exposed bulbs, costumes draped over chairs. It was the same dressing room that had been trashed by the theater vandal, though it was clean now. Or rather, not clean, but the mess was the kind you'd expect from a frequently used dressing room.

Something caught my eye in the corner and I knelt down. With a gloved hand, I dragged my finger through the thick, dark substance. When I held my hand up to the light, the scarlet sticky substance glowed and I stood up, my heart suddenly pounding. "Guys, I've got blood over here."

The team crowded into the room and I pointed to the puddle, then turned to Dumont. "Nash, this is now an active crime scene. I'm going to need to call in our crime scene techs, have them sample this."

"Oh, for crying out loud!" To my horror, Dumont grabbed my hand and licked my gloved finger, then spat. "It's corn syrup and food dye. Stage blood. Get it? It's not real. So there's no problem."

I yanked my hand from his. "Well, give my regards to your makeup director. And get someone to clean that up, it's creepy to leave a puddle of blood, even fake blood, out like that."

Dumont rolled his eyes again. "Shall we continue?"

He showed us the rest of the dressing rooms. There were a few closets, a bathroom that had been updated and remodeled, and another one-way exit to the outside.

Then we went to the control booth, another add-on to the original theater. It was a small, enclosed space above the lobby, accessible by a narrow staircase. We peeked inside. I recognized the woman sitting at the controls, her thick eyeglasses emphasizing the roundness of her face. Her hair was piled atop her head in a tightly wound bun and big headphones covered her ears. It was Freya, the sound and light technician, busily testing things on stage. She blushed when she saw the large group of us crowding into her personal space.

I glanced out at the seats, the stage. "I want to station an officer up here, with her. It's the perfect vantage point to see the whole theater and the audience. Is this the highest point in the building?"

Dumont thought a moment, then nodded. "Yes. There used to be access to the roof, but we secured that door when we built on this control room. Gloria and I have the only keys."

I looked out over the stage as the lighting technician played with shadowy effects. The lights themselves came from bulbs set into big black rigs affixed to the ceiling with thick safety cables and chains. The whole apparatus looked to easily weigh hundreds of pounds.

"Nash, those lights . . . those are new?"

The director nodded again. He pointed to the rigs. "All of that, it's state of the art. The original Shotgun had gas lighting. It would have been very atmospheric but was, as you can imagine, harder to control and often dangerous. After Edison, lighting in the theaters really improved. These that you see here are tungsten halogen, instead of incandescent. The bulbs use a halogen gas; helps the bulbs' lifespan and output."

Freya removed her headphones. In a voice shaking with indignation and fear, she said, "He's right, though we've been having trouble with these lights for weeks. I think your contact sold you a pile of doo-doo, Mr. Dumont."

Dumont's face flushed. He said through gritted teeth, "Call me Nash. And let me deal with that prick. You just make sure everything is up and running by six."

Freya's blush deepened and she and I happened to make eye contact.

It was then that I saw it.

A single gold ball in her left earlobe.

"Did you lose this?" I withdrew the earring I'd found in the burnt-out lobby closet from my purse, carefully unwrapping the tissue and revealing the gold ball still smudged by ash. It was sheer luck, or carelessness, that I'd forgotten to place it in evidence. Freya paled and tried to stand up, but her legs gave out.

"Where . . . where did you find that?" She croaked out the words, her eyes already watering.

"I think you know. Guys, could you give up some space? Finn, you and Nash stay, please." I waited until the tiny room had cleared out, then turned back to Freya. Nash looked thoroughly confused, though it was clear that Finn had quickly put two and two together.

"Why?"

Freya swallowed hard and straightened in her chair. She summoned the same strength that had helped her attack various parts of the theater and hissed, "Because *Waverly* and *Nash* and all the rest of these sheep treat me like I'm a talentless heel. 'Oh, Freya, stick to the lights. You're so *good* at them.' The truth is, they just don't want to see a plain, overweight woman of my age on the stage. They think it will turn audience members' stomachs. Well, guess what? Guess who's been acting for weeks now? Me. Freya Dunlop. I fooled you all."

Next to me, Nash looked as though he were about to keel over from shock. He managed to whisper, "I trusted you. I had no idea you wanted so badly to act. And who on earth would you have played?"

"Obviously, someone with power. With skill. A witch, perhaps." Freya stood up and the three of us, Finn, me, and Nash, all took a step back. She smiled at our obvious discomfort and raised her hands high above her head, channeling whatever spirit goddess she imagined herself to be. "Maybe I'm a witch in real life."

She suddenly lowered her hands and glared at us. "Maybe I'm a witch and I've already cursed you all to hell."

"Lady, this is Cedar Valley, not Salem. You're under arrest." Finn had her in cuffs and her rights read within the minute. Freya stared at us balefully, then lowered her head and began to weep.

As Finn escorted her out of the control room, Freya muttered, "I just want to be someone. Someone who matters."

Nash was angry. "Jesus Christ, what a delusional wreck. Sound and light is everything in the theater. She *was* someone. I've got to find Waverly; she'll have to run effects tonight. Damn it, this just gets worse and worse."

The tour finished, we took our places. Dumont stormed off across the street to round up the last of his actors. Finn and I remained in the lobby, front and center. I couldn't believe what was happening. The front doors would open soon and though we had officers stationed at every entrance and exit, and inside the theater, it still felt as though we were playing Russian roulette with the devil himself. My only consolation was that if *anything* so much as an accidental fall happened tonight, I'd personally see to it that Mayor Cabot's ass got handed to her on a silver platter, dog and all, in the next election cycle.

"This is a bad idea," I whispered into the discreet radio on my wrist, tucked into my sleeve pocket. From across the lobby, Finn nodded in agreement. Even the air felt charged with a strange energy. For a moment, I wondered if the ghost stories were true and the old place was slowly filling with the spirits of the long-departed actors, builders, and audience members. It was unsettling to think that the people who'd last been in the Shotgun when it was open, more than a hundred years ago, were all long dead.

Then the clock struck seven o'clock.

The doors opened.

People streamed in, some dressed in their very finest evening wear, others getting into the spirit and wearing capes and tall hats and Victorian-era costumes. Not shockingly, I knew several of them . . . but if they were surprised to see me, they didn't show it. Everyone was too excited, too jazzed, for the evening. People had been saying for years that Cedar Valley lacked any kind of cultural arts. Sure, we had the library and the history center and the annual fairs and holiday markets, but theater, real theater, had been sorely missed.

We'd set up the metal detector at the interior theater doors, not the front doors, and now people slowed to a trickle, moving through the gates one at a time, emptying their pockets, flashing open their purses. If they seemed concerned by the security precautions, no one said a word. In this day and age, we were all too used to such things at stadiums, concert halls, and airports.

I scanned each face, not seeing anyone who looked like Griffith. If he was in disguise, it was a good one. And if he'd made it in, he'd done so without any obvious explosives or weapons on him.

I saw Gloria Dumont enter, accompanied by the mayor on one arm and a prominent businessman on the other. She looked stunning in an emerald-green ball gown, a delicate diamond choker around her pale, slender neck.

In my head, I reviewed the layout of the theater once more. Front lobby, with a total of six doors. Two back doors at the rear of the theater, and a side entrance door from one of the dressing rooms. The dressing rooms . . . there were six of them, on the smallish side. Then in the lobby, the restrooms, too . . . the balcony seats . . .

I bit my lip. God, if anything happened . . . it would be a stampede.

Ramirez appeared at my side. When I turned to greet her, I nearly gasped. Somehow, perhaps in the restroom or in her truck, she'd managed to clean up and slip into a pair of snug black slacks and a shiny scarlet blouse. She looked as though she'd come straight from home, not from half a day's hard work.

"I thought I could help keep an eye on the guests. Fuego's in the truck, sleeping. Figured I'd blend in a little better if I changed." Ramirez noticed Finn gaping at her from across the lobby and turned away, looking out over the sea of people still coming in through the doors. "This is crazy. That director is a lunatic. He should have postponed opening night until Griffith is located, secured."

"I agree, but it's not my call. All we can do is play the hand we're dealt. That's politics for you in a nutshell: people without expertise and knowledge making decisions the rest of us have to live with." I paused, noticing an older man with a cane slogging through the crowds, his face pointedly out of view. After another tense moment, he looked up and I recognized him; a former city councilor. Not Griffith.

"What do we do if we spot Griffith?"

Ramirez was reckless; she proved that to me on the trail run, and at the pub. The last thing we needed in a crowded theater was one loose cannon going after another.

"You leave Griffith up to Finn and me. Just be ready to back us up if it comes to that. And Ramirez?"

"Yeah?"

"Finn is one of the good guys. He's an idiot, of course, terrible with relationships. Some days I don't know whether to punch him or call his mother, ask her to get on his case. But I'm telling you . . . he's a good man." I glanced across the lobby, where Finn was chatting up a pair of local schoolteachers dressed in low-cut blouses. I sighed. "Contrary to all appearances, of course."

Ramirez was quiet a moment, then said, "Thanks. I appreciate the vote of confidence in him. As you can imagine, my trust in the man is shattered at the moment. But in time . . . we'll see."

Within twenty minutes the lobby was empty again. From inside the theater, I heard the rustle of hundreds of bodies finding their seats, saying hello to their neighbors, gasping in awe at the renovations. Aside from his cast and a few others, Nash Dumont had been religious about keeping people out of the theater until opening night. It worked; intrigue had been building for weeks. I realized to my horror that the theater was filled with almost all of the town's most important people: the mayor and members of city council; city management administration; the wealthy residents who helped keep Cedar Valley afloat with their generous donations to the hospital, the library.

The very lifeblood of this town could be wiped out in one fell swoop.

From inside the theater, a sudden hush descended. I left Ramirez in the lobby and peeked inside. The lights had dimmed and I stepped into a shadowy alcove at the rear of the theater. Looking down, I could see the backs of hundreds of heads, all at a gradual downward decline toward the stage. Looking up, to my right and then my left, were the balconies. Each held eight seats, and I saw to my right that Mayor Cabot and her husband sat front and center in the balcony closest to the action.

A single spotlight hit the stage and Nash Dumont stepped from the shadows into the light, resplendent in a black tuxedo. The audience began a slow clap that moved quickly into a standing ovation, the thunderous applause filling the space with what felt like magic, and *life*. It truly was as though after years of slumber, the theater itself had awoken and would not be held back from anything. It was the sense that tonight's performance was pulsing blood and breath into the wood, the brick, the very fabric in the chairs.

Dumont said a few words, thanking sponsors and his wife, Gloria. From the front row, she stood up and took a quick bow, though it was impossible to pay much attention to the warm-up act. I was too busy scanning the crowd, looking for Milo Griffith.

Even as I looked, though, the room grew dimmer, the crystals on the giant chandelier blinking out, one by one.

And then the play started.

A low rumble of thunder shook the stage. Three witches entered from stage left, clad in black robes, their hair loose and long and studded with twigs. As they began their lines, quite literally setting the stage for the mayhem and intrigue that was to follow, I gave the theater one final scan and slipped back into the lobby. Ramirez had left by then, and Finn had moved to the concession stand, where he sipped from a bottle of water.

"Anything?"

Finn shook his head. "No, and nothing from the rest of the team. Either Griffith is a ghost, or he's not here."

"He's an ex-SEAL, Finn. He spent years learning how to evade the enemy, how to hide out in the open. He could be here and we'd never know it."

For the next several hours, including a fifteen-minute intermission during which the audience stormed the restrooms and refreshment stand, I held my breath. As the scenes changed, and shadows came and went on stage, I could have sworn the heavy chandelier was at times swaying, but the light fixture held fast and true, a testament to its construction.

The understudies for Milo Griffith and Maggie Armstrong did wonderfully, and the whole cast received a standing ovation. From the wings, I caught sight of Waverly in all her golden splendor wiping tears from her eyes, then clapping enthusiastically.

After a few minutes of cajoling, Nash Dumont joined his troupe on stage and took a bow. Though he wore a humble, shy expression on his face, there was a look of smugness in his eyes that he couldn't quite hide.

This was his night, and thus far, nothing and no one had ruined it.

# Chapter Twenty-Four

Chief Chavez slammed his notebook down on the conference table and glowered at us. "So where the hell is Griffith? You were sure he'd be at the theater, and he wasn't. I've got limited resources, people. Jesus, what if he's not even in town anymore?"

It was Friday afternoon, late in the day.

After the play ended and the theater cleared out, Finn and I and the team had spent the rest of the night patrolling the town. We stopped at pubs and restaurants, the movie theater, even the twenty-four-hour high-end fitness club on the north side of town.

No place was too small or too large for us to check.

But we'd found nothing and finally, around three a.m., we'd each driven home for a couple of hours of shut-eye. Then we'd been back at it again, working in pairs, checking and rechecking potential targets.

And now here we were, back at the station, getting our asses chewed out by Chief Chavez.

The whole team sat around the conference table staring glumly at one another. Sheriff Underhill was nowhere to be seen, and I wondered if she'd stuck around all night, or headed out in the evening after the play had started.

Chavez continued. "What's the plan, people? What's next?"

"Look, Griffith knows that we know who he is. Whatever his plans were, they've been momentarily thwarted. But . . . he's not going to give up that easily." I tried to remain calm.

I thought about the maps on Griffith's closet walls, the way one in particular had seemed familiar and yet strange. Then it came to me and with it, a sinking feeling in my gut. Griffith was in the one place that I never wanted to return to. But it looked like I'd have to.

I swallowed hard and said, "The Ashley Forest. Milo's gone to ground at the ruins, in the Old Cabin Woods."

Finn exhaled, was skeptical. "There's nothing there. It's been snowing off and on for the last week. He'll freeze; he can hardly risk starting a campfire."

"There's an underground root cellar that's still intact. He'll hunker down there and use the ground cover to shield smoke. It's dense back there; no one would notice. Chief . . . Griffith is committed to his mission. He's not going anywhere until he sees it through. He's a professional. A few nights in a protected shelter will be a cakewalk compared to the sniper's nests he has been in." I stood, anxious, then sat back down. "We've got to go in tonight, as soon as it's dark. A small team. We'll get in nice and quiet and take him by surprise."

Chavez slowly shook his head, a scowl deepening the lines between his eyebrows. "Those woods are littered with traps and mud pits. You're talking about going into unknown territory with a skeleton crew in pitch-darkness against a Navy SEAL–trained sniper, who has had the last few months to get the lay of the land. You're out of your mind. We go in tomorrow, full force, at first light. Surround the place and flush him out."

"No. It has to be tonight," Finn said urgently. "Gemma's right; Griffith won't wait any longer. Whether the theater was his target or not, he's going to make a move tonight."

The chief stood and leaned forward on the table, fixing his gaze on the five of us. "My answer is final. We go at dawn. Prepare a tactical team. I want all roads in and out of the Ashley Forest guarded by two-man teams. I want a tracker, with a fresh dog, ready to go by five o'clock. Everyone wears a vest. Get maps of the forest, especially the ruins. Understood?"

"Yes, Chief," I muttered.

Chavez exhaled. "Good. Get a move on."

Outside the conference room, Finn and I looked at each other. I read the unspoken words in his eyes and nodded, just once. Though it might cost us our jobs, we were going into the woods. Tonight.

For all his faults, and he had many, Finn knew his people. Within ten minutes, he'd managed to convince Armstrong and Moriarty to join us. Armstrong was an easy sell. And Moriarty was always up for an adventure, especially if that meant sticking it to the man.

Even when the man in question was Angel Chavez, a chief he admired and respected.

"This could get us all fired," I said by final warning. We were in the alley behind the police station, Moriarty taking a smoke break, the rest of us ostensibly keeping him company. Our voices low, our eyes peeled for anyone entering the alley at either end. "I'm serious. I think catching Milo Griffith tonight is worth the risk but you all need to be sure. You need to be one hundred percent in."

"I'm in." Armstrong bummed a cigarette from Moriarty and clamped it between his teeth. Armstrong's eyes were mere slits, his voice a low growl. "I'm going to tear Griffith's head off."

"Yeah, I'm in if Armstrong gets first dibs on the thug. A father needs that kind of opportunity. It's healing." Moriarty lit Armstrong's cigarette, then yanked it from his partner's mouth. "Give me that, you'll hate yourself if you smoke it."

"No one's getting first dibs on anyone. We take him in by the book, nice and easy. It's the only chance any of us have of making it through this with our necks intact," Finn said. He ran a hand through his dark hair, glancing behind him at the setting sun. "The chief won't fire all of us. He'd have no detectives left. That's a move he can't make."

I glanced at the sun as well, watched it move fast in the western sky, dropping farther and farther down. I pulled a map from my back pocket and flattened it against the alley fence. "We need to be in place by nightfall. Moriarty, you take the entrance on the north road. It's the farthest from the cabin, but all along Griffith has done the unexpected. He could have an escape vehicle stashed there. If you find it, disable it. Armstrong, you take the trail on the western edge. It's the cleanest route to the cabin. Griffith may try to elude us by doing the obvious, running right back into town. Finn, you've got south, and I'll take east. There's no trails or roads, so we'll have to hike in. We'll approach the cabin and try to catch Griffith by surprise."

"You really think we should split up?" Finn looked doubtful. "Chavez was right; those woods are a death trap if you don't know your way around them."

"It's our only shot. There's no way that four of us traveling together will take Griffith by surprise; but, if by some miracle we did and he escaped, the easiest routes out of the woods would be unmanned." I folded the map and stuck it back in my pocket. "Right. We've got about forty-five minutes before that sun sets. I want everyone in black, with vests. Backup flashlights and batteries. It's going to be dark out there."

"Where do you want me?"

I spun around to see Jimmy standing in the shadows. He stepped forward, a sly smile on his face. "I've been shooting since I was twelve years old. I'm sick of standing on the sidelines. I want a piece of the action."

"Son, step the hell down." Finn put a hand on the intern's shoulder and gripped it, hard. "You don't know what you're getting into."

"I'll tell the chief."

"No, you won't. You don't want to spend the next six months with the four of us as your enemy." I tried a gentle smile. "You've got what, one more semester left at the community college? Finish school and then apply for the academy in Denver. We'll put in a good word for you."

"I'm going with you tonight *and* you'll write me a letter of reference. The best damn letter you've ever written."

Sighing deeply, Moriarty tried. "Come on, Jimmy, get with the program. You're a civilian. We can't let you join us, period. No matter how much we'd like to."

Jimmy smirked. "What are you going to do, lock me in the trunk of your car? Sun's setting. Tick tock."

I sighed, frustrated but knowing we couldn't waste another second. "He's right. Jimmy, you're riding with me. We're putting you on the third-floor balcony at the Montgomery house. You'll have eyes on the whole forest. Grab four pairs of night goggles from the supply room and four flare guns. You'll have to sign them out, but no one will question it; just tell the officer you're working with me on a special assignment. Meet us in the parking lot in three minutes."

"What the hell am I going to do with flare guns on a balcony?"

"We'll have the flare guns. You'll have your phone. First sign of trouble, one of us will shoot. At that point, it'll be all on you, Jimmy. The second you see a flare go off, you call in reinforcements." I was talking fast, shepherding Jimmy out of the alley, praying the others would hustle and get in place.

We were nearly out of daylight.

# Chapter Twenty-Five

Edith was shocked to see me, clad in black with a ski mask rolled up on my forehead, a man with a backpack of supplies by my side. I had to hand it to her, though; she didn't ask any questions, just nodded when I asked if Jimmy could make use of her attic and balcony for the night.

She murmured that Tom had left Colorado that morning, headed to an audition in Los Angeles, then on to Seattle for the television pilot. She seemed more relaxed than the previous times I'd seen her over the last few weeks and I wondered if she was finally simply having a moment to herself to catch her breath.

I left them in the foyer, counting on Edith to get Jimmy up to the third floor. As I raced out the front door, I heard her ask him if he'd like coffee and a slice of pie, and I allowed myself a brief smile.

Jimmy would be just fine.

Once I was inside my car, driving to the edge of the forest, the smile slipped away. What the hell were we doing? If we survived the night, there was an excellent chance that we'd all be out of a job come morning. Chavez would be furious and rightly so; we'd disobeyed a direct order, and worse, allowed an intern to be party to our insubordination. My stomach rolled as I had a momentary vision of the sun rising behind Chavez as he swore in four officers to replace the four detectives he would shortly be throttling.

The moment passed as I turned off my headlights and pulled

the car over to the side of the road. As the engine fell silent, the first thing I was aware of was the near-total darkness that surrounded me. Outside the car, it was bitterly cold. The thick cloud cover would work to my advantage, but it took a few minutes to let my eyes adjust to the dark.

The second thing I noticed was the silence. Though it wasn't late, the trees seemed asleep, still and unmoving in the night air. I crossed the road and stood at the edge of the woods. If my calculations were correct, I was directly east of the old cabin ruins, where the homesteader and his dog had died all those years ago.

I lifted a foot to step into the forest, then stopped. What if we were wrong? Was this a fool's errand at best and a dangerous mission at worst?

No.

I was right; I knew I was. Finn, Moriarty, Armstrong . . . they all knew it, too. Griffith had to finish his evil scheme and he had to do it soon. Everything he'd done up to this point was built on feeling, on meaning. The further he got away from his grandfather's timeline, the further he got away from the symmetry that seemed to fuel him.

Griffith wouldn't let that happen.

Before I crossed into the woods, I turned to the south. A mile away, the sharp turrets and sloped roof of the Montgomery mansion stood in silhouette against the deepening indigo sky. The rear of the house was dark, save for a couple of lights on the second floor. It was impossible to think that all those years ago, I'd run from that house into these woods, run all the way to the ruins, chased by a witch of my own creation.

I'd moved that night in blind terror, fear driving me instinctively deeper and deeper into the forest.

It would not be the same tonight.

Tonight, I was the hunter.

As I slipped on night-vision goggles and began to walk, I kept the beam from my tiny flashlight dim and low to the ground, praying it would pick up the glint of a steel animal trap should there be one in my path.

Besides the traps, there were the mud pits; shallow pools of a quicksand-like substance, created from the loose soil and numerous creeks in the area. I'd come across a rabbit caught in a mud pit years ago, in a different forest. I'd tried to reach him with a long stick, tried to save him. But the more he struggled, the quicker he sank. Just before he went under, the terror in his black eyes faded and without a sound, he slipped beneath the surface. The mud settled back into place and I quickly left, chilled by the resignation in the poor animal's eyes.

The forest remained quiet; each step of my boots on the ground seemed to echo for miles. Every few feet I stopped, spun around, sure that someone was behind me. Even if Griffith was there, would I know it? Or would the feel of steel at my throat or a gun to my temple be the last sensation I felt in this life?

*He's a former Navy SEAL.*

*He's trained in stealthy, tactical maneuvers.*

*And he's been one step ahead of you the whole way.*

These were the thoughts that occupied my mind as I walked, carefully, slowly, through the darkness. Somewhere to my south was Finn.

And ahead of me was the old cabin. I stared at the tumbled chimney stack, the still-blackened and collapsed cabin walls. To both my horror and relief, a thin column of gray smoke traveled out of the chimney, quickly swallowed by the clouds above.

Griffith was inside.

I took another step and then stopped. A footfall behind me, then a hand over my mouth, an arm around my belly, and a voice in my ear that whispered, "Don't move a fucking muscle."

He continued. "Do you understand? Nod if you understand."

I nodded and the arm that held me rigid slowly relaxed, though Finn's arm stayed around my waist. He spoke directly into my ear, his breath cool and quick. "He's booby-trapped the cabin. I almost tripped a wire back there. Knowing his skills and affinities, he's probably got the place, himself included, if necessary, wired to blow. We won't get in."

"Then he'll have to come out," I whispered back. "This ends, tonight."

Though Finn's face was impossible to see in the black night, I felt him nod. "You got any ideas?"

"Let's draw him out with the flares. He's not going to risk getting trapped in that cellar in a gunfight. He'll want to use the forest as cover."

"And once he's out? We may lose him."

I sighed. "I don't see any other options. We've got the road and trail covered."

"Count of three?"

"One . . ." We readied our flare guns, both aiming at the chimney. I took a deep breath. "Two . . . three."

We shot simultaneously, the flares lighting up the night. Almost immediately, from somewhere inside the ruins, came return fire. Finn and I dropped to the ground and covered our heads. Just as quickly there was the sound of someone crashing through the woods. Griffith wasn't bothering with stealth now, just speed.

He was on the run.

"He's going north, toward the road." I yanked my radio from my jacket pocket. "Armstrong, he's headed your direction."

Just as quickly, though, the crashing stopped and somewhere to our left, to the west, came an eerie dragging, thumping noise. I put the radio to my lips again. "Moriarty, be on the lookout. Suspect is moving your way."

Beside me, Finn swore. "We're running blind, Monroe. We could be headed into a trap."

"Come on, we're losing him," I hissed back.

Ahead of us, the noises stopped. Then came a horrible clacking noise, like giant teeth chattering together, and a terrible scream filled the air. We froze. The scream went on for a long time, then suddenly stopped.

"He's stepped in a trap," I shouted. "We've got him."

We raced west on the trail, in the direction of the scream. After five minutes, Finn grabbed my arm and I stopped. He said, "We should have found him by now. Where is he?"

I scanned the forest, letting my night-vision goggles penetrate through the multiple layers of trees and shadows, shadows and trees. "There. On the ground."

It was a steel animal trap, only it was no leg that was caught in its jaws but a thick log the size of my forearm. Finn kicked it and spun around, his gun raised. "It's another trap, Gem. He faked the scream."

Anger, frustration, and fear collided in me all at once.

"Come on! Show yourself, you damn coward!" I shouted into the forest again and again, but the only answer was a steady breeze moving through the trees, rustling the pine boughs.


"We're screwed." Moriarty pounded the hood of his car. We'd gathered there in utter and total frustration. "We lost the son of a bitch. Nabbing Griffith was the only thing standing between us and unemployment. It's been nice knowing you, kids. Me? I'll be fine, my pension is secure. But you, some of you have families. Nice things, a boat," Moriarty added meaningfully, looking at Finn. "Responsibilities."

"Griffith can't have gone far. Maybe he circled back to the ruins," Armstrong muttered. He leaned back and crossed his thick arms. "What I wouldn't give to have three minutes with that little psycho . . ."

Finn started to get in on it, too, when I suddenly said loudly, "Jimmy."

The three men looked at me with questioning eyes. I gestured to the car. "Get in. Something's wrong. Jimmy was supposed to call for backup when he saw the flares. Where's the sirens? Where are the troops?"

Finn smacked himself in the forehead, nearly knocking his night-vision goggles off his head. "Damn it. The balcony doesn't get cell reception, remember? That's why you climbed down the side of the house and injured your hands."

I breathed a sigh of relief. "You're right. He just couldn't get reception."

Then I realized something.

The Montgomery house was the nearest structure to the Old Cabin Woods. Hadn't I run from the house to the ruins myself, all those years ago? If Milo Griffith was going to double back, he wouldn't return to the ruins and his nest in the cellar.

He'd head toward the mansion.

Toward Edith and Jimmy.

"We have to get to the Montgomery house. Griffith is there, with Jimmy and Edith." I grabbed the car keys from a surprised Moriarty. He tried to protest, telling me it was a stick shift, and I waved him off. "Get in the damn car. Don't you see? Jimmy would have gone inside, found a house phone. He's a resourceful, scrappy guy. He'd have found a way to summon help . . . but he didn't, which means Griffith must have him. Maybe Edith, too."

As I rolled onto Fifth Street, I turned off the headlights and let the vehicle coast to a stop a few houses down from the Montgomery mansion. It stood in all its glory at the end of the cul-de-sac, dwarfing its closest neighbor, still a good half block away. The house was black, every light turned out, including the front porch light, a light I'd never known to be extinguished in all my years of knowing the Montgomerys.

We exited the car and crept, two by two, down the street. Moving silently, we mounted the front steps and then carefully, gently, I tried the front door.

It was unlocked, and the door swung inward to reveal a pitch-black interior.

Finn and Armstrong entered first, with Moriarty and me covering them. Once inside, I gently closed the door and we stood a moment, taking in the hushed air, the ticking of a nearby grandfather clock, the sound of the wind, picking up now.

The wind.

I peeked into the living room and watched as the white lace curtains billowed out, and then in, over and over against the sill. I risked a quick look with my flashlight and saw shattered glass at the bottom of the curtains. Muddy footprints tracked away from the glass, moving across the pale carpet and toward the door at the end of the room.

A single bloodied handprint graced the doorframe.

From upstairs, a deep series of thumps and then a single, piercing scream followed by a muffled shout.

"Careful. It could be another trap," Finn whispered. We took the stairs two at a time while Moriarty and Armstrong moved to secure the first floor. We reached the second-floor landing and paused, listening. The thumps continued above us.

*Third floor*, I mouthed and pointed up. Finn nodded.

I listened another moment, then said, "Attic. They're in the attic."

We found Edith Montgomery slumped outside the attic door, a deep cut on her forehead. She appeared to be concussed; her eyes had trouble focusing, and she couldn't grasp who I was. I pressed the edge of her bathrobe to the cut and whispered I'd get help as soon as I could.

Inside the attic, sounds of a struggle could clearly be heard.

I was frightened for Jimmy. Griffith had already proven himself to be ruthless.

"On three," Finn whispered. He counted off the numbers on his fingers, and when he reached three, he opened the attic door with a kick, then stepped back as I trained my gun and flashlight on the space within.

I gasped.

On the balcony, Griffith had Jimmy in a choke hold. The killer had him over the edge of the railing. As the clouds parted, I saw in the moonlight that Jimmy's face was a bright shade of red. He was slowly suffocating from Griffith's forearm.

I approached the duo, keeping my gun trained on Griffith's head. "Don't do this, Milo. It's over. You don't have to hurt anyone else."

"It's not over until I say it's over. You pricks ruined my plan, you ruined everything. The theater was supposed to be mine. And now this jerk attacks me." Griffith tightened his grip on Jimmy, leaning farther into the railing. I saw swelling on Griffith's face and realized that Jimmy must have gotten a punch in before Griffith incapacitated him.

Good old Jimmy.

"We can talk about all that in here. Just bring Jimmy back into the room, Milo. Then we'll talk," I said. Out of the corner of my eye, I watched as Finn slipped into the room, staying close to the wall, hidden in the shadows. If he thought he could tackle Griffith and save Jimmy, he was sorely mistaken.

Finn hadn't been out there; he didn't know what I knew. The balcony was too small, too rickety. The whole thing would crash down if anyone moved.

And then someone did move.

Jimmy reached up with what must have been the last ounce of his strength.

He went for Griffith's eyes, viciously jabbing a finger into each socket with horrifying force.

Griffith let out an animal-like scream and made the dangerous mistake of leaning even farther into the railing, desperately trying to free his face from Jimmy's hands. With a long and terrible screech, the rail pulled away from the house.

"No!" Finn and I shouted in unison, both moving desperately toward the balcony.

But we were too late. To our horror, we watched as Milo Griffith and Jimmy tumbled down over the edge and into the dark, cold night.

# Epilogue

In the end, the chief had no choice but to keep Moriarty, Armstrong, Finn, and me on staff. Once Jimmy was out of the hospital, the chief hired him, too, as his new personal assistant, though he'd be working one-armed for a while, at least until the cast was off.

We all signed the thick white plaster, even the chief.

Jimmy, and Milo Griffith, had been lucky. The slanted eaves of the Montgomery mansion, the same eaves I'd carefully shimmied down in the bright light of day, had slowed their fall. In addition to Jimmy's broken right arm, he had bruises and scratches all over his face and neck. Griffith had broken both his legs and his collarbone, and nearly lost his vision from Jimmy's brutal self-defense move.

We'd let Lucas Armstrong do the honors that night. He'd read Griffith his rights and then arrested him as Griffith lay on the ground, moaning and writhing in pain. Armstrong skipped the handcuffs and instead sat with the killer, softly humming *Amazing Grace* in an incredibly off-key performance. Griffith's moans increased in volume until it was too hard to take, and I left, moving inside.

My team had it under control.

My team. In a night that had seen incredible highs and lows, the words felt good to say out loud. Armstrong, Moriarty, Finn . . . even Jimmy. We had each other's backs. The fact that their belief in me was strong enough to risk discipline, even dismissal, to get our man nearly brought me to my knees.

Griffith eventually went on to confess to most everything. He'd worn a padded suit the night he stole the dynamite from the Bishop Mine, knowing if there was video surveillance the costume would throw us off track. He did not admit to killing the rabbit at the mine, though it was clear his cruelty knew no bounds. The chase and escape down the alley the night of Caleb's murder; the subsequent bank robbery and killing of Esposito; the drugging and beating of Maggie Armstrong: Griffith copped to all of it. He even admitted that leaving the Nambu pistol behind at the scene of the Esposito murder was theatrics, pure staging. Both a red herring, and not. A prop, Griffith called it; a prop, and a weapon.

At the end, as we interviewed him at the hospital, he was proud of his mission, as he called it. I'm convinced he truly did want to get caught; after all, his background in the military had provided him with all of the necessary training and tools to avoid detection.

But all of that, the confessions, came later.

That night, I got Edith down from the third floor and into an easy chair in the living room. Her cut had stopped bleeding but her confusion remained. Telling her that Caleb's killer had been caught would have to wait until a time and place when she could understand that tonight, at least, justice had been served.

I next saw Edith three weeks after the night at the Montgomery mansion, on the morning of my wedding. In a sweet and sentimental nod to tradition, Brody had spent the night in a bachelor's suite at the Tate, and so Grace and I were alone at the house when Edith stopped by.

"You look good," I whispered in her ear as I hugged her. There was a softness in her eyes, a sense of peace. She smelled of cinnamon and vanilla, without a whiff of cigarette smoke. "Did you quit smoking?"

"Yes. It's been eleven days. I think it will stick this time. I want to thank you, Gemma. It means the world to me to know that Caleb's killer will spend the rest of his years in prison."

We moved into the kitchen, where I poured Edith a cup of tea.

She continued, "But it also breaks my heart. Milo Griffith, like his grandfather, was the product of circumstances beyond his control. War does terrible things to people." Edith smiled sadly. "That must sound trite, coming from me. I've lived a privileged life."

At our feet, Grace tugged the hem of Edith's pants. Edith bent down, lifted the baby, and kissed her cheek. She went on, "Anyway, I'm putting the house up for sale. I can't possibly live there, not after everything that has happened. I'm selling it all, the house, the land, all the furnishings. Even the art. And I'm using the proceeds to start a new business, here, in Cedar Valley. It will be a center for veterans, a clearinghouse of services. Job help, mental health, that sort of thing. I think I'll name it after Caleb. 'Cal's Place.'"

"He'd love that."

Edith smiled, this time a broad, toothsome grin. "Yes, I think he would."

"There's something I've been meaning to ask you. Those strange noises and lights that you saw and heard, in the forest, have they stopped?"

Edith thought a moment, then nodded slowly. "You know . . . they have . . . Isn't that strange? Was it Mr. Griffith? Did he cause them?"

"No, he denied any knowledge of them. And it wouldn't make sense that they would have originated with him; his entire being is about stealth, surprise, not revealing who or where he really is."

Edith gave the smallest of shrugs. "It's a mystery, then. Maybe the Old Cabin Woods truly are haunted."

She glanced around the kitchen, at the dozens of programs and short vases, most already filled with white roses, and set Grace down on the floor. "Are you ready?"

"I think so. Clementine stayed late last night and did a few last-minute things, then picked up and dropped off the flowers this morning. She'll be back in an hour to help me get it all down to the Tate."

Edith leaned forward and sniffed one of the bouquets. "I've always loved roses. What I meant was, *are you ready?*"

"Oh. Well . . . yes. Yes, I'm ready. Of course I'm ready."

Edith glanced at me, one perfectly groomed eyebrow arched. "Well, I'll be there about five. Let me know if you need anything. There's always all sorts of last-minute crises that pop up come ceremony time."

"Thanks, but this is one wedding that will go off without a hitch. Brody's been waiting a long time. He deserves a flawless night."

"And you? What do you deserve, Gemma?"

I bit my lip, surprised at the question and the fact that I didn't have a ready answer.

After a long moment of silence, Edith nodded gently. "I'll see myself out. Try to relax today."


The next few hours passed in a blur. Grace went down for a nap while Clementine, who'd arrived just after Edith left, finished up with the flower arrangements. The Tate was taking care of catering, decorations, and drinks, but I wanted to line the aisle in their grand room with the small vases of white roses. While Clem worked on the flowers, I soaked in the tub, doing my nails, shaving my legs, and letting my hair set in the hard plastic curlers I'd found tucked behind a roll of toilet paper under my sink. I think they'd last been used in the late 1990s, but what the hell, they worked and were free.

After the tub, I quickly steamed my dress and then put it back in its plastic shroud. Grace woke and I got her a snack, a fresh diaper, and a traveling outfit. She'd wear an adorable white flower-girl dress I'd picked up, with tiny rosettes across the bodice, but there was no way I was putting her in it until about thirty seconds before the ceremony started.

Clementine and I caravanned down the canyon, she with the programs and flowers, me with my dress, my baby, and an overnight bag. Brody and I would stay the night at the Tate, while Clementine skipped the reception and instead brought Grace back to the house and stayed with her, and Seamus, overnight. An official honeymoon would have to wait; Brody was due to spend much of December in Tanzania, on-site for a client. He'd be back by Christmas, but it would be a long, lonely month.

At the hotel, we settled ourselves in the small suite attached to the great room. Clementine, with her pink-frosted hair and champagne-colored minidress, looked like a cupcake. I wouldn't have traded a thing about her for all the money in the world.

Julia and Laura arrived. My grandmother was having a good day and the women played with Grace while I did my hair and makeup. The curlers had worked, and by the time I was finished, I had to admit I didn't look half bad. My dark hair was pulled up and back into a tight and elegant chignon, a few loose curls framing my face. My eye makeup was smoky and dramatic, so I skipped the lipstick in favor of a light balm.

Finally, I stepped into the tiny bathroom and slipped into my dress. As I zipped it up, I stared into the full-length mirror, surprised at the sudden tears that threatened to fall. The gown was beautiful, all lace and pearls, with a high neck and long sleeves. I turned to the side, taking in the low scooped back that went down nearly to my tailbone.

I was a bride, no doubt about it.

The tears that I desperately tried to choke back, knowing they would smudge my makeup, came from the knowledge that my parents should have been here. They should have been the ones walking me down the aisle or playing with Grace, their granddaughter.

But they weren't here, and marrying Brody was something that I'd have to do alone. It was my decision; there was no one to give me away or ask permission of.

I would stand on my own two feet as we exchanged vows, as I suddenly realized I'd done every day since my mother and father had died.

"You have it in you, kid. You always have," I whispered to the mirror. Then I stepped out of the narrow changing room and spun around. "What do you think?"

Laura, Julia, Clementine, and even Grace clapped. Clem, perhaps most shocked of all to see me dolled up in a gown, yelped, "You look stunning! Beautiful!"

"Thank you." I blushed, already eager to slip out of the heavy gown and into the lighter, silky dress I'd brought for the reception.

I checked my watch as the lodge's wedding coordinator poked her head in the room.

"Everyone's ready, Gemma. They're all seated, with a glass of champagne per your request. A bit unusual, most people wait until cocktail hour, but we aim to please." Her smile was tight; it was clear I had been a less-than-typical bride.

At least I hadn't been a bridezilla.

"Okay. Let's get this show on the road."

We gathered outside the great room. The doors were cracked open a few inches and as I peeked through them, tears once again welled in my eyes. Nearly a hundred people sat in wooden chairs on either side of an aisle lined with white roses. Friends, family members, Brody's four sisters, work colleagues . . . The room was filled with people who loved and supported us. From where I stood, I couldn't see Bull, or Finn, or even Chief Chavez, but I knew they were in there, somewhere.

It was as though I were about to step into one long, big embrace.

And on the far side of all of it, standing next to the officiant, a roaring fire behind him, was Brody. His wavy hair was combed back, his beard neatly shorn. He wore a black tuxedo with a red bow tie and a white rose in the lapel of his jacket.

Intense emotions had already flooded his face. This moment was as much his as it was mine, and for perhaps the first time in my life, I knew I was exactly where I was supposed to be. For all our ups and downs, all our doubts and struggles, all our fights and betrayals, we were family. We were in it for the long haul. I knew with every fiber of my being that when the end of my life came, no matter what else the future held, I would never regret the walk I was about to take.

Fighting for our love, for our family . . . it meant something.

It was something I could be proud of, for the rest of my days.

In that moment, I chose Brody.